THE
MONKEY
LINK

ALSO BY ANDREI BITOV

Life in Windy Weather (1986)
Pushkin House (1987)
A Captive of the Caucasus (1992)

THE
MONKEY
LINK

A Pilgrimage Novel

ANDREI BITOV

Translated by
Susan Brownsberger

FARRAR, STRAUS AND GIROUX

NEW YORK

Translation copyright © 1995 by Susan Brownsberger
Originally published in Russian
Copyright © 1994 by Andrei Bitov
All rights reserved
Published simultaneously in Canada by HarperCollins*CanadaLtd*
Designed by Tere LoPrete
Printed in the United States of America
First edition, 1995

Library of Congress Cataloging-in-Publication Data
Bitov, Andreĭ.
The monkey link / Andrei Bitov ; translated by Susan Brownsberger.
—1st ed.
p.   cm.
I. Brownsberger, Susan.   II. Title.
PG3479.4.I8M66 1995   891.73'44—dc20   94-18864 CIP

CONTENTS

FROM THE AUTHOR

Nothing in this book is fictitious except the author.
—The Author

The author asks the blessing of the superior of Motsameta Monastery, Father Tornike, and of Father Zenon, painter of icons.

The author thanks the Biological Station of the Zoology Institute of the U.S.S.R. Academy of Sciences, in what used to be East Prussia; Mr. Badz Zantaria, of Tamysh, Abkhazia; the Kulturreferat of Munich; and the Wissenschaftskolleg, Berlin, for making it possible to write this work.

The author thanks Rosemarie Tietze and Susan Brownsberger for their endless patience and valued suggestions.

The author thanks as well his friends and comrades for the friendship, generosity, and tolerance shown to him in various periods of his life as he and they gained shared experience: poet Gleb Gorbovsky; writer and poet Yuz Aleshkovsky; artist, sculptor, writer, playwright, and director Rezo Gabriadze; architect and artist A. A. Velikanov; artist B. A. Messerer; and especially Bella Akhmadulina and the great singer Victoria Ivanova; as well as Dr. V. R. Dolnik, professor of biological sciences; writer and traveler G. Y. Snegirev; poet and singer S. G. Saltykov; writer Leonid Gabyshev; art critic Andrei Eldarov; artist and restorer Sergei Bogoslovsky; physicist Ruslan Jopua; writer Daur Zantaria; world record holder Marlen Papava; and many, many others.

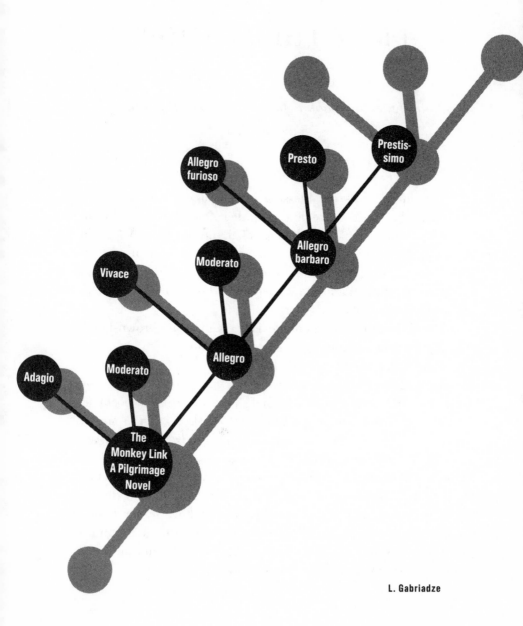

Adagio

Moderato

Vivace

Moderato

Allegro
furioso

Allegro

Moderato

Presto

Prestis-
simo

Allegro
barbaro

The
Monkey Link
A Pilgrimage
Novel

L. Gabriadze

THE FIRST TALE

Birds (Catechesis)

Two men went up into the temple . . .
—LUKE 18:10

"He said" or "I thought"?

I wouldn't want to find that this had style.
That is, I wouldn't want   .   .   .   .

.   .   .   .

.   .   .   .

.   .   .   .

.   .   .   .

.   .   .   . instead of what I'd like to tell you.
Moreover   .   .   .   .

.   .   .   .

.   .   .   .

.   .   .   . in what I plan to say.

We live on the floor of the air-ocean. Among houses and trees as if among mussels and seaweed. Here comes the crab, his bottom shell scraping the asphalt, his armor-clad neck immobile; only by accident, as he crawls over circumstances in his way, will he look up—there above is the splashing sky, and suspended in it, barely moving her fins, is a bird. Birds are the fish of our ocean.

We live on the border of two habitats. This is basic. We are neither one thing nor the other. Only birds and fish know what it means to have one habitat. They don't *know* this, of course. They belong. I doubt that man would meditate, either, if he flew or swam. To meditate, one needs a contradiction that does not exist in a homogeneous habitat—the tension of the border.

There is constant conflict and incident on this border. We are tense. We relax only in our sleep, in a kind of scavenged safety, as if under a stone. Sleep is our way of swimming, our only way of flying. Behold how heavily man treads the earth . . .

As if in pain. Perhaps the asphalt underfoot is too hard, or his shoes are too tight, or his workday is too long, or his shopping bags weigh down his arms. That is how he walks.

"Behold the fowls of the air . . .

". . . they sow not, neither do they reap, nor gather into barns; yet your heavenly Father feedeth them. Are ye not much better than they?"

"Are not two sparrows sold for a farthing? and one of them shall not fall on the ground without your Father.

"But the very hairs of your head are all numbered.

"Fear ye not, therefore, ye are of more value than many sparrows."

Fear ye not . . . It's easy to say.

In some sense, I fear, that text states all we know about birds.

Birds are strangely absent in our lives, although unquestionably visible to the naked eye. They seem to fly at the periphery of our consciousness, as if painted on the very inside of the bell jar with which we have capped the inhabited world. Naïve as such concepts now seem, the heavenly canopy is in fact the precise inner boundary of our knowledge, although it was once declared the outer. This opaque bell jar, which we carry with us, wobbles faintly at our every step. The birds fly always at the rim of it, and we cannot draw near to them—there is a curvature out there, a bend, a slip . . .

So birds exist and do not exist. After all, by nature we watch our feet. Looking up is a luxury. From Aristophanes to Hitchcock, it's not birds that exist but the concepts to which they give rise. We can examine a bird only when it's dead. We can shoot and

eat one. But there's no contact. This is the same as with the
heavenly canopy: we know by now that the sky doesn't end there,
but for everyday life the earth remains flat, and visibility is capped
by our sphere of experience, as if by a lid.

I will venture to assert that we have less contact (in the
physical sense) with birds than with any other living creatures.
It's hard to imagine that you have touched and caressed one, or
that one has pecked you. They just fly around. We have much
more experience of direct contact with the more remote groups
of creatures diminished by the perspective of evolution—with flies,
let's say. The airplane still doesn't make us think of a bird, but
the helicopter looks disgustingly like a dragonfly. Hitchcock spent
his childhood in a taxidermist's shop—birds pecked not in self-
defense but on the attack. In art, the bird is a naturally surrealistic
creature.

I was here on the Kurish Spit, at the biological research station,
for the seventh time. Or maybe it wasn't the seventh, but seven
makes a round number . . . I had first fled to this place from 1968,
as if to a foreign country. "But this shore had already been won
. . ." Since then . . . There's no getting used to it. Each time, I'm
surprised by what I see here again. Supposedly, the reason I come
here each time is that I've forever remembered what a unique place
it is on this earth, and how resurrectingly wholesome it is, making
no threats and imposing no demands, existing so independently of
you that it doesn't even reject you—that is, the kind of place where,
in the marvelous words of Olga S., "soul is miscible with body in
all proportions." That feeling is probably first love, even though
expressed in the language of chemistry . . . Supposedly, that's the
reason I come—and each time, I forget the reason. Suddenly I'm
here. This place recalls a homeland I have never seen.

Little cannon-smoke clouds were drifting across the sky.

Who had been shooting? The smoke had forgotten the shot;
the artilleryman, his cannon. The little clouds were in pairs, like
the cheeks of babes who had slid down from the laps of Madonnas
to play. The trees, however, were somewhat confused about the

wind in relation to which they grew. Some of them were especially submissive to it and grew away from the sea at a forty-five-degree angle. That angle then represented the constancy of the winds, as graphically as a textbook illustration . . .

(The mention of the textbook is very much to the point. For, after my grade school course in "non-living nature," I would never again see the ideal ravines, hills, and steppes of those illustrations . . . but would perpetually experience the torture of growing up, when everything proves to be not quite as portrayed: not so pure, not so exact, not so expressive of the word that names it—not a ravine but a type of ravine, not a forest but a type of forest, neither fish nor fowl, neither the word "ravine" nor the word "grove." But here everything remained in that very state: sea, dunes, clouds, bushes, sand, wind. This unconditionality turned out to have two odd conditions; more on this a little later . . .)

. . . But after smashing against the dunes the wind blew in all directions. The trees, bred to the habit and memory of the line of least resistance, became confused and didn't know what direction to grow in, began growing every which way. They hindered the wind more than they submitted, and thereby altered their assignment. They formed a tangle of live windfalls, growing crisscross, like an anti-tank barrier—x's and y's in all directions—the equation was unsolved.

The bus stopped, and I got off.

First of all I should see Doctor D.

I was allowed to sit in the corner.

In front of me sat six pairs of students, the backs of their heads unintelligent.

He paced the classroom with his hands folded behind him, back and forth past the blackboard. His manner of walking made him somewhat taller and thinner than he really was. He picked his feet up slightly too high and bobbed his head slightly forward at every step, peering as if his eye were placed at the side, like a bird's, and because of this his profile dominated his appearance. He would wheel about so swiftly that he was again presented in profile. As if running along the top of a picket fence. At last he stopped running, faced the blackboard, and drew a straight line. The sound of the chalk seemed to lag behind . . .

"Let's take . . ." he said, with that lagging *screek* (which, despite years of lessonless freedom, I instantly remembered with my whole hide), "let's take"—*screek, screek, screek,* he drew a square—"a closed space."

And he gave us that same sidelong look, as if he had won.

Not a spark of recognition did he read in the gaze of his audience. He retracted the animation of his own gaze, as if retracting his head into his shoulders.

"Which is to say," he continued dryly, "a space bounded on all sides. Hermetically sealed. No access. Nothing in it."

The square on the blackboard became slightly emptier than before. It gave off a whiff of loneliness.

"And let's put a bird in it."

From the severity with which he had drawn the square, I had thought him capable only of straight lines, and now suddenly, with vivacity and ease, in one flourish, he drew a little bird in the corner—in profile, naturally. A girl in the front row giggled.

That was the first assumption. The assumption, as everyone knows, is what the theory rests on. It was also the first oversight. How could the poor bird have gotten in?

"What does she need first of all, in order to continue to exist?" He waited a moment, to awaken the idea in his audience, and gave the answer himself: "Air."

So saying, he erased a little window, with his finger, in the upper part of the square. Everyone sighed—as if the air had whistled into it. The little bird was saved.

"What next?"

And he added a tiny cup of water.

Thus he furnished the bird with everything essential, and the array became appallingly large and elaborate. He anticipated her needs like a young Creator. They were endless. By now the black-board was covered with formulas somewhat more complex than the O_2 and H_2O with which all had begun, though not yet suffi-ciently complex to look like the modern idea of science. The bird, however, already felt cramped in the space allotted to her: she was overgrown with paraphernalia and family. Yet this was the only spot where she could still so much as perch, because the entire space that the lecturer had furnished for her to live in (so empty and small to begin with, on the huge empty blackboard) was now pinched, squeezed, hemmed in on all sides by formulas for her existence; the area outside it was developing the negative pressure of an insufficient knowledge of life . . . and by now the joyous biblical beginning—air, water, food—had been left somewhere far behind. Science begins with that which is truly complex and im-possible to grasp—the beginning—but abandons it somewhere at the bottom of grade school in the form of axioms and lemmas, and ends with merely that which can be learned by any Ph.D.

But it's a long while since anyone has begun at the beginning. To succeed in a narrow major specialty, you must not hesitate to begin with its furthest possible continuation. I was moved by the attempt, in this lecture, to seek meaning. The lecturer himself seemed to be surprised, and to find something for himself in this rare opportunity. Specialists are inclined to suspect everyone of an interest in their own subject (the "fascination" device, long ago exhausted in novels about science)—their neurosis has a touching, pathetic nakedness. And while the men students aren't listening to him, and the women students are mechanically writing, and I'm reflecting on his resemblance (a flattering one, from his point of view) to the subject of his study (in the banal sense that owners resemble their dogs); while we're distracted and not listening to him, he inconspicuously crosses the border of the popular, the well known, the obvious, whose veil he was just about to lift, and enters the domain of special knowledge, the specialist's private shell, the ecological niche of ecology itself—and by now we aren't listening to him, not because we're distracted, but because we no longer

understand, for we have missed, once again, the long-dreamt-of
giddiness of crossing from the perceptively visible to the mentally
graspable. We aren't listening to him . . . a convenient transition
to a new thread of the narrative.

I could have heard and understood this as far back as grade
school. How strange that humankind did not understand some of
it along with me, a little schoolboy! I had finished that school,
had even finished college on my second attempt, I was well past
thirty before people started talking about the things that surround
us and have always surrounded us—about nature, about the
things we can't live without—about air, water, and food. So what
else was new? But it did turn out to be new. The conversation
itself turned out to be new. Nowadays it's so faddish that it seems
recited by rote, as if even the danger of having nothing left to
breathe weren't really a danger: "They put a scare into us, but
tomorrow, and the day after, we're still breathing!" Tragedy has
degenerated into loose talk, a way of leaving everything as it was.
And suddenly we have the dreadful thought that it may be more
promising to ban a subject than to talk it to death after the ban
is lifted. Ours was a hungry era at first, we were in no mood for
it, and suddenly we've eaten our fill, we're alive, food is not vital.
    Time passes, and unrelated things begin to fall into line . . .
After the war, fish multiplied in the lakes and streams; the forests
were untrampled, mushroom-rich, berry-laden; Father and I went
bicycling and encountered no traffic, not a soul. Empty sandy
roads and the twitter of birds. In what year did everyone start
going down to the dacha, everyone start taking mushroom and
berry walks, everyone start fishing? It happened gradually, of
course, but also suddenly . . . I remember it by the suburban
trains, the way they were suddenly overcrowded, packed—suddenly one year. We needed to live through the ten years after the
war before we could stop eating the essential second plate of soup
and thinking of taxis as decadence, and suddenly one year we all
started going to the country—was it '55? '56? Why, it had always
been all right to go to the country, no one forbade it—but suddenly
it had *become* all right. To shoulder a wonderful little box and
go ice fishing.
    This happened in Russia, this I observed, but over in the
West, where we hadn't been, which we were reading about, it was

all idiosyncrasies, eccentricities, high living: someone didn't eat
for six months, someone ate a car, someone crossed the ocean
without food or water on a rubber raft, someone crawled into
caves, someone into a crater, someone walked all the way across
Germany on his hands, someone finally climbed Everest, someone
set sail without rudder or sails.

But earlier, too . . . yes, a little earlier, if it hadn't been for
the war . . . The North and South Poles, the balloons, the dirigibles,
ever higher and higher—it had happened earlier, too, this peculiar
cocktail of adventure, sport, and science, but for some reason
especially after the war. When something became understandable,
when we all understood something—understood *something*, but
didn't understand what. And that "what" began to slip away,
irretrievably. Time, too, is a living being; it, too, wants to live its
life. Every so often there comes a time when humankind lives as
one person; in some sense, this is indeed a Time. We grow old
together, rejoice together, understand together. Later we don't
understand what has become of all this, where it has disappeared
to. Someone realizes that the state of commonality is over, lost,
beyond return, someone senses it before the rest—there is a wave
of suicides, someone casts off in the emptying boat to overtake
the romantically colored ideals. But that movement, too, left
strange things in general use: flippers, masks, large beads, the
vogue for sweaters and jeans, new forms of sport like archery and
waterskiing. Some people began to tame lions, or to live among
wolves or monkeys, some people began to do time studies on Stone
Age work processes, after fabricating tools on Stone Age models
and withdrawing from civilization (in all such exercises one is
troubled by the small two-way radio in the plastic bag, and the
possibility of heavenly rescue by helicopter—the umbilical cord
compromises any escape). Strange people. Their behavior was
puzzling. They might be suspected of publicity seeking. But your
suspicion was tinged with envy: He's broken out! Here we are,
shoulder to the yoke, and he sets off to hike around the world—
anyone would be glad to do the same. The strange part is that
there were only a handful of these eccentrics. To earn the right,
they had to be surprising. But to surprise this work-worn, stifled
world is hard. In the adventures that become famous, you are
struck by just one thing—their simplicity. Why didn't anyone
ever think of this before? It makes you envious. You, too, could
have done it. And somehow you see all too clearly that you can
no longer follow. The gap, the breach, is already cemented over

and guarded. This world is hard to surprise. As the poet wrote:
"It's not easily surprised by your words, not impressed by the
look on your face . . ." Yet we may well be surprised by the things
that do impress this world, how simple they always are, how
seemingly obvious, within reach of anyone. So here we are, living
in a world more impressed by natural behavior than by the formula mc^2. I maintain that this shift, rather than the long list of
naturalists of all centuries, constitutes the essential history of the
science of ecology.

We live in a world of people born just once. We are not
witnesses to the past, not participants in the future. The instinct,
memory, and program of the species have grown weak within us,
as weak as the connection of the times. This very weakness (so
extreme that we have lost our connection with nature) is where
the human seed springs up. Man originates exactly where any
other species dies out. No warm fur, no terrible teeth, no lupine
morals. Trousers, the bullet, religion . . .

How strange, I thought, grasping the experience with difficulty, assimilating the conclusion with ease . . . Let's take a bird
and solder it into a box . . . The trajectory of scientific thought
reminded me of the chaotic flight of a moth. Clumsily conspicuous
at the end of the trajectory was the conclusion that had suggested
itself at the very beginning. How comical, I thought. Examining
his own hands with bewilderment, man discovers that birds have
wings. Opening his mouth in surprise, he finds that birds have a
beak. Has he "discovered" that birds have wings and a beak—
or that he himself has hands and a mouth?

Humankind, I thought, you're incapable of comprehending
any other biological existence. Each time you make the terrible
effort to do so, you comprehend only your own . . . But would
man comprehend even his own existence if he did not try to
comprehend a different one? Man's capacity to know another
nature strikes me as catastrophically small, yet there is nothing
nobler, or more necessary for human consciousness, than to spin
our wheels in this effort.

Ecologists, too, have many of the accoutrements of science,
of course. Laboratories, test tubes, retorts, automatic recorders,
freezers—the whole Laputan environment, the background
against which the white-coated scientist poses, juggling cult objects. But we don't know what he's pouring into what in the
photograph—or whether he's mocking us. The priest of science
is bathed in fluorescent light, he peers profoundly at something

he's supposed to have some knowledge of, while we have none. This is what makes us an enlightened society, that we revere what we don't understand. I'm not being ironic—it really is a mark of enlightenment. But we don't revere *nature*. We revere science.

At last we have an emerging anti-science that reveres nature.

And really, why does he wear such a knowing expression in the universal photo on the magazine cover? A true scientist's expression (in my naïve conception) should be frightened, shocked, confused. For, in his field, he knows everything ever known up to now, up to this day, up to this second—but beyond this he knows nothing. No one does. He is at the cutting edge of science, where knowledge stops. The world's top specialist, if he truly seeks something beyond this, is the very man who knows nothing. Everyone else will have to study and study to catch up before they know as much as he does—they know a few things, but he knows all. He alone has some idea of the extent to which we know nothing. Then why does he stand frozen in the photograph, looking as if he had some idea what was there, beyond, in the next moment? Smug, brightly illumined among the sparkling vessels and mad blinking indicators—but, after all, he's in the dark, he's supposed to have the inspired face of a blind man, a Bruegelesque blind man falling into a hole . . . Every second he lowers his hands into the magical black box—what velvety, absolute darkness! No one even knows whether he can pull his hands out of there, out of his vent hood. But he plunges them in and pulls them out, though he is ignorant of what's in there. Sharper than a razor is the edge between his mind and what occupies his hands, as they putter about so boldly there in the dark of luciferin light.

What certainty makes him so certain?

This tale has both its heroine and its hint of a love story. Clara. No, this wasn't a commonplace, business-trip affair—it was tenderness, a kind of pure love—and its steady glow relieved my loneliness as a journalist. Clara was young, clever, and beautiful. She loved sparkly things and tobacco and could count to five. She loved another man. Valerian Innokentievich was elegant and young. She snuggled up to him like a cat. (The simile is very much out of place: cats weren't allowed within gunshot. Ornithology.) I suppose it's already obvious to the uncorrupted reader that Clara . . . (Ah, Clara! Parentheses in prose are a written form of whispering.)

I remember an exercise in the sixth grade, in a grammar that bore Academician Shcherba's name: something about a girl and her beloved parrot, how she woke up in the morning and he greeted her. It was an exercise on something, say, the pronouns "he" and "she," but to us, by then, all exercises were about the same thing—the quadratic trinomial. We all covered up the word "parrot," I remember, and had a remarkable amount of fun with the resulting text.

Many years later I am presented with an opportunity to write a composition on this topic.

Certainly this was a kind of jealousy, when I was too shy to touch her but she kept plucking Valerian Innokentievich's sleeve to make him stroke her again and again. No, the secret of the feminine disposition is indeed a secret: the seriousness of our intentions is our weakest trump. Valerian Innokentievich was pliant and indulgent. He belonged to a younger generation than ours and scrutinized us with sharp, clever eyes, exploiting the advantage of his birth as if we had followed rather than preceded him.

But enough about my rival. I brought Clara sweet tidbits, gave her cigarettes to peck apart. Crooning, insinuating myself into her trust, I moved a step closer every day. Even the cat loves a kind word . . . (The cat again. Why does this word keep sneaking up on my Clara!) My constancy was appreciated—by now she marked my arrival with a glance. No, her heart still belonged to another, but as a woman she found my devotion flattering. She condescended. By now she might have been angry and upset if I had failed to appear someday at dinnertime. I held this sly device in reserve for a crisis in our relationship.

But enough about myself. Love is knowledge. I came to know three things with Clara's help. If it weren't for these, it wouldn't be worth telling about our relationship here.

Clara was tame; that is, sufficiently unafraid of man to allow him within arm's length. But she wasn't just tame, she was also a *crow*; that is, a creature wild and cautious, different, *not* man. For this reason she was finicky in relationships, and at arm's length there was a qualitative boundary (to give her time to recoil, fly away) which only the initiate could violate. One day . . .

. . . she was sitting on the rung of a stepladder propped against our kitchen wall. It was a convenient rung for socializing: Clara's eyes were at the level of a man's. She gutted my cigarette, I reached out my hand . . . She flinched, threw me a sidelong look, sized me up, and decided not to jerk away, not to take off—just stepped lightly along the rung. My hand fell on bare wood.

I experienced a heartrendingly childish emotion—I so wanted to touch her. I suddenly realized that I had never in my life touched a bird. In one instant, a host of propitiatory thoughts flashed through my mind: how man needed animals, how I'd never had an animal of my own when I was a child (my childhood suddenly appeared more pathetic and impoverished than it had been), I recalled the one baby mouse who had lived with me for a week and then escaped after I'd almost taught him to walk on a knitting needle (he escaped from his glass prison over that same knitting needle), I remembered my dusty knees when I crawled out from under the wardrobe and realized that he had escaped forever . . . I decided that this time, without fail, I would bring my daughter a puppy . . . Offering all these prayers, unctuously repeating "Pretty Clara, clever Clara," I lightly touched her claw. She didn't move.

"Clever Clara, pretty Clara," I murmured, stroking her claws more and more boldly. She paid scant attention but permitted me. Cautiously I lifted my hand to stroke her where she might feel it better—she recoiled, sidestepping away. I was allowed only to kiss her hand.

"Stroke her beak, not her head." Doctor D. was standing behind me. How long had he been watching?

"Her beak, you say?" I was embarrassed to be caught. "She'll grab me!"

"No, she won't. Not if you stroke her beak. She's a predator. With a predator, you have to caress its weapon. Then it's not afraid. Now, you did start out the right way—the claws are also a weapon."

A thought, if it is a thought, enters the mind instantaneously, as though it had always been there, as though a place had been vacated for it. It doesn't need to be understood. It provokes no doubt.

"Good Clarra, nice Clarra . . ." I stroked her beak. This was a much more substantial caress than on the claw. She liked it. She narrowed her eyes, rubbed against it. A crow's expression does not incline you to sympathy. By nature, a crow looks angry. The Creator had not provided Clara with any means of showing joy, tenderness, love. She could not smile or purr or wag her tail. All the more touching, then, was the stern maiden's helpless effort at cordiality. Like the crow in Krylov's fable, she had almost dropped the cheese . . . And the delighted thought that Krylov was as accurate as Lorenz flew through my mind with the sweep of Clara's wing— Krylov's name means "wing" in Russian—and flew away. It was true: what Clara seemed to like best was "Pretty Clara." Though I no longer understood why she wasn't pretty. It didn't strike me as funny, I said it quite sincerely: Pretty Clara. Flattery would be impossible if the flatterer himself didn't enjoy it—it wouldn't be worth his while.

Now the doctor added, "Do you remember, I was telling you about the ethics of animals? Well, man's original, animal ethics apparently included an injunction against harming those who trusted him. The dog, and then cats, pigeons, storks, swallows— all of them, in varying degree, became intimate with man through

this peculiarity of human ethics, without being purposely domes-
ticated. Notice that man feels no instinctive love for the truly do-
mesticated animals—chickens, pigs, goats."

I was delighted. "You mean, only trust evokes love?"

"Did I say that?" the doctor asked doubtfully.

Clara was clever, of course, but the doctor wasn't stupid, either.
To tell me such things was to stroke my beak. How gratifying it is
to have a human conviction given back to us in the form of a
scientific law! This means we don't trust ourselves. We need science
to convince us of what is native to us. At the very least it's strange,
this split between the human and the universally natural. From
this crack grows ecology, and fills it.

"Good," I said. "We love those who trust us. But the most
impressive fact about this trust is that it's displayed by a creature
with a completely different nature. This touches us. We don't forget
for a moment that we're people and they're animals. We look down
from above. What about them? Who do they think we are, if they
trust us?"

"That's a complicated question. I hold to the viewpoint that
when they live with us they think of us as different creatures, but
exclude their own master from our species."

"Who do they think he is?"

"Probably a leader of their own species."

"What, can't they see?" I said indignantly. "Clara thinks I'm
a crow, you mean?" I flapped my arms like wings, and Clara shied
angrily. I recollected myself immediately and tried to stroke her
beak again. She turned away. As if hurt.

"Not you, of course. But Valerian Innokentievich—quite possibly she does see him as a crow."

"A man-crow?"

"No question," the doctor said. "Precisely. A male crow."

"Well, excuse me"—I grinned—"but nature can't be that
blind! How could he be a male—sorry, I mean a crow?"

"Well, picture to yourself . . ." the doctor said.

Arguing, we moved off into the dunes.

(Clara died, but not because of a cat. She was pecked to death by ravens. Not crows, but ravens.)

. . . A thought, if it is a thought, enters the mind instantaneously, as if it had always been there . . . This, too, is a thought. "One thought after another! Pity the artist of the word . . ."

Thoughts in ecology are satisfying primarily for this feature: they are obvious. Unfortunately, this doesn't mean they've occurred to you of themselves. Though you may well think so. I don't know why, but this characteristic of a thought strikes me as its most appealing virtue. Russian is rather a clever language, admittedly more inclined to witticism than to thought, until now. Again—Pushkin alone . . . For him, to think is natural; he has no need to shout "Eureka!" every time. The zeal and splendor of an upstart thought, as it strives in isolation to rise above the surface of reality, are evidence, first and foremost, of how rarely a thought enters its triumphant possessor's mind (where every notion has necessarily been immobilized and named). Paradoxicality, showiness, and sophistication begin to emerge as all but independent features—the thought's desire to be recognized and accepted supplants its function, the brilliance of its secondary characteristics dazzles its meaning. This is a general tendency in our country. Even the writing of poems, for example, has become so technical that poesy yearns for an inspired amateur, while the ability to say anything new is incompatible with skill, it's akin to ignorance. In sum, only if we begin from the beginning, over and over again, can we say something new. It cannot be learned, it has to be *unlearned*. Who is that, looming there on the horizon, never getting any closer? That windblown ecstatic with glowing eye and pounding heart, forgetful of everything we've all been memorizing since infancy? . . . The *amateur*. The amateur waves the white flag of ignorance at us: Come here, here I am! On the flag, a haphazard rag knotted to a branch, is the inscription *I love the alive*. In our world so ceaselessly in motion, spinning its wheels in its constant development—*progressing*—if there is anything with the power to regain its own meaning, which has been complicated to the point of loss, it is amateurism: the distance from

Lamarck to Lorenz is bare of cover, the two centuries between them have been trampled flat by the dizzying development of science. The only absolute genius was a monk who sowed two beds of peas . . . the amateur gardener Mendel.

There is a happy regularity in the fact that the truth recedes as you draw near to it, and if you are really dying to get at it, you will have to content yourself with assorted litter picked up along the road. Truth, like the Muse, is a woman—she herself yields, and it's the wrong man every time. Her choice is hard to analyze. You'll scarcely get anywhere with her by calculation— you must have feeling. Force rules out knowledge. How rapidly we come to know the non-essential! The essential, even now, is almost as remote and as close as it ever was. Goodness only knows what contraptions are flying around in the sky, but as for birds, we hardly guess that they exist. Clever machines grind away, supposedly liberating our minds—and we begin to construct for ourselves, in parallel with the super-bomb, facts which the primitive mind assumed without proof: that everything alive can at least feel something . . .

Twentieth-century science has badly scared the truths. They have flown away, like the birds that people are so clumsily trying to trap here on the Kurish Spit. Man was never so scornful of the monkey as when he came to believe in his own origin from it. Intolerable arrogance. Modern ecology, I think, isn't even a science, but rather a reaction to science. A natural, normal reaction (in this respect, too, it's a natural science). The handwriting of this science awakens within us a concept of style, in the same sense as in art. In studying life, ecology itself is alive; in researching behavior, ecology itself acquires behavior. This science has behavior, an unavoidable ethical aspect. Its limitation is an ethical limitation. Not everything is permitted. Not everything is worth thinking, not everything is worth understanding. Amateurism teaches a lesson by casting its natural and seemingly uneducated—*enlightened*—glance on the alive only when in immediate contact with it. And then easily finds words for its concepts. Niche, geographic range, pyramid . . .

The pyramid means who eats whom in what sequence. You can fail to see the structure only if you've climbed to the very top of it . . .

Food, territory, age, energy, population, birthrate, mortality . . . Excuse me, but what's scientific about this, what's new here, where's the discovery? This we know anyway, this is just life.

Exactly. Our mind-set is prideful: only if a thing is already known to us do we believe it exists. But what is already known, what is not yet known, and what will never be known constitute a single, irreducible reality, in which no one thing is essentially more important and no one thing less important. Sometimes I can't help chuckling when I picture to myself the shapeless fragment, so randomly gnawed at by knowledge, that we keep in our heads as a vision of reality. This fragment, however, seems to us quite smooth and round, all-inclusive. To hypothesize a reality that engulfs our atom of information is a heroic scientific feat. The spiritual meaning of a scientific discovery lies not in broadening our sphere of knowledge but in overcoming its narrowness.

To look underfoot and then at the sky—that is the first scientific method. To scuff pensively at the floor and try to read the answer off the ceiling, where, as everyone knows, nothing is written. This we can understand.

In the vista of my mind I study with great empathy an Austrian man, no longer young, as he wanders down a path in a small, doubtless tidy and pretty Austrian village . . . He lifts his head and gazes at the Austrian sky, almost the same color as ours. He sees there a bird calling noisily, let's say a jackdaw. What, in point of fact, is this man doing? Counting crows. This laughable pastime—proverbially synonymous, in our country, with thumb twiddling—absorbs him for long decades. Why is the crow calling, where is she going?

The sea is deep blue, the sky is sky-blue, wormwood is bitter, the wolf gray . . . To adopt a posture of submissiveness; that is, to bare his most vulnerable spot for the crowning mortal blow, exhibit his Achilles' heel . . . Poor beast! How terrified he must be, and how humiliated, as he screws up his eyes and waits for death . . . But—poor winner!—that will never happen. The winner will roll on the grass, howling resentfully, cooling his white heat, sheathing his weapon . . . Oh, if only the loser would flee like a coward! One could interpret this as a violation and chase him from the territory, snapping insultingly at his heels. But no. That sniveler, that whelp, that freakish scoundrel is still standing with his eyes shut and his neck arched back, exposing to his enemy the temptingly pulsating carotid artery. At this moment of submission the moral prohibition is switched on, full force. Each receives his punishment: the loser for weakness, the winner for nobility. Let us note that both are professional killers, for whom death and blood are as work and sweat for us.

The doctor had just told me Lorenz's fable about the Lion, the Crow, and the Wolf. The conversation had led us away from the sea into a thicket. Our feet kept sinking into the sand.

"Well, and what happens in the end?" I asked, truly impressed by this turnaround.

"Nothing," said my doctor friend. "He'll roll and wallow and snarl for a minute, and calm down. The loser will quietly leave the territory, without a backward look."

"The territory?"

"Why, yes. I've told you that predators have their own hunting grounds, with strict boundaries."

"But . . ."

Truly: but . . . The gentlest of doves, symbols of kissy love, with palm twigs in their little beaks, birds incapable of harming anyone, armed with nothing but a beak that would hardly even peck apart a beetle and claws that don't even dig up dirt . . . well, unless you separate them, they'll peck each other to death. And the winner certainly won't pause over his toppled, dying enemy. He'll finish him off by hammering him with his gentle little beak. And he won't cease his bellicosity after his enemy's death, he'll pluck him naked and rip him to shreds. He is feebly armed—he has feeble ethics. When dealing with individuals of his own species, he has no moral barrier.

"A dizzying idea!" I exclaimed, pouncing on the part I needed. "All my life I've hated doves—"

"You've no moral right to condemn them," the doctor said darkly. "They're not subject to our moral judgment."

We were past the forest, which had hidden the dunes from view. They opened up, unexpectedly high, losing their yellowness in the distance and acquiring an alive, greenish-gray color. Their fluid outlines, too, were alive. They grazed there like a herd, lightly rubbing sides, screening each other with their round humped backs, and sticking their heads out. With my every step they swayed before my eyes like a caravan of elephants walking ahead. That alive color reminded me very much of elephant hide.

We walked through the underbrush, and as it diminished toward the boundary with the sand we kept scaring away jackrabbits. They started up from their burrows at the last moment and sprang away right under my feet. In childhood I had cherished a special fondness for them and had made a particular game of being a rabbit. I'm a city person, no hunter—I had never before had rabbits scampering underfoot. I examined my revived childhood with deep emotion. When they took off, they didn't race away from us into the forest, for some reason, but across the open to the dunes, and I was fortunately able to follow them with my eyes. Only the swiftest creatures have that slow way of running—the animal always seems to be dallying in his escape, looking over his shoulder as he runs. Actually, he's flying, not running. There isn't much commotion in his flight, it lacks the flash of paws—which is why the sequence appears to be in slow motion. The leisurely rabbits quickly disappeared from view, however, as we were to verify when we scrambled up that same dune. The rabbit would fly up the dune—grayish yellow against the yellowish gray—and on reaching the edge he would vanish in the sky.

"What about rabbits?" I asked.

"Rabbits are feebly armed. In a fight among themselves they can injure each other very seriously. You haven't had occasion to see this?"

Yet another rabbit flew up from under my feet into the deep blue sky. The underbrush melted away, we stepped onto bare sand. Underfoot, it did not resemble elephant hide; it was bright yellow.

"Have you?"

"Yes."

I parted with the bunnies of my childhood, I hugged them, the little stuffed creatures, and wept. This was an unnecessary disillusionment. Who would have guessed that *rabbits* were such beasts! But not wolves . . .

"Have you seen wolves fight?" I asked balefully.

"No. I haven't seen lions fight, either." The doctor was a sensitive man. "I did see a fight between ravens. The loser exposed the crown of his head—so the winner grabbed his own beak with his claws, as if he wanted to pull it off, lest he use it as a hammer."

"That's funny," I said, picturing this very vividly. "Just grabs himself by the nose . . . Ha, ha."

"By the nose is funny," the doctor said. "By the beak is serious."

"To sheathe his sword?"

"Most likely."

" 'Crows do not pick crows' eyes'—is that what it's about?"

"Well, yes," the doctor said evasively. "Maybe. I wasn't interested in that. Although that fable is about people, of course, like all fables."

"Well, what about people?" I asked, with burning curiosity.

"What about them?" the doctor asked, as if he hadn't understood.

"Are people powerfully armed?"

"What do you think?"

"Far more powerfully . . ."

The doctor only humphed.

"You don't think so?"

"You see, I *try* not to think so," the honest doctor said reluctantly.

"It costs you some effort?"

"It's worth some effort. You and I just analyzed a classic example. Lorenz made his discovery by overcoming the gravitational pull of anthropomorphism." Glancing at me with faint hope and discovering that I understood nothing, the doctor continued, "Anthropomorphism is the error we make most frequently in studying the animal world. Which is to say, we endow animals with our own traits and interpret their behavior on the basis of our own experience. This is why it took so long for us to gain any concept of even wolf ethics, for example. We discussed them more in human terms than in wolf terms."

"So you're saying—" I joined in.

"I said what I said," the doctor retorted crossly. "Please don't interpret me. I said it because we always have a tendency that is the reverse of anthropomorphism, so to speak. It's not a tendency in the general public but in us, in specialists who have begun to know something in our field. It's . . . what should I call it? . . . zoo- or biomorphism. We begin to transfer our knowledge and experience from the realm of the specialized to the realm of the universally human. You've just seen the errors people make when they sin through innocent anthropomorphism. The fabulist's innocent sin, however, has inflicted incalculable harm on the animal world. Hard to calculate, but also a mistake to underestimate."

"I notice you have something special against fables—"

"I read somewhere, and I completely agree, they're a servile, slavish genre. And besides, I don't find them at all funny or clever. Why contrast an ant with a dragonfly? Or rather, I do find them funny, but absolutely not the way the author would want. The more illiterate the fable biologically, I've noticed, the shabbier and more plebeian its moral."

"Well!" I said. "That's a rash remark."

"No more so than yours on animals . . . Or maybe I did go too far. Again, that's not my concern at all. Or it's my exclusively private concern, so to speak, which comes to the same thing: for a scientist, his specialty must be sharply delimited. Nevertheless, the freer and more abstract a writer's design, the freer it is from concrete, specialized errors. For example: 'Once the Swan, the Crayfish, and the Pike undertook to play a quartet.' This fable in no way contradicts—"

"It was other animals who undertook the quartet. Krylov had these pull a cart. You've twisted the two fables into one—a device not permitted in criticism, either, if I may say so."

"I'm not a critic. I don't know how the morals of these fables differ. To me, they both have the same point: the fundamental variation among biological species prevents us from transferring the characteristics of one to the characteristics of another. Beasts are not another humankind. They're separate creatures, just as independent biologically as man. These fables even have a certain ecological nuance, which Krylov catches: the animals can't play their cart . . . or can't drive their quartet, forgive my sophomoric humor. These are fables about the absurdity of anthropomorphic transfer."

I burst out laughing. "Well, now, Grandpa Krylov will never strip Lorenz of his primacy. That's not what he meant at all."

"But it's what he said. I find no other objective meaning in them."

Once again our conversation came to a dead end. We had gone far astray. Breathlessly we scrambled up the dune. The world was painted in two pure colors, yellow and sky-blue, a surrealist's dream. The surface of the dune was very neatly corrugated, like the sandy bottom in the tidal zone—yet another indication that we live on the bottom in a direct sense: these ripples had been made by the wind. Pitilessly we destroyed this flawless surface, on which lay no human footprint. The surface in some places was hard, as on a sandbar, and we left flat, regular, barefoot tracks. In others it suddenly sank underfoot, the sand crumbled, and instead of a footprint we left a shapeless cow hole. So from one step to the next we didn't know which foot would land solidly and which would go through. The wind blew the sand off the crest, stinging our skin; transparent small corpses of beetles and spiders, dried and bleached by sand and sun, rolled down the slope. An occasional blade of grass stuck up, bending away from that solid yellow. A magic circle had been drawn around each—little sundials growing here and there, it seemed, and somehow the idea resonated mysteriously with the sand, perhaps from the association with an hourglass. I myself figured out the origin of these little circles before I could ask the doctor a superfluous question: the blade kept bending under the wind and striking its sharp little tip against the sand, tracing an arc. Thus, being rooted at the center, it drew an ideal circle in the course of the day, as it bent in all directions in the wind. Poignant, that private domain of the grass blade! Now and then a faint bird track, too, without destroying, as ours did, the loneliness of this surface, made some sort of geometrical contact with the grass-blade sundials. And above the yellow, against the blue, a faded butterfly unsteadily fluttered past. Little black beetles stung like the scorching sand, they looked like sand, they were sand brought to life. Ladybugs in fantastic quantity, implacable, marched across ,the desert toward the sea; their dried-out dead little spots rolled downhill. To say that it was quiet is to say nothing: we carried our sandals in our hands. Suddenly, sticking up from the sand even more rarely than the grass blades, there would be a low, pink-and-blue microflower, soft and delicate.

> *The violet poured her scent on the air,*
> *The wolf worked his evil in the pasture.*
> *He was ferocious, the violet dear.*
> *Each follows his own nature.*

"Yes, exactly." The doctor's voice sifted down to me from above, along with a fine stream of sand. "That says the same thing, more accurately and briefly."

"It's Pushkin," I said. "He's never inaccurate. A genius."

"I didn't know. I don't see any evidence of genius in it. The fact is obvious. Accuracy is no merit, inaccuracy is a sin."

"But this is humor," I said, surprised by the doctor's narrowness.

"What does he want with humor?" the doctor said. "It amends inaccuracy, of course. But anything stated with final exactness has no need of humor."

"But is there such a thing—final exactness?"

"In your field, I don't know. But in science, yes."

"Oh, really?!" I put as much irony as I could into this retort.

"Lorenz, now, the man we were just talking about," the doctor parried. "Which is he, serious to the point of inexactness or funny to the point of exactness? Neither. Simply exact."

I concurred and found a gambit: "Yes, he's exact. But then, what to do about man? You evaded giving an exact answer. Can man be exact in defining someone else's existence, if he's inexact in conceptualizing his own?"

I was pleased. Right on the doctor's heels, one more step, and I stood on the summit of the dune.

I had managed to catch him with my question on the way up—a good thing, for I would have forgotten it here. To say that a view opened up is, again, to say nothing: I dropped my sandals on the sand, to free my hand for a gesture that I did not make. I looked now at one sea, now at the other, but I could also see them both at once. On this windy day (as I discovered it to be, at the summit) the western sea was sapphire, with very white, cloudlike whitecaps, apparently motionless. It was so blue that it completely robbed the sky above of color, as if draining it. So that when I looked at the western sea I felt slightly topsy-turvy, as if standing on my head and looking at sky underfoot. I looked at the eastern sea: exactly the reverse. The sky was soaking up the sea's color. Faint, feathery whitecaps still remained, but the decolorized water, very quiet, kidskin-calm, was losing its surface and resembled a celestial haze. The western sea was real: salty and bottomless. Floating beyond the horizon was prosperous Sweden, three hundred miles away. The eastern sea was a shallow, almost fresh inlet, with the Lithuanian shore only thirty kilometers away. But neither Lithuania nor Sweden was visible from here. The two seas were equal and boundless, deep and salty-looking.

"True, I didn't reply to your atomic bomb. That's what you had in mind, isn't it, when you thought of man as being so extremely powerfully armed?"

East and west, sky and sea were still spinning in my head, and I didn't have my feet on the ground. I really didn't, in actual fact, but I realized this only later. I nodded.

"You see, a weapon of mass destruction can't be considered an armament in the sense we spoke of . . . If we draw biological parallels, as you so tactlessly push me to do, we may discover some analogy with the weapon of mass destruction in the mechanisms that regulate the population of a species. This is a far more complicated field than the one we've touched on . . . But in general, certain phenomena which until recently have seemed mysterious receive their explanation . . . how shall I put it? . . . The genetic code contains . . . This will be hard for you. Briefly, certain things have been provided for in nature . . . But the bomb—after all, that's a purely human phenomenon, and without your forcing me I wouldn't begin to draw such an analogy . . ."

I didn't understand it all, for I was deafened by the vision I had gained here, but with a reporter's assiduousness I did not retreat. "Well, all right. Let's give up on that. But is man a biological creature?"

"In three indisputable manifestations: like an animal, he multiplies, eats, and dies."

Oh, that phrase impressed me!

Death is somehow inherently characteristic of this place, though in every respect it's a true paradise. I have already mentioned the extraordinary mix of soul and body peculiar to it. I don't know whether there are many such points on our globe—I had never seen one before, and I have seen no other since. And whenever I've returned here (returned, not come . . .), I have discovered it, in the same persistent meaning. I promised to explain this peculiar feeling of geographical non-existence, and have twice postponed it—I couldn't explain it to myself.

I have said that everything here is the way it was in our first textbook, that here at last we resolve the almost unnoticed, childish disillusionment of disparity. What we are taught does not match what is real. This is the very point of our education, forming the first little crevice of experience, deep in the subconscious. The flow of life will erode it to the size of a ravine, itself perhaps more like the textbook ravine than a ravine in nature. Oh, that ill-printed illustration, where color crept onto color, obliterating and redoubling the line! That apocalyptic ravine had been stripped bare— it looked like a dead tree, a streak of lightning, the brain! Our youthful romantic images smashed like waves against the concrete shore of reality. When we visited an extraneous second cousin once removed in a famous port city, we saw neither ships nor sea; on the zero meridian we will discover neither a line nor a zero; we truly do not see the forest for the trees.

Everything here in this preserve had been preserved, geography included. Sea, bay, dunes, shores, forest, grass, sky, and birds—not only were they present here, in very close proximity, but they also matched the secret images that we associate with the words when we pronounce them to ourselves with our eyes closed: "bay," "forest," "birds" . . . A reification of concepts, a realization of the dictionary.

Space seemed smaller here by one dimension. At the expense of the one, the other two were fully exposed. Tighter here by one, but roomier by two . . . Since the theory of relativity is hard to explain through any example accessible to us in experience, mathematicians suggest that we imagine a comic character who exists in two-dimensional space. To tell the truth, he's no easier to visualize than the theory itself. Here on the Spit, however, I could exist almost like that more-than-flat man—in profile alone. I have to say that the poor fellow's existence, though he has been cheated of a dimension, can only be envied.

I could, for example, naked as Adam, walk out of my cabin to the western shore and start north along the sea, at the edge of the tide, without meeting a single person. And walk thus for an hour, two hours, three—the whole day, all night, always meeting no one, always going the same way, north, as if along a compass needle. I walked until I tired of it, for an hour, let's say, or two, north along the western shoulder of the highway . . . and when I did tire of it I turned around: crossed the highway and trudged back, this time down the eastern shore, this time strictly south, but again along the edge of the water, again along the highway, again keeping boundless water on my left and the highway on my right . . . The Spit ran south to north (along a steady straight line, on the map or from the sky) for a hundred kilometers, yet where I lived it was no more than a kilometer wide. So I, too, on this geographical knife blade, strolled only north or south, balancing between west and east.

From my early school years I remember those poignant zoo-geographical maps, covered with profiles of wild animals, according to their areas of distribution. Since these were visual teaching aids, the animals were the main thing you had to be able to recognize on the map, and this led to an utterly catastrophic violation of scale. Belgium and Holland together would be covered by a bunny, with a scrap of Denmark fitted between his ears. A ram with fabulous doughnuts for horns would stand with his front feet on one side of the Hindu Kush and his hind feet on the other. Not to mention the elephant (the proportions of the animals were more strictly observed on such a map), who easily covered any of the newly developing countries. Without meaning to, the map greatly exaggerated the place of wild animals in the modern world, thus overriding for a long time, in a child's consciousness, any anxiety about their fate. Well, on the Spit, even that map was remembered as not being much of an exaggeration. Not to mention jackrabbits, because I already have, but each time I took a walk I had every chance of encountering a roebuck, and if I was lucky, a fox or even a boar. When such an animal openly crossed the road within a few feet of me, running along a parallel that intersected this naturally demarcated meridian, and he wasn't in scale but what they call "actual size" on this narrowest of all lands I had seen—then the scale changed, the animal truly did almost cover the Spit from sea to sea. I recalled the map every time, and smiled indulgently at my loss.

That is also why the birds fly so eagerly over the Spit, dipping their wings to both seas. They fly above the exposed meridian and temporarily switch off all the locators that help them map their flawless route with such precision across forests and mountains: north in spring, south in fall. The birds relax on autopilot over the Spit. All clear, just keep on flying. The birds spend the night on the Spit, gather their remnants of energy for the remainder of the journey . . . All in all, the Spit is the largest port on the world's air-ocean, unequaled in its bird traffic. Here the bird researchers have built their nest. Here, too, a diffuse human consciousness has spread its snares and traps.

No matter how man has rigged himself out technologically, there are some basic items he has been unable to reinvent. The latest model of car rolls on wheels like a wagon, food is prepared in a pot over a fire, and the freshest fish, even from the newest seiner, are caught in nets. Birds, too—the fish of the air-ocean— are caught in bottom nets, just like fish, the deep-water birds. In the air-ocean the law of Archimedes grows weak, and universal gravity grows strong. Here a cork just barely pops up—a cork from a champagne bottle, at that—and fishing floats sink, rather than soaring up as they do in water. These nets look strange to an outsider, rising as they do from young forest against a background of sand dunes. From a distance, with the light gleaming through it, this fallen, truncated, four-sided pyramid may look airy and azure, harmonizing with the classical topography of the Spit in its own way. Up close, when you see the massive logs used as stretchers, and the rusty cables used as bracing wires, which have a hard time raising the weightless-looking nets to a height of nearly fifteen meters, you begin to realize, with a modicum of justified relief, how difficult it still is for man to carry out simple construction decisions with his own hands, how awkward and primitive man himself still is. And although the researchers don't net these birds for their daily food, but rather band their legs with a weightless little ring, record them, and release them to the ocean, there is a kind of justice in this still-primitive hunt, an equality of rights, perhaps, between bird and ornithologist, a modicum of morality in this seining. (Here I can readily imagine the shrug of their shoulders: they would gladly get a more modern rig—given the chance.)

In summer, only foolish little strays drift into the nets. The traps are turned around when spring is over, their mouths facing north in anticipation of the fall migration, the seiner's fall voyage. After the initial Martian weirdness, your eye grows completely ac-

customed to the traps. They even add something for you, when
you mount the dune and survey the whole surrealistic landscape
of sand, sky, and sea—an empty net is quite fitting here, spread
out in these barrens as if a flood tide had recently been and gone
. . . The eye grows accustomed, and so do the birds who live here.
They are perched along the crosspieces and bracing wires—au-
dacious crows!—on the brink of a threatening perdition. But no
less audacity, with an equally blank stare, can also be seen in people
crossing a street, for example. A man won't walk into the path of
a car any more than a crow will fly into a net.

The local residents, too, mainly fishermen and the families of
fishermen, are accustomed to these nets. Except that they find it
comical and wasteful for a net to serve other than its intended
purpose. So ridiculous, this pastime of idle scientists, who none-
theless get paid (though admittedly not very much) for doing nothing, while the fishermen slave on the seiners, taxing their bulging
muscles . . .

But a considerable mental feat was required of me, too, in
order to surmount this step when I tripped on it, and to discover
that my sneer wasn't essentially much better than the local one.

There are numerous ill-starred areas of the human mind in
which we all have the illusion that we are specialists in some
degree. The illusory accessibility of our pursuits is a target for the
ignoramus: he hits it.

And really. After the traps, the next facility to arrest the
tourist's attention was a certain shack known as the "Markovnik"
(in honor of Mark, who had built it). Chinks of daylight showed
through it; round boxes were mysteriously arranged on its roof;
indoors there were clicking instruments, which looked extremely
complex; the multitude of different-colored wires, forever in a
tangle, was awe-inspiring. And here I note privately that the standard of complexity for my entire life has been, and still is, the
sewing machine, which I was forbidden to turn . . .

Those mysterious round boxes on the roof, for example,
proved to be merely cages, open to the sky, each with just one
bird in it, hopping along radial perches. A system of wires con-

nected these perches to electrical measuring devices, which clicked every time the bird hopped to the next perch. Mark wanted to know which of the perches the bird hopped to most willingly and often, and at what time of year: the northern perches? the southern? . . . He was studying the guidance of migratory birds.

That's all? But what a wonderful installation!

This is what I, who am wholeheartedly on their side and have been graciously admitted to their habitat—this is what I catch myself thinking . . .

The last time I came, I was lodged in an attic over the "staff room," where laboratory work was done. For an attic, this was luxurious—actually, the second floor of the largest building at the observation post. It was piled with old nets and various research rubbish. I wandered around the attic, happening upon strange items—say, a bundle of glass eyes in various sizes, from owl to sparrow, for stuffed birds . . . I enjoyed it here. I paced up and down the long attic, past the nets, in a tense creative silence. If I grew bored with meditative pacing, I could walk out on a peculiar little bridge, the landing of an outside staircase, and gaze from on high, with a captain's squint, at the view that lay open to me. I saw dunes and forest and sky, and the trap with resting birds perched on its wires. I could gaze thus for a moment, as if in deep reflection, and return with a sigh to my manuscript, which hadn't made one line of progress. As it turned out, I accomplished a great deal of work in that attic, half a novel. I discovered this with surprise when I got home, and my attic existence took on the color of special happiness and success. This time, too, I was relying on the attic again, for I had exhausted all other methods. Therefore, when the attic proved occupied I felt it cruelly, as a blow to my last creative resources. The sole cause of my silence lurked in that attic.

The attic now had a far greater population than when I lived there. It was banked with cages of young birds, who had been raised in such a way that the starry sky was the one thing they would never see in their lives. Research Associate N. was studying the role of the starry sky in their overall guidance system . . . Every morning I sourly watched her haul the cages down from the attic so that during the day the young birds would be in the air and sunlight, conditions more natural than her experiment. And every evening, when it began to grow dark, I watched her haul them back indoors under the attic sky, in exchange for the starry one. The staircase was narrow and steep, with wobbly railings . . . the cages were bulky and awkward, so that she couldn't see where she was going . . . my glance, as it followed poor N., was not friendly.

"Don't you think," I said, catching her yet again at this clumsy pursuit, "that you've been studying the effect of carrying the birds upstairs every day, rather than that of the starry sky?"

Receiving no reply, I trudged off to my cabin.

This cabin had graciously been made available to me by a staff member who was away on vacation. It had been built "for himself," with great respect for his own taste. The builder's personality was imprinted on everything I touched here: the mark of the craftsman. Skill in the practical arts was especially characteristic of the inhabitants of the research station. The very presence of skill, in our day and age, had always been important evidence to me. I recognized that it was not in vain. It meant that their main work, although invisible to the philistine and never understood by me, also contained this trait, since it was so dramatically revealed along the periphery . . . The construction materials had been found on the seashore. The walls were papered with maps—geographical, historical (the Children's Crusade, the Ottoman Empire), and nautical—on which, every once in a while, I discovered with surprise the very cabin in which I was staying. Everything folded back, jackknifed, the little table, the little chair, the bed, occupying no space, extremely convenient to use . . . I made up games with the owner's personal belongings and found no use for my own. Such a cozy space, my thoughts parasitized on it.

And I walked out, away from the cabin—to drift around the premises doing nothing, stretch my legs on the narrow paths with the staff members, who drifted around doing their jobs. Once I noticed Associate N. carrying a small, flat box for trapped birds, and followed her into the "staff room" to see what she had caught.

It was not a migration season, the catch was haphazard. She had only three little birds. The business of measuring and recording had been repeated a thousand times; I always liked these practiced motions, which could develop no further except into virtuosity. A bird in the hand, in everyday life, is a more than rare phenomenon. Here, the hand seemed to have been invented just for the purpose. How conveniently, how precisely the empty hollow of our hand conforms to a bird's little body, duplicating it! How rapidly and efficiently all this was done: the aluminum band was pressed around the tiny leg, the journal entry made, the wing measured . . . Now N. blew on the back of the bird's head to part the feathers and determine its age, then tossed it upside down into a narrow, diaphanous bag, the pan of special scales. The bird weighed its eighteen grams. Next, with a luxuriant gesture, she flourished the bag from the open window . . . The little bird easily slipped out, dipped swiftly three times in unexpected freedom, and flew away from us forever.

I poked my finger (stiff and clumsy, compared to a bird) through the net. The last remaining bird glared at me with its angry little bead, then painlessly but courageously pecked my monstrosity of a finger.

I wanted to ask Associate N. whether the shock of banding would affect the bird's later life (how would you like it if they did it to you!)—and this time restrained myself. I did not ask.

"What a nice little bird," I said lyrically, removing my finger from the net.

"Little bird!" N. said scornfully. "How many years have you been coming here? You might at least learn the name of one bird. At least this one! After all, the station is named for it!"

"What is the station called?" I asked.

"Go outside and read it."

I went outside. On the building was carefully written: *Fringilla*.

Fringilla—that's just a finch. I have long known the word "finch," I never recognize the bird finch. I'm always much more a member of my own generation than I suppose. I don't know; what nuances of history or progress or the age can excuse these mental blind spots? Bird, tree, bush, weed . . . it's just never reached the point of personal acquaintance. How cheated I always feel in the forest! Look, a bird fluttering up from a branch . . . What kind of branch? What kind of bird? "Animals have no name. Who ordered them named?" How I value this poet, who has found an excuse for me. Actually, my ignorance does not inhibit me from a mute and prayerful delight in nature, if I happen to notice her . . . But —what poverty and destitution!

Birds? Crow, magpie, sparrow . . . Maybe the chickadee . . .

Flowers? Rose, daisy, snowdrop . . .

Butterflies? Cabbage butterfly . . . (Goodbye, Nabokov!)

At this point my twelve-year-old daughter enters, and in keeping with this text I continue the quiz. "Tell me, but don't stop to think, just list them: what trees do you know?"

My daughter, in some surprise, but obediently: "Spruce, pine, birch . . ." Pause. "Maple, oak . . . Maybe the chestnut?"

My daughter is honest, she doesn't go on to name the ones she doesn't know: elm, beech, ash. Those are words, not trees.

Next: "Weeds? . . . Dandelion, plantain, burdock . . ." The rest are just weeds.

"June bug, dung beetle . . ."

"Shrubs . . . Mountain ash, lilac . . ."

How quickly the series slams shut! She knows no more than I do. She knows just as much as I do. Her generation will not correct the errors of mine. It will assimilate them.

"I forgot the ladybug—that's another beetle . . . I know the birds better!" she said cheerfully, and then rattled off my ignorance, word for word, like a prayer: "Sparrow, crow . . . I know some sort of chickadee, and a little parrot . . . I haven't seen a bullfinch, but I do know the bullfinch . . ."

Silence.

"I know the woodpecker . . . The goose. I don't know the duck. Oh, the chicken. A chicken's not a bird."

"Don't you know the stork?"

"Pictures don't count."

"The seagull?"

Silence.

"Fish?"

She brightened. "I don't know any fish at all," she said. "Not a one. Is a swan a bird? . . . You know who I know!" she said. I brightened. "The flamingo!"

It's the time, of course. The swell of data, the flow of communication . . . Perhaps we keep our heads this empty so that someday we can stuff them with valuable, practical information? Otherwise we couldn't fit it in? I don't believe this. I remember too many makes of cars and televisions, more than the weeds and trees. Ignorance is ignorance. In the Space Age, a few individuals have been in space, even if they don't know the names of living things. But I haven't! It's I who don't know, not everyone . . .

So this, for me, will forever remain irreducibly strange: it is *natural* for us not to know these things. I couldn't like a man who learned the names of mice and grass blades by rote, out of snobbery, in defiance of everyone. He would be as insanely precious as a madman, unnatural in his very naturalism. *Artificial.* Not to know, in the age of science, is as natural as breathing. This astonishes me. There is always someone who knows something that not everyone knows. Surely, not everyone can fail to know the same thing?

An existence in just two dimensions—only lengthwise and (an existence not very accessible to us) only upward—emphasizes the relationship between the top and the bottom, brings us close to the ideal of a homogeneous habitat. Within every skeptic, behind the mask of disbelief, there is a sighing romantic. "White the lonely sail . . ." Romanticism is bound up with the idea of existence in a homogeneous habitat, an existence inaccessible to us by nature. Poets gaze enviously after sailors and aviators who have realized a dream. There, at last, an idea is realized in pure, undisappointing form—"as though the storm brought rest." But no, not fully realized . . . They get there, but they don't belong. Only in their vessel and only as a group and not forever: the corruption of return, the soul disillusioned by falsehood. "Give me nothing more! Just a boat and an oar! A boat and an oar . . ."

The only homogeneous habitat accessible to man is the realm of the spirit. The supreme thought is accessible to each of us, various people at different points in time and on earth can think it, all paths lead to it, but once achieved, it will be one and the same thought. Only at the very summit will we possess the definitively common nature that cancels loneliness, the common nature with which we are born . . . If someone has reached Truth and someone else is about to reach it, it will be the same Truth, their paths will cross. We are definitively equal only at the very bottom (dust) and at the very top. The rest is journeying. Pilgrims, when they grow weary, look at the sea and the sky—the horizon recedes, and the sky is always as high as ever.

Thus I interpreted to myself the unfathomable idea of the supreme—thus I daydreamed on this most estranged of earthly surfaces, where the threads of all four dimensions had grown thin, almost invisible. Two of them had worn through. Should the last two wear through, this earthly cloud would fly away, it seemed.

But the Spit's narrowness, which essentially eliminated one dimension, could not, even together with the timelessness of sand, water, sky, and solitude, have created this effect, the homogeneity of habitat that I nearly experienced here. And all the other explanations I found for myself were partial—did not explain . . . For example: this was the westernmost point of the empire, no longer Russia, more likely Germany, what used to be East Prussia . . . But I had been farther west. There the earth became Poland and was Poland, but it was nothing more; that is, this unheard-of condition of the earth (neither Russia nor Lithuania nor Germany nor

Prussia nor Poland) also didn't extend into the West. Or another explanation, more basic than the state: the regime. This territory was under a dual prohibition, that of the preserve and that of the frontier. Here was an unpoetic but realistic reason for its solitude, untrampled landscape, wild animals. But again—not for its incorporeality. I also found a more unexpected reason for this land so organic and harmonious: it was not so created by God, it turns out to have been so created by man. Here the notorious noosphere seemed most justifiable and noble. Man, on his own initiative, had planted forests on the Spit and loosed wild animals. Not even a century had passed since the origin of the Spit I was now admiring. This was hard to believe, so natural to the Spit was its current appearance. Feebly extrapolating, I tried to picture what it had been like without man—that is, without pines, birches, and blackberry bushes, without moose, roebuck, and boar: the inhuman wind furiously prowling the dunes, rolling them from place to place, blowing them eastward, straggly inhuman willow branches quivering in the wind, birds inhumanly flying over . . . There would be enough here for a ballad, a piercing ballad howling like the wind —but only one. The poet would wrap himself in his cloak, squint into the distance, and grit the sand in his teeth, whispering the great line, as expressive as the naked Spit—and then drive away in the same carriage, rolling up the blind and fastening it shut without a backward glance. The immortal poem had already seen all, with its own sighted lines . . . No, I hadn't seen the Spit that way, and I didn't mourn it. Grounds for pondering whether one is always right to mourn the departed. Not all waters have flowed away before our very eyes . . .

But even this surprise, that the land was partly artificial—like the fact that it was not mine, like the fact that it was forbidden— still did not explain its peculiar incorporeality. There was yet another cause, finally and truly the last: this land was not land at all. A principled cartographer could have refrained from putting it on the map, or should have looked for a new symbol, neither land nor water, a kind of dotted line. The Spit did not meet the criteria by

which we define dry land, or at any rate not the basic criterion
from the standpoint of science, which believes criteria and not eyes.
From that literal standpoint, the Spit was not land but sea. It was
ocean floor, a hypertrophied sandbar thrusting itself above the
water. A strict scientist would say that it was no more land than
is the back of a whale that has surfaced from the water and will
presently dive back down. He would smile condescendingly. The
usual mistake—confusing human time with geological. From the
standpoint of geology, the Spit has thrust itself temporarily above
the surface of the World Ocean, for a time so brief that it is, indeed,
more comparable with the whale back's existence as dry land than
with any geological epoch, even the most fleeting. It is a truly
fleeting formation, this Spit—driven by the wind, it is drifting
toward the mainland at a fabulous speed, tens of centimeters a
year. Man tries to capture this geological instant: it is beautiful.
He plants forests, designs a monstrous dam shielding the Spit from
the sea. When he finally halts it, it will no longer be the Spit. It
will be a dam.

This did serve for an explanation. It turned the surprising into
the convincing: there was nothing of the mainland here. That this
was not mere suggestion—the special condition of the earth's surface on the Spit—is proved not only by reverse logic, the inability
to state causes and the primordial quality of surprise, but also by
the following fact, which caught up with me even later: there is a
mainland pimple embedded in the spiritual purity of the Spit. In
its flight, the Spit has overtaken a small island and hasn't yet left
it behind. On this fragment of mainland amalgamated into the Spit
you will feel a difference. Here other currents run through the earth,
here everything, even the sky, is more banal, more carnal and
malicious; here the fishermen have settled, gnarled people with
stunted, gnarled dogs running around (apparently a special breed,
under the constant influence of the wind). Here the air is different,
the rains are different—this is land. And the local inhabitants really
do seem to live as though on an island, they don't think of the Spit
as dry land. Almost disdainfully, if not fearfully, they squint at it

from their kitchen gardens as though gazing into the distance, at the sea. An alien thing—not theirs.

To the best of our knowledge, man is incapable of imagining anything that he hasn't seen in some form or other. His mental images of hell are far more developed, differentiated, and detailed than his images of paradise. Moreover, hell is well populated, so to speak, with ourselves and our acquaintances. We seem to understand hell.

> We need only depict in cramped intimacy and simultaneity (on one canvas, let's say) the things we have met in everyday experience—and the ghastly proximity of a saucepan, a rose, and a slug in the sink (my landlady's charming little courtyard in the Crimea, where I am writing this page . . .) will be suffused with hellish meaning. Nor have the birds flown from this narrative. In Bosch we are sure to meet both bird and fish; the most horrible thing is that the expression he gives the bird's eye is not frightening, but always so curious and good-natured.
>
> Almost the main feature of Bosch's hell is a complete inventory of the household objects and tradesmen's tools of his time. They look so real, they must have been reproduced exactly. The unclean are building their tower with all the devices, and according to all the rules, of construction technology. The sinners are being heated in saucepans and skillets that must have been used by every housewife. Simply, these everyday objects and implements are many, all at once, in one glance. What scares us in Bosch's hell is its similarity to life. The Promised Hell . . .

Our vision of paradise is so meager and unattractive as to bring on the puckery taste of boredom: tabernacles . . . Having been on the Spit, and having encountered nothing else like it in my life, I think I can envision paradise with greater certainty. That world, too, is indistinguishable from ours, nothing we haven't seen has been invented there, but much of what we've seen has been eliminated. That world is innocent and free, it is passionless, there is neither pain nor hope in it: it has been divested of our relationship to it: it exists, but in our absence, seemingly even in its own absence. Existence in that world is so astonishingly unburdened because we're not there, and when we are, we're no longer ourselves, as it were.

I don't know why the thought of death comes so easily in this paradise. Perhaps because paradise itself, after all, comes after death. Because death has already happened . . .

From that day on, and every day, I walked away from my blocked typewriter and, just over the threshold, found myself in a place where I had nothing to write and no reason to write, because to see was enough. To see, and to thank fate for giving me eyes and for what my eyes had been given. I took several steps across the sand toward the sea, knowing that beyond the next small dune with its tousled hairdo of sedge I would see the water. This sense of expectation, although satisfied every time, was always just as keen: I walked halfway around the dune, a final, very strong gust of wind in the little gully seemed to hold me back, and suddenly I was standing on the shore and realizing, again, that the whole time, both up in the cabin with my typewriter and while I was walking, the sea had been roaring, and the roar had lured me out to see what was roaring: it was the sea roaring. I took exaggerated deep breaths and inevitably gazed into the distance.

"Would that I could always gaze like this . . ." That banal phrase conveys my preoccupation quite accurately: after the phrase came a sigh, and I was no longer gazing at the sea. I was occupied with the question: What sets the limit on enjoyment if there are no obstacles in its path? I didn't have to hurry anywhere, there was nobody to hurry me. For less than half an hour, less than five minutes—I don't think it was even a minute, more like half a minute, with the last seconds strained and artificial—I had squinted into the distance. Then I uttered that mental sigh, and all was over . . .

When we turned back, I asked the doctor what he thought about this.

"Forgive me for changing the subject . . . But we've walked and walked along the shore, completely absorbed in conversation, we're absorbed in it even now, and yet for the last five minutes I've been wondering when we'd turn back. We're not hungry or tired, and to all appearances we're not bored or in a hurry; the shore is practically identical all the way, the terrain won't change before tomorrow . . . Yet I was thinking: We're going to turn back. What happened and what ended, that we turned back? What constant operates within us to determine our degree of satiation and the duration of our every action? Suppose there's nothing to bind or obligate us . . . We can't give a whole lifetime to the pleasant freedom of conversation. But imagine you're in love, you're walking with your sweetheart. Again, you'll turn back. You'll wait under the clock for thirty minutes or an hour, in the doorway all night —but not till the New Year. You part at dawn. Time for the young lady to go home. Mama, and all that. But she had the same mama an hour ago, you know, and it's been time to part for many hours, yet at this precise moment for some reason the time has definitely come. The nightingale or the lark? After which exhortation—count them—does Romeo finally leave? Why not earlier or later? Why is it that I didn't think about the time while we were walking, and I'm not thinking about it now, yet we're already walking back? What thought made us turn?"

"That one, I think, made us turn in the present instance," said the doctor, who was precise in everything. My discussion was so unscientific that he ignored it. All he could talk to me about in this connection was the biological clock. But that was a different subject entirely . . . "You see, the biological clock is . . ."

I listened to him, and the thought troubling me now was this: What is the concern of science, and what is not? Couldn't my question be studied with precision, calculated, explained? Which law, out of the many laws, does science pluck out for study?

"The next one," the doctor said.

"Beg your pardon?"

"We look for the law that comes next, after the one we have discovered."

"Then don't you think you'll inevitably get sidetracked?"

"Beg your pardon?" the doctor asked.

"I mean, you begin to study a phenomenon, you discover a certain law, you feel your way from that one to another, from that one to the fifth, and so on. Haven't you forgotten about the phenomenon you set out to study?"

"Ah," said the doctor. "No, we haven't."

"Certainly not." I grinned. "You study birds, you get interested in migrations. You study migrations, you get interested in the energy factor. You study . . . metabolism, is it? . . . and you focus on changes in the birds' weight. You study fat in birds. By now you're studying fat, don't you think?"

"But had we studied all this before?"

"But does a bird have eyes? and wings? does a bird have a bird's brain?"

The doctor burst out laughing. "Tell me," he said, "you weren't ever a *D* student, were you?"

"I was," I said.

So I would go down to the sea in order to find the doctor on the shore, if he had just gone down, or else he would follow me out, red-eyed from a sleepless night doing calculations. His numbers didn't add up, my letters didn't form words—without saying hello we would continue yesterday's conversation.

I lost all shame. I abandoned myself to the ambition of the nimble student. I asked him the questions I hadn't asked as a young child. I might not get an answer, but I was delivered from my complex. All the questions without whose answers I had refused to understand anything further and received an "Unsatisfactory." Does an insect feel pain? does a bird think? does a tree feel? do animals have a sense of humor? what happened to the intermediate evolutionary links; that is, why did man skip a rung on the ladder? has evolution stopped, and why? what do so many mosquitoes eat when I'm not here? can parasites be eliminated from the biological chain without harm? do birds have external sexual organs? And all these, quite quickly, came down to certain of the treacherous questions, which, in turn, came down to one: What is man?

He had no answer to this question. Only oblique reservations.

"In the sense you mean," the doctor said at last, "there can be no answer. Man equals himself. He is incapable of more. God alone, if He existed, could know what man is."

"Are you sure He doesn't exist?"

"I don't think He did."

I was about to open my mouth again when he said, "Let's not speak of Him in vain. That commandment does not contradict science."

I am not very strong on useful information. All that he knew as a specialist, all the precise facts that I might have gleaned from him, flew in one ear and out the other. I've always been interested in how they put the jam into "pillow candies."

What I learned from him about his work could perfectly well fit on the flap of a dust jacket. "A little about a lot," or "nothing about everything." In New Zealand, it seems, they have a bird who during the mating season builds a house on the ground, with a door, and when courting the female he comes to the rendezvous with a flower in his beak. Or that birds have always known the earth was a sphere, they knew before people did, and yet when migrating they take the azimuth from the assumption that the earth is flat (perhaps I already have it mixed up). Or that birds don't get sick.

That last bit of information I experienced with somewhat greater emotion than the other entertaining bits. The assertion completely contradicted another one I had devoured the day before (naturally, I took everything on faith)—namely, that all birds are sick, there is no bird not sick.

"It's just an illusion that birds flutter around gaily," Associate N. had told me with a tinge of melancholy. (She was returning from the traps, carrying a quivering catch, in a special flat box, with a net stretched across the top and a sleeve at the entrance.) "Overhead, they're all feathers and cleanliness. Anyone who held them in his hand, as we do, would see that the poor things are swarming with parasites, covered with scabs and wounds."

These burdens behind the outward cloak of lightness (of course they're light—they soar!) had evoked my trust and sympathy. The doctor clarified my bewilderment for me: That's all external, and this is the truth: birds do not get sick in the same sense as other warm-blooded creatures, including us: they do not get sick with a temperature. It can't go any higher. Now I fully understood those 108 degrees, a little of what I remembered from school. Birds live at the limit (the price of flight). Their metabolism takes place at the limit of intensity possible for a warm-blooded creature. They are always at fever pitch and in a fever. Our slight fever of 100° is their 110°—that is, death. This is the sense in which birds do not get sick.

I suddenly saw the true narrowness of life—which we all complain about with such vigor, precisely so that we won't see its full extent. (Our difficulties are all temporary, we don't want to see that they are the norm, that sometimes there is war, for example, when people do not get sick, almost like birds.) On this rarest of earths, where oxygen is diluted to exactly the proportion that we can breathe, where we have barely enough fresh water, even our body temperature is confined to an interval as narrow as a ray of light, where T° ≤ 108°. This entire space is divided and redivided into niches and geographic ranges, where, though we fly and gulp from morning to night, we have barely enough food to maintain these 108 (98.6) degrees, where getting too cold or too hot—like not getting enough to eat and drink—means death. All of this is close up and very real, all is crisscrossed and interconnected, so that if you had time to tear yourself away from the urgency of feeding, when you necessarily feel your existence is unique—if you had time to reflect, even then you couldn't separate your own existence from the rest. Are you a separate body, or a part growing on a common one? You will never be able to say for sure.

Here is a bird. A large bird. Look into her side-bulging eye—
you'll never meet her gaze. The little birds are the ones with the
vivacious bead-eyes that we think we understand. This bird has a
red, wild, fearsome eye. In the sky she is beautiful ("now touching
her wing to the wave . . .")—here in your hand she is ugly and
frightening. She is so definitely not one of us that you won't lapse
into any sin of anthropomorphism here.

This was a seagull (the staff argued, trying to determine her
species). Seagulls do not get caught in traps. She had been brought
in by a boy named Sasha, a Junior Naturalist acquainting himself
with his future profession at the research station. He was ruddy,
round-cheeked, dark-eyed, youthful, healthy, his mother's pet. The
seagull was shockingly unlike him. He was excited, and endlessly
repeated his story.

Like Ivan the Fool catching the Firebird, he had caught this
seagull with his hands. He had dived like a goalie and tackled her.
Honest! He was walking along the seashore, the whole flock took
off, and she was just sitting there. He dove. Tackled her, honest
. . . He didn't believe it himself: Can you beat that, a person who
catches seagulls with his hands! . . . His heroic deed was fading in
his own eyes. No one had criticized him, but no one had praised
him, either. "I've been carrying her for two hours!" he said, hurt.

"But she'll die of cold!" someone said.

This surmise brought immediate action . . .

Privately I have often noted a certain dignified unsentimen-
tality in practical work (and have liked it more sentimentally each
time). Thus the staff of the research station, who themselves had
a very monotonous diet of mush and concentrates, would boil and
chop eggs, scrape carrots, and so forth, every day, to feed their
feathered captives what they themselves did not eat. They reminded me of parents whose children will never emerge from
childhood. Or, for instance, not one of them had the slightest pang
of conscience about disemboweling a bird for his own inane experiment, yet if any unforeseen loss occurred they were extremely

vexed and grieved. One day too many birds flew into the trap, the staff failed to free them in time, and many birds perished. So they ate them! This wasn't just professional chic, an exaggerated lack of squeamishness toward living things, a professional freedom from philistine ideas, an ability to eat both crow and fox. (There is no poisoned or inedible meat! Yet another peripheral discovery I made for myself in their habitat. A reminder, in case you're ever starving to death in the forest—anything can happen.) It was also, although unconsciously, a matter of atoning for a sin before nature, where nothing perishes in vain. They transmuted this precedent into a hunt (the wolf is not bloodthirsty but hungry when he procures his food), they expiated their sin by ritually harmonizing their mistake with the ecological system, by pretending they had trapped these birds for food.

. . . They chopped up a hard-boiled egg, and one of them skillfully held the seagull, skillfully opened her beak, and tried to feed her. The seagull had no idea that they wished her well. Nor had she any idea that her refusal of food threatened her with death. She could not imagine that she was in the arms of a professional and not one of her feathers would be harmed. She probably assumed they had caught her to eat (if in trouble you can eat a seagull, too, although they taste terrible). She saw herself surrounded by people utterly unlike seagulls, and did not see the rescuing sea. She did not want to eat, she passionately expelled this rescuing food as if it were poison. The hero found himself on the sidelines, bewildered, and he stared distractedly at his empty hands that had caught the bird. After dinner the seagull died. The staff attempted to "find a niche" for her, too, in the name of the integrity of the ecological system—they gave her to Clara. Clara was indignant, however. She expressed her indignation in a very human way: cawed, flapped her wings like arms, maintained an outraged silence, and turned her back on caressing exhortations. I didn't go asking questions about the true nature of her outrage (the bad food), for in my own way I shared Clara's feelings.

With a mortal terror filling her crazed eye, this choking seagull stands before me as a generalized symbol, so to speak, all birds in one. This one-bird, if we were unused to their existing on earth at all, is a monster, a terrifyingly huge freak who cannot actually exist. She has just two spindly legs. Her feet are claws. Her coat isn't even fur but flat, coarse-haired bones, which cannot be called by any name we already know, and we invent the word "feather." She has a small, serpentine head with unseeing eyes at the sides; she can't look at you with both eyes at once. Her mouth and nose are combined into a horn, which she opens with a loathsome sound. We can find no word for this and will label it conditionally a "beak." Instead of arms or forelegs she has two fans—even we might think them beautiful, except that they have this streamlined, hump-backed, unnatural torso affixed to them. But if these unnatural parts are intimidating individually, what a monster this is in the aggregate! Take an insect—toward which we all feel an instinctive squeamishness and hostility—enlarge it to the size of a cat, and you will understand the aesthetic emotions you actually experience when you first see this one-bird.

I went out to the gulf. If the seashore was alive with surf, with all the attractive, ever-changing flotsam in its tidal zone, with the jaggedness and ruggedness of its forested dunes, then the bald, unforested shore of the dead-calm gulf was peculiarly empty and lifeless. The lines here were different from those on the sea—peculiarly smooth curves, flawlessly drawn. Here the towering dunes came right to the water, stopping abruptly at that maximum angle, which immediately led me to think of mathematics. Free-flowing dry matter. All this was flowing, falling—just touch it. But no one did, and it stood in an unthinkable sultry equilibrium. Above the scorching daytime heat of the sand the air was shimmering, turning this already dreamlike scene into a mirage. I was standing on the crest of a gigantic sand wave, ceaseless in its agonizingly slow race toward the mainland: here it smashed against the inert smoothness of the gulf exactly as the sea smashed against the shore. It was dizzying, this reversal of my habitual concepts, the smoothness of this sandy steep slope under my feet. Here was a place to launch gliders and paper kites . . . Those webbed, soundless airplane-ghosts would suit the landscape almost better than birds. The wind moaned in my rigging. I stepped into the void and experienced the emotions of Icarus. The sand caved under my feet, curved around my calves. In three giant steps I flew down to the water from an altitude of thirty meters. A river of sand overtook me and buried me knee-deep. I had added my millimillifraction, hastening the Spit in its race: behind me, the sand was spilling delicately, leveling my tracks. A few steps away, by the water, a dead bream lay on its broad side, with its upper side eaten away. Its death, still in progress, seemed to be the only life here. And now, motionless as a glider, the bird who had died yesterday slowly floated overhead. There used to be a fairy tale like this, about a man who sought a land of immortality . . . He thought he had found it. Nothing changed or grew old there, and time did not pass. But it turned out that once every thousand years a bird came and carried off exactly one grain of sand, designating that thousand years as a second. The man was disillusioned. Even in that blessed land, there was time . . . Yesterday's bird, overhead, was from that tale, I thought: the implacable sand grain of my time was gripped in her beak. I leaned back against the dune without pulling my feet out, as if I had grown into the sand. What I saw had no name. I saw water, I saw a fish, I saw sky, I saw a bird . . . they had no names. I didn't know that they were called water, sky, or bird. Perhaps this was fish stretching before me to the horizon, and the fathomless blue above my head was bird? Perhaps what had died in front of me was the water, and the sky had evaporated, vanished from sight? I had no way of knowing that the world didn't stop beyond the horizon. Words, at last, were as empty as the weightless chitinous integuments mingled here with the sand. So they were empty after all. I had become separated from language, which keeps droning at me that the world exists, that it's everywhere I go, it's right here. And, as always, I sighed, I pulled away from the dune through whose eyes I had momentarily looked at what was in front of me. I extracted my feet from the sand, one at a time. The fish was a fish and was called a bream, the bird was not sky but a seagull, what stretched before me was not fish but water, under the name of gulf; oh, and the sky was air, its own airy ocean. Beyond the horizon was Lithuania, invisible to me but solidly fixed. The sky alone had no horizon, beyond it lay the unknown, although that, too, had been stratified by someone into domains and terms—but those words live only in the textbook, and that is why we can still sometimes see into the sky, with this wordless kind of vision. I was confounded by the fact that everything had been named, pinned down by knowledge not contained in the things I saw. Which do we see: objects, or the words naming them? At least it is clear that the world we are coming to know has no reciprocal tie with our knowledge. Even if it is reflected accurately. Our knowledge merely reflects the world. But the world does not look in that mirror.

The mirror is man. You can lift your hand to your eyes, of course: My hand. Or look at your feet: My feet . . . But a man by himself, when he looks before him, does not see himself, and especially doesn't see his own eyes, any more than a mirror sees itself. But even the things you can see on your person, as belonging inalienably to you—hands, feet, navel, below the navel—are not you, after all, they're an envelope, a body, you're inside . . . Look before you—you're not there. Perhaps you are what you see before your eyes?

The sky was empty and ceased to be empty. All at once many birds flew over, a flock. The sky became empty. When one bird flew over, I saw one bird. Exactly one. How many had flown over just now? Ten? More. A hundred? Fewer. I don't know exactly how many there were—fifty-five, fifty-nine, I didn't have time to count them. But one thing is certain: there were a finite number, not one more or one less. I could not learn that number, and no one will ever learn it now. But since that number was exact and final, it exists, as though someone knew it . . . "But the very hairs of your head are all numbered . . ."

One bird, and then all at once many, but how many? . . . The unit—that is the number I know. One—that is the count I keep. Dividing by one is reality.

"I think I can guess—although with difficulty—what you're getting at," the doctor said. "Science really does have a certain inherent narrowness. Its concern is not so much world issues as things that can be accurately established. But your complaints show a certain incomprehension of the genre, to use terminology close to your heart. For us, a brilliant idea we can't prove or confirm by experiment is unprofessional. It's dilettantism, or leisure at best. Taken on faith, a beautiful idea can carry you far astray, beyond retrieval. There needs to be an element of sluggishness, as it were, in the ethics of the true scientist, who has ideas by the bucketful. Actually, to some extent, we do have a gap in our thinking, between the unit and the multitude; but the multitude is also taken as a unit, in some sense. Then again, the unit is taken as an element of the multitude . . ."

We were walking along the shore and not seeing the sea. Yesterday there had been a "box gale"—assorted curiosities were spread out on the shore like wares on an endless display table. We walked along this market row. Wooden boxes were less common than bright plastic. We might find a keg or a pail, also lightweight and colorful. If we were lucky, it might even be undamaged, washed from the decks without reason. Here and there lay plastic balls— fishing-net floats, beautiful. The balls had survived intact, but we did not know what to do with their definitive form and lost purpose. We walked along, developing an idea, and suddenly a certain want of attention crept into the idea: there was something red or blue up ahead, attracting us. Studiously we avoided quickening our step. The idea rigidified, narrowed, and seemed to find its natural conclusion: this was half of a scarlet plastic pail, a vertical section. The intact side of the pail had been turned to us out of spite. We passed by this fraud—and a fresh idea gathered fresh force. A fresh apparition of a fresh item, up ahead, delineated the next pause or an unexpected turn of the subject . . .

"Haven't you ever thought about the nature of man's craving to gather things? Mushrooms, berries, birds' eggs, collections? Or the gifts of the sea?" the doctor said, kicking a yellow float. It rolled back down into the rising tide. The surf was listless after the gale. "To understand what we inherited from our ancestor, we need to know what our ancestor was like. Morphologically, man isn't very specialized for procuring a particular food. His original ecological niche was the gathering of fruit, herbs, roots, eggs, small animals, and coastal flotsam. Such a method of subsistence is inefficient and requires vigorous, varied activity. In contrast to many other species (herbivores, for example), man possessed limited food resources. Hunger was a permanent state . . ."

Thus he resisted when I tormented him about man, but then lightly spilled his secrets himself. Even though he was full of a noble determination not to exploit his experience as an ecologist and ethologist by applying it to man, still, he himself was a man, and he couldn't help thinking about the same things I did. Thus, without meaning to, he had already told me enough. In some respects his ideas were so convincing to me, I believed them so easily, that this very ease struck me as the best of proofs. With a dilettante's enthusiasm, I was already using as my own many of the concepts he had taught me. Our conversation would follow this pattern:

"You're saying"—I would seize on a remark of his— "that . . . Doesn't it follow that . . . ? Then don't we have to conclude . . . ?"

"Yes, I suppose you could say that," the doctor would agree reluctantly.

"Then," I would say, "we can hypothesize . . ."

"Yes, that, too," he would agree stolidly.

"It turns out that man . . ." I would say, heading into the homestretch.

"No," the doctor would say, and easily rebut me, with arguments to spare.

I would retreat temporarily, nodding.

But by now he was used to the freedom of our conversations. Little by little I had corrupted him. His imperative was weakening. I don't think this was because I was persuasive; all these ideas had been languishing within him for a long time, unusable. At first he spoke only of primitive man. In this connection, he might let slip such definitive sentences as: "Man has a low fertility rate compared to other animals."

Or: "Flourishing species strive to increase their numbers and territory as much as possible. Man is a flourishing species; his urge to settle in new places and increase his numbers is natural. By the beginning of our era, the number of people on earth is estimated to have been two to three million . . . That was the antique world . . ." He sighed pensively.

"Malthus . . ." I said. Sand gritted in my teeth, and now we turned back.

The doctor's attitude toward Malthus was complicated. History beckoned him. The ecologist in him was tempted by the epochs that showed through in the distant past, where vain details had been effaced and the count was kept not by decades but by centuries.

"Why do you think Alexander the Great stopped? . . . No, no, his military machine was flawless. There was nothing in the world that could resist it. Simply, he had gone so far beyond his geographic range, and he had won so long ago the lands sufficient for the further consolidation and prosperity of his own country, that the biological purpose of his aggression (to expand the territory for a flourishing population) was completely exhausted. By the time he reached India and Central Asia he was a traveler, almost an amateur ethnographer: he arrayed himself in the national garb of the new lands that had nominally submitted to him. There was nothing he could do but leave, with no likelihood of reaching the subjugated country ever again . . . He could not turn back, he seemed to have forgotten where he came from. His death was obscure. Thus all aggression miscarries, establishing only the necessary boundary to the expansion of its geographic range."

"Interesting," I observed. "It's been a fairly long time since we had a war. Could modern tourism be viewed as sublimated aggression?"

"Are you saying this to me, or am I to you?" The doctor was tempted. Like Alexander, he could no longer stop. He measured history in imperial giant steps. The same had also happened, as the doctor saw it, with a later people, the Norse (thus he was creeping into epochs closer to ours, while I, like a hunter concealed in his blind, didn't breathe or move or interrupt). The Vikings had also possessed military might, comparable to Alexander's. They had had no equal—they could have gained a world much more livable, from our standpoint, than their cliffs and fjords. But from the biological standpoint they behaved more logically than Alexander. They were strong enough to seize Europe, yet they discovered Iceland and Greenland, which Europeans find uninhabitable, and reached the northern shores of America before Columbus. They expanded only within the limits of their natural geographic range, the northern seas.

I had always wondered at the evident relief with which a man comes down . . . You no sooner gain a height, spiraling upward like a bird, than you immediately drop like a stone, mistaking some utterly inedible piece of trash for a gopher. But I, too, could not stop: "The history of Russia begins with the Vikings."

"Even though north, it wasn't their geographic range," the doctor said. "Russia Russianized them. Their regime ground to a halt."

"As in the humorous saying," I said. " 'Come here—I've caught a bear, and he won't let go.' "

"That's it, that's it," the doctor agreed.

"But why did the Tatars bog down in Russia?" I went on.

The doctor humphed, chewed a moment, and concluded, "The steppes ended."

"Did you think that, or did I say it?" I exclaimed admiringly.

But he was lured no further by my admiration. He stopped, like Alexander, having gone too far in his confidences. He fell silent and gazed into the distance.

The sea, toward evening, had become utterly calm and still. Lacquered. As if replete and thicker than water. For a long time now, although I spent hours wandering beside it every day, I had not been seeing it . . . In addition to box gales, there were also "bottle gales," which cast up bottles and flasks from whiskeys and gins I had never seen or drunk. There were "amber gales," which cast up a crumb of amber on their last wave. For a long time I had only been looking under my feet, in the hope of finding a piece of amber "as big as a child's head," or a whole canister, or at least a flat little flask, but I had stubbornly failed to find anything of the sort with which the lounge at the research station was crammed (once they had found a keg of wine, still good, and once a large jar of black caviar, unfortunately already spoiled), not realizing that an ancestor was guiding me in these quests, that this was my excursion into man's prehistoric niche . . . I found a "chicken god," a stone with a hole in it—my ancestor might have worn it to protect his chickens—and that was all. For a long time, it turned out, I hadn't been seeing the sea, hadn't been looking up, had been settling rather rapidly into my forefather's niche. The evening sea turned a grayish pink, fading opalescently toward the horizon, and there it melted away, ran dry, in a line so gentle it was revealed only by the delicate sharp stroke that defined a tiny steamboat. The sun was setting, implausibly large and red. I couldn't tear my eyes away . . . I did—and saw at last, right under my nose, a Swedish beer crate made of dark cerise plastic, with three unfaded gold crowns on it.

Inspired by the crate, I turned homeward. "So be it. Good," I reasoned. "If gathering was the ecological niche of primitive man, and if he has abandoned that niche, made his way up the pyramid of life to the very top, expanded his geographic range to its utmost, and crowded out all the other biological species to settle all the territories of the earth, then what is his niche now, his geographic range? What can we designate as the ecological niche of modern man? The planet earth itself? Can we express it that way?"

"That's somewhat tautological." The doctor shrugged. "But yes. If you like."

All this was reminiscent of an experiment with Lorenz's fish . . . They construct their little houses in opposite corners of the same aquarium and draw the property line straight down the invisible mathematical middle. If one neighbor trespasses, even accidentally, the other fills with fury and chases the trespasser—out of his own territory, all across the trespasser's territory, and into his house-cum-fortress. In his own home the cowardly trespasser gathers rightful energy and darts out, extremely agitated, to pursue his instantly timid rival all across the aquarium, driving him, in turn, back into his house. Once there, the rival gathers strength . . . And so on. The pendulum of war, set to swinging by the chance violation of a boundary, is damped remarkably slowly. The enemies keep this up for hours, until the same invisible boundary has been defined. Then, after halting on it for a moment, nose to nose, they separate as if nothing had happened, nibbling grains of sand and pretending that they have simply come out to graze on the borders of their properties . . . Thus we ourselves illustrated what we were talking about.

"Good," I said, tightening my grip and continuing to drive the doctor homeward. "Then from another angle"—the beautiful crate slapped rhythmically against my knee—"we can discuss the earth as a single ecological system, as the ecological niche on earth of life itself . . ." (The doctor had not objected so far.) "Can we say that by the moment when man appeared on earth the evolution of life, as it were, had also been completed?" (The doctor still said nothing . . .) "By that moment, the earth as a whole was a perfect, well-developed, reliable, definitively balanced ecological system, where everything was interrelated, forming a closed cycle which in no way disturbed the precision of the overall balance of life or the feasibility of constantly renewing the earth's resources, and in which primitive man, the gatherer, fitted harmoniously and without wrecking anything yet. Is that right? So far, I'm not contradicting?"

"Yourself or me?" the doctor said in a bored voice, as if waving me off with his fin.

"Logic."

No, that was another breed of fish, another game: in order to take up residence in his house, I was driving him into my own. For this I had to begin by moving out . . .

"Man has abandoned his primitive niche, where he existed on an equal footing with the other species." (By now I seemed to be saying this myself.) "Is it possible to say—this time not in the sense you reproached as tautological, but in a more adequate definition—that man's ecological niche is precisely the 'safety margin' of the earth as the most general ecological system? That is, his niche is a certain interval in the earth's existence, from the era of man the gatherer up to a world catastrophe that will result in the death of everything alive? At the beginning of the century, there were one and a half billion of us. By the end, there will be six."

"Malthus again!" And again the sand gritted in the doctor's teeth. "Space can't be measured by time, as you are doing. Ecology studies only the ecological systems already extant. Only in this sense is it a science."

"Man should feel somewhat awkward," I said, as though the doctor and his ecology were to blame for all this, "if not ashamed: to be the crown of Creation, and understand this only as meaning that he was born to use Creation."

"One doesn't have to call our earth a creation. For the rest, however, I agree with you. There is a certain awkwardness. But we aren't the only ones conscious of this nowadays, you know. There's an obvious shift in awareness in this direction now—"

"You're a scientist," I said, bearing down. "A person who knows reality and assesses it soberly. Can you really believe that man is capable of stopping? So far, he's just been gaining speed.

Technical progress is a process, not a program. Man has long been a biological creature only in the three indisputable aspects you once mentioned to me. For the rest, he is no longer nature but her doom. Mankind is ruled by the laws of economics, not of biology. Even the conservation measures being undertaken now are economically disadvantageous, and I don't think they're any more effective, on the whole, than little old ladies from an English society for the preservation of animals—"

"You shouldn't talk that way about little old ladies," the doctor said. "Their work is nowhere near so trivial as you think."

"Never mind," I said sardonically, "the time may come for a society for the preservation of old ladies, too . . . Tell me honestly: which is more to your taste, a naked, icy earth over which the sun rises in vain, or . . ." I threw a sidelong glance at the sea. The enormous sun, as it neared the horizon, had acquired an irregular pear shape. The smooth water looked like scarlet silk . . . I pitied the sun, although in my predictions it survived. "Or a green earth inhabited by birds and beasts, with rivers and lakes full of fish, with man gathering roots, and perhaps with the wise dolphin, who didn't start down our unwise path?"

"I understand your anti-humanist thought," the doctor said dryly. "Don't say aloud the rest of what you meant to ask me. Yes, I used to ask myself the same question . . ." The sun rolled faster and faster, like an apple, toward the horizon; it flattened out against the surface like a water drop; contrary to expectations, it failed to sizzle as it quickly slipped under, leaving on the water a unique gray light with a condensation of pink . . . "The question is devoid of meaning. Then there wouldn't be anyone to look at this happiness—"

"Come, now!" I exclaimed. "You even say that? Surely everything alive on earth rejoices in life!"

"Yes, but only man is capable of appreciating its perfection in full measure—"

"But—"

"Don't be too quick to drop the bomb you have in your heart. We don't know everything. As for a hellish thought, even an unspoken one, we don't know what else is factored in with it, or what form it will develop. Just now I made a confession to which I had no right as a scientist . . ." His faint smile still reflected the sunset.

Thus we reached agreement on the outlook for mankind, with no doubt that something depended on our decision. We groped for an exit from our own speculation. Sometimes it seemed to us . . . but every time, if we even came close to envisioning it as a reality, this path, too, would ripple and vanish into thin air. All measures were inadequate. Man positively refused to understand his true situation, for he was solely preoccupied with things that were immediately urgent, or seemed so to him. The present was breaking away from the future. Vanishing in this break was the dear past, the environment that had come to us by inheritance. We went so far as to set ecology up as a totalitarian government over mankind, where, in the medieval manner, a hand was chopped off for a chopped-off branch and a head was severed for the head of a jackrabbit. All this we did in the name of man . . . Only thus would *they* finally understand us! . . . "They" were everyone else but us. Upon sober assessment, our cabinet soon fell.

Dethroned, we returned home and climbed the dune. The sun popped up from the sea for an instant, only to plunge back down. The sand lay pink on the dune top. A long velvet shadow fell on the slope concavely, inside out. Night, awakening, was stirring in the gully between the dunes.

"I would never have believed that Malthus lived in the eighteenth century," I sighed. "Carriages, groves, string quartets, gowns with trains . . . Air . . . what air they must have had then . . . Little streams babbling . . . the bumblebee buzzing . . . shepherds and shepherdesses, the reed . . . but he wrapped himself in his gloomy cloak and swayed in his carriage, thinking his black and distant thought, unbidden by anything around him . . ."

"Don't you think it's strange," the doctor said, "that we've spent the whole evening talking, right here in primeval nature, without meeting a single person—and what have we talked about?"

"Yes, what a place for it! We sin, we sin!" I laughed, grateful to him for that "we." In my hand was the Swedish beer crate, attesting my intention to live.

Hardly had the sun made its final departure into the sea when opposite to it, on the gulf side, without waiting for dusk, the moon burst out from behind the sand dune—as if our two heavenly bodies were seesawing on the Spit, with their invisible plank laid right across it . . . The moon's face was green. Goodness knows what she had seen, there at home, before coming out to us.

Probably it was she who made me toss and turn so, unable to sleep: her frightened light was beating in through all the cracks. I sat up and looked out the window. Small storm clouds were racing across the moon's already melancholy brow. She disappeared for a second, hidden by a thick cloud, only to pop out with an even more venomous flush. "The moon went behind a cloud"—I repeated the tranquil phrase to myself and was seized with laughter. The moon never went behind any cloud! I mean, just picture where the cloud is, where I am, where the moon is. It would be hard to give a more laughable example of distorted scale! "The sun hid behind the hill . . ." Why should it suddenly make me giggle like this? . . .

Now I saw the true self-sufficiency of the sun, which, if you please, "will send us its light," "its fiery greeting." Hogwash, I thought. There's no way the sun is concerned with that. It doesn't send anything to *us*. It's wholly concerned with itself. Little does it care what we are, what kind of dust drifting past . . . The single nail by which hung our whole earthly life began to wobble loose in my mind. Man's arrogance and insolence were first fully expressed in language, if only in these simple forms. Man somehow feels that everything he uses is directly related to him. But that is truly laughable. "Nature's storeroom," "natural riches," "the conquest of nature," "black gold," "white gold," and whatever other kind of gold . . . I sorted through this fresh evidence of man's banditry, all the prints his unwashed fingers had left in the language. I was lying on my back, and my face was grinning separately and complacently—flooded, if you please, with moonlight . . .

I was wakened by a heavy thunderclap splitting directly above me, practically in my own head. In the pitch dark, it was so sudden that I didn't realize or remember where I was, what was happening to me—or even who I was. A living thing, capable of feeling fear and not wishing to die, had awakened in terror; it did not know that it was I. Following the crash and vibration, as if grabbing me by the throat, came a total, black silence, in which there was nothing but prolonged terror and strangulation. A blinding white light rang out, illuminating the matchbox in which I slept—and me, kneeling on all fours on the bed. I truly thought I saw my own self, my body, as if I had abandoned it, still a short distance away, in a quandary whether to return or not. Immediately afterward a blow slammed on the roof. The roof grunted, but strangely enough it held, yielding and moaning a little under the solid stream of water flooding down on it. In this swish and roar a new light rang out, this time reddish as it penetrated the layer of water coursing down the pane, and again everything stood still in utter blackness and the steady drone of the flood. Now the next thunderclap struck, so close that it seemed, again, to be inside my skull. I was wide-eyed awake, but that only increased my fright. And then the lightning began blazing and flaring with such frequency that from one flash to the next I never saw the light fade—my hut was enveloped in pink and white flame. By this light I could make out the map over my bed: all the little veins of rivers and railroads, and the little circles for cities. A flash—and I read the meaningless word "Amsterdam." No such city anymore, I thought indifferently, Holland is already washed away . . . I'm not sure whether I had any clear idea what might be happening—the deluge, a collision with a comet, an atomic bomb explosion, the atmosphere was tearing off, or I was going crazy—but one thing was clear to me: this was *the end.* "The living end!" I said aloud, to give myself courage, but gallows humor did not rescue me. I didn't know what people usually did in a situation as unique as the end of the world. Again, one thing became clear to me: not for anything did I want to die right here, on this bed and in this cabin. Moaning with terror, still on all fours, I crawled off the bed and butted the door open with my forehead. This was right, to have crawled out on my hands and knees. The downpour was like a wall, and in any other posture I wouldn't have been able to breathe. Out here it was even brighter than in the house, the water sparkled like cut glass. Because of the black trunks of the pine trees, I could tell where the light was coming from. Now I wouldn't die in that house! One thing had been accomplished. But I didn't want to die among these close little pines, either. I started to crawl toward the light, efficiently, aiming for open space. Swiftly, on all fours, I ran like an animal, leaving my new track in the wet sand. In this manner I made it to an open spot at the foot of the dunes. Ahead of me, over the gulf, rose a fiery, pulsing wall. It was red and yellow. A roar mightier than cannon fire enveloped me on all sides. I halted, spellbound by the spectacle of this dense, oscillating, thundering curtain. I had no more answers, I didn't know what to do next, and I started to cry. I was choking on the downpour, but I imagined I was shedding that many tears. I did not want to die. And it wasn't that I had such a great desire to live at this moment, or didn't want to die in this manner—I didn't want to die *as this person.* I was unprepared. In desperation I crawled slightly higher up the dune, as if dragging my bundle of tattered, unexpiated sins behind me like immovable property: the unwritten letter to my mother, the puppy I had never given my daughter, the shame of today's verbosity . . . I don't know why the sins I recalled were so few and innocent. I was sincerely ready to repent of everything. Most likely I wanted, unconsciously, to depart with a better opinion of myself. I had no intention of duping the Most High.

Greatest and most shameful, drowning out all these trivia, was the sin of my unreadiness to stand before Him. I lifted up to Him a bleating, wordless prayer and crossed myself. This astounded and even sobered me. I realized, with a sensation of certainty, that I had done it correctly. But before . . . I well remember that I had never really known how to cross myself: left to right? right to left? how to begin, vertically or horizontally? navel last or second? how many fingers to use? My attitude toward the church was the respectful one of a catechumen—and yet I could never cross myself in church, not only because I didn't seem to have sufficient excuse or reason to do so, but also because I didn't properly know how. Trying to learn, I had cast sidelong glances at the people praying, but either they crossed themselves so small and so often, or . . . In sum, well remembering my perpetual puzzlement on this issue, I knelt at the foot of the dune, before the fiery wall as before the Coming, I was so childishly glad to have managed it all! And so adeptly did I genuflect, so devoutly did I cross myself, that my terror left me. Fear, the scourge of humanity, was washed from me by the water. And I don't remember anything more . . .

I didn't remember when I woke up, either. I walked out into the early morning. The sun was shining. Droplets sparkled on the twigs. Steam was rising from the grass. The bird kingdom was chirping even more furiously than usual. An ant was dragging a fly carcass. Associate N. was hauling cages down from the attic.

Everything was in its place—paradise, as before. Except that the sky seemed even bluer, the sand even yellower. Nevertheless, the morning struck me as insincere: it was pretending to be morning. I sought signs of betrayal and found none. The morning was pretending not to remember, mocking a jealous man. With a wry grin I tried to put up my fingers and cross myself the same way, correctly. My hand would not rise. As before, I didn't remember how. Proverbially: "The peasant will not cross himself until the thunder sounds." At least this joy had not betrayed me, the joy of being overwhelmed, yet again, by the exactitude of language. The somber doctor walked past me with a shaving brush in his hand, then came back.

"I've been thinking about our conversation all night," he said. "The thought occurred to me that there is nothing poorer than a rich imagination. It hypnotizes its possessor with the brilliance of its very first picture—the most banal and primitive, as a rule. In the same way, the pessimistic eye naturally sees a more convincing view. We cannot be sure of any far-reaching causes or effects on the basis of our own experience; we won't live to see the results of our experiment in the course of our one life . . . Such is man's time span—unequal to either history or life. Yet another basis for pessimism. Its other eye. To an honest young man my optimism may seem unconvincing, labored, self-serving . . . But throughout this game we always have a gambit in reserve, which we haven't been taking into account. Give it any name you wish: our ignorance, or the will of the Most High. Yesterday you called man a parasite found in the earth's 'safety margin' (your words or mine?), as if in her skin. I came close to agreeing with you. It may all be true, but none of us can evaluate—not hypothetically, not imaginatively, but practically—the size of that margin. It's like fortune-telling. Yes, a trip, yes, a government house, and of course a woman. But when? The time is not named. Until the temporal coordinate is defined we may hypothesize whatever we like. Anything will fit. And if we can't determine the 'safety' coefficient, we can't determine the role of either man or progress. To the same extent that we can hypothesize that man won't stop, that he'll take the ax of progress and lop off the bough he's sitting on—to an equal degree, we can hypothesize the opposite . . . Since our earth is still large and sufficient for life, isn't our consciousness that she's catastrophically diminished (by instant communications, information technology, and so forth), and likewise our consciousness that she's appallingly denuded and ravaged, merely a form of defense for her? A warning sign, a signal, switched on far ahead of irreversible danger, so that we'll have time to take heed . . . Which is to say, I believe that the speed with which we conceptualize the danger is out of proportion to the earth's real situation. And this, then, to use your terminology, is man's 'safety margin': the guarantee that he will have time to learn from his visual aid, progress. That is, the acceleration of progress isn't excessively great, it's *sufficiently* great, just so that we'll have time before the catastrophe. Perhaps quite soon there'll be a graduating class, the end of man's high school education . . . the setting-up of the experiment in the school laboratory, a false explosion . . . sparks in the physics lab, a stink from the chemistry classroom—no more."

For some reason I felt offended. Offended that he had shot ahead to be the first to speak my words. Offended that I was "young" (even though "honest"). Who was he, to play the old man! Two years younger than I. And then suddenly, as we turned back, our idea hit me. The idea that our conceptualization of reality might prove swifter than reality, and that this was our guarantee, this high reaction rate . . . The idea struck me as new, despite its affirmation of life. Practical experience made me grin wryly. Wasn't I a witness that people don't learn anything! Even if you bash them on the head . . . But "we always have a gambit in reserve," he had said. I liked that gambit.

The morning was delightful. If it was indeed pretending, the pretense was even better than the real thing . . . I walked out to the trap. Its nets, still wet and heavy, sagged in steep curves. In the narrowest part of it there was a kind of final receptacle, where the feathered prisoners languished. There weren't very many. Two or three sparrowlike birds . . . Suddenly I heard a laugh, a rather odd one, unfamiliar but distinct. As though an old man had come up behind me, unshaven, husky from smoking, and just a touch crazy . . . Where could he have come from? I turned and saw . . . No one. I felt impelled to shrug my shoulders, just in case. Then, from the same spot, the same old man let out a distinct, teasing caw. I glanced back angrily and caught sight of Clara. She had taken a convenient, spacious perch, on a bough neither thick nor thin, and was comfortably observing the trap and me. When she saw that I had caught sight of her, she behaved more than oddly. She burst into avid, screeching caws—these were what I had earlier, absurdly, associated with laughter. She choked, capsized on the branch, and swung upside down, croaking softly. Nimbly righting herself, she again broke into violent caws, flapping her wings in delight and stepping impatiently, but with no intention of taking off. I inspected myself. How could I have provoked her to such behavior? This was absurd, it wasn't I who . . . I followed her gaze more attentively and only then saw the large bird darting around in the middle of the trap. Goodness knows what it was—it darted so swiftly—an owl, a jay, a cuckoo? not a magpie . . . a bird as big as Clara. It had landed in the trap, thrashed around in search of the exit, and inevitably bumped into the net. Recoiling, it had descended deeper, closer to the final receptacle, beside which Clara and I were watching. The captive still was closer to the exit than to this end, and the exit was wide open, in contrast to the swiftly narrowing throat of the trap, yet however much the bird resisted, it only moved deeper. Strange, I thought; right now, you know, you could fly out more easily than in . . . Clara was cawing with might and main. And this wasn't sympathy or a summons. As before, it sounded like laughter. She kept capsizing, swinging upside down—"Oh, you're killing me!"—and again choking ecstatically and happily, as if with laughter. Suddenly I realized that this really was laughter. No doubt about it. I remembered asking the doctor whether animals had a sense of humor . . . Now I had my answer. Clara thought this was unbearably funny: a bird as big as she was had landed in the trap. As I've already mentioned, this happens rather rarely—large birds are smarter and understand the trap. Of course there was also a shade of cruelty, a despicable triumph ("Not me!") in Clara's laughter. But indeed it was laughter. "What a fool! Ca-aw!" laughed Clara. "So big! Caw, caw! *Such* a fool! Ca-a-aw . . ." She may even have been so astounded by the bird's stupidity that she felt no personal triumph. "You *fool!*"

. . . How could I keep from chuckling at myself—an even larger creature! . . .

For labor under the sun there is also a reward. We should neither underestimate nor overestimate its dimensions. We should give thanks.

As I pored over the conversations of my two peripatetics, I myself gained some insight .   .   .   .
.   .   .   .
.   .   .   .
.   .   .   .
.   .   .   .
.   .   .   .
.   .   .   .
.   .   .   .
.   .   .   .
.   .   .   .
.   .   .   .

A first-grader of my acquaintance named Julia, who had become a writer while I was away, summarized my whole string of confidences much more briefly, though she hadn't heard them. For reasons of style, apparently, she set her story in a "studio" instead of a school.

Here it is, word for word:

"Yesterday a foreigner came to our studio. He told a lot of funny stories, but we didn't understand him. Luckily, there was an interpreter with him. He explained to us that the foreigner was telling about crows and magpies. It turns out that these birds, who look so much alike, can hardly understand each other.

"When I got home that morning, I thought: How strange! We had such trouble understanding him, and that's just what he was telling us about . . ."

THE SECOND TALE

Man in a Landscape
(the Novice)

Behold the stone . . .
—The Gospel of Thomas

. . . and that's just what he was telling us about.

This place didn't recall a homeland—it was one. And it didn't belong to me. I won't name it. Its anonymity will be my excuse. This happened in 1979. I was here for the first and last time. The description, for fear of being inaccurate, will be minimal. May anyone who recognizes it forgive me.

It was unexpected, this place. Or had *become* unexpected. This had occurred within our visible life span. Before, perhaps, the place had seemed to grow up from some broader locality, to crown it. Now it was strikingly incongruous, impossible . . . for the city on which it was based had already ceased to be. No, this isn't a description after an atomic attack. There is construction here, there is life; the avenue goes straight, always straight, and with no change at all becomes a highway; the same dead-white multistory boxes, occupied and unoccupied, finished and unfinished, all equally unlivable; no people can be seen going in or out of them; you feel as if you're riding through one and the same place—that is, standing still; and here, at the city limit, when the highway finally plunges back into the less developed space of Russia, you have to turn left, and your mind is so lulled by the monotony of the road that you are quite unprepared for perception.

For one thing, there are hills. For another, trees. As though the earth had started to breathe, its breast rising and falling. You, too, begin to breathe in rhythm with the crests and turns of the road, which by now is humanly narrow. Here, snaking along the hill, is the white stone wall of a citadel, and at last you come to its improbably thick and sturdy gates. Inside, on the grounds, everything is different. Level lawns, old trees, a church of God . . . A museum and a nature preserve, a happy home for ravens. Space. First cultured, later a culture park. There are also ancient wooden buildings here, out of character, though very agreeable in themselves. They were moved here from all over the North. You visit the log cabin in which Peter the Great stayed in Archangel. You measure your height and palm against his (a notch on the doorjamb, a cast of his handprint). Gradually you leave behind you the section of the park that has been completely restored and rehearsed. Increasingly often, you come across piles of building materials and trash, with a view of an astonishing bell tower, a masterpiece of Russian Gothic. The peaked polyhedron of its hipped roof is inscribed in a similar polyhedron of construction scaffolding, and although the eye is unaccustomed to it, this multifaceted angularity somehow remains Russian. When you have seen your fill of all the restorations and restorations-in-progress, you may walk on . . .

Oh, this imperceptible transition, from the life-affirming ugliness of construction to desolation and incipient wildness! Weeds. Does the plantain have a unique power to triumph over being trampled? Or has it learned to enjoy being trampled, to prefer it? Burdock, thistle, dandelion . . . Their clean leaves are already coated with dust. Tin cans grow into the earth, turning rusty and red; the text in the scraps of newspaper fades; rags rot away, corpselike, pining for the human body; the dusty thistle is replaced by leaves dusty since birth, so caressing to the touch. This is life taught by death. (Here I saw a red toothwort, obscenely poking up through a trash heap. All my life I have carried the toothwort with me as a childhood horror, like the words "war," "fascist," "solitary confinement"—though it later proved to be merely a plant. It grew for me in 1944, behind the mess hall of my first Pioneer camp, and we called it an earth cancer.) How wonderful, the way nature

struggles with the civilized layer! These trashy flowers and grasses
are her infantry, winning back the earth for her, in order to restore
their own culture. Wilderness is not this desolate. Nature is desolate
only where something has previously existed, even if a beautiful
park. The raspberry canes, now small and wild, had escaped into
a ravine, and I followed them. A festering brook flowed there, and
a new board had been thrown across it.

Climbing uphill from the new board was a rotten staircase,
steep and high, with one railing collapsed and the other crudely
repaired. Up here it was shady and gray, with a dankness in the
air. Everything still gave the appearance of having escaped from
cultivation, especially the green leaves. The leaves weren't green,
although they were no longer dusty. They were as tinny and colorless as the leaves of an artificial wreath in a neglected graveyard.
But you had only to reach the top at last, climbing past the missing
steps, and there, indeed, was the graveyard with the trashy wreath.

Culture, nature . . . tall weeds, fallen crosses. A haggard face.
It was painful to imagine what it must have been like here some
three or four centuries ago, when the builder first came. How graceful, finished, and exact it had been. The sumptuous skeleton could
still be seen through the tattered rags of drapery: the bank was
just as steep, the river just as wide, and just as unexpectedly the
bank receded, leaving below it the soft green lake of a flooded
meadow, and in the distance it turned suddenly as if at a shout
and froze in the far-off blue of the forest, as though the river, in
swerving, had switched banks, the left becoming the right, and the
right the left . . . The sky, too, probably remained as before, although perhaps just slightly faded. What lines there had been, if
they still remained! Such lines that the abbot and the builder had
sighed, deeply and in unison. Their doubts had vanished: Here!

Nature could offer nothing greater. The perfection of her offering was plain to see. Such places call for a temple, a citadel, a
city. Within a century or so, people had mastered this space, made
themselves a part of it, and it had become *civilized*. Now the finish
and perfection of that civilized space could only be inferred—from

the "entrance area" (no longer the entrance to a monastery, but to the "grounds"), where everything had been restored "as it used to be." In its newness and tidiness you could see the dispatch of the "plan." They had used whatever paint they had on hand, the lawn was somewhat less than a hundred years old, and the boards and logs still remembered the haste of the woodsman's ax. But it's all right, never mind. Time (and not much of it!) will pass, and, before everything here begins to fall apart again (this time even faster), there will indeed be an interval when it becomes almost "as it used to be." Time also labors, after all, like man: at first perfecting, and only later destroying. Such a curious quantity of boundaries! Wilderness bounded by a civilization returning to the wild; the wilding civilization, by civilized space; the civilized space, by ruins; the ruins, by wilding gardens; the wilding gardens, by wilderness . . . Everything here was in mutual transition, mutual schism.

I scrambled up the precipice. Never will you see such abomination of desolation—not even in a tangled windfall—as in a ruined cultivated space! Oh, how much wilder than wilderness is incipient wildness! The wind murmurs triumphantly in the garbage pit that was once a church and a graveyard. Wreaths toss, tin cans roll about, a newspaper gallops like tumbleweed. Heaps of bricks and filth grow up. Ravens take wing, circling over the past, not the present. And layer shows through layer, structure through structure.

Now, skidding and detouring from layer to layer, you find yourself at a sudden overlook. A sharp whistling breath (by no means a sigh of relief) penetrates your smoke-filled chest: you can see *all* from here! All as it used to be. My God! How does it always survive, this unique point of . . . not of view, but of origin—where you wake up and recall, yes, *recall*, how the world used to be?

But don't attempt even one step to the side! If you should have the good fortune—no, the honor—of finding yourself at such a point, it will be unique. One step to the left and a flock of tower cranes has pecked apart the space on the horizon. One step to the right and you plunge down the cliff, into the garbage pit and dumping ground. One step back and you land on, or tear your trousers on, barbed wire.

Culture, nature . . . But who had destroyed all this? Time? History? Somehow the who and when eluded me. If only I could see him with my own eyes, grab his arm and twist it behind his back . . . Somehow he hadn't crossed my path. I hadn't met the perpetrator of the destruction, any more than you meet the author of a joke . . . The only people around were those who guarded this place or loved it. But who disliked all this, when we all loved it? Who disliked us this much? . . .

I was gazing from a unique point.

No, something remains in this world!

Oh, if only I'd known that I wasn't seeing and understanding it the way I'm writing it now. If only I'd taken to my heels! . . . I understand and see it this way *now*. It's hard not to confuse past with future, right down to their sequence in the present, if space itself, which seems to us more objective, has confused them (the times) this badly.

I lurched to a stop, too anxious, or shy, or timid, to take even a step. The unsteadiness of my pose could be attributed to the uniqueness of my viewing point.

And there he sat. The destroyer of the last point . . . Holding a brush, in an implausible pose, on an unsteady, tilting stool. I hung over his shoulder. He turned around . . .

I won't venture a description. I was so non-existent in his eyes that I don't know why I didn't vanish. To say that he looked at me with fright is inadequate; with terror, incorrect; with horror, inexact. For just a fraction of a second I was suspended in his swaying stare. But his stool swayed, too, his brush jerked, and he hurried back to his earlier point, never noticing me. For just a second he swayed on the thread of my stare, like a tightrope walker regaining his balance.

Once more, nothing connected us. He went right on sitting and painting from the unique point at which I, too, found myself.

The woman I loved wasn't there to enjoy the view with me . . . But it was a long time since I'd had her with me!

The bottomless pit is not empty, and emptiness is not a bottomless pit. I went flying through both.

I was enraged. Specifically, at this painting automaton. He had blocked my unique viewing point. The landscape under his brush utterly failed to match the uniqueness, the chosenness of the site. Something wrong with the color . . . He was apparently proceeding on a diagonal from the upper left corner of the canvas to the lower right. The deep blue forest at the upper left, the silver horseshoe of the river bend in the middle; in the lower right corner, invisible to the painter and clinging like a stuck bristle, sat the painter himself. The upper right was blank for the sky, undepicted as yet, unshadowed by either cloud or cross or bird. In the lower left was a dark blur. I glanced over my left shoulder. This was uncalled for, as though he could paint something that was behind him, as though by glancing over my shoulder I could see my own self . . . There, growing up from a trash heap, was the terrifying, taut phallus of the toothwort. I shuddered. That, too, was a stare. Who could have expected this moss-face with the easel to look at me just that way. The way she used to! She wasn't there. He was.

He already knew I existed, even though he hadn't turned around again. I had gotten through to him. The taut thread between him and the landscape loosened and went slack. His unsteady, inspired figure, which had been clinging to the corner of the canvas, relaxed and sagged. His stool remained steady, his shoulders drooped tranquilly, his brush lodged in his palette. This was the final evening hour when the sky brightens one more time, like the candle that flares before burning out. On his canvas, dusk was already falling. He resembled a fisherman who hasn't had a nibble all day but, at this very moment, has decided to reel in his line, still twitching the float . . . I had nothing to fear. My recent sensitivity balanced my effrontery.

"I didn't disturb you?"

"You did, you did!" he responded crisply, and laid his brush aside with relief.

"Then allow me to—"

"I have, I already have."

"I meant, to ask a question—"

"I meant nothing else."

"Bear in mind, I'm a layman. That is, forgive—"

"I'm willing to believe you. If you weren't, you'd see right off that I, too, am a layman."

His pride, for which I saw no basis, offended me. But I contained myself.

"Why don't you say something?" he said, attacking. "Or don't you like it?"

I saw him clearly: not a man to whom you could say what you thought.

"Oh, I do. It's a splendid view."

"View!" He curled his lip disdainfully.

"I warned you I was a layman, you know. View, landscape—do they differ?"

"Fundamentally!" He took the bait. "The view is what you, too, will see. The landscape is what I saw. The view, strictly speaking," and he looked at the painting and sighed, "can never be painted."

"Beg your pardon?"

"By anyone," he elaborated proudly. "Who has painted the snowy mountains? Or the forest?"

"Shishkin," I said, without hesitation.

"Hardly." Everything about him gave me to understand . . .

"I really don't recall any successful mountains," I said, correcting my position slightly.

"There, you see! Can you possibly paint something that's equal to yourself, has the same significance? Who has painted the desert? The sea?"

"Ayvazovsky," I said, of course.

"Hardly!" He was indignant. "Say Turner, and even then I'll argue."

"Why, what's wrong with Turner?" I said with aplomb, unsure that I wasn't confusing him with Teniers. Do you mean the Elder or the Younger, I wanted to ask, to impress him—but fortunately restrained myself . . . "But Levitan, Vasiliev? They did all right with forest, didn't they?"

"I'm no great fan of Levitan's . . . The color, you know . . ." He squinted warily at his own canvas. "Storm clouds," he said meditatively.

I looked at the sky. It was clear.

"They did all right with storm clouds. With field, but not forest. A field is already a sea. They didn't do well with a clear sky." He repeated my glance at the sky. "But with storm clouds, highlights, reflections . . . Justified abstractionism." He pursed his lips. "Self-expression." He scorned "self-expression," it appeared. "No, no one painted the view! What they did succeed with, partially, wasn't the view but the mood."

"Impressionism?" A display of shrewdness.

"If you wish. Presentiments, premonitions . . . Pre-sentiment, at best. But they considered themselves objective—that is, we're the ones who consider them realists. I mean, they were always justifying themselves. They gave the justification that things happened that way, they pled the reality of experience, even the most fleeting. Photography was vanquishing them, and they fought it."

"Well, even I know the qualitative difference between painting and photography," I said, slightly offended.

"Do you? Well, well . . . But I wasn't abusing photography. You just thought I was. Photography did painting a service of the highest order!"

"Which service is that?" I asked, as if condescending to his orthodoxy.

"A direct service. Photography identified the things with which painting should not concern itself. Because they can be achieved mechanically, by a device. Photography was what engendered the Impressionists."

"From their opposite?" I guessed.

"Very opposite. Photography is one thing, Cézanne is another, as a certain wonderful Georgian artist has said. Cézanne is another . . ." And a small cloud of admiration and sorrow covered his brow.

I grinned. "What have the movies engendered for us?"

"That's beyond my competence. Perhaps we should stop writing novels, eh?"

"Why, what do novels have to do with it?"

"For you, they make the point clearer. What I meant was, the landscape painter merely individualizes the view. He can't mirror it; he can only be mirrored in it. Are 'view' and 'indi*vid*ual' from the same root?"

"No," I replied, putting both Shishkin and Teniers and photography into my firmness.

"But it fits. And in my view . . . See? 'View' again . . . The landscape artist individualizes the view, not only in the sense that he introduces his vision and his individuality . . . but in the sense that the view itself, when recorded in a landscape, is obliged or forced to become partial in relation to itself, stand motionless against its will, acquire expression: light, wind, other meteorological conditions . . . Hm," he said with surprise, "there's a twist! It's exactly the other way around in a portrait. In a portrait, to paint the model's inner state is to equal Shishkin in taste. It would be absurd to paint a portrait of a man who was furious or sobbing or laughing."

"Doesn't Repin have a Cossack laughing?"

"As I say. That's a detail. That's genre, at best. That's character, not a portrait. A portrait is a universalization, the essence— well, the inner state. A landscape can't be universalized. Who are you to claim an understanding of the inner state of the sea or the mountains? Now, you mention Shishkin. He's the proof. Landscape as the portrait of a view doesn't exist. Did Shishkin paint a portrait of a tree?"

A kind of sorrow, for which I saw no reason, creased his brow. His wretched beard quivered.

"What's the matter?"

"Cézanne . . ." He spoke as one speaks of an aching tooth.

"What about Cézanne?"

"Later, later . . ." He waved me off, as if to say, "It will pass in a moment." He looked wistfully at the easel. "Already it's turning out badly."

"Now, now!" I made an effort. "It's very nice. You've found the only viewpoint, in my opinion."

"You found it, too."

"Well, that's no great credit to me."

"There, you see. You're nowhere near so ignorant as you say." He threw me a swift glance, both murky and sly, and then regained his composure. With the squint of a master, he forced himself to apply a fuzzy little dab. Immediately the stool lurched underneath him, but he kept his balance.

Flattered, I launched into a pupil's flattery: "Why did you decide on just that format? I've always wondered—"

"A window. It's a kind of window. Painting, in my opinion, is a window. Or a mirror. A mirror's a window, too, after all. A window through a wall—into the world. And that's how the painting will have to hang later. On the wall."

"I understand," I said, although I didn't quite. "Canvas, format, perspective, eye. The frame of the viewfinder . . . Choosing a viewpoint . . . But the point on the canvas . . . the point from which you began to fill it . . . where is it, and why?"

"Fill it!" The artist shivered with distaste. "Next you'll say *draw* it!"

"All right," I said, getting cross myself, "*paint* it. Can you show me the exact point from which you began to paint this canvas?"

"That's a complicated question. It all depends on the model. A bird, for example, you have to paint from the beak."

"What kind of bird?"

"Birds in general . . ."

"But here?" I pointed at his canvas.

"It's already a failure," he said evasively.

"Why a failure!" Again I had to be careful of his pride! Really very careful.

"A failure because I started from the wrong point!" he said balefully, taking down the canvas.

"From there?" I pointed toward the river.

"You guessed it." The color showed through his gray bristly tangle. "You guessed it! I'm not an artist at all! I don't claim to be! That's not what I come here for!"

"What do you come for?"

"You wouldn't understand."

"You're too severe," I said resentfully, "both with yourself and with me. The way you talk, nothing at all can be painted: neither landscape nor portrait . . . But still life?"

"*That's* possible!" he exulted, all of a sudden, as though he meant to abandon landscape and undertake a still life, then and there. "Even you don't see how right you are! A portrait is possible too. But only for the few. The geniuses! The Leonardos! Has anyone ever painted an animal?" he shot at me.

"A bird. From the beak," I said, quoting.

"A bird is a remote creature," he said, incomprehensibly. "Let's take a wild beast. No one! Except perhaps Dürer. His rhinoceros. But he drew him from a grid. That time he was drawing, rather than painting. It was the first rhinoceros in Germany, perhaps in Europe. Dürer was astonished. Not as a genius, but as a normal person. It's his *astonishment* that comes through. And what a draftsman he was! What draftsmen they were then! Any expedition artist . . . Sometimes I think they were the *only* artists . . . The ones who wanted nothing . . ." He fell to muttering and forgot about me.

"Dürer," I said, "drew a wild beast?"

"Oh, yes! He merely wanted to record it. He treated the line as a letter of the alphabet. And the result was a brilliant, apocalyptic beast!"

"Aren't you contradicting yourself?" I said insinuatingly. "Just now it was impossible to draw a beast."

"Not in the slightest!" he exulted, gleefully packing up his belongings. "You can draw him. You can't paint him. Impossible. This, incidentally, is why painting became art."

"But people do draw!"

"You aren't a writer, by chance?"

"By chance." A forced confession.

"Well, then. If I say to you: People do write . . . ?"

"Don't you mean . . . can't we conclude . . . that a thing you can learn isn't art?"

"There, you see."

"But if you study and study and study?" I said gladly.

"Not enough."

"And if you work and work and work?"

"Even less."

"But if you just suddenly . . . out of the blue . . . understand, as it were—"

"Get inspired?"

"All right."

"Oh, yes!" he exulted. "Perhaps," he sighed. "Once."

"But what can we do?"

"God knows."

"That's all?"

"Not enough for you?"

"Too much for me."

We burst out laughing, and together we descended into the ravine.

"Now, you mention genius," he said, although I hadn't mentioned it. I had already walked across the board, he had not. It was night in the ravine by now, and rotten wood was glimmering.

His inspired eyes twinkled pale and bold from deep in his encroaching hair. "The geniuses always painted the Madonna and Child. They succeeded with the Madonna—never with the Child. Have you noticed? Oh, it's such a mystery! You won't understand right off . . . We see the genius as an especially perfect incarnation. The ordinary person, we say, couldn't have done it, but the genius did—a hundred percent. Horsefeathers!" (What made him fly into such a rage?) "The genius is the ultimate failure as an incarnation! Not from our point of view, naturally. From his. A failure on both the vertical and the horizontal. What a genius has behind him (and that's where the Genius Deity is situated, after all—behind him) is immensely disproportionate to his so-called yield. (You know, on dining-hall menus they give the 'yield' . . . the percentage of meat in the hamburger?) Something we admire will be an utter dissatisfaction and unhappiness for a genius. *He* knows the percentage! He is incarnated to the extent that he succeeds in painting the Child. If, God forbid, we recognize a genius during his lifetime, we kill him by depriving him of this very dissatisfaction. More often, however, we simply crucify them. That's much more rational; we inherit everything, including even the flattery of our admiration of them."

At last he walked across the board. Am I dealing with another genius? I thought wryly. His words sounded a bit too full of suffering. But he really was a genius . . .

Having crossed the board as if crossing an abyss, he paused again and began rummaging in his fisherman's bag (a gas-mask carrier; how had he kept it intact?). Of their own volition, out came a bottle of Kavkaz port (0.8 liter) and a glass (one). He offered the glass to me: "You won't refuse?"

"I don't drink."

"Has it been long?"

"A while."

"Well, that's forgivable."

I started to insist: "I don't drink port—"

"Then don't. I'm not forcing you," he said caressingly. The glass, of itself, turned up in my hand. Suddenly I felt the heat of his mysterious power.

"You're a genius," I whispered.

"Genius and villainy are two things . . . There aren't any geniuses now. They won't work. You can't paint just the masterpiece you're left with. Can't paint 'La Gioconda' alone. Can't write the selected works first, can you, now?"

"Oh, no! You're right."

"Overproduction is a condition of genius. Who needs Dickens's thirtieth volume? Or Tolstoy's ninetieth? What, hadn't they expressed themselves in their twelfth? Wouldn't that have been enough for us?"

"You're exaggerating, I think?"

"Yes. But I'm not a plumber. I don't want to say the right thing, I want to tell the truth. Is *Don Quixote* enough for you out of all Cervantes? *Hamlet*, out of all Shakespeare? . . . Now, you're a professional. How many books have you really read?"

"But how many paintings have you failed to see? In the Louvre, in the Prado, in our storage vaults?"

"In our age there are books, traveling exhibitions . . . We have it easier, seemingly. Although paintings aren't illustrations, to be looked at. You have to *see* them."

"You have to *read* a book, too."

"That's what I'm asking. How many books have you *read*?"

"Well, I haven't read *Don Quixote* . . ."

"And *Hamlet*?"

"That I've read. Recently."

"How old were you?"

"Forty."

"Thank you. And the Bible?"

"Why are you interrogating me?!"

"Don't be angry. I was even older before I got van Dyck and van Eyck straight. Learned who van Eyck was. Can you imagine?"

"The Elder or the Younger?" This was insolence.

"As if you knew!" he scowled. "You, too, know just the one and have heard of the other. And I'm not asking you what van Eyck painted! So that you won't get tangled up in Annunciations . . . I thought you were a person I could talk to."

His feelings were gravely hurt. He was disillusioned.

"All right," I conceded. "Twenty-seven. I first read the Gospel at twenty-seven. And just Matthew, at that. I never did read the Old Testament, except for Psalms and Ecclesiastes. But I've kept it with me ever since."

"You open and close it?"

"I open and close it." I definitely liked him.

"Are you a Christian?"

I pondered my answer.

"Half, then?"

"Well, except . . ." I stammered. "About half."

"But you're not drinking? Don't, then, I won't be offended . . . Is Mozart a genius?" he asked, after partaking.

"Now *there's* a genius."

"Everything he wrote is genius?"

"Everything he wrote."

"And you've listened to everything?"

"Well, not everything. But a lot. As much as I could."

"Do you know how many of his pieces ever get performed?"

I did not know. He had posed the question as a great mystery.

"Ten percent!" He could not contain his exultation.

"Really!" I was astounded.

"There! Overproduction is yet another evidence that the genius is an imperfect incarnation, this time along the horizontal. Why does he have to keep driving and driving, if he's already fully incarnate?"

"To eat?" Here I had him. " 'Inspiration doesn't sell'?"

"Hm-m, yes." He sighed. "You know what Mozart had to pay for a new waistcoat?"

"No, I don't."

"A symphony!"

The night was fully dark. Here in the ravine, at any rate. We breathed in each other's faces. We illuminated them as we lighted cigarettes. A mosquito swelled, jewel-like, on his forehead.

"May I?" I slapped his forehead.

"Thanks."

We started climbing toward the exit, where the sky was still pale, like dilute ink.

"You should have seen that waistcoat!" he puffed, from below. "A bird of paradise! 'Behold the lily, how she is arrayed!' Mozart was compelled to array himself no worse . . ."

"But of course . . . at court . . ." I responded knowingly.

We came to the construction area. There, it was bald and unexpectedly light. Down below it was still night, totally dark. The scaffolded bell tower was especially bright, and the belfry even shone as if a separate light gleamed through it. "Astonishing!" I wanted to exclaim to someone, as if I'd already forgotten my new friend—

"Oh, yes!" he said to the back of my head. "Our own Russian Gothic. Non-functioning. Do you want to go inside?"

I did want to. He felt confident here. He had some sort of connection with all this.

An enormous wrought-iron key protruded from the door. But the door was bolted from the inside as well. He joggled it and knocked. Cawing, the ravens took off from the bell tower. They made the sky even whiter.

He knocked again and said, "He'll open up in a minute."

From the river, accentuating the emptiness of the dusk, a barge horn lowed like an ox. That farewell bellow almost brought a whiff of leaf smoke.

"But are they . . . or what?"

This remark sobered me somewhat. I pictured it too vividly.

He started banging on the door with all his might.

A gigantic, gray, serpentine creature detached itself from the dusk. I jumped and almost let out a yell. Good God!

"Linda! Linda baby! You devil!" The landscape artist patted the devil affectionately.

She was a Great Dane of dazzling horror and beauty, as white as marble.

"Is Linda tired of waiting?" The tenderness in his voice was extraordinary. "Let's go!" he said decisively, and turned the key in the keyhole. But now another thought overtook him. He removed the key from the keyhole and proffered it to me. "Keep it."

Perplexed, I held it in my hands. This was quite something. The size of our Great Dane.

"Keep it, don't worry. It's a memento for you. When you get the urge, you'll come back."

"But how will they . . . ?"

"They'll find a way. Shouldn't lock themselves in . . . But nobody's there."

Utterly uncomprehending, I trailed after them with the key in my hand. The road went uphill, and I leaned on the key as I walked. The she-devil ran ahead, now dissolving, now precipitating out of the thickening dusk.

"An actress!" he related proudly from above. "I took her to be in a movie today. Next door here. They're doing the Occupation. No, the German wasn't here, strictly speaking. It's a Novgorod scene they're doing. She's playing the Oberstambambramsegel-führer's pet." He laughed invisibly, disappearing into a puddle of night. "Linda, my benefactor!" Evidently she had come running up, and now, as he waited for me, he was scratching her behind the ear. "Seven fifty for a day's work!" he boasted, suddenly right in front of me. I bumped into him. "All the same, it's Baroque," he said, with either sorrow or satisfaction, staring over my shoulder, and I turned around.

From here, from above, we could see the bell tower again. The moon, as red and huge as the sun, had crept up from behind the now invisible river. A dark pink glow wreathed the sharp spire. The church smoldered like a last coal in the night.

We were going somewhere; I did not discuss where. A long, barnlike shadow solidified up ahead. At our approach a cellar window lit up and went dark.

"The refectory," he said.

We found our way in, clattering and stumbling.

"Just a second, I'll flip the switch," he said, and everything lighted up.

This, to all appearances, was a restoration workshop. Carpenter's bench, muffle furnace, shelving with canned goods . . . Bare bulb on the ceiling. On the wall, a movie-star calendar with Alla Pugacheva, and an advertisement for auto races. A huge, rustic bin. Similarly crude and ancient benches. Tiny barred windows stared blindly from the depths of the fortress-thick walls, as if squinting, as if puffy with sleep. Massed along the walls, like junk, like a scattered deck of cards, were layer upon layer of icons, icon frames, iconostases.

"Are you interested in panels?" I did not understand, but with his eyes he indicated the junk heap of icons.

"Oh, yes," I said, of course.

"It's coming, Linda baby, it's coming . . . You go ahead and look in the meantime. Don't be shy."

Carefully I tipped back the carelessly heaped panels, one after another. The thrill of touching them was beyond my understanding.

The painter bustled hospitably. Linda circled his every step. He started the muffle furnace and set a can of food in it to warm up. He opened the bin and leaned into it, head and all; at one point his feet even left the floor. His face was red when he climbed out.

"Don't tell me they've taken it!" His face expressed grave anxiety. Again he disappeared in the bin. Tattered clothes came flying out. Empty, crumpled icon frames and tin cans hit the floor with one and the same sound. "O Lord!" came his sigh of relief. "Who'd've guessed it was buried so deep!"

He hauled himself out, with a bottle of Russkaya vodka.

Standing there with a dark, barely discernible "Saviour" in my hand, I shared his unfeigned joy. "But who buried it?"

"I did!" he said happily.

The canned goods warming up in the muffle furnace, however, were not for Linda.

I can't begin to convey how much I liked it here with him! And how scary it was. Who could have known I would tumble out of my ordinariness and grayness, for no reason at all, just like that, into the *present*. Such an unexpected hole . . . The stool had been spread with newspaper. Very cozily, with efficient masculine deliberateness and functionality, he laid out our feast. Bread, an onion, canned stew . . . the sparkle of two washed glasses . . . the broad-shouldered bottle, standing like a small bell tower.

"I suspected you right away," he said, pouring the vodka. "What a pile over there, and you immediately pulled out the most valuable one."

I happened to be holding the same dark panel with which I had been caught when he finally found his stash. But I did not confess.

"Stand it on the chair, take a better look."

Thus we sat down to a bottle of vodka, the three of us, not counting Linda: Pavel Petrovich (that was the landscape painter's name, after all), myself, and our darkened Saviour, facing us on a separate chair. Pavel Petrovich, perhaps because of his profession, saw no sacrilege in this, and I noticed none at the time.

Pavel Petrovich was not eating his bread but dunking it in the stew gravy and feeding it to Linda.

"It wasn't pride, you know, that made me say I'm not an artist. I go there with a completely different purpose. I'm making contact! Do you understand?"

As yet, or already, I didn't quite.

"I'm seeking my place. Not my own in particular; that doesn't greatly concern me. But *man's* place! You'll never find man in a landscape. One good thing about Shishkin is, I don't think he ever put in a single man."

"He put in bears," I interjected.

"But that's the candy!" Pavel Petrovich decided peremptorily.

"And by the way, he didn't paint the bears himself. What—don't you know who did it? . . . Once even Ayvazovsky couldn't resist. Granted, he didn't do it himself, either. But he asked someone to put in Pushkin for him—"

"He asked Repin," I said, boldly moving my pawn against his bears.

"You should do crosswords," he said, unscathed. "Whoever! And they failed! How wonderful that is! Pushkin stands there out of place, painted even worse than the sea, wearing a grin and holding his top hat away from him. But Pushkin himself, our dear one, our genius . . . how well he himself did all this, in his own painting! 'Farewell, free element'—and that's it, he's gone. All that remains is the gesture, the sweep of his hand. A brilliant standard of taste and pictorial accuracy. Me, all I see when I paint is my own nose. Sometimes I'm tempted to put it in, when the picture's a failure . . . And it's always a failure . . ." He waved away his thought as if brushing off a fly, and frightened Linda. "But every time, I don't paint it!"

"Your nose?"

Linda left him and rested her calf-like head on my knee. This was the first time in my life I'd had anything to do with such a big dog. What a terrifying, though pleasant, weight lay on my knee! In a second she could bite in half the hand that was stroking her—

"She'd never bite," Pavel Petrovich said. I didn't have to say anything to him, he obviously read my mind. "All right. Let's leave the deplorable examples aside. Let's take something that will stand up for itself. Bruegel, now. His *Icarus*. Remember?"

I didn't quite, but I nodded.

"Not the Younger—the Elder. You won't trap me on that. What does he have in his landscape that comes from man? Granted, a divine man. The heel! He has Icarus's heel! You'd never notice it—"

"But what about the plowman?" With his help, I had recalled

the whole painting. "The plowman is there, plowing with all his might. Close up!"

"The plowman! The *plowman*, he says! Of course there's a plowman, a plowman is part of the landscape. He is also, please note, seen from the back. Almost faceless. His identity doesn't matter—that's the point. So he's in harmony, because he's a part of all this."

"There's a ship, too. That's not nature, either."

"A creation is already nature! It's beautiful, a sailing vessel. Though less appropriate in the painting than the plowman. Now, you yourself have noted all the points: the plowman, the ship, and Icarus's heel. Best to plow, sail if you must, but don't fly!"

"But that's a fable already, not a painting," I objected.

"In this case! In this case, it's both. In and of itself, the painting in a Bruegel will never disappoint you, and the thought process— yes, in this case it's literary. After all, that's how they did it then, they told a story. But they didn't forget the art of painting . . . And its laws were operative. Man as an individual, as goodness knows what—as the king, if you please, of nature—cannot be fitted into a landscape. You'll never find such a thing. The heel, only the heel. Or the landscape painter's nose, which he isn't obliged to draw. Far more plausible and appropriate, if you're laying claim to eternity, to stick your ugly puss through a hole that has the sea and a cypress painted around it. That's plausible. But any attempt to paint the individual as an organic part of the landscape will be a wretched parody."

He stopped for breath, pleased with the way he had stated all this.

"I never thought!" He wagged his head delightedly.

"Which?"

"This is the first time I ever understood about Bruegel."

"Yes, it's good," I agreed. "But what to do with a Renaissance portrait? It necessarily has distance, depth, perspective, fields and views and hills and waters—"

"That's entirely different! What does it have in the fore-
ground? A person, a face, an individual. Necessarily an individual!
We sense this. We don't know who he was, when he lived, what
he did—but he's an individual! Without fail. And only back there,
in the distance, do we see where the individual came from, what
world. It's a separate world! The co-o-ordinate!" He always spoke
that way, with an extra *o*. "The coordinate of the person! . . . It's
like a painting back there. The necessary window, the necessary
frame for the second painting. The portrait is one thing, and the
landscape is another. It's all very separate and extremely conventional. The antiquity of it is what gives us the illusion of realism."

I clinked glasses, completely agreeing with him.

"Stand on the seashore like Pushkin, or on the edge of the
plowland, gazing into the radiant future . . . Or like today, when
you came up to me, if I hadn't ruined the view for you . . . What
would you have seen and where would you have been?"

I pondered.

"Well?"

"It was as if I weren't there."

"See? You're right, at last. Now we're getting close to the truth.
Where is man? who is man? and why is man? That's what I'm
concerned with, every time, when I try to reproduce what I see.
I'm making contact."

"With whom?"

"It's obvious with whom," he said angrily. "If only with world
thought. You don't see yourself when you look. And what you see
doesn't see itself, does it? Well, earthly creatures see in order to
satisfy their daily needs. But trees, grasses, mountains, rivers? They
don't see. Haven't you ever imagined yourself a stone or a branch?
Of course you have. You've fastened yourself to the spot, situated
yourself in space . . . And when you did this you were depressed
by the meagerness of the world that fell to your lot for observation.
Each time, without noticing, you continued to *see*, and even hear,
as though a stone or a branch had eyes and ears. You couldn't

possibly deprive yourself of them in your imagination, it didn't even enter your head, did it, now?"

"I haven't imagined myself as a stone all that often, but you may be right . . . Not without eyes."

"Imagine, what ni-i-i-ight!" He howled the word "night" in such a ghastly way . . . "What unfathomable selflessness there is in that blind, deaf, mute existence! Why, all things that exist are connected among themselves, without knowing of the connection. But we *see* it—in a unity which none of the participants in that unity knows! You come out to the shore: water splashing, sand, reeds, the forest reflected in the water—you know they don't think as you do, of course, but you can't even imagine how isolated the stones and waters are. For them, there is no whole! They exist entirely in themselves! Like the things in German philosophy. But there *is* a whole! That's the paradox. You haven't invented it, and it's no illusion: everything we see forms a *picture*. So someone . . . No. Then the picture was . . . No. How could a separate thing, by itself, have become connected? And beauty—beauty is no illusion. Our aesthetics does not, by any means, result from the satisfaction of our vital needs. I spent a winter freezing in the tundra. Nothing out there was suited for any kind of life. I was perishing—in beauty. So *who-o-o-o* then?!" And again, he howled the word "who" in a ghastly way.

"If you mean the Creator," I stammered, "I'm not at all opposed to—"

"Hateful man!" Pavel Petrovich snarled.

"But why? I believe, too . . ."

"Too . . ." he echoed venomously, destroying me completely. "But I don't mean you. You're a decent fellow, if you do think a lot of yourself. *He's* the one I hate!"

"*Who?*"

"*Man!* Man with a capital letter . . . The crown of Creation. He gets into everything, everything's his, everything's for him! Why, he's worse than any animal. Worse. Because in place of a pig's snout he invents all kinds of diggers, from the spoon to the atom. And gobbles, gobbles, gobbles. But to stop, or look around, or notice—"

"True, true," I nodded. "I agree with everything. But if you believe in Creation—"

Pavel Petrovich darkened. "There's no other hypothesis."

"—then man, too, is a creation. But in that case, for what purpose? The crown of creation—this may be something man has said of himself, although to all appearances the book wasn't written by man, either . . . But after all, he's even 'in the image and likeness'—"

"My, how you pick up on things!" On his lips, this was dubious praise. "Very quick. A truly civilized man—that's what you are!"

The blood rushed to my head in an unconquerable wave of shameful recollection. It had nothing to do with Pavel Petrovich . . . In what grade had we studied the author who wrote of that "Man with a capital letter"? To wit: " 'What will I do for the people!' shouted Danko . . ." No. "The grass snake crawled high into the mountains . . ." Again no! "With a cry, the stormy petrel soars like black lightning, now touching her wing to the wave . . ." That was it! "The silly penguin fearfully hides his fat body in the cliffs . . ." "One-sixth of them had formed a square in the grove and were gaily playing"—no, that was already something else, more human, about monkeys . . . Anyway, our literature teacher came down sick, and the substitute from District Education was an especially prominent woman, with a monstrous bust . . . Well, it's just that when we sat scribbling in our notebooks and she walked among the desks, first the shadow of her bosom would lean over the notebook from afar, then the bosom itself, our little head would be lost in that heaving bosom, and only with difficulty, somewhere above, could we make out the peculiar caress in her eyes and the cooing of her bosomy voice . . . This was in a year when I was still just a happy child. My brother was already studying at the university and getting A's. He had splendid handwriting and exemplary lecture notes. As it turned out (this amuses me now), both he, as a sophomore or junior, and I, as a seventh- or eighth-grader, were studying the same thing, the "silly penguin." I had peeked at his lecture notes just the night before, and they told, not for grade school but for college-level comprehension, what Gorky had meant by every animal—the penguin was a Constitutional Democrat, I think, or a Socialist Revolutionary. And now our high-bosomed substitute was asking a difficult question to awaken the initiative of the class, a "killer" question (she was probably finishing up at the same university) about these very animals, about the allegory. Well, no one knew, everyone hung back, because the question was posed in such a way that only the teacher could answer it. I, who never showed initiative, was the only one to raise my hand (which the Gospel would tell me to cut off), in order to impress her . . . I should mention that whenever she asked such a thing she had an encouraging, domineering way of saying, "Think, think!" So everyone's thinking, and I raise my hand. She smiles indulgently, ready to hear my naïve childish guess, and I blurt out, as written, the words accidentally seen and accidentally remembered—but who would have believed how fortunately! Blurt them out as my very own guess. The woman must have been surprised, but I was too embarrassed to remember her reaction very well. She went on to develop an idea "which I had suggested to her." And then when we were all copying it down and she was pacing the aisle, my head was suddenly between her breasts. She was hugging me from behind, patting my head, and saying, "You have a good little head on your shoulders . . . a good little head . . ." But the earth did not swallow me even then, although the infrequent situations of this sort are probably the ones in which the earth does swallow people, nor did it swallow me just now, when I suddenly pulled this out from under a thick mass of subsequent shames . . . nor did it when I recounted the whole memoir to Pavel Petrovich.

My, how that story tickled him!

"No, no! You're not hopeless at all. Not by any means," he said, laughing. "I never guessed."

I didn't think I'd been drinking, but the bottle was empty.

"Well," he declared, noting its total emptiness with gratified reproach, "I, too, give you an *A*. I don't know how you came up with this, but you've managed to ask the most difficult question. You can't imagine how I've struggled over this. The landscape has an answer for everything, even the purpose of man, but why 'in His image and likeness'? No answer."

Now he was inspecting the bottom of his glass, turning it this way and that.

"For what purpose, actually, is man created? This, too, is a very painterly question. Why are artists, too, called creators? Hyperbole, of course; 'master' was better . . . You can't possibly call an artist a creator in the full sense. At best he has re-created, not created. But isn't the Creator—although the term by no means describes Him fully—also the greatest of artists? . . . 'In the beginning was the Word.' And strictly speaking, not even the Word, but Logos, knowledge. Then the image of the world existed prior to the world, prior to the act of creation? And it wasn't just an image of the world, it was even divine . . . The image was God! Do you see what we're dealing with? An *artist*. Always the image comes first, and then the painting. This is the foundation of aesthetics. But the painting, you know, is always *for* someone—for someone who's capable of understanding or appreciating. Well, let's concede that our appreciation doesn't matter to Him. He's above that . . . But no, I *don't* believe that our appreciation doesn't matter! Not because we'll praise, but because we'll understand! To be understood, to be not alone—that is the point of Creation, as also of artistic creation. He was not engaged in pure art, we must suppose. No one ever has been, if we probe deeply. Art for art's sake is pride, humiliation more than pride . . . Everyone who creates yearns for understanding. Then isn't it obvious? What is man's origin, what is man for? To *see* Creation! Not only to use it and be part of it, like all God's creatures, but to *see* it! That is, to understand and comprehend it. This, we must suppose, is the reason why He created us 'in His image and likeness' . . . Otherwise it's incomprehensible. Why make man 'in His image and likeness,' for what purpose? The Creator Himself can't have idolized Himself, that He copied the crown of Creation from His own self?"

He upended his glass conclusively, as proof. "But for whom is a painting created? Oh, an ordinary painting?"

"The people," I said. "People," I elaborated, again imprecisely.

"The customer!" Pavel Petrovich cried.

"But who is the customer of God Himself?" I asked in great surprise.

"The world's image that existed before the world? But that's just a guess . . . It's not right, but . . . After all, the customer comes before the artist, doesn't he?"

He exulted as though he had supplied the answer not to me, this time, but to God Himself.

I had no reply for him. I could only nod.

"If I had been able to pose the question that way," I said profoundly, "that's exactly the way I would have posed it." Privately, though, I was solving a problem: I was translating the proof of port into the proof of vodka, in order to check the vodka equivalent of the amount Pavel Petrovich had drunk. I had almost figured it out, but I wasn't sure about the last fifty grams. Had the port been 0.75 liter or 0.8? Right in the middle of those fifty grams, as I calculated it, lay the boundary between *less* than a liter and *more* than a liter.

"There's a very curious hypothesis about this," Pavel Petrovich said dreamily. "Not a hypothesis, even. A myth. But I'm afraid we're not up to it."

Judging by the haste with which I took offense for my mental capacities, my older friend had already drunk his liter—

"You misunderstand me," Pavel Petrovich said affectionately, reading my mind. "I meant myself, not you. My dog money's all gone."

How I rejoiced at this turn of events! I simply hadn't dared to propose it myself. But *I* had money—I did! Though mine, too, was a little like "dog money." Shoes for the baby, perhaps, or . . . I no longer remember. Who cares! I had, have, will have money!

"But where will you buy it at this hour?"

"Not to worry," Pavel Petrovich said. "This will be enough," he said, taking a five from me. (I had pulled out three of them, all the money I had.) "This will be enough," he said, taking the second five as well, and keeping an attentive and solicitous eye on the third one lest I drop it past my pocket.

He wasn't staggering at all. Somehow he was even steadier on his feet, and gentler, as if the floor had become earthen. Without hurrying, he tidied everything up. He didn't forget to turn off the muffle furnace, either; I needn't have worried. The Saviour "not made by human hands" was put back against the wall, after first being kissed by Pavel Petrovich.

"When you're doing restorations," I said, fearful of asking an imprecise question, "do you also . . . make . . . contact?"

"Of course," he said, standing the panel against the wall at precisely that moment. "But it's different. However good the icon, even if 'not made by human hands,' it was painted by a man. Unlike Creation itself. Out there I'm in contact with the Creator." He said this as lightly as if boarding a streetcar or entering an office. "In here, with a man's faith, sometimes true, sometimes not. Sometimes"—and now he became thoughtful—"even with my own faith."

Order had been restored, in the sense that no vestiges remained. We passed behind the bin and through a small door leading nowhere. The doomed, human sigh of the Great Dane, whom we left behind, echoed at our backs in a new darkness.

We were plunged into the depths of the Middle Ages. The depths were literal, stony, and cramped. Or had I grown considerably broader in the shoulders, and taller? My shoulders scraped the walls, my head counted the invisible beams. Climbing a steep little staircase, I suddenly saw above me a star. The fresh night air burst into my cellar lungs. We found ourselves on top of the wall that surrounded the citadel. Standing on it, one could especially appreciate its thickness. We paused there, emphatically breathing in and out. This was a boundary. On one side all was silent, co-alescing in the night. The monastery buildings, invisible, huddled there rubbing their plump white flanks together and breathing— only the peaked bell tower could still be made out. On the other side, chains of streetlamps extended into the distance, a car honked, windows glowed at regular intervals in the hulking orderliness of the adjacent neighborhood . . . The gulp of air was like a genial glass.

This platform called for a speech addressed to nowhere. Pavel Petrovich took the floor.

"And behold, He created him . . ." Pavel Petrovich glanced to the left and then began gazing to the right: the dark of the monastery and the light of the new development. "He created the landscape and added man . . . Ayvazovsky's mistake! You know something funny? In this case, too, He may not have been the one who added the man, eh?"

"So who did?" I looked to the right and left.

"It's a secret for now," Pavel Petrovich said, his slyness gleaming in the night. "My secret. Or rather, a guess, a hint . . . I'll tell you. But not right away."

"I understand," I said, or perhaps nodded. More likely nodded.

"What you understand doesn't matter, what matters is that you'll understand later," he said rather ominously. "Judge for your-self. The world was completely ready when man appeared in it. Man created nothing in it. He didn't make the landscape. What he did make he made badly, he spoiled. You'll say that telegraph poles, rails, and airplanes became part of the landscape long ago. Pre-cisely: *became*! The wild animal carries a bullet under his skin— and never mind, he lives, with a slight limp. Man didn't create the landscape, but neither did he create the conflagration. Again, nei-ther the desert nor the ashes are the work of his hands, they merely exist where he is. Not by him are the weeds sown, not by him is the sand whipped into dunes. The unity he has destroyed in the landscape is merely a breach through which that unity's laws, which he did not establish, can operate. The surgeon cuts, but who will heal the wound, clot the blood, leave the scar? Who leaves the scar on God's Creation? You will say man—and you will be a thousand times wrong. Man inflicts the wound, the scar is from God. Man!" he howled. "The only word that means nothing!"

"I beg your pardon? But then—"

"Is there anything in this world that can name itself?"

"Why, no," I faltered.

"There's our word! 'Whyno.' What's wrong with that as a name for man? Does the moon somehow name itself? Does the pine? Does the cow say, 'I am a cow'? They have no language, you will claim. But life, existence—are they not language, are they not expression? We are given the language of words so that we may name everything. The stone cannot say of itself that it's a stone, but we will speak for it. And who will speak for us? . . . 'I,' said Adam after the Fall; 'thou,' said Cain to Abel; 'he,' said his descendant, of another descendant; 'I am he,' Christ reminded us all. But where is the word 'man' here? Man is but a pronoun: I, thou, he, they, and finally we. And if he's not a pronoun but man, and with a capital besides, this crown of Creation, climax of evolution, this navel of the earth—then he's merely the agent of erosion, corrosion, putrefaction, every kind of oxidation . . . The stress of nature."

But art? I wanted to say.

"What of art . . . ?" He waved a hand. "Man didn't create art, either. Although this is a uniquely permissible way of stretching the point in order to call him a creator or founder, if only with a small letter. What does art prove? That the highest creation of human hands has consumed almost no material. What has been spent on canvas, paint, paper, and ink? For this, nature suffices in abundance. For engendering yet another nature."

Pavel Petrovich was terrible and beautiful. As though he stood on a mountain.

"And you know what? *Do you know what?* Creative work doesn't even require any *time*! Man does not know time when he creates . . . When he loves . . ." He sighed. "In the face of death, he will discover that he has destroyed all his remaining time—that is, consumed it, that is, he's destroyed *himself*, and now he's dead. Time!" he howled. "Who are you? Are you man, perhaps? Is man, perhaps, a sort of larva, vermin, a landscape moth? Time's larva, death's chrysalis? The way the pharaohs were bandaged? Isn't that true, that they lie like chrysalises? The pyramids are monuments to death . . . All attempts to immortalize, to endure beyond the brackets of time, will prove monuments to death. Fear is already a cult. Everything here will outlive me, you see. 'Everything, even the dilapidated birdhouses . . .' We are indulgent toward the landscape, but only toward the kind that's mortal, along with us—the birdhouses, too, will fall apart soon enough, catching up with us . . . What we don't like is worms. Worms. Oh my God, the worms, oh my God, the worms . . ." he muttered. "It's beginning . . ." he said darkly.

"What's beginning?"

"Time, damn it! Vodka ends—time begins. They flow across. No gap there. Same thing. Time flows, too. The language—the language says it all. Now to open this crypt . . ."

Soundlessly, powerfully, a rancid slice of moon broke through a dark cloud. Pavel Petrovich's eyes blazed toward the moon with a matching light. All unexpectedly, he was dead drunk. With a last, heroic effort he shook himself out of his lethargy. A convulsive shudder ran over his whole body, articulating its disjunct, molten, and fused parts.

"Let's go!" he said decisively, and started to descend as if a trapdoor had opened under him.

There were steep steps in front of him, it turned out, and they led into the thickness of the wall. By now, only his head remained above, once more illuminated by the moon, whose smell was fading; the head turned to me, its general shape reminiscent of . . . The black ball lay abandoned on top of the wall, John the Baptist's head never did roll off the charger . . . The head summoned, and I had no strength to move, no strength to follow him . . . I glanced about for the last time. At my right, asleep forever, was the monastery. At my left, glass and concrete, the city of the future smoldered in life's embrace, the last charred brand of a universal bonfire . . . The moon burst into laughter again. Stirring ominously, like dead men come to life, the monastery buildings closed in . . . I turned my head one last time in the fresh air and disappeared underground. One last star flashed above me, as if it had fallen.

"Careful!" came Pavel Petrovich's caressing voice. "Give me your hand . . . Here's my hand!" His hand proved unexpectedly alive, strong, and warm. "That's the way. We'll be there in a minute."

We moved through this catacomb with increasing confidence. There was even something life-affirming and optimistic in our progress, as though there might be light ahead.

"Well, what's so disagreeable about a worm?" His voice, accompanying me, sounded confident and sober again. "Why isn't a spider pretty? But man dislikes, sees as unaesthetic, finds especially ugly the very things that will outlive him. Outlive not the individual, actually, but outlive man himself, outlive his very species . . . The reminder makes him wince. Weeds, barren ground, cockroaches, flies. They tell him over and over: You will not be, you will not be! . . . Pah, they've blocked it up."

Here I bumped into Pavel Petrovich, because he, in turn, had collided with something. This was a dead end. And it was *dark*! I raised my outspread hand to my eyes—and couldn't see it.

"We're here!" Even his voice became more cheerful.

Is he going to do me in, or what? I thought, equally cheerfully, and at the same time touched my useless eye. My eyelashes twitched under my hand with independent life: I was utterly unafraid, but a voluptuous wave of affection for my independent, self-contained existence ran down my spine . . . Pavel Petrovich kicked the obstacle, and it gave forth a joyful, booming response.

"Semyo-o-on! Simyo-o-on!" he shouted, drumming.

It was a door. What more could it lead to?

"Co-o-ming!" an unfriendly voice said at last, from the other side.

I thought I heard a sigh of relief from Pavel Petrovich: Thank God.

"Who's there?" My voice sounded scared, which surprised and wounded me.

"Oh, that's . . ." Pavel Petrovich shifted impatiently from foot to foot. "A great man . . . Head and shoulders above us. A sage!"

"But who is he?" I insisted.

"Semyon? Just . . . a hermit."

"Well!" This was fabulous! "Is he Semyon or Simyon?"

"I don't know for sure. We'll ask him in a minute." Pavel Petrovich pounded on the door again. As if someone had been standing behind it all this time, a bolt clanked, a hook rattled, tin squealed, a sharp blade of light slashed from the crack.

The blinding fifteen-watt bulb illumined a white rat on a man's shoulder. Simyon was a tall, crudely hinged peasant. His long, taciturn face—now the jaw, now the forehead—stuck out beyond the picture frame; he wore a smeared apron and smelled of paint. Pavel Petrovich took the wordless peasant's elbow and drew him deep inside, leaving me to look around. The cellar was extensive, its far end hidden in darkness. Down the middle, in two rows, huge barrels had been set in cement and covered with heavy lids. The complex and powerful aroma of acid and of briny dankness (as if a sea had died here) did not fit with the paint smell trailing from Simyon. The two men went through yet another small door, where a truly brilliant light blazed. Simyon, brightly lit, glanced at me over the rat, as though verifying something Pavel Petrovich had whispered to him, and they both disappeared.

I stood for a long time. They had forgotten about me. Or perhaps abandoned me? . . . At last I risked peeking in. They turned around as if caught, with suspiciously sober faces. In Pavel Petrovich's hands was an extraordinarily fresh, bright icon; he seemed to be turning it this way and that. Simyon's hands were otherwise occupied: in the right he held a small brush, in the left a gleaming half liter. Little tubes and bottles were clustered in working disarray on a small workbench, under a strong lamp, and the whole room was about the size of a barrel, which we wholly filled. Separately, on the only chair, stood yet another icon, which proved to be the very same Saviour with whom we had drunk. How had it come here? I hadn't noticed Pavel Petrovich carrying anything in his hands.

"Familiar?" he asked.

I nodded. But that wasn't what he meant, as it happened.

"St. Cyril and St. Methodius," he said, turning a fresh icon toward me.

"This is St. Cyril?" I asked, pointing in confusion.

Pavel Petrovich grinned. "You guessed it."

I wanted to ask Simyon how it happened that he, too, was a restorer, but Simyon picked up two glasses and nodded to us to follow him.

Nothing surprised me anymore—I was spellbound. Simyon set the bottle and glasses on a barrel. Leaning hard, he shoved the lid off the adjacent barrel. Out of nowhere a small scoop or dipper appeared in his hand, and he dipped it into the barrel. Pickled cucumbers, no less, splashed in the dipper like small fish. He emptied the dipper onto the lid, and they poured glossily down in a picturesque little heap.

"If only we had some cymbals," Pavel Petrovich said, rather voluptuously.

"They're gone." These were the first words I had heard from Simyon.

"What about from the bottom?"

Simyon said nothing. He cocked his head to one side, as before, and seemed to study me.

"I'll go after them myself," Pavel Petrovich begged.

Reluctantly Simyon consented, and Pavel Petrovich headed for the third barrel. Its lid was off, and he began to rummage with the dipper, leaning down into the barrel the way he had recently rummaged in the bin—as though the barrel, too, held another bottle.

"Hold my legs a minute," we heard from the barrel.

Simyon did not stir, and I was the one who went to hold his legs.

"Pull!" he shouted at last, in the echoing barrel. And there he stood, red-faced and triumphant, holding two cymlin squash. Brine dripped from his hands.

"Where are we?" I ventured at last.

"Didn't I tell you?" Pavel Petrovich said in surprise. "But it's obvious! What, haven't you ever visited a pickle plant?"

Something dreadful, like a smile, illuminated the sullen face of the sage Simyon, and I realized what and whom all this reminded me of. *The Three Musketeers.* The headsman of Lille! This greeting from my favorite author touched my heart, and my delight knew no bounds.

"And Simyon?" I asked politely, accepting the second glass.

Simyon looked away, grinding his teeth and flickering his jaw muscles.

"This isn't his line," Pavel Petrovich said, pouring. "He's above it."

We clinked glasses. I lifted mine in obsequious salute to our hospitable host. He flickered his jaw muscles again and said nothing.

Why was he so disdainful of me? When I'd been warmly predisposed toward him, through Pavel Petrovich. I felt hurt.

I hardly even remember what happened at first, despite the music of the cymlins, but later I remember well. I hadn't noticed where Simyon disappeared to. Well, yes, if this wasn't his line . . . I kept wanting to ask what his line was, but I also kept forgetting. Pavel Petrovich kept talking, and his thought did not weaken:

"Another reason I'm hardly an artist: I want to understand everything, rather than depict it. An artist isn't especially supposed to think. His eyes and hands think, his head keeps silent. He's not supposed to think in words, at any rate. For me, though, if it's not

in words it's not a thought. The artist thinks in images . . . You've
heard that expression? But what kind of thought is that? It's a rock
painter's thought. That's who drew the beast, by the way! Pithecanthropus!"

"Cro-Magnon," I said.

"Oh, yes, that's the one. All true artists are Cro-Magnon men.
That's why they like smocks and long hair . . . to hide their tails.
And their faces—did you ever notice? They all have these narrow,
steep foreheads, their eyes are set deep in the sockets. It's even
truer with sculptors. They're even more cavemanlike. By a couple
hundred thousand years. They have bristles on their ears, on their
shoulders, on their backs. Without fail! The hairy man Yevtikhiev
. . . you're too young to have seen him . . . in the old science
textbook . . . when I was little I thought he was a sculptor. That's
why they like to sculpt nudes, because nudes look like real people
to them, without the fur . . . I don't care for them, to tell the
truth. Do you think I say this in envy? You're thinking: He's a
failure—"

I wanted to say I wasn't thinking that, but to my surprise I
only heard myself bleat. Pavel Petrovich understood me in his own
way and filled our glasses anew.

"I wouldn't trade thought for anything! Not even for their
genius. Although," he said bitterly, "thought is lethal!"

I wanted to ask why, but could not.

"I'll tell you why, right now," he said, munching on a cucumber. "This is a great thought. We are born into a world that
is not boundless, isn't that so? Gradually we come to know it.
Swaddled, we look around with our baby eyes and see our mother.
She's the whole world. Then the world grows to be the size of the
room, the house, the street. Then we become convinced that we
can never get to the end of it. Then they explain to us about the
globe, about continents and countries, about the solar system, the
galaxy, the cosmos. And, having taught us things beyond our power
to conceive, they train us to substitute words for concepts. They
don't so much convince us that the *world* is boundless as that our

opportunities to *know* are boundless. We don't yet understand or know everything, they say, but we know more now than we used to, and eventually we'll begin to know even more, and then one day we'll know practically everything . . . The man with the capacity to think begins using that capacity to strive ever onward, ever further, and this is stronger than a drug, let me tell you. You may not get free of a drug, never mind an idea . . . You may stay there. Like Simyon . . ."

(I looked in the direction he had nodded in, and where Simeon was not.)

"A former commando. He stayed where they landed him . . . And there he began to shoot up. Got hooked. Now he needs nothing . . . They explain to us that oxygen, water, and food are necessary for life, and this, too, will be true, because that's how it is . . . They explain that life on earth is the rarest of miracles, because the combination of conditions making it possible is unique and unrepeatable in the cosmos, that life's range is phenomenally narrow, that we'll perish the instant we lack a degree of warmth, a gulp of air or water. This, again, is true. And only our consciousness, if you please, is as omnipotent and boundless as the world . . . You don't see the incongruity? Not yet? Let me explain. What we live in, what we see, perceive, and comprehend, what we call reality, is also a range, beyond whose bounds we perish in the same way that we freeze to death or suffocate. We think that our reality is boundless, that we just haven't come to know the whole of it yet, if you please. In actual fact, however, our reality is that same range, no wider than the diapason we hear or the spectrum we see. We are alive only within this range. And we *live* only in this range, we don't live in reality at all, only in a *layer* of reality, which, as a matter of fact, if we were capable of imagining its real proportions, is no thicker than a layer of paint. That's where we live, in the oil-paint layer on which we were painted. And the painting is beautiful, for what an artist painted it! What an artist! Leonardo is as incomparable to Him as . . . as . . . Even the comparison with Him is incomparable! *He* painted for us the life whose structure we're

unraveling little by little—unraveling in the literal sense as well
. . . 'So stone by brick we tore that factory down . . .' We putter
around, crawling on our layer, all the while thinking we're penetrating deep inside. We don't have the power to understand that
deep inside there's a reality not ours at all, not allotted to us,
certainly not given to us in sensation . . . that the structure of our
life has another structure of its own, which is certainly not located
inside our life. Newton's law is not confined in the apple, nor
Archimedes' law in the bath. The layer of life that was painted for
us has a structure which in turn is a layer of reality, which in turn
has a structure that is lodged, not in that layer, but in yet another,
or in several, I don't know how many more layers, which again
wouldn't explain anything to us even if we penetrated them. We
had no mission to understand, our mission was to live! And it was
beautifully—Lord, how beautifully!—incarnated. Now a thinking
man existed, now an artist existed . . . The artist doesn't understand. He mirrors. This is beautiful because all he can mirror is
that which was already beautiful. But if in this process he also
understands, if you please, then—assuming that he goes deep
inside—he crosses through the layer. But the layer is thin, no thicker
than paint, and what's behind it? Behind it is the ground, behind
that is the canvas, the foundation, and behind that is the abyss, a
hole, torn edges, and then—dust, darkness, a wall, with a nail and
a string to hang himself by, an untalented signature with an inane
title . . . No one but a painter understands painting, but believe
me, true talent in painting will never go further than the mute guess
that something does exist behind beauty. And yet, the thinking fool
will go there. There they all are—Leonardo, El Greco, Goya, van
Gogh . . . they all went beyond the range, beyond the bounds of
representation, and found nothing but madness beyond those
bounds . . . Cézanne . . ." And again his face twisted in pain, as
from toothache.

"But what *about* Cézanne?" I said with sudden clarity, and
marveled at my metallic voice.

"What about Cézanne? Nothing, really. He had never been a

normal person. You don't know a thing about painting anyway. So let's don't talk about him. Let's take an artist of the word. Who has come closest to painting in words?"

"Gogol." Here I had no doubt.

"Right. But he knew nothing about painting . . . Well, and what happened to him next? See? The same thing. He exhausted the layer of reality that the Lord had assigned for him to mirror, he crossed through that layer and went beyond the bounds of representation. Out there, something else begins—out there is faith. But what faith did Cro-Magnon man have when he was worshipping what he saw? Where faith is, the artist is no more. The artist can't understand this, because he's also an addict, because art isn't just the image of life, it's a way of life . . . Those of us who aren't geniuses always have something to prevent us from becoming geniuses: laziness, sluggishness, society, sins . . . And there's no way we can admit that what prevents us is instinct, the fear of death and the thirst for life. Unconsciously we're afraid of tumbling out of the layer of reality, we want to stay alive. But we'll never understand this, because we'll never concede we aren't geniuses. We have been prevented. Period. The artist's crisis is not circumstances. There are always circumstances popping up to turn you from your path. The crisis is that you've come to the edge of the only layer in which an image can be depicted, and now you want to paint invisible objects in visible colors. No one's advice or prescriptions will help you, no asceticism, no heroic feat. Anything is easier than to continue to paint life, which just now seemed alive and capable of representation—and was indeed alive, and simply remained alive forever for some people, because they laid no claim. It's easier not to drink, not to smoke, to stay away from women, everything that other people are too weak to deny themselves is easier than to paint what comes *next* after the image you've already depicted. *He* painted the landscape for us, painted us in it, but how He managed to do this is not for us to understand. The genius moves with cosmic speed in his understanding, and he tears a hole in the image. The sincerity of his bewilderment and despair is equaled only by the blindness or muteness that befalls him. His guess as to the structure of the world—if it doesn't drive him out of his mind—will strike him quite dumb. The fate of the genius is a cosmic catastrophe, not in the sense that we pity him on a cosmic scale, or that it has a cosmic effect on us, not in the sense that he would have given us something good if only he hadn't gotten trapped in the denser layers, but in the sense that he and the cosmos have a common nature. All our geniuses have exploded and scattered like dust, just as our dear earth is about to do. Humankind is close to a catastrophe on the same scale that every genius has suffered. Except that the artist used to tumble through the canvas, while these people go beyond the frame itself: they're exhausting the landscape on the very surface of the layer. Everything was made for us so that we would live and live out our lives. No more, and no further. Further is death. First the death of the lives we've lived, then of ourselves as well. There was as much as we needed of everything. Which means, no more than we needed. Not a whole lot. Just so much. The supply of temptation included. Lord, *when* will they realize that it's gone—gone? There is no more. *No more!* Where can I get it for you, when there isn't any more!" Pavel Petrovich screamed at me. "God had it figured, down to the last man. Next comes the inspector general. The inspector general's coming! And the inspector general is—the devil."

The might of this idea knocked me dead, though I should mention we had also killed the bottle.

"I don't believe in the devil," I said, suddenly resisting.

"*What?!*" exclaimed Pavel Petrovich—and Simyon, who came flying in from I don't know where.

"I mean, I believe in the Creator, in Christ," I babbled, hemmed in by the two sages. "I believe in them as a reality, that they existed . . . exist . . . But not that the devil exists the way they do. No."

"He doesn't believe," Simyon whispered to Pavel Petrovich in fright. "Then what *does* he believe in??"

"Listen to him, listen," Pavel Petrovich said.

"But the air is swarming!" Simyon flapped his sleeves like a panicked cock, gesturing around at the space where we were.

I recoiled. Pavel Petrovich treacherously nodded agreement.

"Swarming with what?" I said angrily.

"Invisible beings!" He looked around as if in terror.

"I don't believe in the other world, either!" I said stubbornly.

"What do you *mean*?!" Simyon, it seemed, was dumbstruck. Pavel Petrovich was observing us with some interest.

"Just what I say," I said maliciously.

"But if this world exists," Simyon said, his voice suddenly mild and ingratiating, "the other does, too."

"Listen to him, listen," Pavel Petrovich said, delightedly backing him up.

"Like a magnet—you can't cut it in half," Simyon said.

"Like light and darkness!" Pavel Petrovich exclaimed.

"Like life and death!" Simyon said, flickering his jaw muscles.

As though they had sentenced me, and now the time for my immolation had come . . . I was having trouble understanding. It seemed to me they had started speaking in some dead cave-language. Their words all hung in the air, the whole discussion, like an invisible, transparent pane, like a sheet of glass between them and me, with rain coursing down and thickening it, a transparent, viscous, fibrous downpour . . . Now the rat was there . . . now Simyon's face would turn savage with kindness . . . now Pavel Petrovich's face would become inspired and demoniacal, as though it, too, like the glass, had those weeping streams rolling down it . . . and now it would suddenly empty of significance, dissolve and wash away in the torrent, revealing the upturned nose and cantankerousness of Emperor Paul's anti-profile . . . At that moment especially, his small, dimming eyes would fill with an intelligence like madness, and Simyon would be gone again, without a trace . . .

"Who are you?" I kept asking Pavel Petrovich.

Who was he? . . .

"Not even one more rhinoceros! Why hasn't there been even one more species since man appeared? And if we shudder with loathing at the sight of some spider or snake, which existed before we did and will outlive us, then what is the expression in the eyes of nature herself when she looks at us, what shudder runs over her skin? Can you imagine that look? *At us?*"

I was captivated by his intelligence, I was overwhelmed and overpowered by it, though I also had overmuch vodka sloshing around inside me . . . And here is why I was still on my feet. However greatly he swaggered, however long he talked, neither he nor I could alter our original situation: he was performing, and I was listening. And no matter how silent I remained—if only because I could say nothing on his level—I, too, was performing and could not retreat from my role, any more than from my supremacy of position: I was performing as the appraiser, the final instance, the technical inspector of his ideas, the quality-control inspector of his truths. One way or another, I was the person for whose sake he was talking . . . Something irreparable had once happened to him, there was something he hadn't swallowed, hadn't digested, something he hadn't forgiven, to which he belonged without remainder and which he loved to distraction. His jealousy burned in everything . . . What was it he couldn't bear? Culture, art, life itself? Or God Himself?

"The good things in life were not provided in Creation. The good things are the work of our own hands!" Pavel Petrovich's voice rang with desperation. He was no longer closing in on his idea, he was fleeing from it, and it was chasing him. "Enough was provided so that we could fulfill our purpose. Love, death. End of program. Yet we imagine that our knowledge only begins when we abandon our program . . . But since knowledge, like God, is immeasurably greater than we are, neither greed nor appetite nor sensuality nor vanity will suffice for the man who begins to know. Neither Ecclesiastes nor Faust."

Pavel Petrovich emerged through these names as though the downpour had ended, or had dissolved the glass pane. Suddenly I saw where we were. The dim light, the slimy gray walls, the garbagey cement floor. Floating in the barrel was a last huge cucumber, too long for the dipper. Its curious dull tip poked out like a little crocodile. One thing became irrevocably clear to me: we were indeed in the place where we stood, and his discourse no longer seemed to me to be hyperbole. We were indeed on the other side of the layer he had talked about. With some doubt that it had ever happened, I could recall the landscape where we had met. The truth was here, and not there; the truth, which is to say reality, was this cucumber. Madness is not what we can imagine and be scared of, madness is when we're already *over there*, and not here. We were on the other side, and Simyon was smiling at us, because what distorted his face was a smile. He was offering me the wrought-iron key to the church.

"You'll forget again," he said fondly.

Because we, it turned out, were about to leave.

"You're stoned out of your mind!" Pavel Petrovich said admiringly to Simyon, who looked very sober to me. "You could've let me have a toke."

With the same frightening and engaging mask of politeness, Simyon took from behind his ear an inordinately long cigarette and offered it to Pavel Petrovich.

I headed for the door we had entered by, picturing the same scrabble in the wall and then the long-desired gulp of air and sky . . . It turned out I had started the wrong way. We exited through a completely different door, and there was no need to scrabble anywhere—we found ourselves right in the street, on the other side of the citadel.

"Now we'll go to a certain place," Pavel Petrovich said.

"But where? It's the middle of the night . . ." Not that *I* was afraid. My flesh was. I consisted entirely of vodka, it quivered crystal clear inside me.

"We're eagerly awaited." Pavel Petrovich was peremptory, yet he seemed somewhat hesitant as to which way to go, right or left. He was privately weighing and deciding something.

We stood under a solitary streetlamp. The road curved around the streetlamp and went downhill, disappearing among close-ranked trees. Still thinking, Pavel Petrovich took out Simyon's cigarette (this time from behind his own ear), then twirled it and sniffed it. He sniffed—I smelled the sweet flavors infused in the night air here: the combined fragrance of asphalt, leaves, grass, and fog was radiating warmth as it cooled. After one furtive puff in his sleeve, Pavel Petrovich handed the cigarette to me. I inhaled, and we set off.

That is, I had the illusion we set off. Because the streetlamp set off with us too, for some reason, and the road followed along like an escalator . . . Pavel Petrovich, of course, was talking, but I was no longer taking it in. Every now and again I dropped out of his discussion into the neighboring darkness of the street. He would support me carefully by the elbow and guide me back to a course illuminated always by the same streetlamp.

His words flowed along that course like a stream, like poetry . . . But they were poetry!

" '. . . He himself looks very like an ape,' " he declaimed.

I was enraptured, overwhelmed. "A wonderful line . . ."

He flickered his jaw muscles and incinerated me with his glance. As though I had mentioned Cézanne . . .

" 'O vanity! And that's your demigod, / That's man: though master of all good, / Of art, of land and sea, of all the world God wrought, / He cannot live two days sans—' . . . grub." Pavel Petrovich cut himself short and scorched me again with his glance, as though *I* were the very embodiment of . . .

"Did you write that?" I guessed timidly.

Great sadness flooded his brow. He shook his head in unbearable suffering.

"He is ape and Pithecanthropus and Stone and Bronze and Golden and heathen and early Christian and atheist, the tenth century is neighbor to the first, and the first to the twentieth. He wears a necktie and a loincloth, carries a sling and a submachine gun, he is slaveholder, peasant farmer, bourgeois, and proletarian, Greek, Mongol, and Russian—all this simultaneously, all this now. Not to mention that he's both woman and man . . . We judge by the top floor, which he added as recently as our own time, but we don't know which of the floors is actually inhabited in our neighbor. Maybe the fellow driving the Zhiguli is a fifteenth-century Mongolian cavalryman, and maybe the fellow in jeans is a student at Plato's Academy . . . We all bend over backward to be like one another, though we insist on our *inconsequential* differences as individuality . . . And no one can tell us who we are. What can you say about the age of a tree? . . . No, don't saw it down to count the rings!" he interrupted me. "What barbarity! Each little cell of the tree is a different age. Isn't the bottom branch older than the top branch? And isn't a fresh leaf on the bottom branch younger than an old leaf on the top one?"

I didn't know. I was standing in confusion before a wild torrent that had suddenly blocked our way. Pavel Petrovich solicitously helped me step across, for it was only a pathetic trickle leaking from a water-pipe coupling. He was now developing for my benefit a theory of the fragmentariness of life—as distinct from his layer theory, in which I already believed—and was extremely angry at the Creator.

"What a heap He built! Just *think*!" he said, with an urgent new intimacy. "No plan or supervision, helter-skelter, using whatever came to hand. We martyrs, we're the ones who people it with logic and harmony, though they don't come easily to us, for which we then blame ourselves. But it's the most ordinary henhouse— just very elaborate, with annexes, stairs, and superstructures— passed off as a perfect building, since we can't see any other. Bits and pieces—lumped together! But they're all isolated, all isolated!" he shouted. "Unfinished, unpainted, carelessly basted together . . . Stop!" he cried exultantly. "That's what's alive, that's what's tremendous, that's what's great and divine—the basting! The *thread* is alive! *It* is the presence of God in Creation! Why didn't I think of that before!" Pavel Petrovich wept, childishly rubbing the tears around his face.

"What is it? What is it?" I implored. "What's wrong?" I kept asking, barely able to restrain my own tears.

"I'm sorry for God!" he said. With an abrupt, manly gesture he brushed away a traitorous tear, flickering his jaw muscles like Simyon.

I was taken aback. "Well, but . . . how can we help Him?"

"We're the very ones who must!" Pavel Petrovich said with conviction. "He believes in us! *We* don't believe in *Him*, He believes in us. Do you suppose it's easy for Him? Look at us! This is what . . ." And he started to cry again. "No, you don't know! You don't know!" he keened. "Why, He's an orphan!"

"Simyon?"

"*God* is an orphan, blockhead! He's the father of an only son, and He gave that son to us to tear to pieces. How could He, bereft of parental care from eternity, have subjected His only flesh-and-blood son to the same fate!"

This was the last thing I had expected! The drunkenness flew clean out of my head. At any rate, the streetlamp finally came uncoupled from me and stayed behind. Darkness thickened around me.

"Let me explain," came Pavel Petrovich's voice from the dark. "First, a question for you. Adam was created in His image and likeness. Can he be considered a son of God?"

My neck was somehow bobbing loosely in my collar. For some reason I thought an invisible huge hand was about to reach down from the sky, in the darkness, and easily tip my head back.

"He cannot!" Pavel Petrovich exulted. "Because he was created, not born! But Jesus was born! Jesus is a son. I read a heretical little book about this, can't think of the author. You may feel satisfied with a creation, even proud of it, but that feeling can't be called love. Only a dilettante can love his own creation—not a true creator. It's impossible to love a creation, and impossible *not* to love a son. A creation may not satisfy you, but you could hardly correct something in it: once created, it doesn't belong to its creator. Do you reread your books, can you correct so much as a misprint in all the copies? Do I enjoy looking at my own landscapes? . . . Such is the practical possibility of loving one's creation and correcting it. The Creator can't make contact with His Creation after it's finished, however greatly it grieves Him. He can only destroy it. But after all, it's alive! The Lord finds the only way: by separating Himself from Himself, by sending another self, His own son . . . He gives us His only and most precious child, so that the latter will finish what He Himself has been unable to do. Keep in mind, too, that not only Jesus is a man; the Creator, too, though He doesn't descend to us, becomes a man, for He is the father of the man Jesus and thereby offers yet another sacrifice, deifying His Creation, adopting it. And then we, who were formerly a mere creation in the likeness of Him and His son, also become His children, for His son is our brother, through his mother and by blood. But, having become Jesus' brothers, aren't we older than Jesus? Adam is older than Jesus in time. And, like his sons—Cain was older than Abel and Cain slew Abel—didn't Adam's humankind become Cain, when we crucified God's son, our own brother?"

We emerged in the light of the next streetlamp. I tipped my head back again, and now retribution spied us. I needn't have looked up—retribution was not pursuing us from above, although possibly from on high.

Out of the darkness that we had left behind, a paddy wagon drew abreast of us and braked sharply. Two policemen leaped nimbly from the cab. One was already gripping my arm tightly above the elbow. The other raced past me and rustled heavily in the bushes, like a moose.

I looked back. The policeman boldly twisted my arm behind me. Ouch!

"Easy," the policeman said.

"*You* go easy," I said.

"No back talk!" he said.

"I'm not fleeing and I'm not resisting," I said.

"True," he said. "No place to frigging hide."

And he smiled an open, childish smile. He himself was rather small, but his teeth were splendid and large. Why, I could take care of him, I thought, clutching the key to the church in my free hand. God saved me—I could even have killed him with a key like that.

"Give me the key," he said then.

I gave it to him.

"Some key!" he said admiringly. "Where'd you get it?"

I couldn't resist: "It's my apartment key."

The officer, fortunately, laughed instead of taking offense. He was gratified.

"Do tell," he said, affirmatively and contentedly.

"Let go of my arm. I won't run away," I said.

"Got a residence stamp?" he asked.

"Yes," I said.

"In Moscow?"

"Yes."

"Where?"

I named my street.

"You're a long ways off. How will you get back?"

"By taxi."

"You mean you've got the money?" He was sincerely surprised. "You didn't drink it all up?"

"There's enough left for a taxi."

"Show me your residence stamp."

"But I don't carry my passport!" This has always infuriated me.

"Tough," he said, but he let go of my arm.

This officer wasn't bad. The other was worse. Panting, he crawled out of the bushes on the other side of the road. How had he flown across?

"Got away, the snake!" he said.

The fact that Pavel Petrovich had escaped gave me mixed feelings. On first thought, of course, I was glad for him. On second thought, it greatly surprised me that he was capable of such a thing. On third . . . Adam, Cain, Abel, I thought, and grinned, not without bitterness.

"Look," said my officer, holding the key out to his colleague.

"Hm-m, yes," drawled the other. "Where'd he get it?"

"He's not saying," mine reported, "and he's got no passport."

"Of course not," said the other. "No residence stamp."

I almost flew into a rage, but my officer backed me up: "He says he lives in Apothecary Lane."

"Where's that?"

"Near the three stations," I said.

"Oh, you all live near the three stations." They both started to laugh. "What about your friend, he live there too?"

"He's no friend of mine."

"What, never saw him before?"

"No."

"How come you had your arm around him?"

"He was going the same way."

"To the three stations?"

"Why, no, as far as the highway. I was lost, and he said he'd show me."

The other officer nodded encouragingly to mine. "No simpleton, is he?"

"Doing fine!" mine agreed.

"Lost, if you please. And where were you lost, if you even know?"

Now, that was the question! There he had me. That I didn't know at all—where I was.

"Tell us where you're coming from, at least," mine prompted, as if he were really on my side.

"From the monastery."

"From the monastery?! What were you doing there?"

"Taking communion."

"That does it," said the other. "What are we waiting for? Let's go."

. . . You don't have to believe me, but in the end they let me off. I hadn't expected it of them. Still less had I expected it of myself.

I woke up sitting on an ordinary office chair, in quarters

strangely unlike a prison cell. It was the kind of pen in which people keep small animals, like rabbits or, at the extreme, foxes. Through the wire partition that separated me from the duty room, I saw a peaceable policeman dozing at his post. Quartered alongside me, on a chair like mine, was a man I would never have expected here: a solid citizen. He wore an expensive-looking coat, with what I took to be a beaver collar; an astrakhan hat, which set off a very noble gray crew cut; delicate gold spectacles, which glittered fiercely . . . and he was asleep with his massive, very well-shaved chin resting on the (ivory!) knob of his equally massive cane.

"Awake?" I heard the policeman's kind voice. "Come on out."

He unlocked the grilled door to our cell.

"Come on out, don't worry, we have nothing against you." (Never in my life had anyone spoken to me so kindly!) "The major just got here, we're going to let you go . . . Stay put! This doesn't concern you!" he shouted menacingly at my dignified neighbor, who had made some move to follow me. "You'll stay here with me!" The word "me" sounded thin and mosquitolike.

A model and example, I fluttered out of the cell like a little bird, with a censorious glance at my colleague, now already my ex-colleague. I had sobered up, of course, which surprises even me. True, I reeked! The major—clean-shaven, exemplary, with an athletic glow on his trim cheekbones and a university emblem in his buttonhole—squeamishly asked me not to come near and to talk from a distance. I managed to explain the whole thing to him . . . What I like about the movies is that I can tell the police I work in them. Then, of course, come questions I can answer—that is, questions turning into a conversation, into a chat. Not that the major had seen even one of the films made from my screenplays. But I did have, if not my passport, at least my union ID. And it corroborated my address, as well as my name. And I hadn't been fighting or singing or shouting obscenities, I hadn't put up any resistance. At the monastery, as it happened, I had been visiting some artist friends. And artists, of course—well, you understand . . . And this smell I had, it was just a misfortune—my digestion, sort of, or my liver. Drink a kopeck, stink a ruble.

"But why don't you look after your health, if that's the case?" the major said in parting.

"I can't say I've abused it very often," I lamented with blue-eyed innocence.

"But why didn't they see you off?"

"They were drunk as skunks," I said censoriously. "I didn't have anywhere near as much to drink as they did."

I had found the key, as it happened, in a village (a separate conversation about the village—where? what district? it turned out they were practically fellow countrymen). All rusty. The boys had restored it for me, I was going to hang it on my wall.

"Here, leave the key with us. But the Galsworthy that you promised you'd try and get (my wife's really keen on him)—when you do get hold of it, drop in and see us, and I'll return it to you."

He actually tore out a used calendar page and wrote down his telephone number.

I had perked up so much that I even inquired what my bigwig cellmate had done.

"Don't ask!" The major scornfully waved me off.

It was already morning, and not even very early. The sun was warm. The sky was blue. Lord! What happiness this was! To walk out of a detention cell, walk out unscathed, walk out to the air, to freedom—and besides have fine weather! I even felt young and fresh, as though I hadn't gone beyond a liter yesterday but was peacefully returning from a morning swim or tennis game. To think in the direction of yesterday—never mind remember it—was loathsome and terrifying. The part of me that was alive, the only reason I still thought I wasn't finished, was my self-righteousness. After all, how had I managed to persuade them? Why, only by believing the whole story myself. I walked out of there fully aware that justice triumphs, and specifically—this is especially characteristic—in my case. The man with the cane was cogent corroboration of this.

Hardly had the police station disappeared from view, hardly had I inhaled a chestful of air at last, convinced that yesterday's fantastic horror simply hadn't happened, that it was all an inflamed delirium, which I had fortunately overcome, conquered, and forgotten—when there was a determined tug at my sleeve. There stood Pavel Petrovich, drawn, sleepless, chilled to the bone.

"Don't tell me they let you go?" he said in a whisper, glancing around. "I was sure you'd get fifteen days."

"How'd you find out I was here?" I said, nonplused.

"Where else could they take you?"

"You've been waiting for me the whole time?"

"I wouldn't have waited past eleven. The judge gets here by eleven."

"What time is it now?"

"Exactly time for the store to open. Let's go!"

Thus was I punished, and again from on high, for the self-righteousness that had so transfigured me just now! Already we were walking out of the store with two bottles, this time Kavkaz port, I think. Moreover, it was his treat again—that was the surprising thing. For he still had my fives, intact, and he hadn't bought the vodka from Simyon at all, Simyon had owed it to him . . . Now, squinting at the daylight world, and sensing the glances at our dead-white skin and sudden stubble, and clasping to our bellies the petards of Kavkaz as though throwing ourselves under a tank with them, or rather, under the cars and trucks, we stood in the middle of the street and gasped for breath, we would never get across this torrent, and I, for one, really didn't know where to go next, and by now I no longer wanted to go where we were "eagerly awaited," and besides, Pavel Petrovich seemed dispirited after his night . . . No park, no plantings—a hellish neighborhood. New construction that was no longer new, a fifties development. Elephantine buildings with sealed, fortresslike entrances and special old ladies who in that quarter-century had grown up on the benches at the entrances. Even Pavel Petrovich, everywhere the insider, finally seemed at a loss. But you don't know Pavel Petrovich! Nor did I, at the time, know all there was to know about him . . . Our goal was literally a few feet away. He was squinting at those few feet not because he was lost but because he was about to make a dash. Across from the liquor store they were making repairs, or rather, remodeling the first floor into something, most probably another liquor store. The showering star of the welding torch was our landmark . . . A laborer had donned his visor and was welding some kind of structure in a looming black doorway. Pavel Petrovich headed for him confidently. I spinelessly followed, already under his spell again. He approached the welder and said not a word to him—although this time it surely wasn't Simyon but a man he didn't know at all, any more than I did—said not a word to him, just: "Let us by." The welder immediately entered into our situation, with absolutely no mother oaths. He extinguished his torch, raised his visor to reveal his good, working-class face, and readily moved aside, clearing the way for us. He, too, said not a word, just: "But step to the back . . ." I instantaneously completed the sentence in my mind: ". . . so that nobody sees you." But I was wrong again, because the sentence had a different ending: ". . . so that I don't blind you." "Step to the back so that I don't blind you"—the phrase gave me no less happiness than the morning that had met me outside the police station! We walked in. And he truly didn't watch us go, he said nothing further to us in parting but went on with his interrupted work.

At the back of the empty dark hall, the probable future store, stood some sawhorses. On these, Pavel Petrovich—and again very cozily!—laid out our property. The worker (I don't want to call that noble man a laborer) sparkled in the doorway, the only light for the entire premises, and we silently drank our first glass and silently waited for the quite rapidly arriving renewal of our constitutions, and I began to feel good, good again, good all over again, and it seemed to me that the worker was defending us, shooting back at a world that was bad and hostile to us.

"If you want, I'll tell you quite honestly," Pavel Petrovich said, and gave me a look so sad that I didn't understand it.

But I felt so indulgent toward him, in view of the nobility of our worker, our protector, our machine gunner . . . that I no longer seemed to remember (though in fact I did remember) his nocturnal treachery, I felt indulgent and didn't want to hear his excuses, his humiliating lies, and I said, admiring my worker, "Why didn't you offer any to him? Well?"

"He won't have any," Pavel Petrovich answered lucidly.

"Why not?"

"Because he will at lunch break."

"You know him?"

"How could I? I've never seen him before. So, do you want me to tell you?"

"Well?" I asked crossly. I still hadn't recovered from my heroic behavior at the police station.

"In all honesty, I turned chicken. That's why I abandoned you. Now you won't want me to be your godfather."

No, I didn't know this man yet! He was utterly unable to accept the idea that he had betrayed me. No, he hadn't betrayed me. He'd had no choice, it seemed. Owing to a number of circumstances, which he would someday tell me about, he had no right to take the risk. On the other hand, I must understand that I was with him for life and should rely on him as on myself. But if I knew the whole story, if I had any idea what he'd had to suffer in his lifetime . . .

What was this power he had seized, if only over me alone? . . . Unlikely that I was alone . . . I had traipsed along after him again like Gogol's Mizhuev.

What I never succeeded in grasping, and what indisputably got me into trouble, was this: the interval and the dose. That is, I couldn't grasp the law or rhythm by which he varied it: now half a glass, now a full one, now one-third full, sometimes after five minutes, sometimes after an hour. I couldn't swear to the accuracy of the interval, of course, because I scarcely had any sense of time left. But in his implacable, suicidal drunkenness there was some element of power over himself and over the process, and although it was a total mystery how I maintained my equality with him, every time he found it necessary to add or repeat I proved quite able and sometimes even willing to endure it. Both his tale and its stormy whitecaps of ideas, presaging the assault of yet another world system, were somehow subordinated and organized by the seeming systemlessness of his toasts. For he did keep his hand on that arrhythmic pulse! This was hard to believe, and all the harder to formalize as a thought, but he seemed to be drinking through me, not himself, and it wasn't that I was submitting to his desire to keep on, but rather that he was being guided at first by my capabilities, and later also by my potentialities. The dreadful stories of his sympathetic, horrific life were fitted in between these spatially and temporally unequal drinks . . . The fascists set fire to his house; sheep bleated; the flag fluttered over the village soviet; the tractor crushed a drunk in a rut; one night a boar appeared in the headlights of the Studebaker; not until a week later were they found, starving in a cellar and unable to remember the word "mama"; his brother escaped from the juvenile colony but proved to be the "cow"—his fellow escapees ate him fifty kilometers from Ulan-Ude; they found a child's finger in a meat pie at the station lunch counter; his father raped his little sister in a furrow . . . This was a TV soap opera, with all roles played by him. But I did not doubt. Occasionally my feeble mind attempted to calculate the hero's age and was confounded, just as in my attempts to calculate the quantity he had drunk. My companion and contemporary had lived several lives, sometimes reaching age seventy and age seven simultaneously. The events he had participated in, or sometimes merely witnessed, were historical, but then his role and perspective would become fantastic, and, in a complete reversal, the persuasiveness and concreteness of the facts of his personal life would paint the historical fact in the most phantasmagoric colors. But each of these biographical motifs always had the same underlying thought: betrayal. Every time, he was unjustly, illegally, accidentally, intentionally, through no will of his own, et cetera, banished, seized, resettled, imprisoned, punished, humiliated, trampled—at the university, in the army, in the orchestra, in the work brigade, in kindergarten, in the Academy of the Arts—his highroad, his bright path, his calling, his purpose was blocked and cut short. Every time, he was *betrayed*. And however unreproachful I was as his listener, however poorly I understood, I could not be fully unaware of the link between this endless chain of treacheries and the fact that he had taken to his heels last night and I had been arrested. My sympathy for his misadventures and my belief in the truth of the events was inconvenient for him, because the more he talked, the harder he tried to justify himself. And the more I agreed with him, the tighter he drew his own noose. This was not intentional on my part, and the fact that I was rising in his estimation and towering ever higher must have exasperated him.

"You, too, shall betray me," he said at last, softly and overpoweringly, as though leaning toward Judas at supper.

I made no answer, in the first place because I couldn't, and in the second place—

"In the first place is enough," he interrupted my silence. "That's what Napoleon said."

Judas, I think, also remained silent . . . And really, the Kavkaz was all gone. Here, from the darkness, the doorway shone as brightly and the day beyond it was as sunny as though there were sky, not street, just outside the door. That doorway beckoned. The welding sparks, which had seemed so blinding when we entered, now showered whitely in the sunlight. The worker, silent as ever, stepped aside to let us pass.

And there we were, in the sunlight. My sensitivity was like that of a photographic plate. I tried to hide in my own sleeve and wasn't fully successful—the light leaked in around my edges. Pavel Petrovich, saddened by my coming betrayal, no longer spoke of the future, not even the near future. But already we were going "somewhere." A police officer's glance would linger on us, he would consider and assess and let us pass to the next officer. He let us pass in the same way that we passed the glass, in that same unclear rhythm. From this point on I don't remember very well . . . All we talked about now was Russia. A most relentless, most forgettable conversation.

But we were making stubborn progress. Across Russia, at least. Again we were "eagerly awaited" somewhere, it seemed. We were even going to his home, it seemed. He did, it turned out, have a home. And a family. And a wife. She, too, was eagerly awaiting us. But how far it was! Up seven hills, down seven dales . . . On each of the hills a bottle was procured, and in each of the vales it was drunk.

I discovered myself now there, now here. Probably I was somewhere between here and there. "Here" was a green little courtyard amidst Khrushchevian five-story buildings arrayed in a square. A green little courtyard with trees that had reached adolescence in the so-soon-over historical epoch but were not yet fully grown. They stuck up around the playground along with the mushroom sunshades, the sandboxes, and the rocket shaped like a slide, and this made them look like kept-back, overgrown children, just coming home from school to our own era—they had skipped out on the last song. They had outgrown the school uniform, too. In the shade of one of these schoolgirls with knees, in the shade of a maidenly poplar, on a small domino table, after killing a bottle with some gamblers and running out to get another and killing that one, too, we played at a roulette wheel fashioned from a laundry tub belonging to a certain Georgie . . . There, under the sun's mild and caressing rays, I lost all five of my remaining rubles. Pavel Petrovich won them back, after producing, with a sigh, the "three rublee," as he called them, that he had stashed away out of his "dog money" . . . "Seven rubles devote to the purchase of boats, and the last three rublee . . ." Pavel Petrovich declaimed, betting on both red and odd at once, winning on both, and promptly losing everything on zero.

Our losses took us to new distances and led for some reason to a sporting-goods warehouse, which was closed, moreover, for stocktaking. But this was the very place where they really were "awaiting" us. Here, too, Pavel Petrovich was completely accepted and even needed. They greeted him gladly, paid no attention to me. An aging playboy took us into his small office, where Pavel Petrovich unwrapped a newspaper containing something like a miniature book (he had had it with him, apparently, all through our arduous journey—and had not forgotten it, dropped it, or lost it). This miniature book was none other than a freshened panel from Simyon, with the same St. Cyril and St. Methodius as yesterday. Now they shone affectionately and soberly below a Japanese calendar with a Japanese nude, whose artful pose concealed a certain shortness of leg but did not conceal the rest of her. On a gym horse the generous playboy set an elegant table for us, with caviar even. He was setting out bread and it fell off the awkward surface of the horse, I lurched to pick it up, and he waved a hand: Leave it be. But Pavel Petrovich—he tremblingly picked it up and kissed it, saying, "Forgive us, dear bread." Although the dear bread had caviar on it. And when we had seated ourselves on a heap of exercise mats among the skis and rapiers and inhaled the wondrous smell of wood and resin, we recovered ourselves a little. I began to feel cheerful among these clumsy athletic monsters, fabricated by the disciplined workers of certain cooperatives resettled beyond our realm of consciousness—by juvenile delinquents, aged actors, the blind, and other outcastes! Cheerful, and suddenly weepy. And I did weep, hugging the sturdy leg of a vaulting buck remembered from my school days. The kind manager sympathized, very solicitously and tactfully. Comforted, I left with Pavel Petrovich for our next destination, which, as he averred, was just a stone's throw away.

Our stone's throw began in a now wild apple orchard preceding the city's farthest new development. The buildings sparkled in the rays of the setting sun like a spilled box of sugar lumps, overwhelming the remnants of my consciousness with the purity and inaccessibility of the universal creative life. And the orchard, through which we were already walking, was extraordinarily large and beautiful, with its sparse, regular, soldierly array of squat and gnarled trees, each with one gnarled, speckled apple surviving in its branches. We ate the apples as we drank. Here in the thick grass, among the trees, on a beautiful gentle slope, within sight of the house where we were "eagerly awaited," we made our last stop. This was truly a dale, a valley, dividing the next-to-last city district from the last. We no longer had any strength left. We were near our goal. A kind of termination, full of sorrow and happiness, shone in the sunset air that stagnated among the apple trees. Here was the threshold of paradise, the last hesitation line before . . . who knew what. We had come to the end. We drank, and my mind cleared as never before in my life. This was all Pavel Petrovich had been waiting for. As though he had been leading me to this very point for two days, deliberately and unswervingly.

"Now I will tell you what it would have been premature to tell you earlier," Pavel Petrovich said, bright sorrow in his eyes. He laid his hand on my shoulder, the way men doubtless used to lay the sword when initiating a knight.

I was fully conscious of the supreme responsibility of this initiation . . .

"Everything was finished by the time man arrived. Adjusted and wound like a clock. Man arrived in a *ready-made* world. There was no evolution after man. Evolution continued only in his own consciousness, repeated itself in his comprehension . . . But man confused comprehending with possessing, with belonging to him! The world was created by an artist, to be contemplated and understood and loved by man. But why 'in His image and likeness'? If you have some acquaintance with men, there's no way to understand that. The only way you can understand it is: 'in His image and likeness' so that man, too, would be an *artist*, capable of appreciating. The artist needed another artist. An artist can't exist alone. The Creator needed Adam even worse than Adam needed Eve. What is Creation, what is this ready-made world? Only in the artist will you find, if not an answer, then a response, if not love, then pity. I weep with pity when I see an ordinary great painting, never mind Creation. For behind our every ecstasy lurks a sense of doom: we will sell, betray, dissipate, violate, waste! But no, surely we exaggerate ourselves even here. And only the Indians of the Yámana tribe have arrived at this idea—"

"What, what?" I said with a start. "Which Indians?"

"The last Yámana Indian," Pavel Petrovich continued, sorrowfully and solemnly, "died in the Argentine city of Ushuaia in 1962. Tierra del Fuego was the homeland of the tribe. In the middle of the last century, they numbered three thousand people. They had no political organization, the elder's word was law. That is, from our standpoint they were extremely low on the ladder of civilization. Low even in stature, only five feet. And they lived in huts roofed with grass or sheepskins. Yet they had a highly developed language, divided into a great many dialects, a fact which made the work of the ethnographers especially difficult. So nothing remained of them. Not a word, let alone a dialect. Only it happened that before the death of the last Yámana a doctor from the hospital in which he lay had tape-recorded him after all. The Yámana was delirious and talked ceaselessly in his haste to reveal something. The story of that tape is a whole detective novel. The tape disappeared. Later it was miraculously found, in Australia. But that's beside the point. Along with episodes from the great tribe's history, when they deciphered the tape they found a noteworthy Creation myth, which for the first time, I believe, treats our Creator as an artist. When the great god Nikibumatva, as I think he was called, which in translation means 'he who shepherds the clouds,' undertook to create a picture of life, his shadow and devil—Escheguki, I think, which in translation means 'the dank name of the trackless being'—immediately meddled in his work. Nikibumatva knew how to create a form. Escheguki was jealous and tried to equal him in everything, but he didn't know how to create a form and was very afraid of revealing this. Watching closely how Nikibumatva created a form, Escheguki would try to copy it, but even his copies came out ugly and warped. Then he began to pretend that he was mocking Nikibumatva, making things this ugly on purpose to show the absurdity of whatever the great god might undertake. Nikibumatva, being truly great, paid no attention, although Escheguki did his best to vex him. Nikibumatva, for example, created the form of a fish. He made many fish, until he arrived at a perfect dolphin. Escheguki, spying on his work and copying it without talent, made a corrupt form and kept adding fragments of other, incompatible creatures, which had also been perfectly created by Nikibumatva, and when he finally gave up in exhaustion, he had the crocodile. The great god created the songbird, Escheguki the bat. Nikibumatva the butterfly, Escheguki the dirty housefly. Nikibumatva would manage to make ten beautiful animals—Escheguki would corrupt them all and glue them together as one, with his poison saliva. But even Escheguki, despite his enviousness and lack of talent, learned a lot, because his secret desire was not to ridicule Nikibumatva but rather to be his equal. And now, when the great god made the noble wolf, Escheguki tried for an especially long time, but his result was the jackal. And Escheguki despaired, and Escheguki was wroth, and he contrived a gruesome joke. He began to sculpt a creature in the likeness of the great Nikibumatva, and his result was—the monkey. The great god had endured all, just so that he wouldn't be distracted from his great work, but this he could not bear. And yet, since he couldn't meddle with someone else's creation, even an ugly one, and since he couldn't prevent something already alive from living—he had neither destroyed the crocodiles, bats, and jackals nor corrected them, once they existed—so, too, he made no move to correct the monkey, this caricature of himself, but merely sprinkled on him a teardrop of his vexation and a bead of his own sweat, for he was distracted from his work for an instant and wiped away the tear and the sweat with his tired hand. And the two drops scalded the monkey, for they fell right in his eyes. Something began to happen to the monkey. He *himself* began to change, before the very eyes of his creator Escheguki. Trying in every way to imitate and resemble Nikibumatva, the monkey changed and became a man. What had created him was the teardrop and sweat of the great god, and that is why love and work became man's fate: love sees the form, and work creates it. But that is also why man turned out to be merely 'in His image and likeness,' because the great god had no intention of copying himself, for he was a true creator, a far cry from the untalented parodist and caricaturist Escheguki. That is why, to this day, man is two-sided—he was created by the devil, but inspirited by God. He might have become like God in every respect, but he is prevented by his devilish nature, which he struggles against but does not conquer, because his flesh is from the devil, but his spirit is from God."

Pavel Petrovich lapsed into a solemn silence. He filled the glass but neither drank it nor offered it to me, and fell to thinking again for a long time, like the great Nikibumatva, while I remained silent like the monkey he had inspirited, sitting at his feet and gazing up at him in adoration. Now he drained the glass at one gulp.

"You know what I understand, thanks to this myth?" he said. Now he filled the glass and handed it to me (I forgot to mention, we had only the one). "I finally understand the first sentence in the Bible—"

" 'In the beginning was the Word'?" I joined in.

"You do know it all. 'And the earth was without form, and void . . .' So that's what you think, it was the word. Then you writers were the first men, isn't that right?"

Caught. I modestly lowered my eyes.

" 'Word,' in the original, is *Logos*. Knowledge. I've already tried to drive this point home to you, but you haven't yet dared to understand. In the beginning of the world there was knowledge of the world—that is, an image of the world. Which, indeed, is the foundation of creative work, in any system of aesthetics. So comparing the Creator to an artist isn't all that metaphorical, it's accurate. Before the world existed, its image did, and if the image exists, the artist is capable of reconstructing it. In all cases, then, the image is older than the creation, as any artist will corroborate in practice. 'The Word was God . . .' Right? But then who was His customer, eh?"

I didn't know.

"Why did Mozart's 'man in black' never come for his order?

Only because the order had been filled . . . The greatness of a design
is the greatness of its primordial error. The artist's design always
conceals in its foundation an *assumption*, something that cannot
be. This is what life is. Life, too, is an assumption. Life is the
customer, it's primordial, because only life was utterly impossible.
Not only in Creation—you'll find this error in any ordinary great
work. What is false in *Crime and Punishment?* That Raskolnikov
murdered the old woman. He could kill Lizaveta, the second
woman, but he couldn't have committed the first murder—he's not
that kind of man. But would the novel exist if it had been 'according
to the truth,' without the old woman's murder? The novel wouldn't
even exist. From the underlying incorrect assumption, endlessly
rectified inaccuracies are diffused over the whole creation as the
design is executed. This labor of correction and sharper definition
is what creates a work of art. To incarnate an image or a word
means not only to re-create it but also to *falsify* it to fit the design.
The genius's sufferings in this struggle with his primordial assumption are immeasurable, but a genius is a man who has made
large assumptions. Without the design's original falsehood, there
would be nothing; only lifeless matter is exact. For there to be life,
it was necessary to assume inexactness even in something exact—
in the most lifeless matter. Water! That's what reveals the Creator
in Creation, and the artist in the Creator. How does water expand
and contract, boil and freeze, in a manner that is unique and the
most contradictory of all liquids? You're the crossword expert, you
ought to know this better than I do . . . From water came life, as
everyone knows. Well, then, the astonishing thing is not life, but
—water! Water is the heroic feat of a Creator who violated harmony
in the name of life. What it cost Him is not for us to imagine.
Verily, this is what He created! Water . . . From a drop of water
to you and me it's a shorter distance than from lifeless matter to
water. Evolution is merely a novel with an inevitable denouement;
possibly we'll even close the whole book . . . Corrections, insertions,
crossed-out passages . . . There's still another basic insertion, however. Oil! No one has properly explained oil, either—the how and

why of it. But suddenly, after creating life, in the inevitable process of corrections and additions, He Himself laid in a supply of oil for us, for our continuation and future . . . As though we really were supposed to fly somewhere in our future. But I don't like it. What is *this* assumption compared with the greatness of the first water!"

There really was something splashing within and around me, like surf . . . Silvery smoothness, and houses rising to the surface . . . A sudden smell of the sea, like homeland . . .

"The Child," babbled Pavel Petrovich. He, too, was already transparent, dissolving in the ocean as it closed around us. "Oh, if only I could—the Child! . . . No one has painted him yet. Because he's not man, not beast, not God . . . Or maybe he *is* God . . . His face is like great water, ever flowing, its meaning is not of our world. Have you seen a true landscape? Look into his face! You'll be blinded. That landscape shows through in the face of the mother waiting for him, carrying him under her heart . . . There, by looking closely, we might understand something more, if only we could . . . But no, Creation is beyond our comprehension. Only the Passion . . ."

The last glassful turned over within me several times, because this thought was too heavy to lift. I dove like a dark little gray mouse into the depths that glimmered before me . . .

I woke up as if someone had poked me, in the small bare kitchen of a prefabricated apartment. Traces of unfinished construction proclaimed the building's newness. I was lying on a cot, under a small blanket, and my shoes had been carefully removed. Near the head of the bed stood a bottle of beer, beside which lay an opener. This solicitude struck me as revolting. I even tripped over the bottle when I stood up on the linoleum in my socks— stood like Colossus on his clay feet, and with a colossal stagger, too. I went to the rosy window to learn where I was and what was making the strange, animate racket outside the window. I was very high up. Extending away from the window were boundless expanses, no longer urban but Russian. The forest stretched to the horizon. Only near the building did it change to the dense young undergrowth just across the highway, which at that hour was empty. Parting that undergrowth with his powerful chest—hence the marvelous rustle that had wakened me—and racing not toward the forest, for some reason, but toward the building, here came a frightened and maddened moose. I'm not much of an expert, I'm not a hunter, but he was obviously young, even though he had reached full adult size. He raced along, parting the saplings like grass, and the madness in his eyes was visible even from many stories up . . . or were his mighty legs thrusting so randomly and wildly that I only imagined he wasn't seeing anything in his way? Above the forest horizon the red sun stood at exactly the same level as yesterday, when I had ceased remembering anything. Was this the same sunset, or a new sunrise, or the next sunset? Was I facing west or east? . . . But there was no apple orchard in front of me, and it could be inferred that I was facing the opposite direction, if one recalled that the last house where we were "eagerly awaited" had been in the orchard in front of us. In that case, it was sunrise! Veiled in a peculiar, mysterious mother-of-pearl, this beautiful *all* was still just beginning to catch fire . . . So, I was in Pavel Petrovich's house! A terror not attributable to hangover seized me. The moose dashed at me and disappeared from view. I peeled my forehead from the windowpane and set off to reconnoiter, soundlessly, in my socks.

It was a one-room apartment. Quietly opening the door, I found the room just as empty as the kitchen. Except that the walls were hung with an endless quantity of landscapes. Going closer to one of them, I recognized it, not without astonishment, as the very landscape from which this whole episode had started. The next one, too. And the next . . . All the canvases had one and the same landscape. The leaves fell, the sun rose and set, snow blanketed everything, storm clouds gathered and rain poured down, and even in the dark of night, with a single star, its features could be made out . . . Always the same landscape, always from the same point. For all my sympathy, I couldn't call this tolerable art; or, which is also possible, I knew nothing about it. But nowhere in these paintings did I see the spirit of Pavel Petrovich, who for two days had tossed my rickety little boat on his stormy billows. Especially in two unsuccessful ones: there was no excuse for the inexplicable washed-out shadow, the gray blur, that hung directly above the point from which he was painting this landscape . . . His nose! I guessed at last. This was his nose. The very nose that he had explained to me was so unneeded in a landscape. After looking around I turned to leave the room and almost cried out, for now I saw Pavel Petrovich.

In the corner behind the door a wide mattress had been laid directly on the floor; beside it, on his knees, was Pavel Petrovich. He had carefully bowed his head on the very edge of the mattress. And on the mattress itself there was—I didn't immediately understand what . . . something inordinately large and round, covered with a sheet. And over in the distance, in the corner, right by the wall, behind the dune of the sheet, I spied a woman's face. Both her pose and his were so lifeless that I was chained by terror, and the hairs found only in literature stirred like worms on my fuddled head. A mosquito was sitting on her brow. Its swollen belly glowed a separate red, from which I could tell that day had finally dawned. Could a mosquito suck a woman who was dead? still warm? . . . Now I also discerned a vein pulsing on her temple. Then the mountain under the sheet also began breathing rhythmically, and Pavel Petrovich was snoring, barely audibly . . . An extravagant feeling of happiness overwhelmed me. I gazed and gazed at this boundless pregnant face, a landscape of steppe and freedom in which we no longer exist . . . ancient as a burial mound, young as a wildflower . . . And the soothed, gentle little face of Pavel Petrovich . . . And on both, traces of tears from the swift, heavy thunderstorm that had passed in the night . . . Softly, on tiptoe, I left the apartment. The door was ajar, and the lock dangled useless on its last screw. There was still no one in the street. A cock crowed from someone's balcony, and after a moment's thought another answered him . . . Only now did I notice that I was in my socks, but I definitely wasn't going back for my shoes. I headed in the direction of the hypo-

thetical highway, to hitch a ride to where my explanation awaited
me.

I could have found Pavel Petrovich's house from memory, or
more accurately, I could have arranged to meet him at the point
of his landscape . . . I was shackled by an unconquerable fear at
the mere thought of it, every time. Even a return to the police
station (I already had the book) was less frightening to me, though
I never made that trip, either. So the keepsake key is still there,
and I still can't get into the church. Quite a few years have passed,
a lot has happened. Whether I left home or my wife left me, my
lady friend hasn't returned, either. And although I have never
encountered Pavel Petrovich again, all the totally forgotten things
he said during those hellish days when I vanished through his
trapdoor have evidently sunk right to the bottom, or as people say
nowadays, have become embedded in my unconscious. From time
to time and for no obvious reason, they float up to the surface in
the form of stunning illuminations (stunning primarily to me). For
a short while, crushed and exalted by an idea that seems to me to
be my own, I "have my reward," I feel smug. But then and there
I rake out the whole reward, suddenly realizing that this, too, is
not mine, my idea, it belongs to those days, to Pavel Petrovich.
And then the crocodile cucumber surfaces in my mind, or the
gaming laundry tub starts spinning, or the gym horse starts beating
its hoof, or Fujiyama's belly astonishes my eyes, or the welding
torch blazes up in my mind, or I remember Pavel Petrovich's nose
against the background . . . The seasons, marking my years, fly
past as on his landscapes, one idea attaches itself to another, and
even though it's not mine, I don't forget it the second time . . .
Ever since, I've been unable to look calmly at Cézanne—I'm always
afraid I don't fully understand him . . . And when I come across
someone's majestic discovery—necessarily about fate, necessarily
about God, soul, or homeland—I take fright even as I admire it,
because Pavel Petrovich, if only I could re-create him in full, said

it certainly as well and perhaps almost better, said practically the same thing as our prophets—and he said it to *me*.

Yes . . . Things were said . . . But who said all these things, and to whom? Who convinced whom of the truth of what? *When* and *where*? And what happened? What ever came of all these things that were said? What cloud were we living on, where did we fly to, and where are we crawling around now? Poking holes in layers and tumbling out of bounds? Let's fly higher by falling even deeper! In accordance with the laws of the correlation of top and bottom. Realistically applying them to reality, exchanging outer for inner and vice versa, not changing our living space and doing nothing in it or with it, producing nothing . . . exchanging outer for inner and inner for outer, thing for thing, as at a bazaar . . . so that the woman becomes a man, the dead thing alive, the man a woman, and the live thing dead . . . and what's in it for us, what's our profit in this spiritual marketplace? So many times we have soared up and fallen, so many times we've turned ourselves inside out with effort or retreated into our shell, yet where have we opened our eyes the next morning, and with whom? *As* whom have we awakened—there's another question. And who awoke?? It's odd, this groping at oneself: Who's this? To this day, I . . . with my usefulness, which sometimes seems real even to me . . . and other people are so convinced of it, as if by conspiracy . . . they've asked me to come, moved over to make room, invited me to visit them . . . invited me as one of their own, as someone like them, just as good, even better . . . invited me into the world, the people, the ethnic groups, the family . . . I tried, I approached, I was liked . . . When did it end? At what line did I balk, failing to cross it, every time? Who drew this magic circle around me? . . . I balked at an invisible line, beyond which acquaintanceship ended and life began: the ordinariness, the workload, and the disillusionment. Every time, I was obligated to no one: I didn't ask for this, you yourselves invited me, I didn't much want to, look to yourselves . . . Smiling, excessively modest, I entered into the next alien existence as if it were my own. Poets, women, Armenians, literary critics, foreigners, peasants, nouveaux riches and has-beens, classicists and modernists, monks and convicts, whole generations of fathers (who are also the sons)—they all moved over and almost gave up their places . . . I settled down as if in my own place, an empty place, a place occupied by no one, a place needed by no one . . . And only a kindred man didn't move over but demanded that I share with him, not my life, by any means, but a half liter to start with, didn't move over because he recognized in me, or perhaps in himself, the same kind of man, and, just in case, suspected me of a faster betrayal reaction.

Not so long ago, there was plenty of everything. Of earth, of water, of air. One would have thought. But no. They're almost gone. Just another little push and they *will* be gone. Plunder of the habitat. But what's so bad about that? The gold and the precious stones are still in someone's pockets, albeit someone else's. The village lost at cards has not disappeared. Solid matter is guarded by the law, at least to some extent. With more transparent matter, it's far worse. Where is the water, the air? Drained away, evaporated. But there are things even more delicate and transparent than water, more incorporeal than air . . . The spirit! What banditry, as yet undetected, seethes on its many floors! Ideas swarm in skulls as if not alive, as if no one's. No one has caught anyone red-handed (red-minded). And no one has been taken at his word . . .

Where is he? I hope he's alive. But I'm sure he is. As for me, here I sit . . . and I even . . . What is the captivating thing about life? The fact that it's really life! You could never make it up. And if anyone finds these recollections implausible in some respects— all right, some things really have become distorted in my memory, and some have been lost . . . Far more implausible than anything described above is, simply, this morning of alive and eternal life: I am painting it directly from nature, and only a week ago I couldn't even have imagined its future existence . . . Could I, even a month ago, when I feared that my last hour had come, have imagined that it too would pass, and that I wouldn't sleep, drink, eat meat, know women—that I would be writing here, and my hand would refuse to lift and make the sign of the cross, as it used to lift in unescapable sin? Could I have imagined myself in this particular kitchen, which I have never seen before, the kitchen to which I have withdrawn for the night so that this hospitable house won't thunder with my typewriter and wake up my hosts, who, after their laborious peasant labors and yet another family funeral, have fallen asleep at last? Could I have known that in the kitchen where I sit there would be, in addition to me, two baby chicks, one big and one little—they all died, these two are all that's left of the last two broods, but even in the kitchen they're cold, and the little chick keeps trying to creep under the bigger one, though actually he's not big either, but the big chick chases him away, and then, once they're awake, they go clattering single file around the cement floor until finally they think of doing something I would never in my life have thought of: they settle down on my foot, as the warmest spot in the kitchen, and though I'm rattling away like a submachine gun as I approach the long-dreamt-of end, and the noise makes them peep in fright, they don't get down off my foot, they peep but they endure, and who will tell me now that I'm not alive, if I have baby chicks warming themselves on my living body and all three of us are now alive, living, and surviving, as we struggle, albeit with different kinds, but all of us with the cold? No one, and especially not I, would have suggested this even yesterday, but someone knew . . . as surely as I know right now, when outside the window it's beginning to turn gray, and emerging from the darkness is the white wall of the house, and the marvelous English (Abkhazian) lawn (*agazon*), the grass-carpeted farmyard—I know for sure that some hens and a turkey and an endless number of turkey chicks will come running out, right now, onto this delightful glade, and a heifer named Mani-Mani ("Money-Money") is going to stick her face through my door, not expecting me here, and gaze at me as in the painting *The Adoration of the Magi*, and Mama Natella will drive her away and start putting the *khachapuri* in the oven at the very moment I finish this story on August 23, 1983, with a baby chick on my right foot

THE THIRD TALE

Awaiting Monkeys
(Transfiguration)

You drank it! . . . Without me?
—MOZART AND SALIERI

I. THE HORSE

. . . with a baby chick on my right foot

I had hardly put the final period . . .

. . . when HE shook the baby chick off his foot, and before I could think of any such thing he had fetched the white jeans I hadn't worn even once, and jumped into them so swiftly and boldly—I would never have thought it possible—*jumped* into them, with both lower extremities at once, not one foot first and then the other, awkwardly dancing and losing his balance in his haste, but both feet at once. And *zip!* they fitted him like a glove. Fitted even too well, being tight below and binding the male equipage that had lain so long unclaimed. And possibly they could have been shortened a trifle . . .

In the end, I didn't protest. I had harassed and bedeviled HIM enough, just letting him eat a little, sleep late, and stroll down to the sea once a day for a swim. I had not permitted him one drop of alcohol or even one thought of the fair sex . . . I had likewise not permitted him too much time petting all the various local children, pups, and piglets, to prevent the development of what I suspected was his tendency to pedophilia. And this for a whole month!

The only way we could keep it up was by *establishing* ourselves, immediately. As soon as we appeared in Tamysh and were greeted by the populace, a sedate and eager throng who came streaming from the nearby farms and kissed our shoulders in natural expectation of the tradition-hallowed feast—right then, I declared that no, I was writing, we didn't drink. Which, I should mention, plunged them into . . . And if it hadn't been for the prospect of a funeral repast on the other side of the village that very day, I don't know how this would have ended. At any rate, our neighbor Aslan later assured me that it might have ended badly indeed, if men like Alyosha and Badz hadn't stood up for us.

But the next day and again the next, the villagers' manly and unshaven faces seemed to have been wedged between our fence pickets since the day before. Their patiently welcoming gaze expressed confidence that today we would change our minds. But— no, no! we're working, I declared brazenly. Though how could there be any question of work, when HE was so depressed by all this "willpower"! I hid in the house like a prisoner, shamed by the honesty of their gaze. The entire village, all to a man, pitied HIM.

Every other day, for literally five minutes, Aslan checked on my condition. This most worthy young man had early been left fatherless and now bore responsibility for the entire farm and his mother and sisters. Precocious maturity was perhaps his distinguishing characteristic. An invincible, boyish rosiness colored his already knightly features. He would tell us something about his troubles and invite us, without urging, to drop in and try the *chacha* he had just distilled or a joint from the new stash of grass he had just received. He thought it had turned out well, he thought it was good . . . He didn't insist.

Aslan was probably coming to see HIM, not me.

One day he arrived extraordinarily excited and pale. Apparently addressing himself this time to me alone, he asked me, as a man he held in such esteem, to keep an eye on his younger brother, who had recently begun to cause him some anxiety—in token of which he apprehensively sniffed his hands. I had already heard something from Aslan about the brother, but I had thought he was older: he was strong and rich and had shops in Gagra. Aslan was obviously proud of him, as if he dreamed of coming to resemble him in time. But how could I look after him from here, a hundred kilometers away?

The trouble was, he said, he had dreamed of a different fate for his brother, a fate in no way similar to his own. What could he do, they had been orphaned early, all the money had gone for the funeral, all the responsibility had fallen to the eldest, and he'd had to pull a job (and he sniffed his hands again) . . . Just now he'd succeeded in knocking over a train and would have to hide, he had a safe haven where they wouldn't find him. The important thing was that his younger brother shouldn't follow the same path, because he was still immature, a romantic, he could take a notion to do anything. He knew the boy carried a blade, but now he was messing with his six-shooter, too! Maybe he'd even carried it!

I thought Aslan was stoned and playing a trick on me, but it turned out there was no mystery. This was not Aslan. It was Aslan's fifteen-minutes-older brother Astamur, who at this moment wasn't so much running his shop, which was being tended by trustworthy people, as doing time in jail. Taking advantage of their extraordinary resemblance, he had swapped places with Aslan during a visit, in order to go and pull the job. Everything had worked out very successfully: the watchman hadn't been killed, just wounded. But by now Astamur was in a great hurry to let Aslan out of the cell before the changing of the guard—a more trustworthy guard for one less trustworthy. His hands reeked of kerosene because he had just buried his TT army pistol in the vegetable patch, in a well-tended row of weapons, and he had to douse them with kerosene to keep them from rusting. Thus engaged in unaccustomed farm work, he had discovered that Aslan, too, had been digging in that row, whereas he had so hoped that Aslan would go to the agricultural college and remain a true peasant, and now he was so relying on me . . .

And Astamur (if this was not Aslan) ran off to his safe haven where no one would look for him—ran "home" to the darkness and to prison.

The prison was not far away, literally twenty kilometers, next door to a great rarity in our territory, a Christian church built by that "friend of the Abkhazian people" the Emperor Justinian, in the Romanesque style, naturally, in the sixth or seventh century, though of course it hadn't functioned for the past sixty years. We will yet have sad occasion to tell about it . . .

Aslan showed up the next day, apparently with no inkling as yet that his brother and I had talked. He was highly excited and therefore rosier than ever. Aslan invited me point-blank to go pull a job with him. They had to move fast, but Million Tomatoes had copped out at the last minute, and Senyok (this was a drifter who was working in the village that summer) wouldn't do, he had started boozing at the cemetery with the inconsolables. About the great man nicknamed Million Tomatoes, later. About Senyok, later, too. But just now there was no way I could cope, either with Aslan or with HIM, for although HE had been dozing he immediately woke with a start, dying to get in on this affair that was none of his business. Only with difficulty did I succeed in thwarting their instant rapport—and if I hadn't talked with Astamur the day before, I don't know how I would have restrained the two of them.

After delivering a measured lecture that almost put even me to sleep, I decided that it was already too late to sit down to work before swimming, and headed for the sea. I was still having trouble restraining HIM, for he continued to try and break away from me to Aslan, in his instant thirst to go pull a job, knock over a train. I allowed him to peek even longer than usual at a conjugal pair of pigs, who at this hour were always screwing by the Fifth Zantarias' barnyard fence. Everyone in our village, I should mention, was named Zantaria or Anua, with just a sprinkling of Gadlias. The spectacle of the businesslike lovemaking of the pigs, for whom he had always cherished a sympathy I could not explain, was a distraction for him but also an excessive attraction, in my view. I dragged him on, trying to divert him with the more moderate and elevated scenes that appeared along our path, in the gaps between the leaves and the clear blue sky, day in and day out, at a definite hour and minute, like clockwork, tireless, rejoicing in the repetition like children. At exactly 4:15 a gigantic mulberry tree in the Gadlias' farmyard would begin to chirp—the birds were announcing sunset, for, although the sun was still beating down full force, according to their information it was already sinking. At exactly 4:30 a cow who had become separated from the herd and felt homesick would return to the Thirteenth Zantarias' barnyard, locate a familiar break in the fence overgrown with "asparilla" briers (about which we will also have occasion to tell a story, this time a cheerful one), and squeeze into the cornfield, where her mistress, by this hour, was already waiting for her . . . The cow, however, paying exactly no attention to the beating, would manage to snatch two or three ears of corn—and then a fourth and a fifth, while her mistress selected a replacement for her broken stick. And at exactly 4:45, in the last yard, a clean little old lady in mourning clothes would emerge carrying a towel-covered *khachapuri* in the outstretched dry branches of her arms, to place it in the oven (thoroughly heated up by this hour) that stood at the edge of the lawn. Why a stove on the lawn? . . . Carefully affixed to the façade there was a large, institutional-looking glass sign, apparently made on special order in the capital, Sukhum, in the workshop of one of the Zantarias, who dealt in signs for banks, schools, and scientific institutes.

"1880–1983"

was inscribed on the sign, without a name, because payment was per character, and everyone here knew anyway who had died. And 1880 was also the birth year of the poet who said, "Ever more often I see death, and smile . . ." The deceased had been the mother-in-law of the old lady who at this very moment was putting the sheet of *khachapuri* in the oven. But then how old was the living lady? No less than seventy-five, to look at her, but no more than a hundred and fifty, either. Walking past—for the umpteenth time!—neither HE nor I wearied of picturing Alexander Alexandrovich Blok at a hundred and three, for he found more poetry in awaiting his mortal hour, dozing in the sun, than he did in his immortal poem "The Twelve" . . . But already, out there beyond the old lady who was Blok's contemporary, the farmyards ended and the sea lay open to view, separated from the village by a marshy strip of black mud in which a buffalo, also black, lay enjoying himself . . .

So every day we went out to the beach, and HE wouldn't go in the water for anything. Then, just as stubbornly, he wouldn't come out, knowing that after we swam it was over—work would begin. In the water I indulged to my heart's content in something categorically forbidden HIM: I tossed back a few drinks with Pavel Petrovich.

Therefore I couldn't be any too critical today when HE pulled my trousers on without asking and charged straight across the cemetery—where, toward morning, the inconsolable friends of the deceased were still drinking on one of the graves—in order to get there in time (he had figured this correctly and clearly) to grab one little drink with them *in memoriam,* and one more till the store opened. But now the wives began driving the cows out to pasture and herding the farmers home, and he and I just made the first bus into Sukhum.

HE sat impatiently in my brand-new snug-fitting white jeans, on the front seat as if on horseback, it seemed, urging the bus onward. But the bus, since it was the first, made long stops everywhere, waiting for its regular clients with their grunting sacks. And even when the client wouldn't be going today, because the Seventeenth Zantaria's brother-in-law's friend Valiko had promised to pick him up in his car—this, too, took no less time than if the client had boarded and come along, especially since he might nevertheless change his mind about going with Valiko and load his grunting ears of corn into our bus after all.

And while HE wriggled and fidgeted, I, still on the momentum of nocturnal inspiration, noticed a few things with my peripheral vision, though it was swimming from the two drinks. Peaceful, non-dusty, daybreak scenes. Nature has no hangover . . . But someone had stretched out at the roadside so freely, so limply, in the still-cold sunlight: red shirt, and tangled light brown curls that somehow seemed so Russian . . . there was something Russian even in his pose. The bus departed at last, and for some reason I began to worry about this man. What was wrong with him? . . . Now I would never know—I was on my way. And he was back there, left behind. He looked like Senyok, our drifter, who earned his keep around the farmyards by helping to harvest the corn . . . worked on our farm, too, taciturn, bony, always smiling affectionately, a sinking, sunset smile. No, it wasn't Senyok after all . . . And besides, was there really anyone there? In the end, he just flashed by like a bloodstain at the side of the road—the bus was already leaving, I didn't get a good look. But as we pulled away my anxiety kept growing, as though stretching taut the single thread that still bound me to life . . . I could—I could still stop the bus, run back, help him, even save him . . . The terror of the unnoticed event was strangely familiar, strangely comparable with the inexplicable ecstasy of an approaching inspiration—a line from a poem never written by anyone floated up from a tearful fog, my eyes grew wet—

Ever more often I see death, and smile—

but now the bus opened and closed its doors again, and I never did get off, I was listening with my peripheral hearing to snatches of an odd conversation about some sort of Abaz—not Abkhaz . . . Again the Abaz, the Abazinians . . . I couldn't understand.

And HE kept on wriggling and wriggling with impatience, cursing each stop, although by now he, too, was listening to the conversation, which had gradually begun to intrigue him. His blood boiled when he caught the thread, in the blend of Abkhazian and Russian: certain "Abuzinians," hated by the storyteller, had attacked the village again and destroyed the crops . . . HE had always "loved the smoke of burnt stubble." His nostrils flared. Well, but that's how it is. All these things are still a recent memory in this land: raids, fires, curved sabers, rustled herds, captive maidens . . .

"Damned Abuzinians—I'll shoot them all, every mother one!" I heard.

. . . and HE kept on wriggling and wriggling with impatience, showing no mercy for my trousers.

Each detail crowds out another detail. We succeed in reporting one particular only by omitting another particular. An irreparable pity! The whole of literature could probably be described in terms of details struggling for their existence. In this battle the bearers of locks and curls, of swanlike necks and wasp waists, of pantalettes and crinolines, have long since perished on paper swords. No portrait, no clothing—the modern hero is not only "faceless" but also undressed and unshod. Not only featureless, but also pantless. The landscape, too, has been excised.

But it's true! Not only the hero, not only the narrator's dubious "I," but also the author himself (not as a character in these lines, but as a person!) at the moment of the narrative (not when he's immediately writing it down, but when it's actually happening) is displaying himself without this "detail." This detail is also property! It must be *acquired*. Existence in the transitional phase between capitalism and communism collides with this last circumstance. A pair of pants, to be sure, is the very last form of private property, which is why Lenin would have done better to seek his "separately considered country" somewhere in Africa. Russia isn't Africa, but still, I was planning to go south, to our Black Sea subtropics (an imperial brag about climatic zones), and at almost forty-five years of age (a quarter-century of writing) I had no pants. This does not imply, by any means, that I had sold them for drink. Which, incidentally, is not so easy to do. In the good old days men drank away their last shirt, "down to the cross." (That is, the cross, too, was thought of as clothing, and sometimes they even drank away the cross; I remember someone tried to palm off a brass one on Prince Myshkin as silver.) But in our day, perhaps because shirts have become scarcer than pants, men have begun to drink away their last pair of pants instead of their shirt. I think the expression is more likely figurative (the image of the last pair of pants in Russian literature . . .). The image of one's last pair of pants is quite unaesthetic—trying to sell them (which, incidentally, I'm trying to do), not to mention buying them (incidentally, someone will buy)—the expression is more likely figurative, like the expression "I have no choice," which is always used at a moment when people are choosing from not one but two things, a moment when they do have a choice. So I did have pants on—I didn't have *southern* pants. Although it was already autumn, the south should be warm, the velvet season; I hadn't been there for a long time, and my expectations of the south were exaggerated. And lo, a beautiful lady, reluctantly outfitting me for the south, presented me with a pair of white trousers. The only insult to my masculine vanity was that her legs turned out to be longer (mine, it seems, are a bit short)—confirming that if she lived under *other* conditions (meaning the United States, most likely), she could have insured them, like Marlene Dietrich. But the zipper zipped, and I decided that they fitted me just right. I could say a lot more here about the lady ("You'll regret it," she told me in farewell, and indeed I do), but with this I end my striptease and take off the last pair of pants in Russian literature.

Or—put them on. My pants, by the way, were the real thing, even though white. That is, they were jeans. That is, Lees. I was especially proud (anyone who really knows will appreciate . . .) of that company's logo, a tiny thing the size of a laundry tag, not the vulgar blob as big as your whole rear end. True, they were too white . . . A writer's skill, as we were taught in school, is manifested chiefly in his choice of detail. Who can say whether these trousers are needed here?

But *I* needed them!

I *see* them.

And I see them on HIM.

He has deflowered them.

Across his rear end there is already a spreading red stain from the mulberries he mashed on the bus (that's why he was wiggling so impatiently! . . .), but he sees it not at all (and will not soon see it), what he sees is "the Black Sea there, the sand, the beach," he sees nothing but palm trees—for him, this suffices for Rio de Janeiro. He is standing on someone's front steps, under one of those elegant pre-Revolutionary wrought-iron canopies, on a small, quiet, not-yet-awake street in the capital city, Sukhum, where the dust is still lazy in the shade, and "with elbow bent sharp" he is triumphantly blowing a green bottle. Actually, he's drinking from it. And the bottle itself isn't green, the liquid in it is green (I had never seen any like it . . .). He himself is drinking it for the first time, he has never before encountered such vodka, and right on the spot he has joyously christened it "Green Demon." But actually, the vodka is labeled "Tarragon" and bears the color of the herb with which it is supposed to have been prepared. So here he is, joyfully drinking it, in the very first doorway after buying it, and the higher he tips his head back the bluer is the sky, the more golden the sun, the pinker the walls of the houses, the more delicate the tracery of the leaves, and at this moment, as he sees himself, he looks like the mulatto in white pants, even though deflowered . . . and not like the Young Pioneer bugler in the park (which is how *I* see him), in whose shade he is finishing the bottle, though no longer alone but with Daur, who has arrived in time. He and Daur caress pink Sukhum with their gaze. Palms—no shit! . . . Passing in front of them there's even a donkey, or perhaps a policeman—the one carries a watermelon, the other munches a round flat bread, the one will flicker an ear, the other an eyebrow, and that's all.

And you will hear no more about pants, for with this they are out of the story, as the Icelandic sagas say.

"You do as you like, but I'm not drinking any more," I told HIM. He didn't even wave me away, so great was his accumulated contempt for me.

In the end, I didn't protest. I had tossed back so many with Pavel Petrovich, according to the methods of Privy Councillor Johann von Goethe (I use the terminology of the unforgettable Venichka), without giving HIM even a drop, that it was time to take my leave.

So, more or less with clear conscience, I entrusted him to Million Tomatoes, and they trudged off "along the fair curls of day" (Daur Zantaria's expression, from Esenin, I think).

If the facial features of the modern hero have been erased and his curls have fallen out, those of the fair day remain. Its clean tresses trailed in the Black Sea, within sight of the snow-white brow of the Hotel Abkhazia (designed, like the Hotel Adjaria in Batum, by Academician Shchusev for a conference which Stalin had planned for the allied countries but which was held in neither place and which therefore received the name "Yalta Conference"). From here on, so that we won't have such long parentheses, we'll eavesdrop on their conversation at the Café Amra, which juts out into the Black Sea like a white breakwater, opposite the Hotel Abkhazia . . .

"Well, and then it would have been the Sukhum Conference . . ."

"And Churchill and Roosevelt would have come to Sukhum . . ."

"And they would have sat like you and me . . ."

"And drunk coffee at the Amra . . ."

"The Amra didn't exist then."

"The Amra has always existed!"

"Churchill drank only Armenian cognac."

"Since when?"

"They decided it right at the Yalta Conference. Every year, Stalin sent him a carload of the best Armenian cognac."

"Sure, and cigars from Castro."

"Listen, why talk like that! I know Castro didn't exist then!"

This retort indicates that there were no longer two of them but considerably more—more by at least one, the bartender from

the bar next door, an Armenian named Serozh, who was resting
up from the work that lay ahead of him.

"Castro didn't exist, but cigars did."

"Listen, why be a pest! Would you rather they'd had the Yalta
Conference in Batumi?!"

An excuse to find out what kind of cigar Churchill had
smoked—after his requisite glass of Armenian cognac—presented
itself then and there. He had long been attracting our notice, this
man. All but wearing a cork helmet, he was feeding the seagulls
and still nursing the same cup of coffee, with an eloquently silent
escort; as we had conjectured, he did prove to be an Englishman.
We immediately translated our question into language he would
understand: with the help of the word "Chercheell," we poured
him a little more cognac and puffed grandly on his Marlboro as if
it were a cigar. He still didn't catch on.

"You Russians are strange people," he said after the third
glass. "You love Thatcher, you love Chahchill . . . You're strange
people."

We "Russians"—two Abkhaz, two Mingrelians, one Armenian, and one Greek, not counting me—almost felt slightly insulted,
either on Russia's behalf or because he had known Russian all
along. We ordered another coffee.

Not by nationalities but by our coffees were we divided! Two
medium-strong, two weak, one *sade* with sugar, two sultans, one
double-sweet, and one plain no sugar, one for Marxen, one for me
. . . The Englishman was ecstatic, with good reason. This was a
ritual! In the first place, without waiting in line: natives, the right
of the habitué, close acquaintanceship with the coffee chef. The
people in line, out-of-town visitors, say nothing, act timid, don't
object (if they don't object, it means they're from out of town).
"Meess, are you here for a long visit? Haff you seen the dolphins
yet?" The accent is intentional, people in Sukhum have little accent;
the accent is for romance, to inspire fear and respect. A week's
growth of beard (which will come into style only many years later
in the West); a gold chain; a carelessly tucked-in white shirt, un-

buttoned to expose a cross buried in fur; sleeves rolled up as if by chance, below the elbow; a muscular, careless hand, perhaps with a thick gold ring . . . "Ovik, six more, be so kind: two extra-strong, one medium, two weak, one regular!" The peculiar chic of the coffee chef is to ignore the order but fill it promptly and unerringly, keeping it straight, which coffee for whom. The peculiar chic of the man placing the order is to have affection in his voice and severity on his face, and not to dither when paying, so that he proffers a crumpled note with disdain for the money but not for the coffee or the coffee chef . . . After executing this ballet, the man who has ordered is not immediately liberated from his mask. But then, after listening with downcast eyes and modest pride as he is toasted, he is liberated after all and joins the conversation . . .

"He might be reckoned as Jewish, but he might not, either."

"If it's through the mother, he should be. Jews reckon nationality through the mother."

"Well, but through the father it's obvious. If you're a Rabinovich everyone knows you're Jewish, even if your mother's Russian."

"That way they get more Jews. Through both sides. Clever people."

"Yes, unlike the Abkhaz. We just get fewer. If it's through the father you're Georgian. And if it's through the mother you're Georgian."

"Damn Lavrenty! How many we might have been . . ."

"What do you think?" They put the question point-blank to the silent escort.

"Are you speaking to me?"

"Was Jesus a Jew or not?"

"I do scientific, ah, research. This isn't my problem."

"Then what is?"

"I study monkeys."

"And you?" This was to me.

"Listen, why pester everyone? What are you, Jewish or something?"

"I'm not Jewish, I'm Greek. But anyway?"

"Who among us has not been a Jew at least once?" Who said this? Surely not HE?

"It seems to me," I said, treading cautiously, "you can reckon the Son of God by His Father, but not by nationality."

"And you, Serozh?"

"Me? I'm Armenian."

"I'm Ainglish," said the Englishman. "None of you know what a third-category city is!"

The Englishman was just in from Voronezh, and Voronezh, to be specific, was a third-category city . . . But how easy it was to talk about Jews here! Everyone here was in a minority.

But together we already formed rather a large crowd, once more to burst out onto the embankment in the genial mood of masters of life.

This, however, was what I needed the white trousers for! ("No vow is forever"—but I didn't think that one would prove so short-lived.) White trousers! I needed them in order to walk with my arms around my friends and catch the glow of my own self-delight on the faces of passersby. In exactly this state of mind (was it fate, the plot, the laws of symmetry, or simply a mirror image?) we might encounter an even more self-satisfied cohort coming toward us. They were always in an indisputable majority. It was amazing! Like a movie! I felt the muscles of my Abkhazian friends flexing under their tight, freshly laundered T-shirts. By the way, I have seen Million Tomatoes lift a hundred kilograms with one hand, and every second man complained that his muscles took half his time.

And it *was* a movie. It advanced on us in "pig" formation, as the wedge was called in the Middle Ages. That is, in front rode a knight armored in fame, slight though he was in stature. The whole myth, the whole preeminence, the whole unquestionability of the cinema was concentrated in him. On either side, keeping a slight distance behind him, and taller toward the edges, followed his retinue—administrators and female assistants who seemed to be always asking something and taking notes. Mighty, courageous cameramen and electricians feathered this wedge.

My friends tensed, the movie director and I embraced, everything merged, and we were doubled. They had come to choose a location. The action of their film took place in Yalta, but Yalta did not fit Yalta. Sukhum fitted it better. This was a new version of "The Lady with the Lapdog." It was a musical. The role of the lapdog had been accepted by an actress who in her youth had been filmed by Bergman, though she wasn't famous just for that, and the hint of a relationship between the heroine and the little dog, as you yourself understand, would produce a revolution in the Russian cinema.

In our new status as a recognized international cohort, we made the rounds of all the remaining coffeehouses on the embankment. There were about seven of them.

Oh, this embankment! It seems so long, by virtue of these coffeehouses! In actual fact this intensive segment lasts two hundred meters, at most, but to walk it you must spend half a day (and half a day back). You can also spend a lifetime (the same people of the embankment will celebrate your funeral). We were coming from the Amra, from south to north; they were going toward the Hotel Abkhazia (where the director was supposed to unpack), from north to south. But we were walking like normal people, while they had tromped past like elephants. Consequently we (as locals) made them turn back, to examine everything as it deserved. "That's no way to choose a location," we implied.

We gratified our vanity as best we could. All Sukhum exchanged bows with us, the filmmakers went unrecognized. "Who's that?" the director would ask in one or another instance, when he thought our tone was especially respectful. "How to tell you . . . We don't generally say, but everyone knows . . . Well, he's a mobster." This gentleman of sixty, in a snow-white shirt and a cloud of imported deodorant, his face as smooth as if shaved from inside, with his mild, intelligent features and a gaze filled with deference and virtue, was so unlikely as to be enchanting—you immediately had no doubt that just such a man, and only such a man, could be a mafia chief. He was very preoccupied, our capo; his grand-daughter was trying to get into college in Moscow. All measures had been taken, and yet he was very anxious. The solicitous grand-father had notched up eight lives, however. No, he hadn't killed anyone in the last twenty years. Simply because there had been no need. How to explain it to you, it's rather complicated . . . Well, he has three or four shops, let's say . . . He's the owner? . . . No, the owners pay him. What for? Well, not to touch them. But it's been twenty years since he touched anyone! . . . Well, so they pay on time.

The noble mafioso—ah, the leisure of his gait!—walked to his car, not in order to leave . . . No, I'm wrong! Of course he couldn't have walked to the car himself, if he wasn't leaving. He simply spoke, without turning to the man he spoke to. From behind his shoulder emerged Aslan (or was it Astamur? he nodded reluctantly, or perhaps unrecognizingly, in reply to my cheerful greeting). Aslan or Not-Aslan caught the keys, and it was he who walked to the car, opened the trunk, rustled around in it for a moment, and brought out something wrapped in *The Dawn of the East*, oblong, like a sawed-off rifle. This gun promptly fired, of course (in the hands of the unskilled dramaturge), as clearly and tonelessly as the first autumn frost. It was champagne on ice! Talent means talent in everything . . . Our friend the mafioso had been the first man in Sukhum to think of carrying a picnic cooler in his trunk! And now these dusty, talentless boxes, after overstocking the shelves of all the village general stores for several years, had become short-age items. (He hadn't bought the cooler, by the way. He had re-ceived it as a gift from the manager of the cooperative that produced them.)

The champagne fired, striking my heart and HIS. Smoke curled from the barrel. The hand of a professional! How beautiful this was. I couldn't deny myself the hyperbole . . . From the way he managed the bottle, it was obvious that his hand would not have trembled. Then this impeccable cleanness (not washedness), and the lovingly groomed fingernails . . . And the cuff! And the cuff link! . . . The cuff link was perhaps a bit large, though of course it was gold. But not everything at once—someday he, too, would wear a tiny cuff link, with a single pinprick diamond. It takes more than one generation to make the chief badge as inconspicuous as the Legion of Honor.

The glasses sprouted on the table (I hadn't noticed any particular Not-Aslan bringing them), champagne flowed from the hand of the violinist who had never held a violin, the landscape vitrified as we watched: the sun, forever suspended over the mooring . . . the Greek fortress of Dioscurias, whose cyclopean rubble, although this is not the first thousand years it has lain here, always seems to have washed ashore only yesterday in some unprecedented gale . . . the trunk of a plane tree, diseased with psoriasis . . . the blinding path of sunlight on a sea becalmed at this hour, oily, taut as silk . . . the seagull forever suspended over the smokestack of the ship *Taras Shevchenko*, which is also moored forever . . . and the gull's sharp cry will never fade over this landscape, which is suddenly darkening and turning coal black, narrowing in my eyes because overpopulated with happiness.

What I respect in HIM is that he never drinks champagne. "The main thing is, don't drink the bubblies," he was told by a dying old alcoholic, who meant not only champagne but beer and mineral water as well. HE believed the alcoholic, not me. Champagne is my privilege. Once a year I, too, can drink to success, which, by the way, consists only in the fact that yet another time has gone by.

My enchanting mafioso began to talk too much about the movies, addressing himself more and more to the director (the same breed!) and for some reason calling him Federico. By now our fame was running ahead of us like a large dog, like a smooth billow of lazy surf, and ultimately like us (in our own view). Champagne appeared at every coffeehouse. They loved us. The union of art and sport—that's what a movie is, and you couldn't find a better place for them to meet than an out-of-season resort. The beaches and restaurants and hotels stand empty just for them, for the film troupes and sports teams.

We were brought together by Marxen, the former world record holder in pistol shooting. Without ever having removed his telescopic sights from his eyes, he was now a cardiologist and a bachelor who in keeping with his specialty took advantage of all the local widows (those who hadn't lost their charm and had even gained a certain quality of mystery), as the confidant of their autumnal secrets. So far, fortunately, our mutual friend was not treating us; so far we had among us one lone micro-infarct, Daur's, which had flown as unexpected and bright as a hummingbird into our determinedly youthful company . . .

Having made the rounds of all the coffeehouses, we must also stop in at the home of the physician and record holder. Here he would show us his library, this man who had read everything . . . Camus and Borges, if you had only known . . . who would be the first to read you in Russia! He took off his spectacles and exposed eyes so weak that even his hands, wiping his glasses, suddenly seemed as wax white and shaky as a flickering candle. Neither hand nor eye had wavered, however, when he hit 599 out of 600. The director, as always, was running the show; that is, he had started a penetrating conversation about sports. He himself couldn't boast the same achievements in his past and was therefore trying to best the champion in his insight into the phenomenon. Not a chance!

Marxen was born blind and grew up blind in an Abkhazian village. His parents didn't think to put glasses on him (minus twenty, he stated modestly). Children his age were already being taken on the hunt, but why take a blind boy? So one day when no one was home he put on his hundred-year-old grandmother's glasses, seized a small-bore rifle, and darted outdoors, blinded by eyesight and looking for something to shoot. He couldn't shoot the domestic animals, of course. Suddenly, fifty meters away, he saw some wild ducks swimming down the small river. He fired once— missed, the duck went on swimming. Fired at another—same thing. Fired at a third . . . Only on the fifth did he notice that they bobbed their heads after the shot. He checked his observation on the sixth and seventh. Same effect: they bowed their heads gently and shyly but continued to swim in the same column, steady as little boats. At this point a neighbor arrived, cursing as he ran—Marxen had shot all his decoys, it turned out, hitting each one in the eye, and they had continued to float downstream with the current.

"Dark, dark was the night, the rain was pouring down . . ." His father was Georgian and his mother Abkhazian, but his grandmother had been Jewish, a pre-Revolutionary revolutionary, and that was how he came by the name Marxen. His parents were imprisoned in '37, so he ended up in the village with his Abkhazian grandfather. Even then, in '37, he saw things clearly. Marx and Engels—he hated those mothers . . . You yourselves understand, what could he do with a name like that, the little blind son of parents subjected to repression? The only road was sports. He said that the brain, eye, hand, barrel, and target, when he fired, were not just a single line but a taut violin string singing in the wind, and then he took into account the wind direction, and the shimmer of warm air if the sun was . . . It was that hot in Italy, when he . . . Brain and target became a single point, equal to the bullet— he felt the movement of the bullet in the barrel when he fired . . .

The director bit his lip. What the hell did he care about "The Lady with the Lapdog," he was thinking, when *this* was the man he should be doing a film about! A ready-made scenario! The actor—there was no real actor . . . Oh, if only Cybulski were alive . . . Stung by the way the director had so quickly pulled the whole blanket (Marxen) over himself, I asked Marxen to show us his weapon. And now we heard all about the abject situation of the athlete in Soviet sports. He had nothing! He didn't have his pistol—it had been state property, unlawfully classified as a military weapon. Only the stock—that was all he had left as a memento of his world record and twenty years of his life. Embarrassed by the paltriness of the outcome of an entire lifetime, he tenderly unfolded a flannel rag, as though it contained a baby's little corpse. There lay a fantastic bone . . .

It replicated the record holder's hand from within; these reverse dents were unrecognizable, a form unencountered in nature; it was like death. It was, indeed, a death mask, or rather the mask's primordial form, from which the face bereft of life is later cast. The mask of a hand (a mask is also made from the hand of a great pianist . . .). This death was warm, because it was wood. A rare wood, from a tree of rare hardness. Polished by the hand of a skilled craftsman, who had fashioned a one-of-a-kind stock for a unique hand. And then burnished by that unique hand, which had pulled the trigger hundreds of thousands of times. There was no trigger, no barrel. It was empty as a skull. I warmed it in my own hand—this was like a handshake. (Experiencing this sensation for the first time, I had no way of knowing that I would relive it within twenty-four hours . . .)

He had never killed anything but those little ducks. He hated hunting and fishing. But if there was anything he would have shot dead without hesitation, point-blank, it was that bloodsucker . . . As a marksman and a philosopher, he knew what murder was and hated murderers . . . Beria he would have hit from any distance. In the eye. That would even have been easier—the pince-nez would have glittered, he would have aimed at that patch of light. From two kilometers, two miles . . .

"Miles?" The Englishman woke up. "You have Russian miles?"

"*Don't vorry,*" Marxen reassured him. He had just begun to study English. His mix of Jewish, Georgian, and Abkhazian blood made him an internationalist, not merely a hater of executioners.

Carrying on with the choice of a location, we turned away from the sea at last, in the filmmakers' van and the two cars (the mafioso's and the monkey researcher's), and began to climb upward along a river by the name of Water. Something reminded me of something. Wasn't it here that Father and I had caught trout and grayling in the winter of '54, when he was building his sanatorium in Sochi? He fished, and I wandered. This was his pedagogical measure—taking me along to the construction site—and my first exile. They were separating me from my first woman, who had been deemed "unsuitable" at a closed-door family council. I kept writing letters, running to the Claim Window in secret, and receiving no answer. I pacified my flesh with ceaseless bodybuilding, my biceps grew two and a half centimeters. My poor father! He, too, it turned out, was pacifying his flesh by fishing; who could have thought it . . . A man past fifty! (Fifty-two.) At the Claim Window I finally received a letter addressed to him, and read it . . . Papa, I couldn't give it to you open! And when, embarrassed, straying among subordinate clauses, you nevertheless asked me straight out whether I hadn't received by mistake a letter that wasn't mine, I flatly denied it. A quarter-century later, when I was helping you take a bath and almost sobbing over your feeble absence-of-body with its expanding birthmarks, you kept your underpants on, explaining (what words you found!) that a son shall not see his father's shame. What Bible had you read?! We never had one at home in *my* lifetime. We did, of course, have conversations about churls.

"Don't teach your father to fuck," I heard. "This is it."

We braked.

Back then I had seen this house . . . With a mansard, incidentally. Beyond the shrubbery, beyond the plane trees, beyond the lawn, it stands vacant, but as if the vacationers had only just moved out, just now. The house in which the little boy Lavrenty grew up. Right in this thick shrubbery, perhaps, the future Beria screwed his first kitten. She wouldn't put out, she scratched him. And he killed her. Like the priest in the nonsense rhyme. But in the rhyme the priest killed his dog. So he killed him, too, killed the priest. Killed him because they'd eaten a piece of his meat. Even though it was the dog. But he hardly killed the priest for killing the dog. More likely for having her. Especially because he loved—

"He loved her—"

"How could that vampire love anyone!"

"I know the true story on that," the director insisted. "I was personally acquainted with her. He saw her through his binoculars from his mansion on Moscow's Garden Ring. She was walking home from school. She already had round calves, and he couldn't take his eyes off them."

" 'Rather skinny, but her calves were round . . .' " Who had quoted this? Daur, of course. " 'Lately she's become a priestess . . .' " He was spouting "Letters to a Roman Friend," by heart. " 'A priestess, and converses with the gods . . .' "

"Who wrote that?" the director asked, startled.

"Sounds like Joseph," the Englishman remarked.

"Well, he may have heard this story," I replied, on the strength of my personal acquaintance with the poet. "He's always been concerned with such things."

"There's a sea of scandal here . . ."

"A Black Sea?"

We were reclining on the lawn near Beria's house and admiring the open view: on the left the mountains reached upward, on the right the valley broadened downward, implying the sea . . .

The champagne, however, had run out, and the Englishman was limp with exhaustion.

"But when are the monkeys?" He was pushing to continue the journey.

"Tomorrow. Everything will be tomorrow," the researcher explained to him. "Both the monkeys and tomorrow . . ."

Anyhow, HE had been right about the bubblies: champagne tires you out. The Englishman was sound asleep, but the others, too, kept dozing off. Except the mafioso and Daur, who were having a conversation behind me in Abkhazian. I listened: about those same "Abuzinians." I listened: Abkhazian is the most mysterious language! It's the swish of a dragon against a rock. From a time when dragons still existed . . . "I see a world blanketed with institutes of Abkhazian studies," Mandelstam said. Sound is more ancient than speech. The sounds of Abkhazian speech seem to flow together, not into words, but into just one word, however long you like, equal to the length of the whole spoken sentence. As though landscape and action and character and time of action were not divided into subject, predicate, modifier, and object but were all contained in a single word, born anew each time. That is, reality isn't stratified, it's included in the word. The reason no one knows the Abkhazian language, not even the Abkhaz themselves, is that you have to inhale it along with reality from the day you are born. So natural was it for these men today to speak Abkhazian that I could immediately conclude they were both from the village, they had been born there and grown up there. It's hard to believe the language is dying as long as even two people speak it the way Daur and the mafioso do. "Abuzinian" was not a word but a syllable in one or another long word—a word as long as they had breath for. This syllable that I had singled out kept shifting places in the word/ sentence, standing now at the beginning, now at the end, now in the middle. The mafioso's tone was resolute on the "Abuzinians," while Daur was trying to mollify him. Or so I understood. By now I very much wanted to ask about these cutthroat Abuzinians. What did they want, and what hadn't they shared? But everyone except me seemed to know this so well that I felt childishly afraid to ask, lest I lose my "in" status, so flattering and not granted to everyone.

"Is it already tomorrow?" The Englishman was awake.

"It's still yesterday," we answered wittily.

"Yesterday I still have a bottle of whiskey," he replied.

Properly appreciating his sense of humor, we followed him to his hotel.

"No ice," the Englishman said apologetically, fetching a three-sided bottle with a turkey on it.

"He says there are no glasses," Daur translated.

"*Nyet problem,*" said the mafioso, not suspecting that he was translating from English.

Perhaps-Aslan was already bringing glasses.

We discussed, in passing, the subject of ethnic humor. Marxen, evidently wrestling with his own three nationalities, declared that there could be no national sense of humor.

"What's Abkhazian, Georgian, Russian humor? Is it funny or not funny—that's humor."

"Funny to some, but not funny to others."

"That is, funny to a Russian, let's say, but not very to a German?"

"Or funny to a German, but not funny at all to a Russian—"

"Or funny to a Georgian, but not to an Abkhaz—"

"It won't be funny at all to an Abkhaz if it's funny to a Georgian."

"Jewish humor strikes everyone funny—"

"If it's really Jewish," Marxen said.

"You mean the Russians invent those jokes themselves? That wouldn't be so funny."

"What do you have against the Russians?"

"Me? Never. Serozh, is there Armenian humor?"

Serozh considered for a long time and then took offense: "What are you, thinking of those Armenian Radio jokes again? That's not Armenian humor."

"All right, if the Armenians didn't invent the Armenian jokes, or the Jews the Jewish jokes—or the Chukchi, certainly, the Chukchi jokes—then who did?"

"Is English humor also not English?"

"I concur with the view that this is rather a question of import than export," the Englishman said.

We burst out laughing, and the Englishman didn't understand why.

"Something else strikes me funny," he said, gesturing at what to our eye was his luxurious hotel room. "There's so much wood in Russia . . ."

We followed his hand, as if he were showing us a grove.

The whole room really was paneled in wood, or rather, an

imported plywood imitation of wood, more likely Finnish than Russian.

"And look, I can't understand it . . . So much wood—and not one wardrobe. Nowhere to put clothes," he added, reverting to English.

Our jackets were piled in the middle of his careless bed, on which we were also sitting.

"It's perfectly understandable," we said.

"Why??"

"They didn't budget enough."

"Of what, of what?" the Englishman said, with a perfect Voronezh accent.

"Well, economic resources. Money."

"Enough for wood, but not for a wardrobe?"

He began to circle the room, thumping the walls. They responded with the sound of cannon fire. "Why so much?!"

"Funds."

"Funds? You mean your Plan? That they sent you more plywood than money? But extra plywood *is* money, to you!"

We laughed again, and the Englishman couldn't understand why. How could we explain that it wasn't because of his failure to understand our economy? It was because "plywood," in Russian slang, does indeed mean money.

"Plywood is cabbage," someone tried to explain, but this was an infelicitous translation.

"Plywood is plywood . . ."

The translation had been made more precise, and, as if in proof of its supreme precision, all of a sudden the plywood exploded boomingly—fired a shot and fell silent.

"What's that, what's that!" The Englishman jumped up in fright, pointing at the ceiling. Something ran across it again, making a scrabbly racket. We were not about to explain to him that this was a rat, and perhaps also a cat. We said, "A mouse." We weren't about to shame the state.

"Then why such low ceilings?"

"They didn't have enough plywood."

"Meaning money?"

"No, meaning plywood."

"Is this Russian humor?"

"No, economics. They made money on the plywood."

"That is, plywood on the plywood?"

"You're quick on the uptake. But you, unlike us, know what a third-category city is . . ."

"Ah, Voronezh! . . ." The Englishman rolled his eyes dreamily.

We drank to Voronezh. You must agree, this brings our vast expanses together, when an Englishman drinks to Voronezh in Sukhum. It unites the empire.

"Let's call it experience," the Englishman said, in English.

So this was the story. The Englishman had come to the Soviet Union to gather material for his diploma. (We never did clarify which was the diploma and which the dissertation: what we call a dissertation, they call a diploma—or vice versa.) He had come to study our experiment, because in Britain they had something similar. An experiment in keeping monkeys in uncongenial climatic zones under almost congenial natural conditions. In other words, free. He had heard a lot about the monkey colony in Sukhum and felt that this might be where he could garner some experience. But he was told that such an experience was common not only in Sukhum but also throughout the Union, and that monkey breeding was now a practice, not an experience (apparently, as the Englishman realized in Voronezh, they were confusing the concepts of "experience" and "experiment"). Apparently they also confused "practice" with "practicum" and thus sent him to a student practicum in Voronezh, where an experiment had once been set up, "reahlly," with monkeys living under conditions approximating those in Voronezh, but the monkeys had died in a week, so that there may have been an experiment, but in practice there had been no experience, as he promptly reported to Moscow, with the request that he be transferred to Sukhum after all. He reported and reported, all the while living in a student dormitory (oh, you don't know what this means in a third-category city!), until the period of his on-the-job training was up, and then he decided simply to test whether there was such a place as Sukhum, as on the map, and he reached it "on his own expenses"—that is, at his own expense, another project for which it was none too easy to obtain permission, so he had succeeded only through Intourist, as a private party, and now he had met Mr. Dragamashchenka (this, it turned out, was the researcher's name—so we had a Ukrainian in our company, too), and lo and behold Sukhum "reahlly" existed, and Mr. Dragamashchenka had promised he would try to do everything possible . . . but this was the third day they'd been meeting, and he couldn't pay for the hotel this long, it was supposed to be five stars but there was no wardrobe . . .

Anti-Aslan said that five stars were coming right up, and before another rat had time to run across the ceiling he appeared with a bottle of cognac. The Englishman kept counting the stars on the bottle, half laughing and half crying.

"Sleep, sleep, sleep!" the Englishman proclaimed. "You've buggered me to death. Sleep is the shortest distance between two binges."

The director and the mafioso were no longer there.

Mr. Dragamashchenka took my elbow and led me aside. "Would you be able to help me out?"

You can see, he said, what condition he's in . . . ("No more. To sleep," the Englishman was muttering.) On Fridays we have meetings with interesting people. Oh, a small group of research associates get together. A relaxed conversation . . . You can talk on anything you like . . . They know you well, he said with conviction, from which I inferred that he himself had never heard of me before. This did not wound me, however (or had I trained myself not to feel wounded?). After the meeting there would be a light tea, right there in the laboratory . . .

Tea, of course, altered the matter. That was pretty good, tea out of retorts and test tubes. HE was pushing me to consent. You yourself see the condition he's . . . it's embarrassing. A foreigner, after all . . . But you won't be embarrassed by a fellow countryman? In a fellow countryman we understand it, and besides, you're doing fine . . .

Doing fine . . . Friday . . . I had thought it was Thursday. I could be proud of myself. Wasn't I every inch an "interesting person"? Today, at least, I was a very interesting person. Who here knew that HE (I thought of myself in the third person) had just finished something *great*! For me it was still Wednesday, when I had finally, after trying for a month, sat down at the typewriter . . . I had thought it was one night. It was two, as it turned out. Oh, this was a sign! This inspired hope. I still hadn't read whatever I'd written there, but since I didn't remember, it might actually be a text. I remembered that the last thing I had described was the yard—and I had walked out into it.

And walked out of it. Today I could be proud of HIM, too. No small matter, was it—two nights without sleep (I might have curled up for three hours or so, but in that same henhouse, without undressing, like a chick on a roost), forty pages of continuous text, approximately two half liters already, not counting the champagne that I myself had drunk . . . It's not everyone who could, not everyone who would . . .

But today was Friday already. And only noon. Yesterday had whistled past me like a bullet past my temple. We—what was left of the cohort, Marxen, Daur, and I—were riding in Research Associate Dragamashchenka's car. The responsibility I faced had utterly sobered me, and something had become clear. Complications had arisen with the Englishman. It was embarrassing to refuse him, you understand, but the road to the site of the monkey settlement lay past a "facility." What kind of facility this was the researcher didn't tell even me, but I understood that the Englishman was not to see the monkeys. For me, however, the researcher said, meaning me, it could be arranged if I was interested. They couldn't pay me for my talk, but this they could do. Even tomorrow, they would take the institute bus and go, and while they were at it they would check on how the preparations for winter were coming, winter's the main problem for monkeys. Last winter was tough, lots of snow, they had trouble getting through, it went down to twenty-five below in the mountains where the monkeys were and their tails got frostbitten, but otherwise they survived, and if they survived that winter, they'll survive the next ones, too, except of course they need support, they have the little house against bad weather, and they do need extra food, but still they're free, in effect . . . But you'll see for yourself. Are they better off free? No question—if you could just get a look at these beauties! What manes! These are lions, not monkeys . . . The presence of lively emotion in the discourse of the monkey researcher, as he had proved to be, gladdened me. Down at the bottom of my nearly emptied authorial womb something began to stir, rapidly swelling and bulging in the likeness of an idea. Soviet monkeys . . . The liberation of the monkey . . . The Russian monkey . . . A monkey living free, under conditions of socialist society . . . Without a cage . . . Monkey freedom . . . A republic of monkeys . . . Monkey ASSR . . . Couldn't say that— everyone would be offended. The monkeys would not be offended. The main thing was not to offend the little monkeys. I would allow no harm to come to *them*. —No, I could write this, I had to! "We gave them their freedom . . . their manes grew, but their tails got frostbitten . . . they need feeding . . ." There was something to this! I always get pregnant the first time . . . But then I can't deliver for years. The fruits of my womb press down upon each other. The mass begins to ferment. It no longer results in wine—I have to distill moonshine.

    And drink it, too. We each had a small *chacha* at Daur's, where we made a brief stop to change our shirts and take a shower. That was not the purpose, as it turned out. They had turned off the water in Sukhum again, and Daur's shirt was too tight on me. I rolled up the sleeves a bit higher. HE could not refrain from glancing in the mirror, and even I was pleased with myself. I sat HIM down on the can, and while he strained, I chased monkeys. It's a very beautiful place and a picturesque road, they say . . . Suppose I'm going there with about six monkey experts; suppose I ask them about monkeys, the way I asked Doctor D. some time ago about birds; suppose they're of different nationalities: an Abkhaz, a Georgian, an Armenian, a Greek, a Jew, a Russian . . . I could take the Ainglishman along, too . . . don't take the Ukrainian . . . suppose they're inhabitants and patriots of this very land . . . suppose they're amateur historians, as all of them are, here in the province . . . suppose they just happen to tell me the history of the region, and also just happen to start arguing: which of them is a real native, who is more native . . . suppose the argument grows into a quarrel between the Georgian and the Abkhaz, between the Georgian and the Armenian, between . . . no, I won't for the world quarrel with the Jew . . . this is our business . . . "This is an ancient quarrel of Slavs among themselves" . . . and, well, in a group like that, the Jew is more of a Slav . . . but not a Georgian, not an Armenian, and not a Greek, certainly . . . and besides, is a Russian all that far from a Jew? . . . the Jews are more Russian than we are . . . every time, they plan to live here; every time, we don't want to live . . . not that again! you're on your way to see the monkeys . . . yes, but I haven't arrived yet! . . . what do they quarrel about? . . . oh, that's easy, we just have to get the details . . . the Abkhaz, naturally, quarrels about Georgianization, the elimination of Abkhazian schools, the registration of Abkhazians as Georgians . . . the Georgian, naturally, cannot bear this historical injustice and says didn't we give you television in 1978, didn't we give you a university? . . . you said it! you "gave"—you gave because you'd taken, confiscated, first you confiscated and then you gave . . . what could we confiscate from you? you didn't even have literacy . . . well, but for how many centuries were the Abkhaz the kings of Georgia! . . . what! the Abkhaz, kings?! in our country!? ha, ha, ha . . . you Georgians never waged war, the wars were waged by the highlanders—Circassians, Abkhaz, Ossetians—and you were always under somebody . . . under the Persians, the Mongols, the Russians . . . but where were *you*? *you* were always under *us*, you've always been part of Georgia, you *are* Georgians . . . at this point they enter into hand-to-hand combat, it's the start of a national struggle, what's it called—Stalin used it for the first Bolshevik newspaper—*Borba? Zorba? Cobra?* . . . by the way, where's the newspaper? . . . ah, the newspaper . . . we do have newspaper . . . that isn't quite true to life . . . they'd never say it that directly, or else they'd cut each other's throats . . . they say it that way privately, away from each other, to a third person, I mean, of a third nationality . . . and what does the person of a third nationality tell them . . . he tells them they're fighting in vain, because in any case, before either of them existed, there was a Greek colony here (if the person is Greek) . . . or if the person is Armenian he says that back in Assyrian times this was strictly Armenian land . . . now everyone will pounce on the Armenian: oh sure, Nefertiti was Armenian, Napoleon was Armenian, Leonardo da Vinci was Armenian . . . but we have no quarrel here, the Armenian will say; why quarrel, if they were Armenian? . . . the Russian alone remains modestly silent and makes a mental note, because why quarrel about what happened when, before Russia even existed? before Russia even existed, this land could belong to anyone you please, be my guest, but the minute Russia appeared, then to whom could the land have belonged? . . . not *Turkey?* . . . what did you want with Turkish rule? . . . you're Christians: fear God . . . that's what the Russian will never say while they quarrel on their way to the monkeys, having forgotten all about them . . . the Russian is admiring the landscapes, winning them inch by inch from the infidel for his own little book, what will it be called? *Monkey Sapiens* . . . not bad . . . *Homo Bilegus* . . . what's "leg" in Latin? oh, come on! oh, the ones who make shoes for invalids? orthopedists, that's it! so which is it, ortho- or ped-? ortho-dox, peda-gogue, pedi-atrician, pede-rast . . . *Homo Pedis*, that's funny . . . no, *pedi* is children . . . something's wrong . . . coming, coming! I'm ready, I'll be right out . . .

This is what happened. While I was preparing for my talk, Daur had been mainlining at the home of his neighbor, a Greek who was remarkable for the fact that as soon as he and Daur got their apartments in this new building, Daur did nothing, because

he had no money for repairs and because he labored in the arts
(*sapiens sapiens*), but the Greek, because he was a truck driver at
a furniture combine, a workingman, a man with a skill (*sapiens
habilis*), immediately undertook to finish everything in oak with
his own hands—everything—the parquet, the walls, the ceiling,
the bath—it went on for four years, and when everything was done
he took an ax and hacked it all back to smithereens, after which
he became pensive and solitary (I had never seen him this way)
and could associate only with Daur. I, of course, didn't immediately
guess why Daur had withdrawn to his neighbor the Greek's, perhaps
because I occupied his can for so long, but I realized it when we
stood before the audience, which consisted mainly of female research associates under thirty, some of them even pretty (three out
of seven), and there were exactly three of us (HE calculated it for
me, then and there): Dragamashchenka, Daur, and I . . . Dragamashchenka introduced Daur, a man known to everyone in the
city, and Daur was supposed to introduce me, a man known to all
though unknown in the city, and to tell the story, as it were, of my
literary career. Daur boldly stepped forward and said that they saw
before them a man who was interesting primarily for the fact that
he was . . . Here I froze in anticipation, on the threshold of sincere
delight and counterfeit embarrassment, for I have rarely met such
a gift of eloquence as Daur's. As a *tamada*, or toastmaster, he
surpasses all, leaves them in the dust. He's especially eloquent and
witty in the presence of ladies, so that I had often actually envied
him—he so far surpassed me in such situations that I merely ex-
ploited my advantage as his elder and adopted the pose of a teacher,
admiring my pupil and approving his every word . . . Daur inhaled
with his whole chest and did not exhale again. Or so it seemed, at
least. He stood there, chest thrown out, eyes and mouth round, and
we benevolently awaited his exact word. The girl on whom his eye
was fixed began to blush uncontrollably, the sweat streamed down
Daur's face, but his next word was never born. Dragamashchenka
began to applaud, Daur exhaled at last and sat down, and I stood
up.

A man is a man, that is, very weak. I couldn't help blooming like an emphatically luxuriant flower against the background of the preceding orator. If they were biologists, then of course what did they know about biology? And of course, I was the very man to teach them to understand their own subject. I talked to them about . . .

My nocturnal inspiration was still boiling in me. When I finished, last night, I simply hadn't said everything. As always, the things for whose sake you write it all, the two or three thoughts that troubled you so much that they actually sat you down at your desk to express them—these are the two that prove not to have been expressed. Neither Pavel Petrovich nor I, much as we drank, had ever finished thinking them out; I had simply shot through the text and emerged with the two of them in my hands, finding no place for them anywhere along the way. Even Pavel Petrovich hadn't had time to explain them to me.

"The pig . . ." Pavel Petrovich was saying to the young ladies. "Can you give me any reason why we traditionally hold such a contemptuous, ungrateful, and churlish (see there, even I almost said 'swinish') attitude toward this astounding animal?" Pavel Petrovich had apparently decided to pursue his idea of the Creator as an artist who had revealed himself through the creation of water. "Not only is the pig clean and intelligent, it is also the most perfect creature in the natural system of the peasant farmyard. The problem of pollution-free production, which cannot be solved under the conditions of late-twentieth-century technical progress, was solved at the dawn of mankind's development by the invention—I emphasize, the invention—of the Pig! Nothing in the history of human civilization has so perfectly emulated and replicated Creation as the peasant farmyard. It is a painting of Creation, framed by the fence. The fenced vegetable patch—this is an invention equal to the wheel. This too, primordially, was round. Only partition, the presence of a neighbor, gave it rectangularity . . ."

The total unexpectedness of the word "rectangularity" jolted the orator. He glanced all around and chose for himself a little blonde, who didn't appeal to me personally (I had my eye on another one), but both of us (in one person) were picking up signals from a third, a little typist at a publishing house I knew. Her shy invitation embarrassed me: this was someone who should be avoided but not offended . . . "Rectangularity," having escaped his lips, inspired him, and he easily went on to discover a connection among the following words: Russia, kolkhoz, nomads, neutron bomb, "without a single nail," fire, "with dung in their hands," raft and church, "eighteen wars with Turkey—and no Dardanelles," Vikings, Teutons, Swedes, Tatars, Lithuanians, Turks, Poles, Ermak, *"nach Osten,"* swamp, cut a window, Siberia, geographic range, Europe, tundra, horses, hides, women, cattle slaughtering, primitive tribes, moonshine, the freeze-over, dumplings, palms, California . . . "Too bad about Alaska!" . . . Khrushchev . . .

Good God! What nonsense was this! He was performing for that little blonde—roughly outlining, not his own questionable ideas (he'd never had one in all his born days), or even mine, but those of our old friend Doctor D., which the latter had confessed to me just once and retracted the next day . . .

But never mind, talking about Khrushchev is all right now. This is even encouraged, talking about Khrushchev. Let him blab on.

"Khrushchev was always a broad-minded man. Dates didn't count for so much during his regime as they do now. A year or 'one day,' he didn't care . . ." (No, better not talk about Solzhenitsyn.) "The two hundred and fiftieth anniversary of St. Petersburg or the tercentenary of Peter the Great or the centennial of serfdom . . . Alaska or Cuba . . . corn . . ."

"Allow me to disagree with you about Ermak Timofeev," Dragamashchenka put in, rescuingly. "An original but somewhat schematic conception. Granted, we can still make a raft from a log cabin. But a sleigh from the raft!" An obsequious chuckle was heard in the audience. "We're not such nomads—"

"Not nomads!" I flared. "What about all these mass reloca-

tions—Virgin Soil, Young Communist construction sites, the Bai-
kal–Amur Railway? Who but nomads would consent to that?"

"And another thing I didn't understand," Dragamashchenka
said, recognizing that it was dangerous to object or correct at this
point. "Why exactly is the pig the king of the beasts?"

"Because it crowns the pyramid of the peasant's farmyard. It's
the lock. What, above all, testifies to the presence of the farmer?
The padlock with which he chains the gates of his farm. The farm
is *his*. The padlock closes the chain. The pig closes the circuit of
the farmyard, lending it the perfection of nature and revealing the
Creator in the farmer. Because the design reveals the Creator. A
design, in principle, is incapable of embodiment. It's never seam-
less, there will always be loose ends. They can only be tied in a
knot. The design always sticks out. You can't hide it. You can try.
All right, then explain to me, why oil? Why is it that oil, before
man existed, was evenly accumulated all over the earth in these
outhouses of living nature? As though they'd been planned for
future man. Not one of the hypotheses on the origin of coal and
oil has so far convinced anybody, you know. But once the earth
permitted on her surface the development of life and the chain
reaction of evolution, wouldn't she be buried under the waste matter
of life and the products of decay and decomposition, if it weren't
for these tidy little sacks of oil? Doesn't the peasant farmyard
resemble a balanced ecological system, precisely because of the
pig? Hasn't oil played the role of an invented pig for all nature?
All right, then, tell me, why virginity for the human species? in
what other animal species does it occur? and does your mother
monkey have it? What kind of membrane is this, rated for a single
use?"

With this he terminally embarrassed the young women and
seized the undivided attention of all of them at once. The one I
liked was genuinely frightened, however, and seemed to be on the
point of leaving, though she was still irresolute. But the intellectual
typist was gazing with frank adoration, which was exactly what I
didn't want.

"Apart from the explanations you consider mythological—Adam and Eve, the Tree of Knowledge, and the Fall, which dictate the laws of human experience for us even today and define the history of humankind through original sin and the immaculate conception of the Virgin—I'm afraid we will find no sound explanations. And we don't need to. What we need is . . ."

And I stopped, like Daur, unable to recall what I had just said.

Daur was avenged. Or had I saved Daur? If a thing isn't written in time, it begins to come true. Oh, these embraces of the life that once happened to you! A sort of *Toilers of the Sea*, not a text. You are embraced by an octopus, you writhe in the futile convulsions of the struggle, choke in thick layers of existence.

My unwritten novel *Gambling Fever* was happening to me. Omitted descriptions flashed through my mind.

Where is the horse? Who has been forgotten there under the fence, "in his fine red shirt, such a bonny lad . . ." And what is Million Tomatoes?

Million Tomatoes can lift a hundred and twenty kilos with one hand. He has learned Cortázar by heart. He has a beard . . . My God! What contortions! What an ugly face a word can make on the page! It's not right anywhere, doesn't fit anywhere, doesn't belong, and if you'll just listen closely, it doesn't even have any meaning. Repeat any word ten times for practice: what "table," what "chair," why "door"?

Million Tomatoes has had his own dealings with fame. Including those of a great cardplayer. Back in his childhood he lost a million all at once. And since he didn't have a million, but the card debt was unquestionably a debt of honor, he had to lose not a million rubles but a million tomatoes. The winner graciously allowed him to pay the debt in installments. For about ten years, Million Tomatoes carried five or ten kilos at a time. He grew up and became strong, like Crito of Miletus, as he approached the

Olympic Games of 1976, 1980, but now in 1984—no Los Angeles. He was too late with his weights, like me with my words . . .

I was wrong about the pig, that was the whole trouble. The pig may indeed be the lock. It may indeed follow us around, ungrateful though we are, to pick up our shit. But the pig's own shit—there's no place to put it. No place to put that final shit. It's no good!

This kind of thing does happen—all at once and for no earthly reason you fall silent. You stare pop-eyed and say nothing, and it's not the connection between the words, it's not the words you lack—even the letter is insurmountable. You lack speech itself. You are silent for a month, a second month, you begin to be silent for a third. You hear applause, shake hands, reap prizes. Grateful listeners have long been waiting for you to have a drink with them. And two, three, four more people—Adgur-Raul-Rauf in one person, and Million Tomatoes, it turns out—have long been standing behind you like two guardian angels, they have long been impatient for you to finish your talk, to take you and Daur to a certain place where people are waiting just for me.

Daur and I each received the skull of a female monkey as an honorarium. The date of her death had been scrawled in soft pencil on her forehead. One could now date the narrative with greater precision. This was in autumn, and she had died that summer; the year was 1983. I think it said July 17. "July" was written with the Roman numeral VII. The pencil wrote especially well on the bone surface, as if on some very heavy and expensive Chinese paper, so porous, the color of ivory. But the pencil rubbed off. For some reason the date was erased in reverse order, first the year (but I remember the year), then the month, and then for a long time the day was left, suspended in timelessness. Lest I erase it completely, I kept turning the skull different ways—whereby I kept erasing it. Her birth date, however, had not been recorded with the same precision. Dragamashchenka examined her teeth and said that she was no more than two years old. One tooth in the left lower jaw was loose, probably the canine. She was a girl. Her name was Lucy. Or Margarita, I don't remember. Of course, Lucy. Not Margarita. Margarita was the name of the other one. Not the other one they gave to Daur—I didn't even take any interest in the name of that one—

but the one in the audience, whose address HE had time to get, while I stood silent, disgraced by my own silence, and tenderly stroked my monkey on her bald head. HE had time for everything, as Million Tomatoes and I dragged him toward the exit: time to grab a test tube of alcohol from the light buffet that the girls had arranged in my honor, to eat a Greetings cracker with it, and to get the phone number of the one he liked, the one I liked, and the old acquaintance whose eternally inviting gaze, so languid with shyness as to be indecent, I should not answer under any circumstances: she was staying at a resort hotel not far from here with her son, who was in kindergarten.

And so, having been seen to the door by our dissatisfied audience, who continued to wave to us from their laboratory threshold, with modest and perhaps even blue kerchiefs, we rode off in two cars, a Gorky jeep and a Volga 21, climbing more and more steeply into the mountains. And while HE celebrated his triumph by recounting an odious drunk-tank incident which had taken place in my student days and which struck him as entertaining and jolly for some reason—while my friends gave him dazzling smiles and nodded knowingly—I relived my shame. With Lucy perched in my lap, I sadly stroked her receding forehead and looked out the window. Through the vibrating, cloudy little window installed in the well-traveled canvas of our jeep, I increasingly saw the side of the road: a cow warming her udder on the warm asphalt . . . a piglet unhurriedly trying to penetrate a fence, squeeze through it despite the triangular frame on his neck . . . suddenly . . . a man was lying at the side of the road, still wearing the same fine red shirt, with his arms serenely outflung in a way that doesn't even happen . . . and I had seen him somewhere. Million Tomatoes passed me his reefer. I took a reluctant toke, eyeing his inordinately large fist,

with which I had seen him pound a nail into an inch-thick board
. . . But having tried it, I took another toke. "Good grass?" Million
Tomatoes asked proudly. And really, I did feel better. "Good . . ."
I even thought that HE had left me for a seat in the Volga traveling
behind us, in order to tell the same old story to the other crew . . .
"Good"—at last I was able to pronounce a word, though what I
meant to say was "Papa!"

For this was Papa. He was contained in a smallish blue cup
on Mama's lap, as though he had been won in a minor competition,
and my mother was gently stroking him as if he were alive. The
resemblance to a trophy was heightened by the diagonal gold script:
what he had earned the cup for. For his *final* date, he had been
awarded both a birth date and a proper name. This was indeed a
trophy. The only one of its kind, the first, unique. Papa, forgive
me for that letter! . . . Mama and I were in the back seat of this
same kind of car, a Volga 21. We were taking him to our cemetery
at Shuvalovo. The driver was the husband of a niece of my father's,
in other words a cousin-in-law of some kind, or anyway my cousin's
husband, Chereshnya by name, proud of his automobile, his origin,
and his scholarly degree, a nice fellow and basically not stupid,
who played at being a churl but wasn't a churl at all—a kind, ugly
man. He was surprised at the force of Mama's emotion. "What
made you love him so much?" he asked her, with his characteristic
bluntness. Looking forcefully into his eyes, which glinted dully in
the cheerless long face canceled by his nose, Mama said with all
distinctness, "His beauty." Chereshnya, as I have said, was not a
fool, but now he, too, understood.

The return from the cemetery . . .

Again, we hadn't arrived at the promised monkeys.

The tooth came out of Lucy's jaw by itself and was easy to
put back in. I would have to be sure not to lose it, I reminded
myself. And now we arrived.

They were expecting us. The liberated populace had finally
gotten through the fence pickets. They kissed us on the shoulder.
They waited on us. They didn't have bread and salt on an em-

broidered guest towel here, but they did have the towel itself. One dignified woman held the soap and the kettle, another the towel. They poured for us while we washed our hands, and then passed us the towel. Both women, as they later explained to me, were Supreme Soviet deputies, one to the Abkhazian ASSR, the other to the USSR. These were villagers.

And in fact there was a village here. My drunken Russian heart thrilled and sobbed. This was what it meant to have an uninterrupted life of three generations! It meant wealth. Impossible even to compare—I did not tire of comparing. In place of the two-story Abkhazian stone house on pillars or pilings, I substituted our leaning, five-walled log cabin; in place of their traditional *agazon* (lawn) in the farmyard, I imagined a puddle, the clay-and-dung slop trampled by cow and boot; instead of their orchard—fig, persimmon, apple—our modest little vegetable patch with its onions that had once again failed to come up; and instead of their hydraulic pump, our little farm pond, teeming with life like a droplet under Leeuwenhoek's lens . . . The sorrow of the patriot welled up within me, in proportion to my admiration for their well-deserved plenty. The climate, of course. In our country such things don't grow. Here, just poke a finger in the ground—lemons, mandarin oranges . . . In our country we have *winter*. In our country, just try and take anything outside the house. Here they have the kitchen separate, the livestock separate—they can run across the yard on the lawn. In our country we have to keep one flank pressed to the stove and the other to the cow, lest we freeze to death. They have it easy. Thus reasoned the patriot within me, the city dweller who in his fifth decade had guessed the secret of our "five-walled house": it has nothing to do with our five-pointed star, it's the wall in the middle, which divides the log cabin into a lived-in half and a roofed barnyard.

Now the same women passed shot glasses of *chacha*. So we were still standing out in the yard. Not only were the yard, the lawn, and the house theirs, but the elaborate iron gates that locked what was "theirs" were also theirs. And the *chacha* was theirs.

With this slightly different nuance: not store-bought. Theirs and their own—in the sense that they had produced, prepared, made it. But so were the yard and the lawn and the orchard—they were THEIRS, like the *chacha*. It was strong *chacha*.

The climate, of course! Grapes won't grow in our country, under any system. What, didn't they have the Soviet Regime here? Not only did they have it, it was standing before me in the flesh, in the form of a deputy to the Supreme Soviet of the USSR (which, as I had learned in school, according to the Stalin Constitution is the Soviet Regime itself), and its name, through some heavenly misunderstanding, was Sophie. Sophie herself, bashful and blushing, handed me the *chacha* as she had handed me the guest towel before it. What harm had she done me?

Let us describe the blush of her cheeks separately, for such it was—separate. Separate from her cheek, from her face—independent. Her blush was like one more part of her body. Aha! A forgotten word: strong. Just used in another connection, however. But for the same reason. Strong house, strong *chacha*, strong color. We also used to call it a "rustic bloom." It's a long time since I've encountered it on our haggard faces. Even in the countryside . . . So it's not just the fresh air—you also have to work. In that same fresh air. At home in Russia, you'll encounter that kind of bloom only in a traffic cop. Because, rain or shine, he ventilates his rustic gene in the fresh air. The Russian village population, increasingly often, has left to join the police. That's where it survives. The names of our emptied wayside villages, as you ride along the highway from traffic cop to traffic cop, always recall the surnames of policemen, for some reason. But it turns out they recall where the policemen are from. We city dwellers simply become acquainted with the police earlier than with the village. For example, the name of the village AKSHONTOVO flashes past your window on the roadside. Exactly. In your youth you had an encounter with a Sergeant or even (keep going) a Lieutenant Akshontov. He composed the statement and you signed it, seemingly not even for what you had done but for what you had *not* done. Solid negatives:

*un*printable (expressions), *il*licit (intoxication), *in*subordination (to the representative of authority). Or maybe it wasn't Akshontov, it was some other surname. But it's Akshontov who is waiting for you right now, at his post at the exit from the village of AKSHONTOVO. Benevolently he detains you: you have exceeded the speed limit, in your reverie on the fate of the Russian village. And such color in his cheeks!

As in Sophie's. A bloom. Like a flower. And would you believe, through this natural and acquired color, this dark-claret-red, almost-black rose, there also emerged a blush of bashfulness. How could they help adorning the Supreme Soviet with this dawn of the east . . . "With rosy dawn the east was mantled . . ."

Pushkin, of course, first of all. That's another obsolete word —"rosy." In Pushkin's time, they still had rosy cheeks. The word was still usable, for it fitted. And yes, rosiness was characteristic of Pushkin himself. He was the rosiest boy at the Lyceum. Rosiness particularizes him no less than do curls and whiskers. Anyone who even once saw him alive . . . Again, not we.

There was a man here who resembled Pushkin. In rosiness and face. Pushkin's head sat atop the big strong neck of our young host (Sophie was his). The elder host, his father, who was not inferior to him in strength or rosiness, bore a striking facial resemblance to my own father. The resemblance was further heightened by the fact that I had just been remembering him, my father . . . But he was alive and well. He had never been so healthy when he was alive. *Blazing* with health . . . If the Russian language used to have so many exact and varied words to describe health, perhaps we had health, too?

He sits at the head of the table, my father does. Gives the blessing. Hands the reins to his son . . . Now, how shall we describe a masculine rosiness? Their faces are covered with fine cracks, like bark, which is why they always look as though they're making fun of you and winking, because these fine lines radiate around their eyes and mouth on their toast-brown skin, and at that moment you break off a piece of toasty-brown crackling from the suckling

pig, as Voroshilov did in Iskander, and they raise their glasses . . .
to you, it turns out. Evening light falls on their faces as on tree
trunks in the woods at sunset, proving that the bark has no less
life than the leaf and flower, and as I look at their . . . quit choosing
your words like a beggar! as I look at their *honest* faces . . . I
cannot condemn either their unmistakable guile or their self-
satisfaction.

We are upstairs, in the formal half of the house, where no one
ever lives. It has a parquet floor. It has carpets and crystal and
polished furniture. It has daggers and horns worked in silver. It
has a beautiful painting on the wall: a tiger is chewing up a young
woman, and her breast is bared to the moonlight—she gazes at us
with frigid farewell. But this is not Rousseau. It's an original.

Here, everything is store-bought. The most expensive. What
they don't use. What the rest is all about. No worse than other
folks'. As good as other folks'. Better than the neighbors'. Their
life and work hum busily on the first floor, at the level of the sinful
earth, for the sake of building this domestic paradise on the second
floor—where none of them live during their lifetime, not so much
because they're unworthy but because they don't have *time*. Too
much happening downstairs to go running up to the second floor.
Although right there, beyond the salon in which we sit, I can also
see the main bedroom—again, a suite of furniture, with Arabian
linens and silken coverlets, everything the best and most expensive,
for "simple human happiness." Again, they don't sleep in it, they
sleep downstairs, they're worn out from a day at the plow and
collapse on a sagging cot. That they don't sleep here is not a con-
jecture or a figure of speech, in this instance, for the floor is spread
with a layer of nuts and persimmons—the farewell sun reaches
them now. Finding an angle of vision through the crack of the
slightly open bedroom door, I admire this sudden painting until
. . . Until Sophie notices my gaze and closes the door. This, then,
is the question: Why did she close the door, so that I wouldn't see
the bed or so that I wouldn't see the persimmons? Was it the
violation of order that embarrassed her, or the conjugal bed?

Sophie and her older sister-in-law (the one who is a deputy to the ASSR) and her mother-in-law and yet another aunt, all of them in braids, have lined up at the far end of the table and are benevolently surveying our masculine repast. Seniority among them is by age, not by rank. When the mother-in-law, who is no deputy, notices anything that looks to her like a violation of order, she whispers to the ASSR deputy, who whispers to the USSR deputy, and the capable Sophie comes running, now with cheese, now with chicken.

Why, how can I help loving the Soviet Regime here! When she reaches her imperial arm to the most out-of-the-way place and caresses her disgraced poet with an unexpectedly motherly caress —as though she weren't the one who had chased him here, out of her sight. The good thing about a machine is that it operates without intent.

Not only is the Soviet Regime here, it has been here repeatedly! Khrushchev himself, without formality, used to sit in the chair next to mine, where the father now sits. And this is why the whole village is so overgrown with greenbriers. My memory being uncertain, let's call them asparillas. Once a year, in spring, when still soft and green, these briers become a delicacy. The rest of the year, they're just briers. Khrushchev visited right at asparilla season. He loved the flavor, which he had never tasted before. Having no reason to plant corn in Abkhazia, because everyone here had been raised on cornmeal mush, he daydreamed aloud that asparilla, possessing such a foreign name, could fetch hard currency for the country. This was jotted down and then also taken under advisement by the local leadership, which naturally was not far away—that is, in the very same room where we are now. And a campaign was launched to introduce the new agricultural crop. Asparilla ceased to be edible the very day after he left, but Abkhazia became impassable because of the greenbriers. Khrushchev was dismissed and the asparilla receded, remaining stuck on the borders of the fields like a natural fence. Thus the ferocity of the local fences is not due merely to agricultural necessity or kulak character.

So that's the source of their wealth! This yard was blessed by that visit, and ever since the toilers have been untouched. And they've taken advantage of this niche, to toil. Without the regime you get nowhere . . . You have to be friends with it. Time preserves interesting monuments after a ruler: a Ukrainian Crimea, but also a corn boundary that has advanced two hundred kilometers farther north, and asparilla fences!

I don't know whether Fazil Iskander has recorded that story in his encyclopedia of Abkhazian life . . . but here I can no longer avoid acknowledging how much he's bothering me! And I have no intention of writing *better.*

Mine is a different story: I had almost lost Lucy's tooth again . . .

I should watch myself, and especially HIM. What all didn't I tell him! I ordered him under no circumstances to drink wine, which was exactly what everyone was drinking, after having paved the way with the shot of *chacha.* "Wine will ruin you!" I told him impressively, allowing him to sip *chacha* just a little at a time (in violation of custom, which, as a guest and an exception, I was allowed to violate) from the clouded little glass. "At least don't bother me!" I told him disgustedly. "Have something to eat!" I advised him, like Mama. He mustn't fall apart in such honest company! Let's call it a sense of dignity. Especially since our hosts had someone with whom to compare us. Not only had Nikita Khrushchev been here before me, but the President of the United States had also meant to come, though he didn't, Yevtushenko was a frequent guest, and other writers, foreign ones . . . Greene? Böll? . . . Yes, I think they were the ones. Hemingway did not come. That Englishman was a pretty good drinker, yes. But again, only *chacha.* Then it was surely Greene.

They drank to the peoples. This is a special toast, perhaps just a local one. With no reference to "internationalism" or the "friendship of the peoples." Pre-Soviet, apparently—a traditional toast. God, it says, so created the world that there are peoples . . . Chechen, Jewish, Moldavian . . . and thank God! this is good, that there are peoples. Well, as the only Russian here, how can you *not* drink, finding yourself in a fortunate (for you) minority!

The good thing about the tradition of toasts is: you can't outfox it. You can vanquish the table only in honest battle. How can you not drain your glass to the peoples, to the earth that gave us this table, to the parents who seated us at it, to the ancestors who uniquely chose our parents, to the living (may God grant them health!) and to the dead, who are alive right now, in that glass of yours; to all who are not with us at the moment, though they're with us all the same, and to those who are . . . it's such a remarkable gathering of people! that you must drink to each individually, and only when the toast is to you yourself may you accept it and not drink, modestly lowering your eyes. But if you keep in mind that no one has the right to rise from the table until the whole series of toasts has been completed, without a single omission (and the toasts are drunk by the glassful), and that to get up for a slight need is shameful for a man, you will not be surprised that diseases of the bladder are quite prevalent in Abkhazia, a fact which also allows me to hint to the gathering that the Abkhaz may possibly have a great kinsman in the astronomer Tycho Brahe, who wore a silver cone in place of his nose, which had been cut off in his youth in a duel, but who died quite old, though not by the saber or dagger but from the rupture of his bladder, for, when he was invited to be a court astronomer in a strange land and didn't know the customs of the court, he did not allow himself to get up from the table, just in case, not knowing what was correct there and what wasn't, and such implacable adherence to purely Abkhazian traditions could only mean that his mother had been an Abkhaz or an Ubykh . . . and this hypothesis of mine is heard out with unexpected attention and accepted on faith—that is, as fact.

How strong a man is when there are few of him! When he must prove to the world that he exists, and besides must not doubt it himself. Any outside corroboration will seem like a buttress. Just yesterday they so little doubted their own existence that they stole horses and women from each other and sold them. The women were renowned, and they ended up gracing harems so far from their homeland that if you so desire you can now trace the most unexpected kinship on your mother's side. The famed janissaries or *seyfülmulûk* will suddenly turn out to be from our village, and even Napoleon is only a stone's throw away. After the *mekhad-zhirstvo*, the suicidal exodus of the Abkhaz into Turkey at the turn of the century, Abkhaz and non-Abkhaz began to be counted differently: kinsfolk were counted on one's fingers. Thus, of the Ubykh tribe, cousins to the Abkhaz, not a single man was left. They had departed, scattered, and vanished, along with their horses and women, weapons and pots and pans, songs and dances, customs and language. The language no longer existed. And if a certain German, who had never even heard of the Abkhaz and Ubykhs, hadn't collected folklore in Central Africa, if he hadn't come across an ancient Negress who began to tell him fairy tales in a dialect he did not know—that is, a nonexistent one . . . The German did not garner the fame of a Schliemann or a Dahl, but ("boundless is the fame of the Teucrians") I see no feat more heroic than the rescue of another's fame. As a girl, the Negress had been sold into Egypt and worked as a servant in a certain harem, which a party of Ubykh women entered—in proof of which she lit up a pipe . . . The German tape-recorded her unintelligible senile babble. Freed of a duty that even she had not recognized, she then and there entrusted her unburdened soul to a pitying God . . .

"So what did you say was the name of the Quiet One?"

The Quiet One? . . . Ah! The name Tycho sounds like the Russian for "quiet." It's good to drink to the peoples!

"He was a courtier. His ancestors went on a crusade to the Tomb of the Lord, and one of them came home leading a beautiful woman, supposedly a Turk, whom he had rescued from slavery. Nothing is known about her, except that she smoked a pipe and was Tycho's grandmother."

"It's very possible, if she smoked a pipe," they agreed. "Do you think she was the one who trained him not to get up from the table?"

"It's very possible," I agreed in turn. "But his dying wish was for this inscription on his gravestone: 'He lived a wise man, died a fool.' "

And this proved correctly understood by all. We rose from the table at last. I could now be pleased, not only with myself but also with HIM: all except our hosts were so drunk that I could only admire the way HE easily, without staggering, glided down—in my jeans, which showed especially white in the pale dusk—onto the lawn, which had turned from emerald to dark green.

But if only that had been the end!

Here on the little meadow, now that the outlines of the yard were hidden by dusk and all these buildings didn't look so solid and new, my patriotic introspection on the subject of someone else's wealth was not so unnerving to me. Why bemoan lost traditions and spinelessly plunge myself into poverty? . . . Tradition is by no means our wealth, and wealth is indeed a tradition. So I concluded, as I measured the depth of the field to which the guests, preserving their masculine dignity, were disappearing one by one, as if for some other purpose. And when I had measured it precisely, when I found myself in the strictly Russian board shack, when I was chasing away the image of Tycho Brahe's inglorious death—I suddenly remembered the heavenly northern village of Turlykovo, where all these things had once existed: the well, the pump, the untrampled meadow, the carved porches and lintels. The little village rose up like a temple on a hill, and when you climbed up to it you did indeed find yourself in a temple, from which you could pray to all of God's world, which immediately came to you, immediately encircled you, not tightly but intimately, this world that was quite enough for you. The forest that hugged the field stood like a monastery wall, and on the lone pine rising above it you could make out an obvious cross. People had lived there! And—it had existed! . . . They did not live there now. The temple had been abandoned with a weird, shocking suddenness: spoons in the sideboard and a little frock hanging in the wardrobe . . . What a bombing that was! Come on out, crawl out, it's all over! . . . That was how it seemed, that the handsome residents would suddenly emerge, making a joyful noise and exulting that nothing had been destroyed, everything was intact . . . Except . . . They would never return! That was the terrible thing. They would never again want to . . . As though collectivization were, indeed, Russia's notorious primacy in the invention of the neutron bomb: everything is safe and sound, man alone is gone. We will yet return to Turlykovo! I had time to think, with a glad shiver down my spine,

and now the lawn began to shiver beneath me just as gladly, powerfully, and gently, and from somewhere *over there*, racing out from the dusk of the farm buildings, with a startled neigh, came a *Steed*. Oh, what an animal this was! A bird! A creature! The creature, the horse, not believing his own feet, shot toward us, right into the orchard. He didn't know yet where to go, but his soul was already flying along. He seemed hobbled by the might of his own body, he must first disentangle himself, trample his way out, burst out of his own self, the next dungeon after the one just abandoned. His color was already indistinct, but his coat shone: now his croup, now his flank reflected the not-yet-risen moon. He was just on the point of fully believing in his freedom, he let out a triumphant neigh, he was about to dash away, but now he abruptly shied in fright, mistaking an apple branch for I don't know what. The apple struck his muzzle, and he crunched it up with childish delight. And it was as though his heart could not bear three happinesses at once: freedom, motion, and an apple delivered right to his mouth. His flank heaved convulsively, as if from a race. He had been rushing around in this horse paradise, he had been flashing among the now white tree trunks like a zebra, and the apple had flung itself between his teeth; the moon-green juice streamed down his muzzle, and exulting over all this, startled and fearless, was his sidelong, neighing eye. If there are apples, there is also a paradise. If there is a paradise for us, it will have a horse. Otherwise, for whom are the apples and why is there a paradise? And if the horse is in paradise, we, too, are in paradise,

so we stood in a circle around the horse, and modesty simply streamed from our host, and my thoughts on the meaning of wealth struck me as pathetic, for this was a Steed. All those definitions of what was theirs and their own, created and acquired, turned out to be small-minded Marxist confessions. Yes, of course this horse had been bought, but not like a television or a carpet, and not even like an automobile. He was not for need. He was for racing. He wouldn't win yet this year, but he would win in the future, no question, and

you don't look at the woman you love, or your child by her, the way you look at a Steed;

there's a normal, safe, everyday envy that is fun to excite in your neighbor, through your harvest, for example, or your wife, or your growing son, or your new car, but there's an envy as huge as a Steed, it prances inside you and tramples your soul, an envy with green apple foam on its lips, an envy you have to be a little more careful with,

and this is the moment when the host presents his guests with the farewell horn. That horn was the size of an elephant tusk.

It held exactly two bottles of wine.

I was still thinking the horn would start around the circle . . .

But the host, the young one who looked devilishly like Pushkin, demonstrated how this was done—it was for one man—downing the contents of the horn in a single breath, without pausing. And as they refilled it and I tried to guess who was next, and as his father, who bore such a rare, such a fraternal resemblance to my father, except that he had lived a different, parallel life, secret from me, with its fresh air, toil, and health—as his father glanced at me in such a fatherly way, benevolent and encouraging, and chuckled as though covertly pleased with me,

most likely I was thinking inscrutable are Thy ways, O Lord, and I might, perfectly well might, be his son; a great hand had reached down from heaven with the little seed of me on its palm, and I had been conceived in Anapa (*Ana-pa* in Abkhazian means "outstretched hand")—so that was a fact. The Japanese count a man's age from his conception, so why couldn't Anapa be my homeland? But that chance event would be the only one, and doom you to your fate . . .

The horn was held out to me, and even as I tried to beg off, HE was already struggling to get at it. I implored him, I grabbed his arms, I asserted with good reason that this would ruin him, he couldn't handle it, he would disgrace himself, he would get smashed. In vain! He wrenched himself from my clutches and seized the horn. Feeling himself to be a horse, he all but neighed. He kicked off his sandals, apparently for greater resemblance, stamped his bare heels on the Abkhazian *agazon*, and declaimed: "Earth, help me!" And so, deciding that he stood on the soil at last, he applied himself. I could only watch with trepidation. He drank and drank, and the horn kept lifting him up. Even when sober, I can't tip my head back too far, for fear of dizziness. How did he have the breath! . . . His head tipped back, the horn rose higher and higher. Standing, literally, on the earth, he saw the moon come up all of a sudden, as if jumping out from behind the horizon. There was something predatory in its curve, as in the leap of a snow leopard seizing its victim. And thus, not so much holding the horn up as holding on by it, he dangled from it between earth and moon, like the Young Pioneer bugler in the park, and simply froze, trumpeting his last, victorious drop. To the sound of a friendly, approving ovation, he remained standing. Well, well, I thought. Let's see what you do now. But even now he didn't immediately fall down, he was still able to hand the empty horn to the next man with a triumphant gesture and leave the arena without staggering.

Getting him into the car was harder. He crawled around the lawn on all fours and wept. "The tooth! I've lost Lucy's tooth . . ." he wailed. No one but me understood him.

He calmed down at last and drooped his head on my bosom. Lulled by the jolting of the automobile, he hugged Lucy's skull the way a child hugs a toy.

Before we reached Sukhum he woke up, suddenly clear and decisive, for he had heard a gentle neigh. He asked to stop. Everyone was glad to relieve himself slightly of the Abkhazian one-for-the-road, but this wasn't even what he had on his mind. He asked whether the resort hotel gleaming beyond the railroad track wasn't the one where . . . and they confirmed that it was. The very same, how had he guessed? A terrible thought flashed through my mind. Under no circumstances could this be allowed! But then and there he confirmed my misgivings, declaring that he would ride no farther, he would spend the night at the resort. How I hoped that our Abkhazian friends would not allow this! But, after deliberating briefly, they deemed him to be of sound mind. I was restraining him with my last strength, but he had always been stronger than I. "Fuck off!" he shouted angrily, and tore himself from my drunken arms. And ran.

He was running, he thought, like a horse. Straight across the railroad tracks and the asparilla thickets; there wasn't much left of my jeans. And when he had finally crashed through the last reeds and sedges and thundered across the pebbled shore, he flopped into the sea without undressing and began to swim. "Fuck off!" he repeated with each stroke, in reply to my choked appeals. I didn't have the strength, I faded and was left behind.

He swam quite far along the moonlight path, emitting epic snorts like a folklore steed and admiring himself in the phosphorescent bubbles, as if he were all of this, both sea and horse and moonlight path. He felt like mineral water poured into a goblet, although he looked more like a dropped-in Alka-Seltzer. He dissolved in the night and came up on shore with a faint neigh, as if born from the sea foam, right across from the resort hotel with all its windows shining. He was purposeful. He was aiming for the apple.

I implored him. This was the very thing he would never forgive himself. He must not do this under any circumstances. This was degradation. The Fall. Stop!

"Fuck you!"

And he was right. He had done it to me . . .

It was I who was wet, dirty, and drunk, while HE, agile as James Bond, stealthy as a snow leopard, was instantly in a dinner

jacket, with a rose in his buttonhole, and it was HIM she saw, not
me, to judge by her ecstatic glance as she accepted the rose he had
just barbarically plucked from the main flower bed; it was they
who together, immediately, without even exchanging a word, ran
to the beach holding hands, ran off into the night, into the darkness,
into the sea, he with the neigh that befitted him, she with happy
squeals; it was they who undressed as they ran, dropping their
tunics and mantles, peeling off everything; it was they who splashed
and played like Triton and a naiad, phosphorescing for each other
with their white behinds, kissing and hugging in the open sea, well
aware that it was only they who saw the hotel with all its windows
shining, while it, poor fool, did not see them—it squinted, peered,
but did not see . . . and here, in the surf, in sight of everyone, he
hit the bull's-eye at last.

He overturned the night on himself. Fuck that night! . . .

. . . and the sea, and the hotel, and its shining windows, and
all prose, and the horse, and the apples, and the horn, and the
peoples, and the moonlight path, and the sky, and the stars, and
Mother Damp-Earth herself, who in this instance consisted of already cooling pebbles, and the already invisible bushes that
shielded them from the lighted promenade, and the promenade
with the vacationers' excited voices carrying from it, and those
vacationers, and their voices, and the globes of the streetlamps
above the voices, fuck those whispering lamps, fuck the border
tower, fuck the searchlight strolling along the coastal strip but
solicitously skirting them for the moment, and the cicadas still
droning for the same reason, and the breeze gusting up, and the
wave rushing in, and the wave rushing out, now the stars, now the
pebbles, now the surf—and the sea, the sea, the sea!—to Greece,
to Mediterrania, to Rome!

II. THE COW

August 25, 1983. Six a.m. Mediterranean landscape. Very clear. Swept pink shadows. Morning flotsam on the beach. A body. Wearing something that was once a pair of white jeans. Barefoot. Sandals—one in his hand, the other just lying there.

Two men appear above him.

"Turned up his toes . . ."

"Do you mean to say he's not alive??"

"I don't mean to say he's not dead, Doctor."

"But he's hanging on by one sandal."

"Which means that he's half dead."

"But not that he's more dead than alive!"

"All it means, Doctor, is that he's dead drunk."

"Really a very curious expression, you know . . . Does it mean . . . ?"

"That's it! You've nearly guessed it. The question is, what is a drunk—dead or asleep? Out cold, out like a light . . . what *is* he?"

"Don't you mean, honored colleague, that there's life, there's death, but there's also *pause?*"

"Very close, Doctor. Should he be considered a corpse or a body?"

"It turns out a drunk is neither?"

"What is a drunk . . . There's yet another complication to this question, Doctor. The question is, of what does a deadly sin consist—the sin, or death?"

"Perhaps the answer lies in how much he drank?"

"Well, yes. A drop kills a horse, a liter kills a man . . . Nevertheless, you're not telling all, Doctor."

"I think I've expressed myself quite clearly, honored colleague. Everything depends on the dose."

"The dose . . . A lot is a lot, a little's a little. That's experience, not a thought. The principal condition is rhythm. In the beginning, time gave a shudder. Ticked and got started."

"The time of the action? You think it's like a clock?"

"There now, what kind of scientist are you! And you call yourself my colleague. That's like HIM thinking he wrote us . . . You assume you're smarter, do you? I see, I see. Then tell me, how long will this go?"

"How long?" Doctor D. automatically glances at his watch.

Pavel Petrovich bursts out laughing, satisfied. He tosses up a flat little cobblestone and catches it.

The bay is as round as a plate. Overnight the sea has completely stilled and solidified. Replete and smooth, it is so abundant that it even curls up at the edges, like a kind of oversized jellyfish.

"Here, let's play a game," Pavel Petrovich says, getting set. "If you guess, the bottle's on me. If you don't, the bottle's on you."

"In the first place, how could I guess? And in the second place, where would I get a bottle?"

"As Napoleon used to say, in the second place is enough."

"What does Napoleon have to do with it? Do you mean the cognac?"

"Your taste isn't bad." Pavel Petrovich laughs. "Let's play for a Napoleon."

"I'm not good for a Napoleon," the doctor says, pulling out first a three-ruble note, then a five, then a one.

"Now, this is a man's conversation. So, a bottle?"

The doctor still isn't sure. "But you know, this is somehow . . . the last of my . . . Yesterday, you see, I also somehow . . . spent a fair amount . . . Colleagues, you understand . . ."

Pavel Petrovich sighs and flings the stone into the sea in a fit of temper, without looking. But the stone goes hopping over the thick water as if alive, like a frog. And hops thus all the way to the horizon.

"Doesn't that remind you of anything?" Pavel Petrovich whispers mysteriously, leaning toward the doctor's ear.

"Well, yes. Childhood, of course. I couldn't do it. I could never get more than three skips. I was so envious of people like you!"

"Nonsense," Pavel Petrovich mutters carelessly. "A matter of practice. Precision of gesture, no more. Still, I am a sculptor, you know."

"You don't say! I've never seen a live sculptor before—"

"You've seen a lot of dead ones, have you? No offense meant, it's a joke. Ha, ha."

"Oh, that's all right. It's not very unfunny."

"You're a fine fellow, Doctor. In any profession, a sense of humor can't hurt. But you specialize in birds, if I'm not mistaken?"

"Birds, yes . . . How did you guess?"

"Why, I was sitting in the bushes and saw you admiring a feather. Creatures with a great sense of humor, they are."

"You've noticed this, too? You don't say! One really has to know them well."

"I do know them pretty well. But don't be so surprised, it's just that I made a living from songbirds as a child. Now, you chose to speak ironically about clocks, Doctor. But you know, I didn't throw a mere stone into the sea—I threw a visual aid . . ."

Pavel Petrovich holds the pause, relishing it, but Doctor D. holds it, too.

"You noted that the first skip was long, the second a bit shorter, the third . . . well, and so on. What does this mean?"

"Well, if you want to switch to mathematical language, it's a linear graph of negative acceleration."

"Really. I'll have to remember that. But all the same, it's a superficial description. Doesn't this remind you of a clock pendulum?"

"Not in general, no. Well, unless you hang the stone on a thread—"

"Oh, but why hang it, Doctor? That's like the Armenian riddle, you know: it hangs, it's green, and it cheeps. You know the riddle? Good, good. But your mathematical point, about acceleration, is exactly what I had in mind. When the pendulum gets to the end, what does it do? *It . . . stops.* And in order to stop, what does it do? *It . . . slows . . . down.* Do you follow?"

"Naturally. The damping of the pendulum."

"Damping. Excellent! And what does that imply?"

This time, too, they both hold the pause.

"It implies that even a clock, in order to run, must stop, every second. Unlike time! A clock is mere rhythm, no more. It arbitrarily beats out the twenty-four hours for us. It doesn't measure time. Every thoughtful person knows this. But a clock isn't so naïve as that same thoughtful person believes. You, for example. Do you think I felt offended by you? I felt offended for the clocks. The master craftsmen."

"Master craftsmen? I in no way touched on craftsmen. A clock is a clock. It runs."

"That's exactly it! How does the master craftsman differ from the scientist? He has *feeling*! Clocks . . ." Pavel Petrovich snorts disdainfully. "What other article has man complicated so unnecessarily as clocks? How hasn't he decorated them! What chimes, what repeaters! And what hasn't he crafted them from! Crystal clocks, porcelain clocks, gold clocks, straw clocks. Water clocks! Man has—well, he's simply made clocks from everything. Finished one, started another. Why? Even in our own century, when there are no craftsmen left, only industry, what clocks haven't we invented! Already it's hard to recall the ones we had in our youth. Remember how proud we once were: anti-magnetic, shock-resistant, waterproof . . . Where are those windmills today? Now even the electronic clock is yesterday . . . Now it has a radio, a computer, and a television built in. Why so much?"

The doctor still isn't taking the bait. And Pavel Petrovich goes on.

"Because, and only because, what people measure by the clock is not *time*, but their *relationship* to it! A clock is a ritual cult object, not a practical one. You're late or on time, not because you use a clock, but because you need something or you don't."

"Bravo!" the doctor responds. "That's true. You're right about late arrivals. Speaking of which, I've been engrossed in our conversation, and now I'm late. Where are we going, by the way?"

And indeed, the round bay on which they met is no longer visible. A long, boring strip of shore stretches ahead, and the rim of the sun has already thrust up from behind the mountains.

"You're late?" Pavel Petrovich says cheerfully, greeting this as his own victory over time. "Good, good. You're not too upset, I take it. But where was it you needed to go?"

"Oh, my colleagues wanted to show me some sort of relict grove and then take me to see the monkeys—"

"The relict grove!" Pavel Petrovich exults. "Why, that's exactly where we're going. You may not even be late. We'll even meet them all there."

"Still, it's an amusing twist. We got talking about clocks and forgot about time."

"Re*mark*able! A remarkable twist! We haven't even begun to talk about time. Now that you're not in a hurry, we can talk a while. If this interests you, of course."

"How do you come to have such an interest in clocks? Is it professional? Are you interested in them as a sculptor?"

"A sculptor . . . Amusing. I can see the scientist in you. Your observation is accurate. Thanks for the idea. But of course. Above all, a clock is a sculpture. A conventional kinetic sculpture, if I may use the language of the avant-garde. A monument to time, as it were. To what else has man erected so many monuments? Lenin and Stalin together didn't dream of so many. I once had occasion to repair a clock with Lenin—"

"What? Is there a Lenin monument with a clock?"

"Oh, no, a regular mantel clock, it struck the Kremlin chimes. I was working as a watchmaker then—"

The doctor laughs happily. "I think you've made a monkey of me, Pavel Petrovich."

"Oh, but no, my dear fellow. You don't believe me, but it's true, I did work as a watchmaker. So I haven't made a monkey of you yet. Would you like me to? Let's play this game. If you guess how many skips, you owe me a bottle. If you don't guess, I owe you."

"Excuse me, how do you mean? I don't follow. If I guess, I *lose?*"

"How truly distrustful you are. Truly the scientist. Your logic suffocates you. You yourself said you couldn't guess. I'm offering you more advantageous conditions. Risk-free, from your point of view, I might say. Well?"

Pavel Petrovich is already holding a suitable stone.

"Well, all right." The doctor chuckles. "Do you really want to lose, rather than win?"

Pavel Petrovich looks sad. "Yes, I want terribly to lose. But I never lose. Believe me, it's actually boring."

"But I'm going to pick at random—and you've lost."

"Oh, how I'd like to hope!"

"Well, as you wish."

"Well?" Pavel Petrovich freezes in the posture of the "Youth Pitching Horseshoes." "Remember, in Pushkin? 'Briskly the youth took a step, And he crouched with one hand on his knee . . .' "

"Well, eight."

Pavel Petrovich throws.

"One, two, three . . ." Doctor D. counts. "Six, seven . . ."

The stone suddenly halts and sinks—like a stone—to the bottom. As if diving. As if alive.

"Eight," the doctor says, with a somehow childish plaintiveness.

"It's even hard to conceal how distressed I am," Pavel Petrovich says, accepting the money from the doctor. He disappears in the bushes.

And the doctor, deep in thought, scratches his nose.

It's hard to say exactly what he is thinking. We are eavesdropping and spying, no more. But his expression is eloquent. On first thought, the prospect of a drinking spree makes his nose itch, as usual. On second thought, he is not such a fool as to hope for Pavel Petrovich's return. On third thought (there being no hope), he hadn't planned on drinking first thing in the morning. Why, he had even run down to the sea with the intention of having a swim at dawn. He fully looks the beachgoer, although basically he doesn't care for either swimming or sunbathing, since by occupation he spends his whole life on the beach. So he can take it or leave it. Lest his research associates succumb to laziness, he must set an example: at home he doesn't swim or sunbathe. But here it's a different matter. Here he can indulge. He is wearing shorts, tennis shoes, and a silly little cap with a long visor, with a towel around his neck. And he hasn't even gotten his swim. That odd man . . . On first thought, Doctor D. has never met anyone like him before. On second thought, the man is suspiciously reminiscent of something—far in the past, but it happened to the doctor himself . . . Doctor D. tries, and simply can't recall. Suddenly abandoned by Pavel Petrovich, he strolls along the water's edge, along the shore—always in profile, in profile, bobbing his head and picking up his tall, thin legs—and his long visor further emphasizes his resemblance to the subject of his studies, the bird. Thus he strolls and meditates, and this time we can definitely state that he is meditating on Pavel Petrovich, because he is hunting up the flattest stones on the whole pebbled beach and trying to throw them, but they just won't skip for him. Again, they sink like stones: straight to the bottom.

And now he laughs, content with his loss.

Resolutely he strips to his underpants, in order to take his swim at last, then and there. But having undressed he does not go in the water. He sits down and looks at the sea, once more somehow contriving to be sideways to us.

Thus he sits naked, like a big plucked bird, and now he is probably comparing the seas: his own sea, a northern one, the Baltic, with this southern sea, the Black. No comparison! A deficiency of birds. No sand. The gray color of the pebbles in the littoral zone ruins everything. It's not just the fauna, somehow things are worse here with the flora, too. Still, he has to walk as far as the so-called relict grove. Before . . .

Before the sun hits the beach. It has already fully risen from behind the mountains and hangs above them like the moon. It lights the whole sea, and the sea becomes truly *black*. Black as oil, as mercury, as amalgam, as a mirror . . . as shoe polish, as a shined shoe. Something of that sort. The doctor changes his mind about swimming.

He vacillates a moment longer, whether to return or to walk ahead. Toward where the relict grove is. If that odd man wasn't lying . . . But even if he wasn't lying, how far is it?

He sees a bird at last. It's only a seagull. But still.

And he walks toward where the seagull is. Ahead then, not back. He paces like a crane, his visor nodding northward.

Why has he come here? Strictly speaking, to play hooky. To have a swim. He doesn't feel like swimming. The relict grove and the upcoming excursion to the monkeys don't interest him all that much. The monkeys don't interest him because he has no expert knowledge of them. They hold some interest for him only in connection with the human population. Apropos of this, ever since a certain moment (again, somehow mysteriously connected with Pavel Petrovich—he does have something to do with this!), he has more and more often been thinking forbidden thoughts. Unprofessional ones, but so alluring . . . He has suddenly discovered that, if he is honest, he has long since lost interest in thinking about birds. Only one animal is interesting to think about—man. And the more interesting, the more terrifying. Or rather, the more terrifying, the more interesting. This is his scientific adultery.

The Black Sea doesn't interest him, either. The only thing about it that interests him is the sulfur. That sulfurous bottom layer, which continues to grow, leaving only a few dozen meters for surface life. That layer interests him, again, from the standpoint of the activity of the human species. But whether because the people here in the south are all lazy and incompetent, or because there's a kind of secrecy . . . so far, he has obtained no information on the dynamics of the sulfur layer more precise than what he himself already possesses. And no one is suggesting where to obtain it. More likely, they themselves don't know.

The monkey colony itself doesn't interest him. Nor, especially, do their experiments. To begin with, none of their work is up to the mark. This Dragamashchenka . . . They say he has an off-limits laboratory, something to do with man. But he just won't talk. Won't talk because he doesn't have anything, or because he doesn't need to? Secrecy, or the appearance of secrecy? Dragamashchenka is no biologist . . . But he doesn't talk, as a professional. Yesterday, though, Doctor D. himself talked. Cracked, spilled his secrets. He shouldn't have argued about man yesterday. He had one drink too many with them. Not surprising, when that girl in white . . . Regina, was it? . . . was hanging on his every word. They have much better liquor, by the way, than he has at the station. One and the same Academy of Sciences, you'd think, but the liquor is different. Why should monkeys get better liquor, as if they were bosses over the birds?

This thought should cheer the doctor, for, again, it is not about birds and monkeys, but about man. And for that reason, of course, he will go on the excursion to the site of the natural monkey settlement. In the first place, he has never seen primates in a herd, close up. He is very tempted to take a good look at the structure of their society . . . The monkey is free in Russia, under socialism! We're not free, but the monkey is! The story is that freedom immediately led to the blossoming of their secondary sexual characteristics: their manes grew thick as lions' manes, and their gluteal calluses blossomed like roses. But their tails got frostbitten. It's

Russia, after all, even though without cages. And, too, they can't feed themselves, they require supplemental feeding—vestiges of socialism already . . . Hm. He will have to go.

But here we are already violating our own precepts—we're beginning to think for Doctor D.

All we can state with confidence is that he suddenly emerges from his reverie and starts to hurry. Because there's something up ahead. A lot of seagulls, a racket. Looks as if there's even a man . . .

With Pavel Petrovich, we somehow find it easier to think what he thought. It's much harder to predict what he will say.

In the first place, we increasingly see Pavel Petrovich face on, unlike Doctor D. Perhaps because he's always talking, and we're listening. Face on, he's shorter and wider than the doctor, even more so than he actually is. So it seems. They're nearly identical in both height and weight, but the impression is quite different. By the way, it has been very amusing to observe the two together: one always in profile and the other face on, one tall, the other short, one gaunt, the other not exactly fat but tubby-looking, and apparently with a bald spot, for some reason, in contrast to the doctor, although this is untrue: Pavel Petrovich definitely isn't bald. It has been amusing to observe them together, and it's too bad they have parted so soon.

Having received the money, Pavel Petrovich goes charging into the bushes face on, like a little wild boar. Squat and sturdy, he barrels along in a straight line, as if meeting no obstacle, as if parting not only the bushes but also the houses and fences. And he pops out onto the highway, right at the bus station. Sprawling around it is a modest, dusty little bazaar with two roosters (feet tied with a bootlace, eyes rolled up from the utter horror of life), three watermelons, and a bundle of *churkhcheli,* but he doesn't stop to look at all that, he goes straight up to a wrinkled little old man who has an inordinate growth of gray stubble and is dozing under his inordinately large cap (the kind that was once nicknamed an "airdrome"), so that his face is completely indiscernible behind the stubble and the cap, but Pavel Petrovich sweeps all this aside and achieves swift understanding, rather divinely, even. And now, holding a dark bottle corked with a plug of newspaper, he looks like a Partisan ready to fling himself under an enemy tank. He dives into a fence, just as he did into the bushes, and promptly finds himself on the shore, but in a completely different place— the very place the doctor is now approaching, alerted by the racket of the seagulls.

There is a dolphin on the shore.

He has been dead quite a while. The flies are already hard at work on him. By now even the gulls don't seem to want to eat him, they are merely circling and screaming, impressed by the event itself.

It is indeed an event.

Doctor D. stares vacantly at the dolphin's flank, which is streaked with tints of walleye white and mother-of-pearl . . . "streaked" is the wrong word . . . "traced" is wrong, too . . . "shimmering" is wrong, "gleaming" is wrong . . . there's no right word. It is unlike Doctor D., professionally observing the death of an individual, to have thoughts about it, about either the death or the individual. But now for the first time he has suddenly, unthinkingly, fallen into a reverie. Is the dolphin totally dead? On first thought, of course, he isn't alive. But is he all that dead?

The morning light lies freely on his skin and slides off like a glance. His flank has dried, and as it loses its own warmth it is taking on the temperature of the environment. As if the sun were licking up its warmth, and not vice versa. The dolphin is no longer reflecting but isn't yet absorbing, either: the water has dried from his flank, but the light has not. The unarguable fact of death is bewildering precisely from the scientific point of view. A liberation from the biological program, from the previous servitude of feeding and multiplying. A release. Go to sleep. Rest. The doctor feels like asking, "What's wrong?"

The dolphin remains dumb. Not, ultimately, in the sense that he is "dumb as a fish" (the doctor, as you are aware, knows that the dolphin is not a fish). He has nothing to say. And specifically not to you—to him, the doctor.

The dolphin holds his peace. As if he's still waiting for something, and it hasn't come.

"This one won't come back to life," Pavel Petrovich says.

The doctor has been so engrossed that he is genuinely frightened. The silence breaks—the seagulls burst into screams.

"But he may rise from the dead."

"Don't be a fool!" The doctor, in fright, covers his privy parts for some reason and then is embarrassed to have done this.

"I understand," Pavel Petrovich says, with a fitting expression. "It's a real shame . . . But I've been waiting for you a long time. I haven't opened it." He displays the bottle.

"You could have, even without me," the doctor growls, rather rudely.

He is no less shocked by Pavel Petrovich's return, however, than by the spectacle of another's death.

"I could not," Pavel Petrovich replies. "The money was yours, after all." And he thrusts the change into the doctor's pocket.

"But you won?"

"I played for the bottle, not for the money," Pavel Petrovich parries, with dignity. "Let's go around the corner, we'll drink to the memory of God's servant Dolphinarium."

"Dolphinarium? That's not his proper name, it's—"

"I know, I know. Anyway, let's get out of here," Pavel Petrovich says, nudging the doctor as if toward an exit. "I spotted a nice place—"

"Around the corner?" The doctor is still sarcastic, still resisting.

"Yes!" Pavel Petrovich laughs. "Around that one over there!" He points to a small nearby cape.

"And he certainly isn't God's servant," the doctor continues. He is already following submissively. "You and I are God's servants. But he—"

"*We* are not God's! We are uprisen servants, the worst of

categories: servants, but not God's. But he—yes, you're right. He's not a servant. But he's God's. God's creature. What bastards we Russians are—how can we use the word 'creature' as an expletive? 'Creature' means created by God! That's our godlessness talking! A viper spewing from our lips!"

"But creeping things are also God's creations, you know!" the doctor protests adroitly.

"Damnation! God forgive me! The devil made me say it. How easily I bit, old fool that I am!" He is sincerely distressed. "But in truth, it's one more proof of our irreverence toward Creation. Again, I'm right! But that, let me tell you, is a topic. That's not so simple, the reptiles . . . This way, please . . . Right this way . . . A splendid little spot."

They make themselves comfortable.

Pavel Petrovich is like the Magic Tablecloth. This is a fairy-tale spot, between the roots of a large pine. It even has sand, all strewn with needles, cones, and other charming detritus of life. So Pavel Petrovich sits himself down as if their surroundings were of his own making, produces a tumbler he has scavenged somewhere along the way, noisily pulls the cork with his teeth, and fills the glass more than halfway.

"Here." He offers it to the doctor.

"With nothing to munch on?"

"Even the press will suffice for me." Pavel Petrovich sniffs the paper cork expressively. "For you, however . . ." He glances around quickly and reaches for an herb of some sort. Plucks it and holds it out to the doctor. "Sniff, then drink, and then sniff. It's a great help. You can chew it, too, no harm in that, but it's not strictly necessary. People like it either way. A matter of taste."

The doctor both sniffs and chews. And sniffs.

"What marvel is this?"

"I don't know the Latin name. We call it 'dullvein.' "

The doctor is amused at the way Pavel Petrovich greedily catches up with him.

"So it wasn't even corked, just plugged. Really, couldn't you have taken a sip along the way?"

"But how could I!" Pavel Petrovich is sincerely hurt by such a suggestion. "Now, you mention the reptiles. 'Reptile,' in our country, has long meant a policeman, and not the noble snake. Either way it's unfair. To both the cops and the reptiles. An insult, as you have justly noted, is always reciprocal. Infelicity in a simile is an insult! As you see, style is a vital thing. When I was—"

"What, have you found time to be a policeman, too?"

Pavel Petrovich frowns. "Why, yes. An Investigator for Especially Important Cases. An executioner. I used to shoot unfortunates in the dungeons. I'd choose the most unfortunate and shoot them." Pavel Petrovich flickers his jaw muscles. "What do you take me for?"

"Not for a rept . . . I'm sorry, but you weren't a snake, were you?"

"Don't be silly! A snake *catcher*. I was a snake catcher, understand? Well, let me tell you, they're the noblest beasts. They wouldn't bite for the world, not for the world. Unlike you . . ."

"Come now, Pavel Petrovich! Among us zoologists, the word 'reptiles' isn't an insult at all. The legitimate name of an order of animals, no more. True, they certainly aren't beasts, as you choose to call them. 'Beast' is a synonym of 'mammal.' "

"I know even that, Doctor," Pavel Petrovich says, resentfully pouring another. "Creeping things crawl, and mammals breastfeed. And you won't mix me up on the animal species. Better *you* tell *me*: to what species does the lancelet, for example, belong?"

"You know that, too?!" the doctor says delightedly, taking a sniff of dullvein.

"Now, you mention death . . ." Pavel Petrovich says, taking a sniff of cork. "But have you ever been in the desert? What a noble, dry death it is there! The wind blows away all those little skins, twigs, skeletons. The rustle alone remains, like a sigh. The plants—they even rot beautifully. But we? I can't get that dolphin out of my mind . . . What do you think he died of?"

"I don't know. Possibly of natural causes. Stupidity, an accidental wound. He was still very young."

"How did you decide that? He was full adult size."

"I know nothing about dolphins, but there are a number of shared attributes. In the baby lion and the baby elephant, so to speak, the mousling and the froglet, the human youngling and the unknown beastie. Oh, the steep brow, short nose, round eyes—it's all been programmed into our emotion so that we'll drive ourselves to feed them, defend them, not hurt them . . ."

"Provide them with shoes, clothes . . . Well, you're a wonder, Doctor! Not a word about love. But that's where all the toys come from! Not *for* children, but *from* children. I hear you! So his own kind couldn't have hurt him?"

"Not only couldn't they have hurt him, it's even strange that they lost him. To the best of my recollection, dolphins live as nuclear families, like people. In four generations, moreover."

"What's a nuclear . . ."

"Husband, wife, children. But the grandmother and grandfather, too. And they also have the great-grandfather and great-grandmother."

"Brilliant. You're not fictionalizing? But how did they lose him?"

"How would I know? I'm a scientist. I have to know *already* in order to infer something *more*. Well—he became engrossed in a game. Got hit by a propeller. Dived too deep, drank too much hydrogen sulfide, and suffocated . . . But most likely it was the overall environmental picture. He no longer wanted to live."

"Committed suicide? How could a beast, God's creature, not want to live? That's unscientific, Doctor. As you say, it's built into him—the undeniable desire to live. Only man can fail to want to live. You yourself curse anthropomorphism, and yet you yourself are lapsing into it."

"No, it's not I but you who are lapsing into anthropomorphism, Pavel Petrovich. You so dramatically express your dissatisfaction with the human species (I mean in the biological, not the social sense, as you are aware), and in spite of myself I have to agree with you in many respects, yet all you're doing is magnifying man. Suicide is actually very prevalent in the animal world. Mass suicide, moreover. We, meaning *Homo sapiens*, are the ones who see suicide as an individual act. For the self-replicating systems called living organisms, the termination of the individual—that is, death—is merely an evolved characteristic: they are merely links in an unbroken chain of descent . . . Their purpose is not their own life but the continuation of the genus and species. After fulfilling their purpose they have nothing to do in this life. Not only the very noble scorpions you saw in the desert, my dear Pavel Petrovich, and not only the males, whose purpose, as you yourself say, is briefer, and not only the humpback salmon you caught on Kamchatka. The mechanisms for regulating the population of a species are extremely diverse and quite unknown. Unfortunately, we make our own monstrous correction in them."

Against his will, Pavel Petrovich is curious.

"Let's suppose there's prosperity. They've had good weather, a lot of food, few predators. All the progeny have survived, the flock has grown large. On the return trip, during the autumn migration, the young ones seem to become foolhardy. They perish from all sorts of causes—bump into high-voltage wires in flight, let themselves be eaten by anyone who feels like it. Just as many arrive as the last time, as many as permissible and necessary, because it's by no means certain that the same accidentally favorable circumstances await them there, and an extra mouth may prove, as before, to be no earthly use. Now let's suppose there's poverty. The flock has multiplied according to its normal tendencies. But they've had bad weather, little food, many predators. The loss of each individual becomes super-important for the existence of the whole flock. Remarkable things happen. The individual becomes strong, wary, bold, and ready to sacrifice himself for the sake of his neighbor. Yes, his very self-sacrifice is a sign of the desire to live. Man's activity destroys these regulation mechanisms. Then the animals simply can't live, they develop depression, and yes, they commit suicide. Fling themselves up on shore, like whales."

"You think he committed suicide?"

"It's conceivable."

"Inconceivable! You yourself say he was too young."

"Don't young people commit suicide?"

"He lacked a library, that's what!" Pavel Petrovich declares decisively. "A great-grandpa, that is. After all, what's the remarkable thing about the dolphin family? Why did they, as a community close to us and possessing far more resources than monkeys, fail to take our path? They're not a family but a floating library, with the experience of four generations on one shelf! Great-grandfather! Great-grandfather is what man has always lacked! Have you ever noticed that a man's lifetime, even if full-length, is exactly one generation short of a century? From this comes our whole misfortune; from this grows man's ungovernable history, like rust. A century is a natural measure of history, but we never equal the century, never have time to be either a great-grandson or a great-grandfather, and therefore never see how an affair began or how it ended. We participate only in the process or the result, we witness either birth without death or death without birth. We, it turns out, are those 'individuals' of yours, whose death is a matter of indifference to life. We do not know the sole measure of time: *justice!* But the dolphins know."

"Great-grandpa told them?"

"Yes! Exactly! Your human irony is misplaced. Among dolphins, a century swims as one family! And all are witness to each other. Among dolphins, the history of the family doesn't diverge from the history of the species, as it does among men. There exists but *one* justice—the sole measure of time. But among men there is a constant arrhythmia of family and species. The history of mankind is separate, and hostile to man. Hence *history*, may it be damned!"

Pavel Petrovich puts a great deal of venom into his pronunciation of the word "history."

"Justice is too subjective a concept." (The doctor's words.)

"Objective! And the death of the individual is by no means a matter of indifference! No, I can't . . ." Pavel Petrovich lets out a sob. "Surely you understand that the mother no longer has her son, the grandfather his grandson? That his dolphin death has indeed broken your famous chain?! And his lone death may signify that we have already destroyed all the dolphins! We poisoned the sea, and the first to perish was the weakest—the great-grandfather. He failed to survive. We've reduced their family by the great-grandfather. Now that they have three generations, like us, they will no longer be able to live. You and I have just seen the great-grandson perish. Perhaps, being illiterate, he intended to come up on dry land, like us? Without his great-grandfather, the great-grandson not only has perished but will not become a father, either! Dear God! what ni-i-i-ight!" Pavel Petrovich cries, rocking as if from toothache. "What did he see, when we looked at him?"

"He saw nothing."

"I understand. He's dead. Like everyone else, you don't even believe in the soul: that it's still nearby and gazing at itself from above . . . But the dead, too, look at me. They themselves don't seem to want to look, or to see me, but I feel myself behind their closed eyelids . . . And such darkness presses down on me, hems me in! After all, we *live* in darkness! We have simply been illuminated. From outside. By the sun. By the source of light. The tiny lantern . . . Imagine how dark it is inside you. In your stomach, your brains, your innards . . . your heart! Like in a tree, in a stone. What do they see? They exist in primordial night."

"Well, but trees see in their own way. They not only sense warmth, they also feed on light."

"Oh, that's obvious. A blind man sees, too, in some such sense. If only with other organs. I mean something different . . . I can't explain it even to myself, let alone to you. My point is that we exist in darkness as in death, and in death as in darkness. We don't see objects—we see the way the light falls on them. We ourselves, on earth, where we exist, among our own selves, live in darkness. And being dead is a more real state than being alive. Because the dead man doesn't see the objects surrounding him: he himself is an object, merely illuminated from the outside. He doesn't see the way the light falls; for him, the source has been switched off. Does he see the light itself? Isn't he made of absolute darkness, in his own mind? Isn't it the dead man who's a particle of light, while we are merely a clot of darkness? In death we become a habitat, a homogeneous one, like water or air, but even more homogeneous: light. In life we are separated from one another by opacity, life is not homogeneous, it is scattered like peas. Oh, if only life were a habitat! There would be no death. So our habitat is death, not life. Non-existence is homogeneous. And life doesn't end with death, we live in it, in death. Death isn't separate—it is the habitat of life. Like water for fish, like air for your birds."

"Good heavens, Pavel Petrovich," the doctor exclaims. "Are you saying this to me, or did I think it? Brilliant! Well then, is a fish or a bird more dead than we are?"

"Ah, how precisely you've captured the thought! Bravo, Doctor! Yes, the bird is more dead. She is dead when flying. Not in vain is she death's herald among all peoples. What do we know of her sensations in flight? Now, you, Doctor—you know all about birds. What does she feel in flight? Is she not swimming in death? And later she will alight—to live alongside us a while, to catch her breath. Incidentally, is the phoenix a man or a bird?"

Doctor D. considers at length. "More likely a bird . . ."

"What would you say as an ornithologist: might the phoenix perhaps be a species that has its biological niche (I use your terminology) at the boundary of two habitats, death and life? That is, not on but in the boundary."

"A boundary is a line," the doctor objects. "A line, in a mathematical sense, has one dimension. That is, there's no way it can be a niche."

"You won't muddle me, Doctor! The phoenix is a man in the form of a bird."

"No, it's a bird in the form of a man!"

"Neither. Our phoenix is merely a representation of the phoenix, it's a phoenix in the form of a man."

"Now, that's more exact. But then he's a phoenix in the form of a bird."

"You're somewhat muddled, Doctor."

"You're *trying* to muddle me! Let's sort out who said what to whom—"

"You'll never sort it out now." Pavel Petrovich is pleased with something.

"It's nothing but a metaphor. Unscientific," the doctor says crossly. "The main point is that the phoenix burns and is reborn in the fire. In a physical and chemical sense, life *is* combustion."

"Oh yes, decomposition. I, too, went to sixth grade, Doctor! In the sixth grade I was still going to school, it was the seventh I didn't go to. For man, it's first life, then death. But for the phoenix, it's the reverse: first death, then life. The phoenix is simply a man in reverse."

"Simply? . . . Then he's in the form of a bird."

"That doesn't matter anymore. Tell me, which is more important, the head or the wings?"

"More important? . . . The distinguishing feature."

"Which is?"

"In man, the head. In a bird, the wings."

"That's all?"

"Yes, and that settles it. No either/or. The phoenix is both a man and a bird."

"Neither. He was a woman."

"Oh yes, the tits." The doctor laughs. "Is the sphinx a woman, too, in your opinion?"

"That's your thesis, Doctor, about the distinguishing feature. But the distinguishing feature of a woman is hardly her tits."

"You've caught me again, Pavel Petrovich . . . Another thing

I've been trying to guess, ever since childhood: how does the mermaid make the transition to a tail? In all the illustrations, the artists skillfully avoid answering . . .''

"Bravo, Doctor! I'm downright delighted what an unspoiled person you really are, even though a scientist. You actually seek an answer in art? Well, you don't know and we don't show—not because we don't know, but because we avoid showing."

"But why do 'you' try so hard to avoid it?" the doctor says ironically.

"For aesthetic reasons."

"Ah."

"Tut-tut! Again, you have only one thing on your mind, Doctor . . . I was thinking of the more ethical side of the aesthetic."

"Pavel Petrovich! Have mercy on a fool. What does ethics have to do with this!"

"A lot indeed, young man! Why should it be, do you think, that in the phoenix, the sphinx, the centaur, and the mermaid, the human part is the head and breast, while the privates, excuse me, are not human?"

"Oh, so that's your ethics! Anthropomorphism again . . . again, apartheid for the animal world! But if it's the other way around? The body human, but head of an animal?"

"That doesn't happen."

"It does, it does!" the doctor exults. "Even in that same ancient Egypt, if you recall . . . Don't you remember, what's his name, with the bird's head?"

Pavel Petrovich becomes sad and very silent. With relish, the ironic doctor develops his theme—everything he can possibly recall. The sphinx, he says, is nevertheless male, and the mermaid is not a fish, and certainly the centaur is male, because he has a beard, although there are also women with beards, but if you just look under the centaur's tail he's male both ways, both as a man and as a horse . . . that being the case, it would be interesting to know which he prefers, mares or . . .

No, the doctor shouldn't carouse like this!

"Prefers! Women, of course," Pavel Petrovich states, with knowledge of the issue, and just then an idea strikes him. He rises up vertically, like a swallow. "De-e-e . . . de-e-e . . . de-e . . ." he bleats. "But there was such a god of death, and his name was Ptah. And he was from *over there*, but the ones you're always looking at under the tail, they're from *here*, from you and me. That's where ethics comes in! There's a boundary, but no such thing as a *distinguishing* feature! Your distinguishing feature doesn't exist— that's what! So death doesn't have one, either."

"What, may I ask, are we arguing about?" the doctor puts in.

Better he hadn't. Pavel Petrovich falls upon him, diving not like a swallow but like a hawk, like a kite.

"We are not arguing—we're educating. To argue alone is even more harmful than to drink alone. *A* is for alcoholism, and *O* is for . . . ?"

The doctor frowns. "Pavel Petrovich, you poeticize everything. You've convinced yourself that poetry is accurate. But poetry is the very greatest inaccuracy. It's a pack of inaccuracies, poetry is. Masterfully inaccurate, if you will. And as for the bird, she's supported not by an element but by an object, the air that she compresses with her wing stroke. Through the air column she's supported by the earth, the *earth*, like you and me. She doesn't hover in an element, in death, she wants to live—that is, to eat— so she flies. That she alights to 'live a while' outside her airy death, as you choose to put it, is complete nonsense, since many birds even screw—that is, they '*live*,' as we politely express it—right in the air."

"Well, but to screw, as you choose to put it—to screw is to die, don't you think? What is more like death than this ultimate ecstasy? Don't we, in our bawdy, polite Russian vernacular, use the verb 'finish' for this? To 'live' and to 'finish'—don't you hear?"

"You're reasoning like a male animal, Pavel Petrovich."

"Who am I to reason otherwise?"

"The female may have a different opinion."

"Oh, the female may even be death itself. At least, we always die in her. Weren't you talking just now about the termination of the individual, about the unfortunate fishes and spiders who die in the moment of fulfilling their purpose? But notice: most often it's the males. And the female, nearly always, executes the sentence. We males do have some remote idea of death from our experience of love. They do not! No, death is unknown to them. We're mortal, but they're immortal. Immortal because they *are* death. They are homogeneous and eternal. They are more ancient than we. They slumbered, *existed*, in that eternal and absolute darkness before the light. We didn't. And won't. And don't need to!"

"My Mephistopheles!" The doctor laughs. "Have they really vexed you so much? Yet for all that, they're your instrument."

"My Faust! They'd drive even the King of Darkness crazy . . . Here again, you see how right I am. He is, after all, king of what? Of *daaark*ness! Haven't we, dear Doctor, been neglecting our sole comfort?" And Pavel Petrovich looks at the dark bottle against the light, to determine how much he hasn't neglected.

"Haven't we been neglecting the sea?"

"Why neglecting it? There it is." Pavel Petrovich points to the smooth expanse with a gesture as generous and careless as though he had beckoned it into existence. "The sea is always there, help yourself."

We will omit their long squabble on the subject of whether it's better to have a drink first and then a swim (Pavel Petrovich) or to have a swim first and then a drink (Doctor D.), inasmuch as Pavel Petrovich originally favors just having a drink, in the belief that *chacha* will equalize the temperatures of the body and the environment more quickly and accurately than other liquid procedures, while the doctor believes an altogether monstrous thing, that it's better to have a swim and nothing more to drink at all— for which he pays by having a drink both before and after swimming, while Pavel Petrovich pays only by swimming. Moreover, Doctor D. swims a long time, with the breaststroke, and Pavel Petrovich a short time, with the overarm stroke.

"Now, about the nature of squeamishness," Pavel Petrovich

says, blissfully drying off. "You were saying that it's a gene memory of the source of disease. An innate fear, exaggerated through primordial ignorance. And I agree with you, it's exaggerated. Just as I agree with your scientific conclusion that there's no inedible meat, especially poisonous meat, in nature. Protein is protein. I would even give courses in non-squeamishness, for people who think themselves enlightened. Have harmless grass snakes and tarantulas go crawling after them . . ." Then and there, apparently to prove both points, he catches a mosquito and eats it before the doctor's very eyes. "Have them bathe more often and launder their socks. Nevertheless, this squeamishness vis-à-vis mice and spiders is different in nature from what you say. It's not an innate fear in the individual but an unconscious hostility in the whole species: *they*, the rats, cockroaches, spiders, et cetera, will outlive *us*. That is, when we ourselves have outlived our usefulness, they will remain to populate our earth without us. But who says the earth is ours and not theirs! They're more ancient than we are, they have outlived everything and everyone that existed before us, this is their earth, not ours. The dolphins, they won't outlive us. We'll outlive them, and without them we'll become even worse. Do not animals regard us with horror, the same way we regard insects? The dolphin alone still finds within him the strength to trust us. The reason he's even smarter than man is that he's better . . ."

Pavel Petrovich draws breath. And the doctor butts in:

"If you constantly resort to the notion of a Creator in your constructs, you raise the usual question of the imperfections in Creation, the system of evil inherent in it. And, already foreseeing some of your arguments and proceeding from your system of coordinates, I amend your discussion of squeamishness, with which, in principle, I can't help agreeing: namely, that 'squeamishness' is a more private concept than 'disgust.' Now, I don't remember exactly how this goes, but in the Old Testament—you correct me, please—there was something about the 'seven plagues of Egypt,' which included both snakes and insects. That is, if snakes and insects are indeed God's creations, they're somewhat ambiguous as a punishment. And for that reason the disgust they inspire will take a form less personal and superficial than mere 'squeamishness,' and more fundamental."

This obvious oversight makes Pavel Petrovich feel very gloomy. He could, of course, apropos of this, regale Doctor D. with a brilliant retelling of his Indian legend about Nikibumatva and Escheguki and the creation of the world, inasmuch as Doctor D. hasn't had the opportunity of hearing it. But Pavel Petrovich is not the kind of man to repeat himself, as a matter of principle. And this is the tack he takes:

"As concerns the imperfection of Creation, we haven't yet reached the point in the plot where I'll be able to state this for you and you'll be able to assimilate it. Much will become clear when everyone finally understands that man didn't come from the monkey at all, but the monkey from man."

"How's that? Don't you mean . . . ?"

"No, I do not." Pavel Petrovich shakes the bottle, and his face grows stern. "This is our fault, Doctor, yours and mine. Disgust and squeamishness are on your conscience and mine. We are charmed by that which is lighted, and terrified by that which lies in darkness." So saying, with a broad, graceful gesture, Pavel Petrovich unfurls before Doctor D.'s eyes a view of the sea (now slightly bluer), and with a threatening finger he points down, either under the ground or to the sea floor. "As you see, we're extending our topic and revealing the interconnection of all things. Of course, the Creator didn't literally create everything on earth; evolution worked on a few things, too. Sometimes He may have been distracted from earthly affairs for a brief hour, but who shall say what God's Hour equals? And when evolution was working alone, it didn't improve Creation but merely exposed and exaggerated every mistake in it. The Creator did His work enviably well. And afterward, Envy did the work for Him. Envy with a capital letter, and you know whose name that is . . . Evolution is as saturated with envy as a fruit with juice. Take all those dinosaurs and brontosaurs, who trampled the earth as thoroughly as men have . . . Evolution can accumulate only catastrophe, when in His Hour the Creator shall turn his attention to His Creation. O Lord! What a ca*taaas*-trophe awaits us . . ."

Since Doctor D. is poised to give an expert speech on evolution (with which he himself, however, is not thrilled), Pavel Petrovich is forced to abbreviate, if not the size of the impending catastrophe, then the pause appropriate to its scale . . .

". . . then it was He who created Beauty in the world. That which lies open for us to see and admire is beautiful. That which hides in darkness, as if actually ashamed of its own ugliness, is hideous. Evolution, or more correctly, mutation, works with impunity underground and in darkness, generating giant monsters and reptiles so hideous that they perish at one glance from us, if chance casts them up on a lighted surface. Death, too, has its own small zoo. Even death can't do without life."

This time Doctor D. succeeds in venting his indignation:

"This isn't even anthropomorphism, it's narcissism of some kind! The 'beautiful,' if you please, is merely that which we recognize as beautiful. But what do we compare, and where do we derive our criteria? Everything alive is in hiding, if you will, and won't poke its head out without special reason. There's a hypothesis on the origin of sleep, quite unproven, but I like it: sleep isn't for rest at all, it's for survival. If you've managed to eat your fill—hide, lest you get eaten. That is, be still, die, sink into the darkness you're fighting so hard. What is sleep but a small death? And we practice sleep far more often than coitus—although that, too, leaves us inclined to sleep—"

"What is sleep without dreams! How will you explain dreams, if not as the struggle of light and darkness! Perhaps you yourself, awake, are being dreamed by someone . . . And you are safe, in your dream, from poorhouse and jail, / you are stealing sleep, when the guards arrive. / They'll fold up your bunk. But still by day / you'll see men almost not men, woven of night. / And like a scrap of freedom, in your bosom you keep warmth and sleep's last mirage, that it's a game, and you lay down your bet . . ."

"True, true," Doctor D. says contentedly. "I said you were a poet. But have you sat in prison, too? . . . But shouldn't we move on, shouldn't we be getting to the relict grove?"

"Have I sat in . . . ?" Pavel Petrovich starts, and immediately becomes himself again. "But we're sitting right in it—in your relict grove!" He waves his arm to the right, as much as to say that the creation of the grove has cost him nothing.

The doctor is stunned. The pine under which they are sitting is the outermost tree in the grove. Pavel Petrovich settled down first, facing the grove, and has long been admiring it, leaving for Doctor D. only the view backward, to the shelterless shore.

"Not really! You had me under a spell . . . All right, then, let's be on our way!"

"Let's change places instead. We still have some left. You'll look at the grove, and I'll look at you."

As he changes places, Pavel Petrovich once again examines the bottle closely, gauging its contents, and his face expresses dissatisfaction; he begins to rummage through his pockets, as though, by sitting for a long time, he might have acquired some money. The doctor does not take the hint and does not produce the change so nobly returned to him—he lets Pavel Petrovich rake all the crumbs out of his pockets.

"You don't smoke, do you? I don't either. But I suddenly have a strong urge." Pavel Petrovich busies himself intently with enriching the mixture, plucking out unneeded crumbs and blowing them away. "You don't have any newspaper, either? Oh, well. We'll read the local press."

And he begins to unroll the cork. It turns out to be an unexpectedly good-sized scrap of newspaper, which he scans attentively.

"It's worn at the creases," he complains. "The thread of the narrative is lost. *Aprasnua Apsny Zantaria Akademia Anauk Achyrba* . . . From there on, it's obliterated . . . Written in Russian letters, but not in our language."

"I almost thought you knew Abkhazian, too."

"The Abkhazian language is impossible to know. Only the Abkhazians know it."

"That difficult?"

"That ancient."

Pavel Petrovich cuts off a suitable small piece. Adroitly, with two fingers, he rolls himself a cigarette.

"Well, I don't think I'll strike a spark by rubbing two sticks. We'll have to go swimming. There won't be enough for two doses apiece. So let's have it after instead."

They swim for a while.

"By the way, what occurred to me while you were swimming . . . The modification of the landscape in the direction of beauty may have happened with man's collaboration."

"I don't follow." (The doctor's words.)

"But what is paradise, in your opinion? And for whom was it created? For Adam, our great-grandfather."

"What, do you believe in those fairy tales?"

"What else am I to believe in? Why don't you look at the grove you were so eager to reach! Isn't this paradise?"

We, too, will look. And we'll be at a loss for words. Shishkin, that German, muddled all the pines for us. There is shadow. There are pines. Sand sifts in fine streams through the roots of the outermost pines along the shore. A small cloud is caught in the treetops. Doctor D.'s soul overflows with northern, home emotions. He feels clean and young. Full of health and strength, ready for a scientific feat and for the future in general, which these ancient relicts specifically reaffirm, for some reason. There is no old age in these pines. Only the triumph of sobriety. "My God!" the doctor exclaims to himself. "I'm alive!"

"Thus it was before man," Pavel Petrovich proclaims solemnly. "Since the creation of the world, some seven thousand years ago. Not these trees, of course, but the same kind. Yet these . . . may perfectly well have seen the first Christians."

Doctor D. looks at Pavel Petrovich sideways, like a very large chicken. His profile expresses the same great surprise. This is like the moment just before a sudden cloud hides the sun, or just after: the irony that always illumines the doctor's profile is obscured by a cloudlet of perplexed belief. You can't mean . . . but perhaps . . . but what if we're still early Christians? . . . And why not? We babble like uncatechized heathens. We overthrew the idols and idolized Christ. Overthrew Christ and idolized man. The time has come to overthrow ourselves, too . . .

Pavel Petrovich is carefully carrying a single match that he has picked up on the shore.

With his fingernail he marks an invisible line, quite close to the bottom of the bottle, and looks sternly at Doctor D. The doctor takes a modest sip. Pavel Petrovich prepares himself for his last swallow like a samurai preparing for hara-kiri. He strikes the match skillfully on the bark of the pine tree and inhales, blissfully rolling his eyes and turning his face to the sun. Then he sits down cross-legged and stands the bottle between his feet. Tenderly stroking it, with his eyes half closed, he begins to sway quietly, taking microscopic little gulps and equally short drags. He croons softly, contentedly:

> *Eine kleine Papierosen*
> *Nicht spazieren nach zurück!*

The doctor pricks up his ears. "What, were you in the Occupation, too?"

"In the Occupation, no, but I was a prisoner," Pavel Petrovich says carelessly. "But you don't have to believe me, Doctor."

With his eyes still closed, he offers him his home-rolled cigarette.

"What's this?"

"Happy hour, Doctor. *Nicht spazieren* . . . Tell me, Doctor, what population-regulating mechanisms (I learn fast, don't I?), apart from Condom and Malthus, does *Homo sapiens* have? War?"

"War, too. All the ones that other species have, plus. The

human species works only on this one thing, you might say—the development of these mechanisms. And even with these he's a failure. Because man, if you please, has 'tamed' nature. How can you tame her? when you're part of her? It's a form of suicide. Lopping off the bough you're sitting on. 'Tamed' nature has replied by depriving him, first of all, of his natural regulation mechanisms. They continue to operate, of course, but weakly. Without the implacability of law. They've shifted to the status of 'factors.' We used to get a lot of help from epidemics, wholesale deaths of all kinds: plague, cholera . . . They'd wipe out half of Europe at one go. Our valiant medicine interfered with that . . . And of course there's war. But even war no longer copes, however highly developed the means of annihilation. Meanwhile, there have also been other factors at work. Do you know that the automobile, quietly and slowly but without respite, has killed as many people as both world wars? But fertilizers, and medicines . . . Our society's effort at 'creation' "—the doctor puts very heavy quotation marks around this word—"has become a much more effective war than war itself. War as a method has begun to be obsolete, as is manifested by the invention of the atomic bomb. The unusable weapon. It has buried war. War has become pointless—it can't be won, it can't be ended. For the moment, the only thing working right is the growth of the megalopolises."

Pavel Petrovich throws him a satisfied glance. "But you're a humanist, Doctor."

"And . . . and . . ." The doctor actually chokes with laughter. "And . . . a pacifist!"

"I envy you," Pavel Petrovich says, watching the doctor roll around in a fit of laughter. "What a high you've caught!"

Doctor D. stoops, freezes, and does not fall. "Hear that?"

"Regrettably, no."

Doctor D. presses his ear to the grass near the empty bottle. "Napoleon's losing something again," he reports.

"That's the grass talking . . ."

"No, the bottle! The grass just goes bss-bss-bss, bss-bss-bss."

"Grass always speaks softly."

"Sh-h-h! I hear it . . . Lovingly, like so: you? me? here? yes? . . ."

"Stop!" Pavel Petrovich commands. "Watch out, don't put yourself under a mantra!"

"Why interrupt!" Doctor D. says resentfully.

"Enough's enough, that's all," Pavel Petrovich says, with great sadness. "I haven't caught my high."

How strangely they have switched roles! Pavel Petrovich has suddenly become the Joey and Doctor D. the August. The sea is their circus ring and carpet.

Doctor D. leaps around the carpet like a monkey, his hands nimbly catching something invisible to us, perhaps a butterfly, perhaps a housefly, perhaps one of his little birds . . . Pavel Petrovich watches him with affectionate sorrow.

"To catch . . ." Choking with laughter, the doctor continues to catch air in his hands. "A high . . . I caught it!" Slowly, one finger at a time, the doctor opens his fist. "It flew away, flew away!" the doctor chortles.

And he catches it again.

"D-d . . . D-d . . ." Pavel Petrovich, his eyes half closed, is moaning in great distress. "D-d . . ."

"What?" Doctor D. suddenly wakes up. "You don't want me to laugh so hard?" He is still emitting spurts of laughter, like a boiling teakettle that has just been turned off.

"De . . . de . . ."

"Death?" the doctor guesses, and stops gurgling. But his nose is still spouting steam. "What's the matter, Pavel Petrovich?"

"De . . . de . . ."

The doctor shakes Pavel Petrovich, trying to bring him to his senses.

"Dessert!" Pavel Petrovich says clearly, at last, fixing his eyes on the doctor. "Doctor, you're a teakettle."

At last he, too, has succeeded in laughing. The doctor looks around distractedly, as if for dessert or the teakettle, not understanding how he came to be here.

"Forgive me, Doctor, I'm a bad man."

"What did you slip me?!"

"Grass, Doctor, grass."

"Why didn't you warn me? That really wasn't nice, it wasn't comradely—"

"Without it you wouldn't have caught your high. It *was* comradely."

"Why dessert? Why a teakettle?" The doctor is hurt, like a child.

"Forgive me, Doctor, truly. I didn't mean it that way. Forgive me. For spoiling your high. It made me envious." Pavel Petrovich stands up. "Let's go, Doctor."

"I'm not going anywhere."

"A nation deprived of beer—" Pavel Petrovich intones darkly.

"Stop bullshitting me!"

"A nation deprived of beer is unworthy of the name of nation!" Pavel Petrovich concludes.

And they set off. Northward. Past the relict grove. Without a glance at the sea. Deprived of beer.

Moreover, Doctor D. somehow preserves his profile, as before, stepping along the water's edge as if on fine sand, while Pavel Petrovich, face on, crunches rudely over the coarse, already scorching pebbles.

The sun beats down full force. Doctor D., in profile, wears his visor. Pavel Petrovich, face on, wears a leaf on his cantankerous nose.

They are essentially silent. To the limit of their ability to keep their mouths shut.

"I'm afraid we won't overtake them now."

"Your colleagues? Don't you imagine you've already outstripped them?"

"You're a devil, Pavel Petrovich."

"I thought we'd already distributed the roles. So far, everything's going according to script. You're Faust, I'm Mephistopheles. I, too, have lost a day's work, by the way. I came out to do some drawing and forgot my sketchbook."

"But you're a sculptor."

"Sculptors also draw. Sketches."

"Do you plan to sculpt the sea?"

"Very insightful, Doctor. That's exactly what I plan. It's my secret dream—to raise a monument to the sea."

"In what form, I wonder?"

"In the form of a cow."

"?!"

"But you saw the dolphin . . . It almost got me all mixed up. They call it a sea cow."

"The sea cow is a completely different creature."

"I know that. Surely you couldn't think I'd sculpt a cow, I mean, the sea . . . I mean a cow . . . sym*bol*ically! I'm a realist! The sea . . . in the form of a dolphin! Pah!! Any mediocrity could do that."

"I don't understand."

"You will yet," Pavel Petrovich declares darkly. "You will see. Better you didn't."

"I don't understand."

"Not everyone can endure it."

"I don't know much about art. I'm a rank-and-file scientist. I assume that being a sculptor is a calling. But how did you discover it? How is it possible to be born a poet, a painter, a violinist?"

"People deprived of childhood . . ." Pavel Petrovich says darkly.

"Who?"

"Violinists, I say."

"I'm talking about you. How did you guess that you were a sculptor, specifically?"

"And how did you think to catch birds?"

"It's not the same. But strangely enough, I do remember how

it all began. I mean, I don't even remember, Mama told me—"

"You were born and caught a bird?"

"Exactly! I was just barely walking, everyone was playing in the sand, and I kept walking around a water barrel where the birds occasionally came and drank. And finally I thought to set the lid on the barrel in such a way that the lid slammed shut when a bird lighted on the edge to drink. And I caught one!"

"Well, there you are. And you ask how to become a sculptor . . . According to spiritual affinity. That's not my definition, it's my teacher's."

"You were a sculptor's apprentice? Like in the Middle Ages?"

"Bravo, Doctor! Exactly like in the Middle Ages—our best age, believe it or not. I'm an apprentice of Grigory Skovoroda. He maintained, in particular, that men were unhappy because they didn't find themselves occupations according to their spiritual affinity. He divided all mankind into three parts and came up with the clergy, the military, and the peasantry. He advised us to keep a close eye on the infant. If he joins in the chorus—to the seminary. If he reaches for the saber—be a soldier. If he amuses himself with worms—then plow. When everyone finds himself an occupation according to his affinity, that's happiness for you."

"But then which are we?"

"We? We're illegitimates."

" . . . "

"Peter the Great issued this ukase: 'Illegitimates to be registered as artists.' You, too, are an artist," Pavel Petrovich says, graciously issuing his own ukase. It does not sound convincing, and he adds, "In your own way . . . Aren't you tormented by thirst? Shall we play another, perhaps?"

Doctor D. grins. Without further hesitation, he proffers the change to Pavel Petrovich. "Yes, you and I seem to have found an occupation according to our affinity."

"It's no joke." Pavel Petrovich, likewise without hesitation, accepts the money. "If every man were busy with his own affairs, where would we get aggressions and depressions, which are basically one and the same thing? Instead of the pointless struggle against dissidence and alcoholism, I'd busy the psychiatrist with this: the diagnostics of vocation. The psychiatrist would write a prescription for the minister of foreign affairs: Make paper cutouts of dragons or roses. For the war minister: Straighten old nails. And so on. With retention of salary and privileges. Can you imagine how happy it would make them? Us, too, at the same time. 'The Tale of How One Peasant Fed Two Generals' wouldn't be a fairy tale at all. He'd feed them! If only because they wouldn't bother him anymore. And the main thing is, that peasant would get beer production rolling. And the nation would become a nation."

Doctor D. frowns. "Only let's don't talk about Russia."

"What else is there to talk about! It's all we ever talk about. Doctor, you're not a Jew, by any chance?"

"Me? I don't think so. What does it matter?"

"But you're an intellectual, my friend . . . It does matter, it does. In your place I wouldn't renounce this so lightly."

"And you yourself, Pavel Petrovich?"

"Me myself? . . . Who among us has not been a Jew? . . . We won't make sense of this without a half liter."

"Where are you going?" is all the doctor has time to say.

And he climbs up to a shady spot. The beach is strangely empty today, he thinks. Then why is he thinking about Malthus again? Because, he thinks, it's absurd to be divided into Jews and Russians when together we're an ethnic minority on the earth. It's absurd to be divided into . . . when by the year 2000 all whites will total . . . and blacks even less than that. But of course, the yellow race! . . . The Georgians and the Abkhazians—what *haven't* they divided! It's absurd. To be divided into . . . when for a long time humankind has faced just one common problem. It's like people lined up to see the doctor, boasting of their diseases. Whose hurts worst. But man cannot be stopped, even though he will understand all. Should he believe in the Second Coming, perhaps? A long time ago, someone did toxic-poisoning experiments on bacteria in an overpopulated habitat, he constructed mathematical curves, and mathematically they coincided with the arms race after the Second World War . . . Asymptotically approaching universal perdition. The comparison between intelligent man and a bacterium cannot insult the biologist. Reason must still be used with reason . . . But there's a catch: the time factor. Is he late or in time? If late, he's already too late. If in time after all, just barely. Man must push himself even harder to jump onto the last running board . . . Perhaps it has been necessary for him to hurry so rapaciously with all this armament, for the armament is what has brought in its wake all this technical progress, and without progress, man could not solve the problems of survival he faces . . . Pavel Petrovich is right. Now is the time to switch aggression to . . . Only how to switch it? . . . This the doctor does not believe—that man will come to his senses.

And the doctor looks at the only person on the beach, an adolescent boy. The boy dives resolutely into the sea and splashes about like a happy dolphin calf.

Pavel Petrovich has hardly even been gone. As though he kept it buried somewhere nearby.

"Bulletin," he reports, panting. "There are no people because there's a bacillus."

"Vas is das?"

"The sea is polluted. A gigantic discharge of shit."

"We must tell the boy," the doctor says anxiously.

"You think he doesn't know?"

"What about us?"

"We have our own antiseptic." Pavel Petrovich shakes the bottle. "A smaller petard, of course," he states with disappointment.

Gloomily he takes a drink himself and passes the bottle to the doctor. By now there is something familial in his gestures. As though the two men were sitting in the kitchen.

"But how catastrophic!" ("Caataastro-o-ophic," he declaims.) "A fart below, shit above. Imagine how it's all going to blow up someday!"

The doctor stares dimly into the marine distance.

"Let me explain. You yourself got me scared that the hydrogen sulfide was all the way up. Hydrogen sulfide is the same as a fart. And a fart burns. Didn't you ever set one on fire?"

"You mean everyone did it?" the doctor asks in surprise.

"The whole sea will flame up at once, can you imagine? Whaaat a torch that will be! A pillar of fiiire—that's what it will be."

The doctor giggles. " 'The dark blue sea is burning bright, / From the sea the whale takes flight.' "

"Who wrote that?" Pavel Petrovich says, suddenly jealous. "You?"

"Grandpa Chukovsky."

"Wise. Deep. So he, too, foresaw."

"It's for children."

"Who else! You can't explain this to adults. They've already failed to understand. Do you know what we're all going to die of?"

This is spoken so meaningfully that the doctor decides not to answer. He waits.

"We're going to drown in our own crap!" Pavel Petrovich endures a pause. "And do you know why we're going to drown?"

"Because we *are* crap?" the doctor says gleefully.

"Wrong! You're a misanthrope, Doctor Doctorovich! You've grown quite antisocial there at home in Germany. People may not be quite such turds as you think."

"What, even bigger?"

"Why, no, my friend. Wrong again. For the time being, smaller. We won't even have time to develop that far. We'll drown in it because we don't know how to use it."

"In principle, it's hard to disagree with your metaphor."

"This isn't a metaphor. Let me explain. What is soil?"

"So you mean fertilizers," Doctor D. says, disappointed.

"Let me amplify. What is coal? You're silent. Then what is oil?"

"That's a correct series. I understand you. Except that the

crap we have nowadays is something else. The crap we have now-adays is not shit. It's chemical, imperishable. The littoral zone is the gills of the sea. It no longer breathes—the surf has wrapped this zone in such a quantity of plastic."

"That, too," Pavel Petrovich says. "We have to create a pig. Before it's too late."

They have another small drink, and Pavel Petrovich initiates the doctor into certain details of his plan for transforming the world.

"As you realize, the pig here is meant not in the literal—although why not? also in the literal sense of the word. It's a prototype and symbol. The logo, so to speak, of the project. Project Pig: Retrofitting the World. Sound good?"

"Sounds good!" Doctor D. joins in enthusiastically.

"First of all . . . I don't know what's the first of all, because everything's first of all. Perhaps the hardest thing is to choose what's first of all. That will be our firstmost problem, Doctor: where to begin. But that comes later . . . This won't be easy without a half liter—this won't make sense without God. It's harder to prove that He doesn't exist than that He does. The act of Creation is as prov-able as a crime. The Creator is caught red-handed, snared at every step. Otherwise, how will you explain the constant ruptures in the chain of evolution, the disappearance of the links that you scientists need in your research? Each time, after all, the key item is the very one missing: logically, here's where it should be, but it has vanished somewhere. Catastrophes, you say? But why did they happen at the very point you have marked? Yes, exactly: the whole thing is crudely basted together, it barely holds. And lo, the thread is alive! And someone sewed it! What has to be created is not the crystal lattice but the atom, not life but water, not the elephant but the living cell. And then evolution will suffice, at least up to man. Man can also be produced from the monkey, but in that case it's hard to make man the sole recipient of virginity—merely for the sake of the idea of original sin and immaculate conception. The German is sly. He invented the monkey. But then he had to invent, not man, but virginity! The Lord hung padlocks on the very places where one thing didn't tally with another. Which means He was *present*, He was *meddling* in his own laws. He is always there as a *lawbreaker*. And you wrack your brains over the secrets of the universe. Wherever there's a secret, there's a lock. A divine secret! And we try to pick the lock. Our knowledge has become a jimmy, and we're forcing the very locks with which Creation was locked against us, for your own good. We are all imperialists, colonizers. Not America, not Russia, the human species itself is the colonizer of Creation. By the way, man's calling was to be His Pig. To pick up, clean up, eat up . . .''

Doctor D. brightens. "Bravo!" he says, rubbing his hands.

"And to admire! To admire the work of His hands!"

"To admire . . . perhaps." The doctor is on the point of agreeing, when an idea strikes him. "But do you know which is the most ancient surviving profession on earth? If you're speaking of human callings—in Skovoroda's terms?"

"Hunter, probably. Fisherman?"

"No. Museum worker!" Doctor D. throws Pavel Petrovich a triumphant look.

"Well, yes, he deals with antiquities . . ." Pavel Petrovich finds himself somewhat muddled, to which he is unaccustomed.

"All right, I'll give you a hint. What is man's most ancient tool?"

"The stick. Warrior! Warrior is the most ancient profession."

"All animals fight. Give the stick back to Engels. Even a monkey knows how to use a stick. Man's very first tool . . ."

"Well?!"

"All right, I'll give you another hint. What is the first garment?"

"An animal skin."

"An animal skin . . ." Doctor D. scratches his nose distractedly. "Correct, I guess. I asked the question wrong. What's the first garment in a more modern sense, down to this day? . . . That's wrong . . . What part of his clothing? . . . What cut, model, pattern? . . . Pah! Let me have a drink."

"Oh, don't torture yourself, Doctor Doctorovich. Tell me and be done with it."

"Tell you!" Doctor D. is childishly hurt. "That's no fun. Here! What first garment did man put on, not from cold, or from the rain, or . . . Damn it, why put clothes on at all?!"

"A loincloth!"

"Yes. And why?"

"Wonderful!" Pavel Petrovich says gleefully. "From shame. Not from cold, but from shame! To hide the privy parts. What did I tell you!"

"But that's *not* what it's for! What you said about chastity was interesting, but I'm going to double-check. It may be found in some other animal. But chastity wasn't the reason for the loincloth, not at all."

"Well, all right, but what does your museum have to do with this?"

"Correct. The museum and the loincloth. Do you see the link? No? Now you owe me a bottle."

"But we didn't have a bet." Pavel Petrovich appears to be losing his temper.

"All right. Man's first calling was gatherer. Roots, nuts . . . And the first tool he himself invented—which became the loincloth—was the pocket! In his passion for collecting, man's most ancient instinct."

"Oh! I'm a fool, a fool!"

"Made a monkey of you, didn't I?"

"The pocket, I agree. I'll get even with you for this. This is easy, getting something from your professional reading and then torturing a person."

"I didn't get it from my reading!"

"What, you thought of it yourself?"

"I did. I was collecting amber on the shore at home and thought of it. When I was stuffing the amber into my swimming trunks."

"My compliments. Then I owe you a bottle. Although . . . Let's take it further. If the first garment is the pocket, then what's even earlier than the pocket?"

"That's the stick, now."

Pavel Petrovich cannot hide his glee. "Don't take it away from Engels. I returned it to him forever. Well? It's your own idea! How did he tie the pocket on? . . . A knot! When the monkey thought to tie knots—that's when he became man. Now take it further. You answer me, now. And again, for a bottle. A question no harder than yours. And again, my own discovery. When I worked part-time at a furniture store, moving furniture, I always wondered, how did man invent such inconvenient things? So. Tell me, what was the first furniture, from which everything originated?"

"A chair? More likely, a stool?"

"No-o."

"A bed? More likely, a hammock?"

"No-o."

"What do you *mean!*" Doctor D. is incensed. "Why, as soon as man stood up on two legs, his backbone got tired. Osteochondrosis is an atavistic disease, by the way; did you know? So he sat down, on a stone."

"A stone," Pavel Petrovich says, "is not a stool. And a tree branch isn't yet a hammock. That way I'll write off your pocket as cheek pouches. No, you tell me, what was the first furniture he *created?*"

"A table?"

"No-o."

"Not a wardrobe!"

"All right, I'll give you a hint. A wardrobe is getting warmer."

Doctor D. sinks into a deep reverie. Table? chair? bed? "There's no other furniture."

"Give up?"

"Yes."

Pavel Petrovich solemnly reveals his secret: "A trunk!"

"Why a trunk?"

"To hide your nuts and roots! The trunk is the proto-furniture.

Everything comes from it. Sit, and it's a bench. Lie down—a bed.
Put a cloth on it—a table. Stand it on end—a wardrobe."

"Hang a lock on it—a god," the doctor says sarcastically.

"Now don't get all upset. We're quits. I don't owe you, and
you don't owe me."

"What are you talking about?"

"I say, I won back the bottle. And you needn't speak ironically
of locks. Our job now is to mend them."

"But who's going to do it?"

"The military-industrial complex! You yourself mention the
atomic bomb. What's left for them to do now? All these missiles
and planes will become scrap metal, matter expended in vain. They
already have, the military and the people just don't know it yet.
What has always brought technical progress in its wake? War. It
will never bring progress again. What to do, then, with the ag-
gressive human genius, where to find an occupation according to
its affinity? Will you ever force the knight to beat his swords into
plowshares, make pots and pans out of his armor? Humankind
doesn't plan to become better. It will soon have no place to hide:
there's going to be a kind of worldwide siphon, through all those
holes in the sky . . . And our military will shift from attack to
defense. They'll busy themselves with inventing the Pig. The idea
of non-polluting manufacture is as alluring in its unattainability
as a flight to Mars. If something's impossible—what more does
genius need? Non-polluting manufacture is just as much of a black
hole as war. That's where we can throw all our money, all our
energy, and all our talent!"

"I wasn't expecting such optimism from such an intelligent
man," Doctor D. says. His face, as he speaks, wears a very happy
expression.

"Nowadays the world has grown so vulgar that a pessimist is
always wise. An optimist is either self-interested or a fool. There
are no people. Only the fucking critics."

"Dear Pavel Petrovich!" Doctor D. is in tears. "Believe me, I
am unspeakably happy! This, may I say, is the first time in my life

that I have found support for everything I have left unspoken . . .
Pavel Petrovich! Allow me to kiss you!" He attempts to lay his
cheek to Pavel Petrovich's lips, but somehow nothing comes of it.
He just barely keeps his balance in this difficult new space and
does not succeed in superposing the two projections. "Allow me to
drink to you!"

"I allooow!" says Pavel Petrovich, pouring for Doctor D. "And
to yourself, my pet, as well."

They clink glasses.

And they set off down the shore, arms around each other,
almost as one man.

". . . And there'll be compulsory military conscription!" Doctor
D. is saying. "The soldiers will carry out alternative service. Plant
and conserve forests! Raise animals, fish, and birds!"

"Lenin we'll bury outside the church pale, like a suicide,"
Pavel Petrovich is saying. "But the mausoleum—no, we won't destroy it, we'll preserve it! We'll sink a deep shaft in it and fence it
with a velvet barrier, like in a theater. People will approach, peer
down into this maw, breathe the sepulchral chill, and remember
the millions murdered. We won't destroy any monuments at all,
not even Kalinin's. We'll bury Dzerzhinsky, too. And again, we'll
sink a shaft under him and drop him in. Vertically. And roll asphalt
on top. Lay out a flower bed. We'll have the world's first underground monument. I make this assertion as a sculptor."

"But all the other monuments," Doctor D. joins in, "all the
boy buglers and girl athletes, the Sverdlovs and Marxes, the Lenins,
Lenins, Lenins . . . and all the Stalins in the courtyards and cellars
. . . and in the Lenin Hills . . . we'll collect them all and cart them
to some one place . . . and make a kind of Disneyland of our own,
for hard currency . . . they'll stand like Chinese soldiers . . . a whole
army was dug up somewhere in the Gobi, not long ago . . . we'll
cart them off to Kara Kum and Kyzyl Kum—"

"No need to insult the desert! I know a better spot. Nothing
will ever grow there anymore. There's a spot like that near Baku,
where they used to extract oil. That's where we'll send them."

"Windmills . . . solar batteries . . ." the doctor babbles.

"And the main thing, my NUALRU Plan! Alcoholization of Russia. National, Universal! The state can't be restored without the rebirth of the people. The people can't exist without beer. They degenerate. Without beer the nation will become totally besotted. What's the sense of combating alcoholism, especially by Bolshevik methods. You can't go against nature. We're a drinking people, we drink anyway. But good God, *what* we drink! And so, a categorical prohibition against all our cheap fruit wines. Vodka, too, to be of the highest purity only. Fine grape wines, of course. Cognacs, for those who like them. And the revival and universal development of brewing! That's the main thing! Revived pubs and taverns— these will be steps on the staircase of civilization. The drunken peasant will beat his woman because the kitchen hasn't been cleaned up, not because he hates his own life. Pubs must become such that daily life is attracted to them, so that we'll have a model of cleanliness and quality, so that we'll be ashamed of the way we look and live! Can you imagine, in the Kremlin, in the office of the General Secretary—our Andropov, God grant him health!—on the wall of his Stalinesque office, a map of our sixth of the earth, encrusted with semiprecious stones (the expense won't break us), and under the stones, lightbulbs. Andropov presses a button on the control panel. A little star lights up somewhere on Kamchatka. 'Congratulations, comrades!' he says. 'Yet another first-class Palace of Beer Culture has opened in the settlement of Klyuchi!' (That's not far from the Avacha volcano, have you ever been there?) 'But don't rest content, comrades,' he says. 'The NUALRU Plan is proceeding at a slow, slow pace! Reactionary forces are resisting its progress, covertly and overtly. In some places they're still diluting the beer, comrades! They don't let the foam settle!' "

Doctor D. purses his lips in disdain. "Do you like Andropov?"

"Well, but the man thinks nationally! He's made vodka less than five rubles again. Old Crankshaft. Have you tried it? It's not the greatest vodka, of course, but it's 4.70. You've got something left over for cheese and the Metro. He's allowed stoves on garden

plots. This is a major matter! He's allowed vendors at the trains
again: potatoes, dill! But the main point is, he's allowed a monastery in Moscow! Beer palaces and monasteries! That's what will
resurrect agriculture! Ecologically safe farms. Small ones, producing ecologically safe food—that's our future! Exports will grow.
Gold will flow. We'll buy up cheap food products from them in
exchange for our expensive ones—and save and save!"

"We ourselves don't eat, you mean?"

"Personally, I'd just as soon the grub didn't exist at all."

"You eat absolutely nothing?"

"You might say that. Except perhaps to be sociable . . ."

"A most interesting case! I was recently told by a colleague
. . . A very talented physician and biologist, incidentally. He's at
some top-secret place, the Laboratory for the Preservation of Lenin,
I think. They have excellent equipment there . . . To make a long
story short, he's busy developing a hangover tablet, for our spies,
probably. So he says that four out of a hundred chronic alcoholics
live into old age without getting hit by a bus or sticking their hands
into pulleys and gears. They fulfill or maybe even overfulfill the
norm and the Plan, they don't commit violations of social order—
except that they absolutely don't snack, they don't eat anything at
all. They contrive to get from pure alcohol everything they need
for physical vitality. Still more surprising, they produce normal
children, on whom the parent's alcoholism has no effect. True,
science so far has not established whether these surprising traits
are hereditary."

"They are," Pavel Petrovich affirms confidently. "I had a
grandfather like that, too. I can't vouch for my great-grandfather."
He scowls suddenly. "So what are you saying, you think I'm an
alcoholic?"

"Good heavens, yes! Such an alcoholic!"

"I am not an alcoholic!" Pavel Petrovich says indignantly.

"You always return," Doctor D. states, "return to the thought,
to the theme, return with a bottle. You're not an alcoholic—you're
the man of the future! In biology, four percent is a gigantic figure!

Far more significant than the remaining ninety-six percent. Because it's already a mutation! And in our age, with mankind half-starving, with food and natural resources short, we can bet on such a mutation. Because a man who, like an automobile, fills up on fuel (incidentally, a fuel far cheaper and more unlimited than gasoline) is exceptionally promising from the standpoint of ecology and economics. These four out of a hundred may prove to have a great future."

"Future!" Pavel Petrovich says darkly.

And they begin to speak of Orwell. Of the unforgettable year 1984. Will Russia, they ask, live to see the year of the future? . . . Here, out of respect for the censorship, I omit their conclusions. Although I can't help observing, for the future, that one of the interlocutors intensely dislikes Orwell, while the other finds in him . . . I name no names.

"Your Lorenz is more convincing," Pavel Petrovich concludes, even more darkly. "In a minute, in a minute! You'll see for yourself."

"I didn't mean to offend you in any way," the doctor says apologetically.

"I didn't mean to distress *you*. I had intended to bypass this . . . But unfortunately we've already arrived. Here, beyond this breakwater . . ."

"What's that?" the doctor asks in a whisper, so that only the *a*'s issue from his lips: "Wha-a-a-a? . . ."

"How do you like that for a monument to the sea?"

"That"—huge, white, shapeless—lies submissively on the shore. The tide has washed it up to the piling of the breakwater.

"This is the third day she's been lying here . . ."

There is a lot of her. A cow is not this large. She is like a whale. She does not shimmer with mother-of-pearl or even walleye white. The light flows around her, forming pools. Sky, sea—the light falling on the cow comes from all around. No one has noticed the time changing—like the weather. White, gray, sunless . . . She has thought of nothing for a long while now.

"This is right at the boundary of two habitats, between two sanatoriums," Pavel Petrovich explains. "The Railroad Ministry's and the Central Trade Union Council's. Or vice versa. So they can't straighten out whose jurisdiction it is. Any fool can tell *whose* jurisdiction it is! Now you see what I meant about the pendulum, what I meant about ni-i-i-ight! . . . Which is dead, which is deader? Time, unstopping? or the life in it, dwindling since birth?! No, *time* is the corpse! It's time that's dead! Like the cow. And the pendulum is not the stride of time—where could it go?—but the boundary of eternal life and eternal death. The pendulum carries us from that life into this death, like a larva; we suffer metamorphoses, and we use them to measure death, like time . . . Explosion and Chaos! That's the reference model, that's the starting point—that's what I've been trying to drive home to you . . ."

But Doctor D. probably does not hear him. He looks about him with a somehow white and deafened stare. His stare is like the cow. He sees the two sanatoriums. He sees a fisherman who has cast his line on the far side of the breakwater—the man's back may be turned, but the cow is just a stone's throw away from him. He sees a flock of daring beach girls, unenthusiastically playing volleyball in a circle. A creature with two legs, no breasts, and a mustache approaches them, and they start playing more gaily.

"My God!" groans Doctor D. "What are they walking on!"

And he sprints into the sedges near the shore . . .

He returns tall, pale, and resolute.

"I know *where.*"

"Then let's go." Pavel Petrovich is not about to argue.

And they abandon the sea. They walk. They no longer have far to go.

But the doctor is extremely unwell.

"Captain, Captain, hold on," Pavel Petrovich hums solicitously, supporting him with his words and by the elbow. "Well, the cow . . . Well, how to comfort you? . . . Would you like me to reveal a state secret to you? The authentic version of *The Knight in the Tiger Skin?* . . . In 1978, just at the very height of the Abkhazian events—which were also classified as secret, by the way—some tourists found that skin. Moreover, along with the knight. Again at the boundary of two habitats: a glacier and a moraine. But there was a fresh wound on the skull. Their instructor happened to be experienced; he forbade any further use of the ice ax and hurried down to report. But this glacier, in turn, was the natural boundary between two regions, one Mingrelian and the other Abkhazian. Who wanted to claim responsibility for the murder of a Russian tourist? The Mingrelians maintained that the body had been found on the Abkhazian side; the Abkhazians, expectably, on the Mingrelian side. The tourist center certified that not one of their Russian tourists had disappeared. Then, of course, the question arose whether he was a Mingrelian or an Abkhaz. If a Mingrelian had murdered an Abkhaz, the Abkhazian side wanted the body. Either to avenge it or to institute proceedings. But the Mingrelian side wasn't sure but what an Abkhaz hadn't murdered a Mingrelian. In that case, let them turn over both the body and the proceedings. Confused as to who was who, they summoned a commission of local history experts: was he a Mingrelian or an Abkhaz? But the knight proved more ancient than the existing administrative and territorial division. The tourists had done a job with their ice ax, but all the same he was very well preserved, in his tiger skin, for back in those days there were still tigers in this locality. The tiger skin, too, was well preserved, as were the tall goatskin hat à la Robinson Crusoe and, most importantly, his weapons: the knife, the javelin, and the arrows with, significantly, bone tips. And no one had murdered anyone! He himself, poor fool, had gotten caught in an avalanche. However, when it turned out that neither side bore any direct criminal liability, the quarrel flared up in an even more basic form. Establishing his ethnic affiliation would mean resolving the ancient 'quarrel of the Slavs among themselves': who was the real native and who was not. While people from Tbilisi were flying in to see him, the knife and the amulet he wore next to his skin disappeared—and a round-the-clock guard, made up of representatives of both sides, was posted. A visiting poet put forward a brilliant idea based on the tall hat, and imparted it secretly to the ear of the chief of the commission. The hypothesis didn't hold water—but the anniversary celebration of the immortal epic was coming up, with UNESCO and the Hall of Columns, and the president didn't risk ignoring a proposition like this. Besides, the body, which had lain there in peace throughout its six or eight thousand years, was now being subjected to contemporary influences for the third day. There was also the matter of protecting the tiger skin from the local history experts. An army helicopter showed up in short order, and the participants were required to sign a non-divulgence statement. An inquest was held in Tbilisi. He would have confessed both that he was Shota and that he was Avtandil—no place to frigging hide. Certainly he would have confessed that he wasn't an Abkhaz. But the trouble was, this was the first man ever to come down to us in such a state of preservation —that is, much more of a world event than any literary jubilee. While a Moscow commission from the Preservation Laboratory at the Mausoleum was flying in, the knight, who was being kept sealed in the central morgue, suffered the disappearance not only of his tiger skin but also—incredibly—of all his male equipage. The scandal was becoming truly international. If we concealed a discovery of this magnitude from the world, we could be purged wholesale from all international associations, including that same UNESCO —not just from a few anthropological associations. Not to mention human rights! It became clear that to preserve him, especially in secret, in his already somewhat spoiled state, would cost our homeland thousands of dollars a day, even if we evacuated him on an emergency basis to Moscow—but didn't lay him next to . . . It would be cheaper to send a special expedition to some place like Switzerland, where we could plant him under a local glacier, and there he would be found by our mountain climbers, preserving for our fatherland the honor of the discovery . . . But this scheme, too, ran into a whole string of technical difficulties, including customs and passport control. And the knight was classified irrevocably, that is, he disappeared, although the investigation of the tiger skin has continued, and some progress in this direction has occurred: a neck amulet was requisitioned, in the form of a stone with a little Stone Age hole. By chance I received the amulet as a gift."

With these words Pavel Petrovich tears his shirt open to expose a chicken god.

"The cord had to be replaced, of course. Would you like me to give it to you?"

"Oh, Lord!" the weary doctor groans. "How stupid everything is. *Stupid, stupid, stupid!*"

"You don't believe me? Take it, take it!" the very kind Pavel Petrovich insists.

"Do you vouch for the authenticity of the hole?"

"Almost. It may prove to be even more ancient."

"The hole? More ancient than the Stone Age?"

The doctor does not believe a single word—in this particular case, wrongly. Pavel Petrovich hints that the interesting organs may have been stolen by the "organs" themselves, the secret police, for another preservation laboratory, also secret, which attends to the sexual health of the leadership apparatus. Apropos, he begins to tell another trustworthy story: how he himself once ended up in a ward in a VIP hospital, in a department of that very kind, he was working as a blaster and a stone caught him right in the . . .

But he no longer has time to tell the story, because they have reached a city—namely, the capital of sunny and hospitable Abkhazia, the city of Sukhum. Their triumph over space is greeted by the municipal brass band, performing "Amur Waves."

"So this is what we mean by 'brass pipes'!" the doctor says in delight. "I've always wondered what that meant. Fire and water I could understand, but what were the brass pipes? And it turns out they're glory! Meaning fanfares. Meaning triumph."

"An extremely doubtful interpretation!" Pavel Petrovich says sullenly.

"There can't be any other," the doctor exults. "Why didn't I guess before!"

"Why can't there be?" Pavel Petrovich says, perking up. "There most certainly can. The expression 'to go through fire, water, and brass pipes' is no metaphor: it's a technical description of a still."

The doctor will gleefully accept the new etymology. Because by now they are getting very close to the Hotel Abkhazia. The snow-white beauty Abkhazia, so felicitously built by Academician Shchusev himself in precisely this, and no other, spot. And there in the Abkhazia, the doctor claims, is his friend and colleague the Ainglishman, an expert on settling monkeys in the West under unsuitable climatic conditions. He has plenty of everything, all kinds of whiskey-shmiskey, gin-and-tonic-shmonic. No *chacha*, though.

But disappointment awaits them. They are not admitted to the hotel. Possibly because of their appearance. True, they haven't been insulted yet, the police haven't been called, they are not admitted simply as unauthorized persons, in keeping with the sign, which says in red and white UNAUTHORIZED PERSONS NOT . . . Happily at this point Dragamashchenka, who is in a dismal mood, and movie director Sersov, who feels marvelous . . .

And all of them are admitted to the hotel unimpeded.

Dragamashchenka has a talk with Doctor D., the director with Pavel Petrovich. The Englishman, for whom Dragamashchenka, as it turns out, bears direct responsibility, has had something awful happen; the director offers Pavel Petrovich a role in his upcoming film. In the night, in a dream but also in reality, the plywood ceiling collapsed on the Englishman. No, he himself was unhurt, he simply couldn't tell whether he was asleep or awake. Because the plywood fell on him along with a rat and the cat who was chasing the rat. He decided that delirium tremens had set in. He demanded immediate deportation. They're so principled, these English. He insisted on it, and was evacuated on an emergency basis—by now with indisputable symptoms of delirium tremens. And as ill luck would have it, Dragamashchenka had just succeeded in arranging, at last, a trip to the monkey settlements for him.

The movie director, at this very moment, is moving into the vacated room.

And no whiskey-shmiskey . . . Pavel Petrovich quickly agrees to the new role in director Sersov's film.

"I know where we'll go," he comforts Doctor D. "To my friend Semyon." (He pronounces this name somehow strangely, with slow significance: perhaps Simeon, perhaps Simyon.) "I didn't expect to meet him here. Suddenly I looked—and there he was!"

But it turns out this isn't so close. It's rather far from Sukhum, in the large, spread-out village of Tamysh. They curse the city and discuss the charms of village life. Crime is growing in the cities and there's no use fighting it, because it's a biological factor. Punitive measures are inevitable. Therefore the tribunal will exist for a while longer, after they have transformed mankind, but capital punishment will gradually be replaced by mere exile to the cities, which will also fulfill their useful function of garbage pits. The filtration and purification of *the all* will be performed in them, and the city will at last find its natural purpose. The *city* will become the Great Pig of the Future!

But this will not be soon . . . And Tamysh turns out to be far away.

"Some believe, and some do not believe . . ." Pavel Petrovich is coated with dust, as if with fur: his eyebrows, his stubbly beard, even his hands. "Some overthrow an idol, and some create one for themselves. But I . . . I delight in the Lord! I am delighted by Him Himself! And not only as the Creator . . . That, of course, passes understanding, how beautifully He produced all this. What delights me in Him is something else . . ."

Wearily they trudge along the endless highway. Doctor D. plods uncomplainingly, a little behind, as if on a leash. Peers over HIS shoulder. Inspects the dust on his hand with surprise.

"Humanity! That's the astonishing thing . . . He bears responsibility for His every mistake. He is *present.* It's such a mistake on man's part to cast Him far away, to a heaven! He's here! We'll never understand this. He sent us His Son as proof—we didn't understand that, either. And if we're a mistake, He has adopted that mistake. He has set us above everything in this world! Above the angels and archangels! Because they're mere creatures, even though of a higher order, while we're His children. You say that Adam is our forefather. No! He, too, is merely God's creature, because he was not His Son. We're grandchildren of Adam, but children of the Lord. And He has been waiting a long time. He needs us. He still hopes. He believes in us. Can you imagine what *faith* He has! But we've lost faith, we believe in anything at all except Him. We proclaim His covenants, commandments, and laws, we threaten ourselves with them. We've scared ourselves with the Lord, as a boss who would judge and punish us. But that's not what He needs from us. He'd like a bit of our faith and love. A bit of answering affection for a father . . . Haven't you noticed that the father is always the least-caressed person in the family? He works and works and works. Or drinks and drinks and drinks. And simply comes to naught, with never a respite. Papa!" Pavel Petrovich lets out a sob. "Forgive me!"

He glances about him. "Well, here we are at our goal," he says, immediately calm. "It won't be long now. I want you to understand where our common mistake lies. Whether you believe or not is of no consequence. You're a man. But He . . . He got blown to bits by His Creation, or by a land mine. He's not above us, He's in us. We and He are one. And what we must do is not bow down before Him, or squirm in self-abasement, or construct a God-man from ourselves, but become Him, Himself." Again he glances about. "And now the cemetery is within sight . . . Just a stone's throw from here."

From the cemetery comes a lament, a moderate one, not loud or heartrending.

They are burying Senyok, Semyon, Simyon, or Simeon. He disappeared, and they missed him only on the third day. They found him in the ruined church—the same one, seventh-century, next to the prison—already stiff, with the inconsolable rat rushing around beside him. He was wearing his red shirt and hugging a big three-liter bottle of *chacha*, which he had stolen from Mama Natella. It is she who weeps so unpremeditatedly, so honestly and steadily: Didn't I pour for him? Wouldn't I have given it to him anyway? . . . He never finished it off—he reached the midpoint. But neither did he part with it. Someone even speaks in favor of burying them together. Then it is decided to use these very leftovers as his funeral repast.

"Remember, Doctor," Pavel Petrovich says sternly. "The hair of the dog that bit you is everything you drank the day before."

The doctor is still refusing—he keeps struggling to get to the neighboring sanatorium. A certain associate . . . you should have seen the way her son looked at me in the morning . . . But the doctor no longer has any willpower.

"Why do you keep tromping like Napoleon!" Pavel Petrovich says, rhythmically knocking his forehead against the lid of the simple coffin.

And Doctor D. breaks down.

"But why are you crying so, Doctor?"

"I pictured the biomass of the worms . . ."

Such was the death of a Russian drifter, the Holy Fool Senyok-Simyon.

And here at the modest funeral repast, over the fresh grave, Pavel Petrovich lost Doctor D. and blacked out. A body on the lawn. Peace. The soul conversing with the body, the body with God. The empty bottle conversing with the grass:

"Want!"

"Here."

III. FIRE

1. The Cat

The question of who I was had become unusually topical.

HE was going downhill—I was suffering a comedown.

The reunion sufficed for about three days. The embraces unclasped. A telephone call told HIM what he was worth, and I concurred. I had extended the autumn, and now winter was all the more wintry. Yet another November anniversary was blowing in through the windows—the sixty-fifth? sixty-sixth? sixty-seventh. The three days became three years, and the three years flew by like three days. My fur coat fell apart on me. I had never realized what comfort cost! Even eyeglasses can wear thin on your nose, like shoe soles—why bemoan your shoes? Cockroaches converged on the apartment. Snot enveloped me like a conflagration, there were handkerchiefs drying on the radiators. I kept waking up from unfrightening, tiresome nightmares, less and less distinguishable from life.

At first I'd be asleep, things would seem to be all right. Doorbell. I answer it. They apologize, they've come to the wrong place. Never mind, it's all right. I go back to bed and lie down. Damnation! I forgot to turn out the hall light. It's beating in under the door. I go to turn it out, and there they are in the kitchen, with a nice cake, having tea. Very peaceable; they explain that seeing as they have the wrong address, and they've come on the train especially for a housewarming, well, either way, they'll do it at my place, and won't I sit down. I say something about well, it's somehow . . . and they say never mind, it's all right, don't go to any trouble. And all of them so round, provincial, unexcitable, bashful-looking, but brazen. Already they're off to answer the doorbell themselves, and it's some more just like them, and again with cakes. I shove them out, and they grow listless, speechless, they topple over, I'm tangled up in them, stuck, more and more frenzied. I toss out a whole landingful of quilted jackets, felt boots, winter caps with earflaps —those caps were no better than floor rags anyway. The minute I lie down again the wardrobe starts to creak, the window vent swings open, sparks shoot from all the cracks, and there's a whiff of smoke. I ought to close the window vent—I no longer have strength to get up. And already there's a quilted jacket crawling in through the window vent, he's muttering, he has lost his cap with earflaps. He bumps into my wardrobe in the corner, and the bust of Napoleon on the wardrobe starts to topple off. I barely catch it to keep it from breaking. I'm stuffing the quilted man back through the window vent; he expanded when he crawled in, and I can't stuff him back. Sparks shower as from a welding torch, Napoleon gleams bronze in their light, but he has empty eye sockets, as in antique statues. How did I come to have a Napoleon? I've never had a Napoleon in all my born days! He's never stood on my wardrobe . . . I toss out the idol, too, after the quilted man, and carefully close the window vent, but outside the door there is already a hullabaloo, a racket, a commotion—they turn on the light and make merry.

Snot was choking me. I would wake in terror, turn on the real light, but in the same room, and reach for my twisted lump of a handkerchief. Cockroaches would dash out of it.

So this is what it means to be a dissident, I would think with a grin. The main thing was not to confuse the initial phases with the final ones. AIDS was coming into style. No resistance. The snuffles turned into a cough, and the cough into diarrhea. The surveillance methods and my persecution mania coincided. The initial symptoms led to random connections, and the random connections to alcoholism. My soul, not having had its hair-of-the-dog, thirsted to confess. It had someone to confess to, but nothing to confess. In one instance you would become a madman, in the other an émigré. I wanted neither. But still, the KGB was better than AIDS, and I mustn't confuse them. My fame was growing.

People kept visiting HIM. Now wenches, now vagabonds. The vagabonds came, literally, straight from the station. Like the ghost in the old joke, I live there—live there! . . . Someone woke me bright and early: straight off the train. Our encounter resembled the encounter of two tomcats in a doorway. Not without dignity. One could hardly find his reflection in the mirror, the other had an eye on his cheek. Not without rules. For example, take off your shoes in the vestibule and follow me across the grubby floor, right into the kitchen. While I pretended to wash, I was actually considering what to do now, passing my unwashed hand over my grizzled stubble with annoyance. The briefcase he had brought was bigger than he was. His entire property, no less. I can date his appearance precisely. The Korean airliner had just been downed; the day before, an international book fair had opened, and I had met with a Swedish publisher. The Swede was from Amnesty International, and his eyes expressed bewilderment, as if I were somehow behaving incorrectly. As if to say I wasn't in prison yet. The last time, too, he had asked insistently how he could help me. I had disappointed him by saying that all I needed was glasses "like the Beatles'." And here I was, sitting across from my uninvited guest in my Swedish glasses.

"Half a million is yours," he said, opening the briefcase.

How simple! I thought delightedly.

At last they were trying to buy me. My pride was put in its place: couldn't they have sent someone a little more convincing?

He took a toothbrush out of his briefcase, and then a whole manuscript. It was in four folders, each of which was in a separate cellophane bag, plus wrapped in a kind of parchment.

"So," I said, taking charge of the situation. "How long were you in prison?"

"Eight years. Almost eight . . ."

"How long did it take you to write this?"

"A year. Almost a year . . ."

"How many pages in it?"

"Eight hundred. Almost. A little less."

"And you want me to read this in a day?"

"But you won't be able to put it down!"

It turns out you don't even have to take charge of the situation, if it's yours to start with. Who has read this? You'll be the first. How did you find me? Through the address bureau. Have you, er, read me? Uh, no, I heard about you by word of mouth. And what makes you think they'll lay a million on you? Oh, at least a million . . .

His naïveté was equaled only by his experience. He had gone to prison when he wasn't even fourteen. It cost me a mental effort to realize that this was who he *was*. That he had been sent by no one but himself.

"Why the parchment?"

"In case it gets thrown in the water. I've thought of everything. I can still set a Guinness record. I can do five thousand deep knee bends. I can't right now, without getting in shape. But I can do two thousand for sure, right in your presence." He squatted down then and there, in his socks.

I surrendered. "Spare me."

And I couldn't put it down . . .

His eye had been shot out, back in his rural childhood, because he refused to kiss a kitten under the tail. He had learned to do deep knee bends in the punishment cell, to keep from freezing to death. He was in love for life with his grade school classmate, Vera, but had dared to declare his love only from prison, after buying a photo from a good-looking cellmate. And he received an affirmative answer to his declaration—when he opened Vera's letter, a snapshot of her buxom older sister fell out. He decided to escape in order to get married. Having learned the regulations, he yelled to the guard, "Do not fire on a juvenile!"—and caught a bullet in the shoulder. He kept on running and felt that his arm had been completely torn off. The wounded arm was on the side without an eye, and he couldn't see it. Then he took hold of it in the other hand and raised it to the other eye as he ran, to make sure . . .

I was perishing—people kept trying to save HIM. She gave him a kitten, Tishka. Her mittens and fur hat were bigger than she was. And Tishka was even smaller than her mittens. I kissed her on her cold fur hat, on her mitten, on Tishka. Hurry!

Someone disturbed us. Who could this be? I wasn't expecting him at all. A man unique on this earth, in his way. Just like me. Parents—they're only half like you, each like his own half. But this man was just like me, like both halves. My brother, then. Although a Georgian. He was a year ahead of me.

He mustn't see her, she mustn't hear him. It was a one-room apartment. I hid her in the wardrobe, just as she was: in her shirt and fur hat. He was continuing to degenerate into a woman. In proof of which he had grown a beard. Women no longer interested him, as a man. For a year now he had been scouring the medical literature. This was a very rare genetic disease, which was why he felt obliged to warn me. So that from now on I could choose the right parents.

That in itself was a long story. Then he disappeared.

She emerged from the wardrobe wearing only her mittens. Her nipples smelled of naphthalene.

Tishka was the one who had it best. He slept on my jumbled manuscripts.

She was leaving. HE managed—scoundrel!—to kiss her hand. Otherwise she would have stuck it back in her mitten.

She forgot her book—or was it my brother's? *The Tin Fleece of Victory.* A translation from the Georgian.

People do write!

The narrative rolled along in flowing, Nobelesque waves. It licked the shore of Colchis. A small, weary detachment, the last remnant of a mighty army. At its head Jason, wearing a "cloak with a raspberry-red lining," no less. Behind him the man who executes every order in silence, as though his tongue had been cut out in captivity. And behind him, the man who does nothing but scratch himself—the "gallinippers" try his patience. Everyone in turn shivers with malaria. Jason alone is smooth-shaven, reflected in his own shield. Another limps at the end—his short and double-edged sword has chafed his neck, and his "loincloth is festering." And now the mute utters his first word. "The Pontus," he says. Short-and-Double-Edged washes his wound in sea water. They build a campfire. Gleams of firelight play in their sunken eyes. The gallinipper victim scratches his broad Ossetian chest. Sparks fly up without reaching the stars, under which inscrutable Hellas sleeps peacefully, forgetting her heroes. From the page came a whiff of the campfire, and my nostrils flared in helpless envy of this ancient-Georgian Greek.

I made haste to be saved before my time was up . . . I made haste to be baptized. That was the thing! Forty years I had waited, like a Grand Prince—but I made haste. And did *not* die then and there. But how could I die. . . . The Eye had not died when they beat him, as a child, on the "plywood" (his chest) with a "bunk" (a rod from the head of an iron bed) . . . How could I die, when I was barely forty, in this most beautiful place on earth . . . except perhaps from happiness. The Motsameta Monastery, whose name, I learned, means "the believers," stood on a kilometer-high precipice above the Kura, and from the precipice one celebrated that kind of world, and a landscape also arrayed by autumn. The farther away, the clearer the air: at the bottom of it, on the bank of the floodplain, people had indeed gathered to celebrate Sunday, they were starting the shish kebab and laying out lavash and greens, and a happy cow who had sneaked up and stolen a lavash was running circles around the meadow like a dog, fleeing her pursuers, and the victims of the theft were even happier than the thief . . .

"I know thy sins," Father Tornike said, not letting me open my mouth at this first confession in my life. "I can imagine . . . And I remit them for thee . . . But do not forget, from this day hence it will be more painful for thee to sin." And he sighed know-

ingly. I was wrong not to believe him! Gaily I spat on Satan in the
form of a scraper and broom, for which space had been found in
a corner of the church. "Pah on Satan!" Father Tornike proclaimed, and all of us, marching in single file with candles in our
hands, joyously complied. It was easy then for me to spit on him!
Dear Gagi, precious Father Tornike . . . It was easy for you to get
your first prison term, by baptizing the Pioneer camp during swimming! The children climbed up on shore, no longer in their red
neckerchiefs . . . "One glass," Gagi used to say, "will do me for a
company of soldiers." He had to use a little more on me, at the
expense of the Pioneer camp and the potential company. Dear Gagi!
Remember me in your prayers . . .

A certain editor, in particular, was saving me. She was at-
tempting to arrange a trip to Tbilisi for me to participate in a
roundtable on "the phenomenon of the Georgian novel." For a
start, I was given a newspaper assignment. To unmask a false hero.
He had become a hero for Afghanistan, but that wasn't enough for
him: now he had saved a drowning man. As a psychological writer,
I was supposed to prove that he hadn't saved anyone; he had simply,
out of inertia, been seeking "the heroic feat for which we always
have room in our lives." For the liberal lady editor, this would be
a permissible way of criticizing the war in Afghanistan.

I disliked her zeal. And I went.

The man sitting before me was very calm. As an experienced
investigator, I had taken a seat with the light behind me so that I
could see all the nuances of his facial expression, and so that he,
accordingly, could not see mine. From the way he grinned, I imagined he had caught on. A glance sufficed him to complete his reconnaissance and concentrate on a chosen target. This, for some
reason, was a loudspeaker. He oriented himself to it. Well, so I was
a psychiatrist and he had a mania. I felt sure the office wasn't
bugged. I followed his glance. For some reason my patient was
disturbed by a cord. It had been pulled from the outlet and was
dangling somewhat short of the floor. Besides, it was tied in a knot.
The knot had not been tightened. Well, but it was quite impossible

to eavesdrop through that cord! The mere fact that the major had been summoned to talk to me and I was receiving him in an office—even though not my own (but how could he know it wasn't mine?)—made me (a private, untrained, unfit for front-line service) his . . . how do they put it? . . . "junior in rank, but senior in position." This cheered the outcast in me. My junior-in-position had accordingly remained silent and standing. I invited him to sit down and tell me the whole story. "But I didn't plan on saving him!" the major began, not so much with irritation as with genial annoyance. "The thing of it is, it just so happened, the night before, I was reading this book by, sorry, mental lapse here, can't think of the author. Book about one of us. Assistant company commander, he's a hero, and his young lady is this nurse. Well, so what she does is, she saves this drowned man. Mouth-to-mouth. I remembered. I never meant to tell anyone. But Monday morning at the Academy they're talking, how was everyone's weekend, and they knew I'd planned to go on a fishing trip. So I said, Some fucking —pardon me—trip, when I had to dream his horsy teeth all last night. I mean, you know—mouth-to-mouth on somebody. So this fellow in my class, he writes it up in the wall newspaper. I mean, he wrote it up, but the garrison newspaper reprinted it. If I hadn't've read it in that book, about the nurse, the mouth-to-mouth, I wouldn't've dreamed his horsy teeth. I never planned on being a soldier. Thought about it a lot, of course. I was working at the factory, already had my five rating. So I get the notice, I'm called up: Go to training school. Well, so I went. Stopped by the plant recently—well, they all remember me, haven't forgotten, and we had a drink, of course, I brought it with me specially. I even felt homesick for the plant. Well, can't go back now, my qualification's wrong, and anyhow I'm close to retirement. Soon as I finished training I got this urgent call and they put me on a plane. Where to or why, nobody knew. Then the helicopter, and an assault landing. So from my very first day, my first night. Back home they wrote that it started the twenty-first. Actually it was the twentieth. But that's just you I'm telling, in secret. Don't go and print it. We were the first to break into the palace. I can still see it, this blue room, all done in silk. But already empty. Just the one photo album lying on the floor. I looked at it for a minute. All these pictures of his family. Beautiful woman! You know, I'll tell you honestly, in the beginning I wasn't scared at all, it was even interesting. But then after I got hit the first time, I climbed into my armor and wouldn't come out. Our Deputy Political Officer—nothing but praise for him, outstanding fellow—he says to me, Come on out of your armor (my tank, that is) or you'll sit there forever. Well, I got hold of myself, and then I didn't mind. You go on reconnaissance and you can't shoot. You've got one combat knife for the whole squad, can you believe—the master sergeant issued them under receipt. And a forty-kilo walkie-talkie on your back. Your back's all black and blue, sore as hell. But it's necessary, so that they don't notice you. You meet up with some Afghan, you have to finish him on the spot, so that he doesn't report. Well, but since you can't shoot, you place the knife to his ear and pound it, so that it goes ear to ear. Main thing is, keep it quiet. Well, there was this one fellow they didn't kill, they loaded the walkie-talkie on him, like a donkey. He carried it the whole way. Then of course they liquidated him, what can you do. No great satisfaction in it. That Deputy Political Officer, he got promoted, and they sent a new one. Complete fool, still green. We crawled to their lookout—quietly, we had our feet wrapped. I stuck my head up: two men with rifles, by the campfire. I chose which to rush first, and I waved for him to go around the other side and take out the other fellow himself, and he says, 'What?' But I'd already rushed mine, and the other one heard and comes at me with his rifle butt. Took off half my ear. But I finished mine anyway, and the DPO, good man after all, croaked that one from behind. Was I hungry! And they'd just been eating a big flat bread. I broke it in half. It was spattered with brains, but this was a dark night, so I gave the spattered half to the DPO and kept the dry half myself. Didn't matter, he never noticed. Then we both crawled around till morning: I'd lost my bolt when I swung my rifle butt. Never did find it. Later I substituted a Chinese bolt, it fitted, the fellows fixed the serial number for me."

"So they gave you a Hero Star for this?" I asked.

"Nah, not for this, and besides they didn't give it to me, just recommended me. You needed 160 killed, and I only had 129. My DPO, the one I told you about before, filled out the recommendation for the Hero, and he rounded the numbers up. He laughed. Doesn't matter, he says, the Motherland will forgive. But there was two of us, and one star. They gave me the Red Banner of Combat. Now, your editor, she didn't believe it that I resuscitated a drowned man. I noticed that, by the way—he was already totally drowned. The thing of it is, I'm casting my line, I look and there's a sort of a pink bubble on the water. Turns out to be his back. He'd surfaced with his hump up, like a fishing float. Well, so I pull him out—his back's dry, warm from the sun, but the rest of him is cold. I called, Who knows how to pump him out? And at first they'd all crowded round, but soon as I called they all scattered: Get an ambulance. Sure, an ambulance! I tried artificial respiration, didn't properly know how. No luck! Now I remembered about the nurse, in the book. But the fellow must have been good and drunk. So I'm doing all this mouth-to-mouth with the puke. Two hours I struggled over him. Couldn't believe it myself when he came to. At that point the ambulance pulls up. They start trying to find out who and what, but I'd had it up to here, I lit out the back way. Reeled in my lines. Some fishing trip! Our correspondent, now, the only thing I blabbed to him was how I had the fellow's horsy teeth haunting me all night. No big deal. But he wrote it up. You ought to write about our orphanages instead. Such poverty, why, it's terrible! I gave a talk at one of them, free, and later, can you believe it, after my talk, they stood in line to . . . just to . . . touch my hand—they'd walk away and there's the next one . . ." The major turned aside.

To wipe a tear, I thought, but he stood up. "Pardon me," he said, and went to the loudspeaker. He undid the knot in the cord and sat down again, comforted: now there was order. "Well, that's

it," he said. "I haven't told you anything unusual. Anything secret.
Only the date—that the whole thing started a day earlier than
reported . . . but it's not that much of a secret."

We left together. I glanced with scorn at the editor waiting for
us, and silently we walked right past her. Walked right past and
on out to the street—waiting there for me all this time, and waiting
there still, was good old Dryunya, my best buddy, a saintly man.
It was his principle to drink as his hair-of-the-dog the same thing
he'd drunk the day before, in the same amount and with the same
man. The three of us went around the corner, out to the boulevards,
to a Nadenka. At that hour they were still serving. We had one
beer apiece, and then Dryunya argued over who would pay for
whom. The major paid, and we exchanged phone numbers.

Life itself was setting me an example: the Eye, Jason, the
Afghan . . . One had to struggle with himself to make sure that
what he saw before him was indeed what it seemed, and not what
it was. One had to struggle! Make positive efforts! Regardless of
whether they could become reality. I responded. I hired myself out
to chauffeur a certain monk around the country roads of Vladimir
Province. I left the cat in the care of my neighbor the singer. We
inspected the abomination of desolation of ruined churches, and
were desolated. The monk was a venerable thirty years old. His
wisdom and maturity were equaled only by his inexperience. He
was old enough to be my father, young enough to be my son. On
the lenslike Vladimir meadows he gamboled like a calf, his cassock
collecting all the pollen, and there were more flowers than the eye
could see . . . I accompanied him in silence. He felt like asking
me—but couldn't. He wanted me to ask him—I don't know what.
"You see," I said at last, plucking up my courage, "I believe in the
Creator, I believe in Christ, I believe in the Virgin Mary. But there's
no way I can believe in the devil, that he actually exists . . ." "Then
what *do* you believe in!" the monk said indignantly. "Why, the air
is swarming with them!" He gestured expressively, his arms de-
scribing a wide circle, and strode away from me in wide paces
across the meadow. He was soon distant, and suddenly, for the first

time, I noticed that he in no way perverted the not-yet-lost beauty of the Vladimir meadow! A monk—that's the man of the landscape! Moved, I gazed after his small pyramid. It harmonized easily with the landscape: under the cassock, you couldn't see that he had two legs . . . Could that really be the whole problem?! "Sanctified be thy chariot!" he said when we arrived safely. The automobile was sanctified, and I caught a whiff of smoke and burning, this time from none other than me, when I climbed in to drive home . . .

A new guest was already waiting for me by the house. In his little Zaporozhets coupe. Straight from Murmansk.

"We have enough grief without you not drinking," Dryunya told the guest from Murmansk. But the man didn't drink and didn't smoke. And also—as we gradually guessed. Not what you might think in such a case, but just the reverse. Snow-white collar, razor-sharp crease in his trousers, loose pullover hanging from his shoulders, very neat crew cut with glints of gray. Thin, well built, supple. And shaved! His skin . . . a sort of special skin, a generation younger than he was. He spouted Kuzmin by heart. How had he climbed out of his Zaporozhets looking like this? . . . If he didn't drink, he could at least make a quick trip to get a bottle. Oh, he didn't know the city. Dryunya readily volunteered to show him. Oh, he didn't have room in the car: it was packed solid with household belongings, and he had even removed the front seat. We didn't believe him and went out to look. Indeed, the whole car was crammed with books and ironed shirts. " 'Everything I own I cart with me'?" I asked. He indulged my joke. It turned out he was a drifter, turned out he was homeless. He had the car, it seemed, but no residence permit. He had spent the summer drifting. Toward winter he had set out for southern climes, via Moscow, naturally, via me, naturally. A slew of people arrived, Dryunya's family, the Great Gatsby's guests, Rabbit's friends and relations: U.B., a retired KGB colonel, Ustin Benyaminovich, simultaneously a grandfather and grandson (his grandmother was still alive enough to idolize him). Einstein, an Armenian, raw-vegetarian, and janitor, always good for a debate

on the topic, Is vodka a raw foodstuff? And the singing Saltykov
himself, a Saltykov from the sadistic Saltychikha's line, not from
the ones who were satirists and Shchedrins. He walks right in,
singing loudly:

> *Thus stone by stone, brick by brick,*
> *We pulled that factory down! . . .*

Then a young damsel arrived to save me from another who
had arrived just the moment before. Not joining in our party, the
guest from Murmansk led me out of the kitchen into the other room
for a conversation alone together, and—it wasn't immediately what
everyone immediately thought, but to get me to read, in his presence, then and there, his manuscript. Granted, not a large one. We
concurred in our assessment of Nabokov. There I gave him his due.
But in my assessment of his text I was a disappointment, didn't
pass his examination, so to speak. The tête-à-tête was a failure.
And he couldn't hide a slight grimace of disgust when he once again
inhaled all our stink. The women were crying on Saltykov's
shoulder.

> *To water do not speak of love!*
> *She cares not for us, she runs through the pipes . . .*

Water—that was the women themselves, of course. Never mind
about the pipes.

Zyablikov, too, showed up, a Pavel Petrovich in his own way,
a rare guest—and immediately provided drinks all around. He had
smoked all the grass of the Buddhists, drunk all the church wine
of the Orthodox, and now he outdid himself as a psychic.

And in truth, his power of persuasion was colossal. "Absolutely, you have a bug here somewhere. I smell it . . ." Cockroaches,
yes, but I prided myself on not having bedbugs. "Come on, you
know what I mean!" The bug proved to be an eavesdropping device.
Zyablikov half closed his eyes and began making passes with his

hands. "Here," he determined, pointing to the ventilation grille. "Know what you should do?" I still didn't know. "Rip off the grille . . . Do you have any kind of lance?" Well, a poker. "Rip off the grille," he insisted. "Take the poker and *go at it . . .*" He made a savage face. "Crash! Run it through!" He plunged an invisible lance into it and suddenly looked like St. George the Dragon Slayer. There was even something Georgian about his ordinary, snub-nosed face. Dryunya performed the whole procedure, gesture for gesture. They hadn't found the poker—a fragment of my only mop was left sticking out of the mutilated vent.

The girls, without ever choosing, departed with Saltykov and Zyablikov, in complete harmony. And I was left alone with Dryunya, as always. He instantly took it upon himself to propose toasts, and this he did for a long time. I endured it, because he was claiming that I was a genius, and it was hard to outargue him . . . "Our whole misfortune," he sighed, "is that we have absolutely no Salieris!" "Sure," said the girl who had returned after all, "but we have a shitload of Mozarts." We had a good laugh.

HE was offensive—I was offended. The girl proved to be a lady, an ex-wife. Dryunya was a knight. He couldn't bear to see her treated this way. "And what do you have in your briefcase? What's in it? Nothing. Your lousy briefcase is empty!" Anger scalded me. And it was no longer Dryunya who dared to say such a thing to me, but Sergunya, our good old mutual friend.

HE tore Sergunya's shirt and crowned Dryunya with a bowl of lump sugar. They both danced around in a Cassius Clay stance, but they spared the national treasure, never did land a punch. The lump sugar proved to be sharp. Badly scratched and unable to keep his feet, Dryunya was escorted out by the lady, who now scorned me.

At last, I was left alone. Alone, alone! Alone in all the universe! Abandoned, unneeded by anyone . . . I had done it, achieved what I was trying to achieve. "What we fought for has been our undoing." How it all stank!

I went into the bathroom to wash away the shame . . . So this was why it stank! In the washbasin lay Dryunya's huge turd—he had closeted himself to wash the lump-sugar wounds that I had inflicted. "But so uncomfortable!" I exclaimed in delight. "Up high! on one leg! and the toilet right there!"

This was indeed a catharsis, in the sense of a purging. While I was cleaning all this up, it turned my stomach. Oh, God!

And someone rubbed against my leg.

Tishka! Little Tishka! . . . My darling! You're all I have . . . How could I forget you, what a prick I am! But you're hungry! Coming, coming, my pet . . .

This was what I needed. Just what I needed! I needed to feed someone. How simple. I simply had to feed someone. And none of your high-flown . . .

An old man's simple, quiet, deliberate, solitary movements. Take fish out of freezer. Run hot water. Put fish under water. Coming, coming, be patient . . . You can't eat it raw, it has to be cooked just a little . . . Here.

My wife had left, my family had returned.

This was good, this was terrific. Good not to be alone in bed! A book, a cat. No complications. Purr, purr . . . What's that little motor you've got there, where is it housed in you? . . . *"The men still slept in the postures of yesterday's weariness . . . The sleep of the dead. As though they, too, had been overtaken by the enemy's sword and spear. As though they, too, had not departed from yesterday's field of slaughter. Jason began to moan and swing his head like a bull, trying to shake from his eye sockets the sight of the lost battle. Red. All was red. Red waves under his eyelids. Jason started down to the sea. The morning dew washed yesterday's dust from his sandals. The sea, too, was blood. The Pontus Euxinus rolled its dawn-pink waves. A sea of blood!"*

Bloody foolishness!

Decisively I put out the light. Tishka rumbled on my exhausted breast. Patches of light from the Kazan Railroad wandered across the ceiling, diesel engines lowed to each other, and the dispatcher's mild-mannered obscenity, amplified by a megaphone, floated freely over the sleeping capital: "Bastard, where do you think you're going?"

I was happy. I slept.

And woke at cockcrow. I was frightened. Whence a rooster? And where was I?

When a church bell pealed, I felt calmer. Could it be? Already?

But Tishka's heroic snore resounded on my breast. He was decidedly alive. And if he was alive, I, too, wasn't dead. Most likely a decree had come out, and I hadn't even noticed that it was permissible to ring the bell once, in one church, on major holidays. Must be Andropov's doing. They said he had even permitted a monastery. He had permitted a lot of things, though. It was all right now to sell potatoes and dill again, over there at the train, like after the war. And he had permitted people to set up a stove in the garden shed. And he had fitted vodka back into the five-ruble note . . . He might even be a good man, at heart . . . But why was he doing this to me? Perhaps, while he was at it, he had also permitted roosters to be raised on balconies?

Or perhaps, finally, all was over. No Korean airliner, no Afghan . . . Church bells pealing, cocks crowing.

But none of this was true. Someone had been battering at the door for a long time.

Tishka meowed resentfully at the way I jumped up. My heart pounded in the unwarranted hope that this time it was she. The woman, the only one, the sixth, who had gone away forever. "Come on, Tishka," I even said, "let's go meet the mistress."

At first I saw only roses. All covered with drops of morning dew, it seemed. Opalescent, not yet open—I hadn't encountered such a luxuriant bouquet for a long time. The bouquet entered headlong, as if being chased. "You don't remember me, but we've met . . ." I was flattered. To an author, after all, roses are no joke. They are dear, both precious and pricey. To which of those bastards, those party secretaries and chief editors, would some unknown young woman bring roses! This was the reward of disgrace. Roses for my withered laurels . . . Then and there, she asked to put them in water. "Of course, of course! Such . . . roses!" I went into a flurry, tearing off the cellophane. She took the bouquet, almost snatched it. I yielded with some bewilderment. Well, yes, women always know best how to deal with roses . . . Now she'll start peeling the stems, she'll ask for sugar, a hammer, aspirin, a vase, coffee, vodka, cotton, a bathrobe, she'll go into the bathroom . . . She went into the bathroom, carefully straightening the cellophane on the bouquet, and ran water into the washbasin. The sight of the rose-filled washbasin overwhelmed me.

I can't stand people who put their faces too close to mine. As though they were a goblet. Either they're nearsighted, or they're sure they're irresistible, or they have bad breath. My admirer proved to be a writer; she had brought her manuscript, I was right on her way to the station, she was going to meet (she didn't say whom), but not for another hour, and she had decided to bring it by. Even Tishka she put too close to her face. I took both Tishka and the manuscript away from her and hinted that she would be late. She was unembarrassed by this—but embarrassed by my quite insane stare, meeting hers in the mirror over the washbasin. Had she only known that this was laughter! I watched the water run off the cut stems into the *clean* washbasin. Two items—evening and morning—resonated together in it. A rhymed couplet. Good thing there was a space between the lines. What would have happened if I had flopped onto my cot just as I was, without washing, which as a rule . . .

Shit and roses! *Shit and Roses* . . . How's that for a novel! And all to the music of Vivaldi. Just now it was being marvelously sung by my neighbor Victoria. This was the only recording I had, and I listened to it endlessly. Just the day before, it had been involved in this incident . . .

An American professor named Murphy (which proved, as always, to be his first name, not his last) had called to say that he wanted to talk and had a package for me. Over the phone he spoke the word "package" in a whisper. The package proved to be a stereo system sent by my best friend Y., who had recently emigrated

there. Murphy was very handsome. He could not conceal his surprise at the way I lived, although I had spent three hours tidying
up before he arrived. He moved warily, trying to avoid touching
anything, as though even the walls were contagious. Even his chair
he put in the middle of the room so as not to touch anything. I
glanced carelessly at the stereo and thanked him, but he insisted
on demonstrating how it worked, as though he weren't so much
delivering the merchandise as selling it. He even seemed offended
that I didn't properly appreciate the significance of the gift, which
was, strictly speaking, from him. And I suppose I felt hurt that the
professor was preoccupied with something other than his immediate
task—that is, the study of my writing. Like a professional com-
mercial traveler, he pulled a cassette out of his pocket. This was a
good singer, not Joan Baez but another woman, and the system
gave excellent sound. The American talked in a flat, artificial Russian voice, like a German. He somehow wanted to be sure that he
had delivered this specific apparatus to me. He wanted to be sure
that I understood the functions of the buttons. He was making quite
an effort to keep from looking now at my scattered manuscript,
now at my walked-down shoe. A man—a Russian writer carrying
on the tradition, he had been told—whose things lay scattered on
the floor, who didn't have a corkscrew handy and who knocked
the cork out with a blow of his hand, could, of course, put equipment to the wrong use. No, he didn't drink or smoke at all, Professor
Murphy didn't; he still had another appointment . . . But I detained
him anyway. Something about this—the way he sat spang in the
middle of the room, with his feet placed as if in a tub, his broad
shoulders not touching my air—goaded me to action. I thanked
him once again, in more detail, and praised the sound. "But," I
said, "I have nothing to compare it with, I have just one cassette
that I know the sound of." "One cassette?" A certain bewilderment
in his voice gratified me. I knew what I was doing. "Yes," I said
carelessly, "I have a neighbor here who sings." "Sings? . . ." Oh,
his disbelief suited me perfectly! I well remembered, would remember all my life, the impression made by that first sound, that

sound heard for the first time . . . But that's a separate story. Right now this Murphy could not imagine what awaited him. Even recently, after all, I had been just as ignorant . . . Carelessly I handed him the worn cassette (without a box). He inserted it carefully, preserving his almost annoyed expression.

Oh, there are wonderful singers, of course. But once in a lifetime comes the ecstasy of an encounter with deity! The cassette opened with a Vivaldi aria.

No question, my overseas friend Y. had sent me an excellent stereo. Murphy—he immediately became somehow dearer and closer to me—never did have time to change his expression. Caught by surprise, his countenance froze in annoyance. This was exactly what the great blind bard intended . . . by the way, about the blind man . . . but about him, too, later. Yes, exactly, you had to lash yourself to the mast to keep from flying after the voice. Odysseus, the Sirens, afterward came Schubert. Murphy drew breath. He looked about the room in which he found himself. "A neighbor??" You should have heard him. With what palazzi, with what Nices, such as he would never frequent, had he supplied the image of this voice? "Why, yes," I said casually, "one floor up. Oh, you know . . . salt, matches . . ." "A neighbor!" he exclaimed, hastily collecting his things and indignant at my lie, which was the pure truth. I exulted. "The Soviets have their own pride."

Should I now tell about how this happened to me, too, for the first time? About her guide, a provincial music lover who suddenly proved to be blind? About the three people sitting in the auditorium? No, another time.

And yet, now. One must render the angels their due, not the devils. People were trying to save HIM—I was trying to save my soul.

I could understand Murphy. We do have these gaps . . . If he'd never heard of the person, what was she worth? The state of being well informed is always limited to a terminal knowledge of what's best. She had phoned me at a bad time on that occasion, too. I was in no mood for her and her concert. But her voice over the telephone was so powerful! I got my car started and drove her, listening, along the way, as she complained about all these club concerts: They'll be doing well to have three people there! . . . I had had a presentiment of all this vocal pathos. A worshipper of hers, who rode with us to the concert, intensified my foreboding. He was from the provinces, a church watchman. Sometimes he tore himself away to serve his musical idol as well . . . We entered a dilapidated Palace of Culture by the back way. After walking down corridors past mottoes and Outstanding Workers, we approached the greenroom. The artist's expression became aloof and majestic. We could accompany her no longer: she must prepare herself. We, too, decided to prepare ourselves and began to look for the toilet. Now a certain eccentricity in her knight's movements put me on guard . . . First he bumped into a windowsill, then into a trash can. Was he drunk, or what? Then he headed straight for the women's toilet, and I barely succeeded in stopping him. He was blind! That was the problem! He wasn't her guide, she was his. And here in the men's, the correct, john, as I was going, I heard . . . "What's that?" I asked with terror and ecstasy. "That? Victoria!" the blind man said with pride. All the might of heaven pierced the gray walls— and this was only a warm-up . . .

But even the angels won't save me!

Because just as poor Murphy exits—two men enter. With a shared briefcase. Provincials, the same kind, straight from the station. But nice and clean. In worn-down shoes and crooked neckties. They had shaved in the station toilet.

The brothers Goncourt? Ilf and Petrov? I thought with a grin, as they looked for the best place to put down their briefcase. They turned out to be physicists, inventors. A serious conversation took place. One man seemed to be the senior in rank, an adjunct major. He did the talking. The other was more junior, a privatdocent as it were, a lieutenant- or sergeant-docent. He was saying less and less, nodding expressively, glancing at the briefcase, where they probably had drawings of an invention . . . The story, briefly, was this. Yes, they worked at a secret laboratory. They did not conceal

from me that it was KGB. They expressed curiosity, in turn, about
my education, ascertained that I was not a physicist, and explained
that they couldn't really explain to me the essence of their discovery,
which was destined to overturn the foundations, but the principle
was that they were just on the verge of creating a psychogenic
weapon, and as a matter of fact they already had a working
model—an irradiator. Admittedly a weak one, so far. "A hyperboloid?" I asked. They did not catch my irony, but grinned wryly:
Everyone's hooked on science fiction, and so are you. Engineer
Garin, Engineer Garin! . . . But this was in earnest, this was very
dangerous, this thing they were now telling me about in great trust
and secrecy. And the minute they had realized the danger, they
had tried to get out of the laboratory. You yourself understand how
difficult this is, to get out of the system. They were being pursued.
They had been forced to hide. No, they were sure no one was tailing
them at the moment: I could believe them: after all, they did have
some experience (a bitter smile) in how to distinguish a gumshoe
from a shadow. How? You can tell right off. Here they began to
explain the difference to me, in a form even I could understand,
much more clearly than the essence of their psychomachine. "But
do I have someone watching me?" Why, of course! You may not
have a tail, but your gumshoe—there he is. And they led me to the
window. Don't show yourself too much . . . over there, by the fish
shop, in the ski cap, see him? I thought I recognized the wino: he
really was wearing gum boots. It was cold. "But why do you have
a tail, and I have only a gumshoe?" I said resentfully. I was beginning to enjoy this. "Oh, now, don't compare yourself with us!
We have a world-class discovery of importance to our national
defense, and you're . . . a writer." They swallowed the "only,"
recognizing the awkwardness just in time. "But even you have
extensive ties with a worldwide public," they said, turning the
flattery back on me, "that's why we're here." Their point, in brief,
came down to this: I must stir up public opinion, motivate the
public to appeal to the world and warn of the danger threatening
it, attract world attention to the problem. I backpedaled: What

makes you think I have extensive world ties? . . . "Oh, come on."
They grinned again, meaning that I shouldn't play modest. Well,
yes, Murphy had just left me . . . So far they had contrived to stay
hidden. We spend the night in various houses and cities, they
chirped, but it can't go on this way for long. The noose was tightening, they couldn't escape . . . But when *they* get their hands on
the formula . . . imagine what will happen then! In sum, however
ironic their remarks on science fiction, their scenario differed little
from *Engineer Garin's Hyperboloid*—it had just been serialized on
television. A mighty thing, despite all, is literature in Russia! How
many schizos had been generated by this one man, our Soviet
Count, Alexei Nikolaevich Tolstoy! . . . And here, again, was a
question: schizos or provocateurs? No answer. The Eye, by all
parameters, was a provocateur, but he had proved to be an outstanding personage . . . Well, these two were in no way outstanding.
If these two were professionals, I really felt insulted for our native
KGB . . . Or don't they give a damn about me, that they've sent
the very bottom of the barrel? Still more insulting . . . Then they're
just schizos after all—again, a service of the Voices on enemy radio.
Schizos, you know, don't just watch television, they also listen to
voices. Our enemies, too, plant manias in us. What are they
doing—working hand in glove, our enemies and the KGB? To drive
us all crazy? Say what you like, it's the same department. That is,
they're different departments, but say what you like, the same
profession. So which of us have they driven crazy: these two here?
or me after all? "After all, you don't fully appreciate the scope of
the threat," they said. "Imagine them aiming this psychocannon
not at an army, not at a neighboring state—we're still a long way
from such capabilities, though we'll have them—but aiming it right
at you. And we do already have such a device, a laboratory model
so far, but already accurate at twenty meters." They talked, and
surveyed my little kitchen, which isn't even ten *square* meters, and
now their gaze lingered on the mop, which was simply sticking out
of the air vent . . . And now they appeared not to notice it but with
fresh inspiration began to describe the effect of the cannon aimed

at me. Two days of exposure—total paralysis of your will, destruction of your personality. What will? what personality? If you but knew . . . It's only you, in your department, who have that illusion. You alone, it turns out, recognize me. That's something, at least. If you but knew . . . you'd slam shut my case file and throw it away like an unneeded rag. The image of the colorless clerk—perhaps the only man in the world who was interested in my personality, in its significance and even power—deliberating a campaign strategy against me, dispatching provocateurs to me, and aiming the world's first experimental psychocannon at me . . . Think: What does a man have? wife, children, friends, a calling—so I have none of these, all I have is a Citizen Investigator, about whom I know absolutely nothing, while he knows . . . The citizen most interested in me! He alone, and a little stray kitten—that's what I have left! What's happening to me? Is it hangover, or have they actually aimed the cannon?

At this point Tishka appeared and called the detective's bluff. Sidling catwise, sidling with his skinny little back arched at an acute angle, menacingly baring his teeth and hissing, he approached their bulky briefcase as he would a wild beast—another instant and he would tear it to pieces! He filled my heart to overflowing with tenderness and laughter. But theirs, their double heart, he filled with anxiety and unrest. Their gaze began to wander and their speech to falter, well, exactly the way, if you recognize the devil in a dream in the guise of a close friend or relative, and you make the sign of the cross over him, still in your dream—exactly that way, their bodies began to slump and their faces to crumple . . . The courage swelled in Tishka's tiny frame, for though the enemy wore a dull, padlocked expression on its face, it was plainly a coward. Tishka made a dash and sprang back, waiting—not a sign of life! But if you freeze, for a long time and without moving, there seems to be something living inside it . . . A mouse! A mouse, surely, lived inside the briefcase. My Tishka was not such a fool as to mistake the non-living for the living! A magician! Why hadn't I guessed right off, when they were positioning their briefcase so solicitously! Well done, Pusskin, well done, you son of a bitch! You've given my soul its hair-of-the-dog!

At this point I rose and began to wind up the press conference. I recommended that they would do better to consult D., who wrote on science. He had both authority and strength, and what was I, I was a little man, I had no such connections, and it was unprofitable to aim the cannon, such an expensive one, at me. What, don't you know that he's an associate of ours? they said, trying a new device. "I would never have thought it. As liberal as they come—and a collaborator?! Why, it can't be!" It can, it can. "Thanks for warning me." None of that, now, they said, picking up their eaves-dropping briefcase from both sides and shooing off the heroic Tishka. What's the matter, do you think they're bugging you? and they nodded toward my mop. Then you're already off! "Meaning what, may I ask?" Meaning, off your rocker! "You know what you can—" I said menacingly. We do indeed know, you naïve fellow. Why, they'll simply drive a nail through your wall and stand watch at night. Highly entertaining, the way the intelligentsia tumble in the sheets.

I jerked out the mop in a fit of rage, but hard as I looked I found no nail.

The place smelled of fish, shit, and roses.

At that point my wife even returned—to visit Tishka. My willingness to forgive all was exhausted then and there.

"And aren't you ashamed to invite girls to such a shit hole?"

Good heavens! what girls? what made her think . . . ? She sniffed again.

"What whores you bring home!"

Somewhere I had read that perfume was based on the same molecule. I decided to tell her the whole truth.

"You're lying again, like two men! You think I know nothing about perfume?"

This was *ours*, this was *our own*, and this was *all*. She slammed the door.

Dear God! What do you all want from me? What am I, sweet

or something? Can't you see that I'm already totally gone? Or are you drawn by the very smell of carrion? Attracted by the death agony? Do you want to snatch away the last of my vital forces? Drag the threads of me off to your ratholes?? What exactly haven't I given you enough of? . . . But what *have* I given, that I've been stingy with? . . . You've given nothing, in point of fact, to anyone. You've only disillusioned them all. Medicine to your brother? Medicine was not what he needed, and his wife was right to throw it in the garbage: it was no good, didn't help. The Eye needed a million, he was even ready to give away half of it—you didn't give him his million. Did the homeless gay want recognition for his story, or something more? You gave him neither. The provocateurs required your consent to collaborate—you didn't even go for that. You're writing a novel, you say? Why, only Dryunya needs your novel—but you haven't written it, even for him. *Is* your briefcase empty? Is it? Why else did you crown him with the sugar bowl? Well, all right, I agree, I didn't give them what they wanted from me . . . but what did they give me!? But what did you want? Why, I didn't want anything from them!! There, you see. They wanted —and they gave you *themselves*. But I never even asked. You never asked, but they gave. But I . . . but didn't I . . . didn't I give them myself?! You did not, you put yourself at their disposal. Why are you now outraged that they used you? Who are you? just who are you to . . . ? Who are you without them, without your ragged one-eyed troops? You don't love me, that's what. What do you mean I don't love you, darling? You don't love anyone. I! . . . don't love? . . . Or your mother—where's your mother? And the children . . . where are your children? Go ahead, hit me, just you try, hit me. Hit me, darling, at least hit me . . .

What do you mean I don't love you? how can you say such a thing? what do you *mean* I don't love you! when I love you so, so, *so-o* much that . . . that I don't even know what . . . well, and then why do I hurt so much, if I'm as unfeeling as you say? Tishka, oh my Tishka, my little Tishka, oh why does she talk such rot . . .

I kissed Tishka's little face, which was sharp with

bewilderment—there wasn't much left of him in my arms at all, only a bit of fur, and inside it just a tiny ball no bigger than our heart . . . But suddenly his eyes went blank, he scratched me, lunged out of my arms, fell to the floor, and began writhing on his side, beating his paws as though racing in another dimension into an unknown space. For a long moment he hurtled across my spat-upon linoleum, along some insane evolute: in a circle and forward and in a circle again. He ended up in the opposite corner of the room, under the wardrobe from which Napoleon had fallen in my dream. Tishka, little Tishka, what's wrong? He was alive, though. He was all wet, a third his own size, but his flank was heaving, he was breathing.

I telephoned her. "Tishka," I said. She arrived immediately, as though she had been standing outside the door. Tishka, however, had managed to recover completely; in a most amusing fashion, he was playing that my dried-out lump of a handkerchief was a mouse. I had lied, it appeared, for the sole purpose of calling her over. But it turned out that this suited her perfectly. Thus, it suited us both. We dispensed with explanations. I cannot recall how it later developed, nevertheless, that I was at fault after all, having lured her with Tishka.

But the minute she slammed the door, or perhaps not that minute but an hour later, or perhaps the next day—I remember nothing—all I remember is that Tishka was writhing again in his falling sickness, like Dostoevsky. I called her, she hung up. I called everyone I could, trying to ascertain whether cats get epilepsy. Among others, I called Zyablikov, a great expert on animals. Cats, he said, get everything people do, except perhaps not hangover: did I have anything for a hair-of-the-dog? I did not, I didn't have even a kopeck. The mezzo-soprano, as always, rescued me. She said it was worms, wrote down how to get rid of them, and gave me some money.

I remember nothing. At first it even seemed to be getting better, and hope dawned, and the worms even came out. I went around with a rag all the time and washed up. Never in my life had my floor been so clean. But his fits became longer and more frequent, I couldn't watch. If you have ever, even once in your life, lived forty-five years under the Soviet Regime, you know. You know how the emergency medic arrives. Especially the veterinarian. Rag in hand, I rushed to open the door, but it was the Eye with his manuscript. On his own he had taken his briefcase to the Hammer Center (how had they let him in! but they had), and there he had offered his novel to the Italians at the next table, for only a hundred thousand now; he was nabbed, of course, but he had time to dump his notebook, and he swallowed the paper with my phone number, and they let him go. Well, Dryunya and Saltyk, they practically never left; the young woman who had once come with roses resolutely took back her manuscript; the drifter in the Zaporozhets had something else he'd forgotten to ask me; an assistant film director I had met in Sukhum, not so long ago, phoned from Baku, inviting me to fly out immediately and take one of the central roles . . . no, not *The Lady with the Lapdog*, the script has been thoroughly rewritten, the action takes place in Central Asia during the war . . . yes, you might say it's a unique retro . . . no, the director can't even contemplate anyone else for this role, he apologizes for being unable to phone you himself, he's shooting a sandstorm just now . . . no, of course Baku isn't in Central Asia, but this is a movie, you know how it is . . . no, he saw you, and he needs an aristocratic look . . . don't laugh, those are his words, that you had acquired an uncommonly aristocratic look since he last saw you . . . you reminded him of the young Neuhaus . . . yes, of course he's too young to remember him and we know you're not an actor . . . but we'll pay you the highest rate . . .

Tishka began tracing out his circles again. Foam bubbled from his mouth, leaving a damp mathematical curve. What was I to do now? The epileptic fits gave way to a sexual lunacy. He humped everything in succession: blankets, pillows, towels, chairs, briefcases, manuscripts, empty bottles, ashtrays, shoes, umbrellas, the guests themselves. Probably they had all arrived during the time I don't remember. And those two with the psychocannon . . . What about it, maybe they were really doing it to me already, irradiating me experimentally, and they just kept right on increasing the dose, still marveling at my strength, but on poor Tishka here the rays had immediately had a ruinous effect. No one had ever, so dramatically, gone crazy before my very eyes. And everyone gives advice! A nation of counselors, as Y. used to say, the friend who sent me the stereo, which Tishka immediately humped all over. The American professor—Murphy, I think his name was—he simply fled, abandoning the stereo . . . What, can't you summon a veterinarian in this country? You can summon him, but . . . The elephant can eat a ton of fruit, but . . . And indeed, why is it our elephants aren't dying yet? A rich country, no doubt about it . . . Tatarbekov—he said it was quite impossible to launch cats into the cosmos. They're all psycho. Only dogs . . . "Only dogs," said the cosmonaut Tatarbekov, sitting in my kitchen and smoothing the general's stripes on his pant legs to fortify himself. He had been brought to see me, of course, by the Afghan major. We poured a fresh drink, and Tatarbekov went on with his story about the cognac cucumber. "Do you know what a cognac cucumber is? No, you don't know what a cognac cucumber is!" The flask had been made out of foil, the main weight was its screw-in stopper. They hid the flask under an instrument panel when the rocket was being weighed—it proved to be one and a half kilos too heavy, but the flask was not discovered, and one experimental instrument had to be disassembled . . . so out in space, when he unscrewed the flask, it went *blam!* and out there, you know how it is, the weightlessness, and there was this one giant cognac-drop hanging in the air, just like a cucumber, they had to catch it right out of the air, drop by drop.

Then Tatarbekov vanished. Tishka disappeared right behind him.

The ambulance arrived at last. Tatarbekov was gone without a trace. When asked whether cats get epilepsy, they shrugged their shoulders and offered to put him to sleep. I wouldn't, not on any account, but now Tishka himself had vanished. He had long been keeping watch by the doorway, trying to slip out at every opportunity. He wanted time to live a little, like a grown-up tomcat: sing a song, have a look . . . His precocious maturity proved the deadliness of his disease. I would catch him on the stair landing, in other people's entrances and cellars. He stared at me with blank eyes that refused to recognize me, the eyes of a son who has gotten out of hand: he would not forgive me this. His unwillingness to come home was not mere madness, it was the desperation of resolve. At last he had disappeared for good.

Dear God, what kind of man was I, that not a single creature could get along with me! My whole life narrowed and focused and began to happen. She arrived on her own initiative—how had I dared not to tell her anything about Tishka!—we searched together. Zyablikov joined us. "I told you right off it was the cat plague," Zyablikov said. "Was he dragging his feet?" She and Zyablikov developed a mutual understanding. I can always detect this, when her gestures become a trifle more fluid and her glance a fraction of a second more attentive. I followed them through the courtyards, annoyed that I was so doleful and muddleheaded: I could never be the first to recognize that we hadn't been in this specific entrance, or that there was yet another cellar here.

When we warmed ourselves, she would make mulled wine. Zyablikov, he could drink anything at all, anything in a bottle. Once he drank a dose of insecticide sufficient to exterminate vermin over an area of half a hectare. "But why exactly half?" I asked indignantly. "In our country, private plots don't come any bigger," Zyablikov said, proving his case. And in truth, he never lied. For a man like Zyablikov, there's no point in lying. I yielded to him. What did I have, apart from my aristocratic look? I understood her.

But it was I who found Tishka. Better I hadn't! There would have been some meaning in it if he had disappeared without a trace, meeting the fate of a fighting tomcat and not that of an ill-starred Soviet animal. His tail and paws had been broken, and it was obvious at first sight that he wasn't long for this world. He kept scratching me and trying to break away, however, desiring no improvements for himself. She saw him in my arms—then and there, I was to blame for his so calamitous condition. I held him as if holding my own guilt . . . Had Zyablikov held him, he would have been a hero for finding the cat. Had she found him, then she would have been the one: she had found him! Whereas I didn't even know how to hold him in my arms.

But it was I who had to get the car started, I who had to drive it. Because I had the car and she had the cat. He lay on her bosom as if she were the Virgin Mary. My car hadn't started for a month. It resembled its master, like a dog; the resemblance increases with age, people say. Its fenders were crumbling to dust, like butterfly wings. At someone's urging I had stuffed up the holes with discarded nylon stockings to match. A panel of drivers, convened right on the street by Zyablikov, tinkered with my motor. Then we pushed it, the whole street. Then no one was there. Darkness had fallen before the car started, of itself, for no apparent reason. The main thing now was not to turn off the motor—and not to brake, because the brakes didn't work either. "Look," Zyablikov said, pointing to my rear license plate, "a bug!" This was the first time I had seen a bug, one of its varieties. Zyablikov knew all about it. "Your spook was helping start the car. I saw him." It was a round gray gewgaw on a magnet, which had been stuck above the license plate. I removed it and turned it over. Where was the mike? "This is a transmitter, shit-ass!" Zyablikov said. I put it back in the same place, and we drove off.

All the veterinary hospitals had just closed. Searching more and more for one open round the clock, we crossed the capital from end to end. Dear God, what a city this was . . . Only true misfortune will take you through such back streets. The place we live in was revealed. Soggy courtyards and slimy basements. A last matron, wielding her mop in a lighted doorway: "You're just a minute too late, folks, Doctor left just this minute. What have you got, a kitty?" Charitable despite all, this institution.

I was sure that Zyablikov had bugged me. Wrong again. In

the very first courtyard, the police showed up right behind us. First, one walked past as if by chance, eying the car, but we were standing beside it and he didn't come over. Then another; we had only to walk away. Again, Zyablikov was the first to catch on. He removed the bug and put it in his pocket. "I'll prove it to you," he said.

That was how we drove, taking off the bug when we stopped and putting it back when we moved. And every time, a patrolman appeared from under the sidewalk, as though for no reason: wasn't watching us, even seemed to be whistling and looking at the sky. We debated. The story was this. They had noticed that we had noticed, and now their overriding mission was to destroy the secret evidence. This is more important than following you: who gives a shit about you?

So we bowled along. The stocking worked out of the hole in the fender and streamed like an embassy flag. "That's for when the ambassador himself is in the car," Zyablikov explained. "If he's not, the chauffeur doesn't have the right. An ambassador's car is extraterritorial. When you're inside it, you're as good as in the embassy, on the territory of your own state."

Our car was extraterritorial. The traffic police did not stop us but merely watched us pass and went off to a booth to make a phone call. It turned out we had an escort. "Look, look!" Zyablikov pointed out the rear window, and there was a black Volga—following openly, festooned with lights and antennas and all the extras.

That was how we drove Tishka, with a flag and an escort.

This entertained us and enabled us to survive. We were laughing hard. She did know cats after all: Tishka was asleep in her arms and no longer struggling. "It brings us together," Zyablikov said.

It also parted us. We buried him by the Kazan Railroad embankment, and that was when we forgot to pocket the bug in time. It vanished. "They had to have it," Zyablikov said angrily. "Why did you mess up! What a piece of evidence!"

She walked away without a word of farewell, without raising her eyes.

Zyablikov and I were left alone together. "Do you at least have something left to drink?" Zyablikov suddenly looked at me with attentive eyes from which the mockery had vanished. Sighing as if he had reconciled himself to something, he followed me in, although I had nothing left. "Somehow I always get a fiendish appetite at a funeral. There's a reason for the funeral repast." He prowled around in search of cologne, mouthwash, quinine extract, any kind of elixir, toothpaste, even shoe polish—I had nothing, but he found, and started to make, some dried soup. I warned him that the packet was from the last resident, and it had been several years since I moved in. But Zyablikov was famed for his gastronomic fearlessness. "This is nothing. Once I ate the egg of a dragon. It was several million years old." "The egg or the dragon?" I was touched by his attentiveness. "The egg, of course!" he said gleefully. "The dragon would have been another several years older. Well, a brontosaur. In Tajikistan. I was stoned out of my mind and horribly hungry. I set off to the market and bought a hundred eggs at once. Put them all on to boil and fell asleep. I woke up groggy, but my appetite was gone. And I had a hundred eggs, already hard-boiled. In a stupor I peeled them all and sculpted a single huge yolk. And on the surface—I thought for a minute and duly plastered it with the white. Put it on a big pilaf platter. What to do, I wondered. I phoned the local Academy of Sciences. Blah, blah, I said, found a whole brontosaur egg, have it at my house. The entire presidium came racing over in their skullcaps and robes, wearing their orders and medals on top. They sat down cross-legged around the platter and started thinking, arguing about Moscow. Finally they sent for vodka. But I laced it with dope. The venerable *aksakalli* got smashed. Again, fiendish appetite. And in their reverie they ate the whole egg. They woke up: where was the egg? They woke me. I don't know, I said, I went right to sleep . . . and left the egg in your care. I don't know what will happen now, I said. At the mention of Moscow, they were gone with the wind."

This story failed to cheer me. " 'How sad our Russia is'—did Pushkin say this, do you think, or did Gogol invent it?" "Who the fuck knows!" Zyablikov said angrily. "I can't call up the dead. But I can arrange a rendezvous with someone living. Anyone you want." I didn't understand what he meant. But what he meant was his exceptional aptitude as a psychic, which had revealed itself as suddenly as, in their time, his affiliation with Buddhism or Orthodoxy. And he meant that I could rendezvous not only with someone within our borders but also with someone unreachable, like a woman friend of mine overseas whom I passionately wanted to see just then, when my loneliness was becoming qualitatively total. Zyablikov, of course, was an insightful person, though he had also been sufficiently initiated into my life story. I don't know which was greater here, my disbelief that he could effect such a rendezvous or my disinclination to see anyone. Once he had forcibly treated me for headache. I have a virtue: my head never aches (like a Georgian, all I have there is a bone). He twisted my head so hard that for twenty-four hours I couldn't get rid of a very acute migraine. I submitted to this and felt better than I ever had.

"Well," he said peremptorily, sitting me down on the shabby leather couch and sitting himself down on my right. "Where is she?" "I don't know." This complicated the task. He took my right hand and felt my pulse. "Close your eyes." I did. "Think!" I couldn't think. "What do you see?" I saw nothing. I didn't want to lie to him.

This was a strange mixture—my utter disbelief in ESP and my desire to be totally honest in the experiment . . . "Come on!" he said, angrily squeezing my pulse. "Don't resist!" Except for an upright piano (as shabby as the couch), which stood opposite me and which I stared at in surprise before closing my eyes, I saw nothing. The piano lingered under my eyelids as though I hadn't closed them. The nuance of black reminded me of water. The water in the Fontanka River, which the windows of my grade school had faced. I had stared out the window at that water, not listening to the drone of the teacher, just as I was now staring at the piano and not hearing Zyablikov . . . I was staring at the water through the classroom window and thinking that this was a Venetian window

—meaning the shape of the pane. "Where are you?" came Zyablikov's voice, from far away. I grinned. "In Venice." "Do you know
the address?" "No, how could I?" "Then ask!" "Whom?" "Anyone." "There are a lot of them." "The first one you meet!" He was
squeezing my pulse with impatience. "Go on, what's the matter
with you!" "It's awkward somehow . . . And besides, I don't know
the language." "Ask in Russian!" he commanded. "It doesn't
work." I felt guilty. "Board a gondola!" "But what will I tell him?"
"Let him take you where he wants, it doesn't matter . . . Well?"
came his impatient call. "What's up?" "We're underway . . ." "Tell
him to dock." The boat bumped against three steps that were
splashing in the water. The school was opposite. I stepped ashore
by a dilapidated palazzo. "Enter!" I heard, as though from the
boat. "It's strange, there's no entrance here . . ." "Enter from the
courtyard! Go on . . . Is there an entrance?" "Yes . . ." My voice
reached me from elsewhere, faint in the distance. "Enter!" "But
there's only a staircase here, and a small door . . ." "Open the
door!" "But there are only some brooms, dustpans . . ." "Dustpans
. . ." Unconcealed scorn resounded in my ear. "Pah! Go on up!"
"There are two doors here . . . I don't know which . . ." "Push
either one! Well? Do you see her?" It was a rather dim and untidy
room with the look of a bachelor's quarters, somewhat empty; an
office desk and chair stood by the slanting window. Nobody home.
"Nobody home. It's the wrong apartment . . ." "But there's another
room! Go into the next room . . . Well?" Someone scuttled away
from me. In the half-light I didn't immediately recognize his face.
"My brother's here," I said. "He's frightened." "That's normal,"
came the satisfied voice. "Subtle bodies always take fright. Ask if
maybe he has something to drink . . ." My brother, in confusion,
spread up the unmade bed, on which he apparently slept without
undressing, and gladly fetched a bottle from the refrigerator. He
closed the door quickly. I had time to notice that the refrigerator
was otherwise empty. "Well, does he have anything?" "Yes, whiskey." "How much?" "A little less than half a bottle." "Good
enough. Hurry up and pour!" My brother bustled around and

brought two glasses, hastily and poorly washed. Frightened as he
had been by my sudden appearance, he was glad of this temporary
remedy for the situation. He poured hurriedly, his hand shaking.
"Cheers!" he said—this was the first word he had spoken—and
greedily drained his glass. "Well," I heard from the other shore,
"have you drained your glass?" I was still twirling the glass in my
hand, in a reverie. "He has, but I haven't," I reported. "Well, what
are you doing!? Hurry up! Chug . . . chug . . . chug!" It echoed
as though he had cupped his hands like a megaphone and shouted
across a river. I made up my mind at last. "I chugged it," I said.
"You're hi-i-igh"—the loud whisper sounded right in my ear, and
a handcuff seemed to have been removed from my arm. "Now talk
to him about anything you want . . . I'm not listening." I was at
a loss; I didn't know how to ask him or what about. For some
reason I felt unbearably sorry for him. Irretrievability—that was
the word. Like a doomed man . . . When it's not subject to appeal.
When you also concur with the sentence. He was in his right mind,
as never before. And this was a misfortune. Actually, we had nothing to talk about: everything was clear. "Why did you dream all
this up?" I asked, to ask something. "They promised to cure me,
and I stayed"—that was all he answered, and suddenly he smiled
Father's weak and gentle smile. The black waves of the piano
floated before my eyes again. I disembarked where I had been
sitting, opposite the piano . . . Next to me Zyablikov was asleep,
blissfully collapsed. I wanted to ask him why my brother, and about
the nature of this strange degeneration of my overseas girlfriend
from a woman into a man. Zyablikov could not be roused. Solicitously I lifted his feet onto the couch and covered him with a lap
robe. The lap robe, for some reason, was my father's, the one he
used to throw over his chilly shoulders before his death.

All of this was from somewhere else. The lap robe, the piano,
the couch . . . How did I come to have a piano? The piano was
from Zyablikov's apartment, which I hadn't yet visited then. So,
this wasn't then. This happened later. But was the lap robe even
longer ago than this? . . .

I forgot the cat immediately, forever. He didn't fit in either the past or the future. No one had noticed: at first he was simply alive, then he was more alive than dead, then more dead than alive, then simply dead . . . No one had noticed. The good thing about powerful emotions is that you tire of them. After this I could not live alone.

Lord, how good to have hope! Since when have we given the name hope to despair? "That's life," as a certain fond wife said, standing in an accessible pose, when she learned that her husband's father had died.

I unloaded the stereo that my overseas friend Y. had given me. Distributed the money to my wives. And was already en route, aboard the plane, reading the script in which I had consented to play, not the lead role, but a central one. Hollywood is everywhere.

2. The Monkey Link

Hollywood is everywhere . . . Three hours later I was eating lamb's-fry kebabs and washing them down with Czech beer on the shore of the Caspian Sea. Night. Wind. The night was warm, but the wind was strong. It shook the wretched board kebab shack, giving it an extra coziness. When the season ends, the filmmaking begins: we were alone on the shore. Outside was desert, inside we had everything. Having arrived before dawn, I still didn't know how true this would prove in daylight.

I went out to look at the sea, on the pretext of the beer I had drunk. No sea. A yawning black hole, which reeked of darkness and slime. As though the sea had been locked up at the end of the season, like a vendor's shack. Or even as though it had been stolen.

Perhaps this was some local (Oriental? Muslim?) peculiarity, to have everything at home and nothing outdoors. The chef and the waiter were playing backgammon, paying no attention to either the color television (which was on) or us or the stove. They even had a timer! No wonder they also had Czech beer. And it was as though we were the hosts: benevolent film people, deceiving ourselves with art, not too drunk, just enough, since we would be shooting tomorrow.

A diaphanous green insect, the sea's sole representative here, crawled across the beer mug onto my hand and fixed its clever blue eyes on me. I could not withstand its gaze and closed my eyes, trying to hear the surf through the whistle of the wind. This was important to me now, as a musician . . . Leaves. For some reason the shore was strewn with fallen leaves. Strange. I had never seen a sea like that. As if in a dream . . . It *was* a dream.

I looked like Neuhaus and taught piano. My pupil, a Kazakh by nationality, looked like the young Pasternak. I left my wife and married a housemaid, by whom I had a child. I was supposed to lead the baby, barefoot, across the piano, so that he would leave his touching footprints on the dusty lid. (Had something happened to me fairly recently, a lifetime ago, involving a piano?) Outside the window, meanwhile, there was supposed to be a thunderstorm: thunder, lightning, torrents down the windowpanes. My school friend came, an artist who had lost an arm in the war and who all his life had been hopelessly in love with the wife I had left—he came to reproach me for abandoning my wife. We reached no accord, and after insulting me he slammed the door so hard that the glass flew out and smashed to smithereens on the floor. Then my new wife, the former housemaid, arrived soaking wet in the downpour, her thin dress outlined her figure, and much became understandable. "That's life," she said. I suggested this phrase, and it was promptly inserted.

Director Sersov spent half the night expounding his plans to me. They were extensive. I was supposed to write a script for him. It was to be based on an incident that had actually happened. A group of young astrophysicists go on a fishing trip in the mountains on the border of Armenia and Azerbaijan. A snake crawls across the road. They try to drive around it. They look back—no snake. Where has it gone? They drive on. The fishing trip is a success.

But when they pack up their catch, they discover that the snake has gotten into their car. They try to chase it out, but it crawls up inside, someplace where they can't get at it. Can you imagine?! Desert. Heat. The bite of the Blunt-nosed Viper is fatal . . . The fish are spoiling, characters are being revealed . . . Now, suddenly, a caravan. With the caravan, a Sufi. He knows how to converse with snakes. They ask the Sufi to persuade the snake to crawl out. The Sufi prays for a long time, and the snake finally consents. The infuriated astrophysicists start trying to kill it. The Sufi implores them not to do this, but they do. The Sufi is in despair, for the snakes will now cease to believe him. The Sufi curses them, prophesies their death. They send him on, return home, and get drunk.

I liked the word "Sufi," but I didn't like the ending. Yes, having them get drunk is good. But it's only the beginning. They perish one by one, under very mysterious circumstances . . . "Who would allow such a thing?" the director said, sincerely offended, and I settled for the role of pianist.

In the morning I didn't like the landscape. Not a drop of color in its face, not a blade of grass. Man had been here! Riddled with holes, black with grief, exhausted and abandoned—all the way to the horizon the earth was peopled only by black, rusted-out oil pumps. But even they were dead. Their beaks no longer pecked, because there was nothing to peck. And this was the site of the music school in which I taught pianoforte, if you please, to Kazakh children . . . And now I caught sight of an implausibly beautiful pomegranate, peeping out from behind a fortresslike clay *duval*. Within was paradise: roses, houris, and lamb's fry with Czech beer . . . And now I stepped ankle-deep in a puddle of oil.

. . . The baby refused to come to my arms. Perhaps I smelled of oil. It's that kind of smell . . . like blood . . . you begin to be bothered by it yourself. The baby set up a bloodcurdling howl and would not leave his footprints on the piano; the Azerbaijani firemen ran out of the water that poured down the windowpane. The baby was cut from the script altogether, his mother having been paid for a day's work. The result was worse for my image: now I married

the housemaid just because of the dress clinging to her figure. My
wife had been the former Natasha Rostova, but my new wife was
the former sweetheart of the young Sergei Esenin. What a lady-
killer I was! While the Azerbaijani firemen were eating, and then
refilling the tank with water, it was decided to do the scenes in
reverse order: first the wet wife. She was doused from a bucket
that had been specially warmed on the gas. I was supposed to
whisper something in her ear, and she was supposed to cry. I saw
my new wife for the first time, and I didn't like her. Everything
went well, but the director's viewfinder, with the distinct inscription
"Nikon," had been forgotten on the piano lid, which was in the
frame. This ruined the *vérité* of harsh wartime. But the warm water
had been used up, and the actress began to freeze. Vodka was
obtained from the first-aid kit, and the actress recovered. *I put my
arms around her, and what did I see over her shoulder?* . . . A fresh
bucket heating up, an Azerbaijani fireman courting a pretty assistant, people eating fried eggs, mending snags in panty hose,
playing cards, knitting a sweater, selling, buying, bartering, changing their clothes, trying on new clothes and old clothes, stealing,
drinking, drawing, fashioning spoon bait, reeling in their fishing
lines—the cameras were rolling. Retake.

My wife stank of vodka, I of kerosene. "How'd you get so
sozzled?" I whispered tenderly in her ear, and where she was supposed to burst out crying she burst out laughing. I was beginning
to like her. Retake.

And every time, only the first take was any good.

My artist friend slammed the door, the glass shattered, and I,
in confusion, not knowing what to do with it all, began to collect
the splinters—but then abandoned the whole business. The assistants had done an excellent job: the glass had flown out as it
was supposed to, had shattered into the requisite quantity of splinters in the designated spot, I had walked past as I was supposed
to, had picked up a splinter as I was supposed to—but at that point
I began to examine with curiosity the blob of plasticine adhering
to it, for this was what they had used to hold the glass so that it

could fly out, and I hadn't even known that the plasticine was
. . . Retake.

The second pane fell out before he had time to slam the door,
and it gave him a cut on his only arm. First aid for the wounded
. . . Retake.

The third pane was the last one. No more had been provided
for. And it was thick. My friend had orders to slam the door as
hard as ever he could, so that the glass would really fly out, really
smash into a thousand pieces. My friend slammed as he was supposed to, the glass flew out as it was supposed to . . . I had never
seen such a thing, and neither had anyone else. This was a large,
rectangular pane of glass; somehow it fell upright, and without
shattering at all it came rolling at me, waddling awkwardly, counting off its right angles with a clatter, completing turn after turn,
one, two, and only on the third turn, after stopping to think, did
it slowly topple sideways—again, without shattering. I stood open-
mouthed and watched this miracle.

Some things have an idea behind them, and some things just
are. It's a rare piece of luck when there's no meaning. And only in
the movies is there such good fortune.

Something had happened yet again. I could stand no more.

Impoverishment of place. As though this whole solid, tangible,
chosen world were really only a figment of the imagination. It had
flown away just as lightly as a balloon. Atmosphere.

The atmosphere of description is somehow thicker and coarser
than reality. Reality does not survive being described. Either it
perishes or it gains full independence. Or did it ever exist at all?
At any rate, whatever you have described, your only satisfaction
will be that the text is finished. There will no longer be anything
to compare it with. The past has disappeared somewhere, and the
very space is gone.

And who created, re-created, incarnated, anticipated whom—
the horse the chicken, or the cart the egg—will prove conclusively

unclear, as a kind of ultimate conservation measure: so that nothing will infringe on anything, if only in the past. Who came first, did Dostoevsky create his *Demons*, or the demons us? Did Dahl indeed create a *Dictionary of the Living Language*, or had the language itself, by that moment, died? Had Russian literature finished, described all, or did the Revolution happen because all had been described, finished? Rather than guess, let us be in no hurry to settle any scores we may have with reality.

In the end, Columbus did discover India, not America.

Geography is like a wife. Travel is our polygamy. If we had a harem, we could stay in one place.

And so, all the places where I had loved to shut myself up and write a few pages died the same death: one day they entered a text. No matter how many vows I made to myself, on the principle "Don't live where you fuck, don't fuck where you live . . ." Where are Toksovo, Peredelkino, Dilijan, Tiflis, Goluzino, Tamysh? At all events, they have been described. Perhaps they do exist. But I have died for them.

Travel is a different matter. You're not planning to live there. There you're an invader—and that's all. Crossing a space. Cutting across it. A surgical incision. A microscopic section. You dissect the space, or perhaps it dissects you. For some reason it doesn't hurt. An adventure.

When I set out on a pilgrimage, I already know whether I'll write about it. I know what I'll write, and how. In this sense, although geography is finished, I am a professional traveler. I travel solely for the right to compose this or that "journey." I bring home as souvenirs two or three fertilized details; they plump up nicely in my subconscious and send forth the necessary shoots.

One such detail I already had—Lucy's loose tooth.

The rest was mere technicality. The Rafik (there's a delightful word! a hint of empire; produced in Riga) started off crammed with six people including the driver and the author, or eight at most, allowing space for just one Armenian (whose name might also be Rafik), one Abkhaz, one Georgian, one Jew, and then, in tight competition in the text, for a Greek, Pole, Persian, Ukrainian, Tat, Ossetian, Korean, Tatar, Chechen, stray European, American, or African. Dramatic unity was assured: a Russian driver drove the Rafik, and a Russian (the author) also sat in state beside him. It was no longer a problem to lead the conversation from monkey customs to inter-ethnic relations. After such passions, therefore, the attainment of the journey's goal—contact with the free monkey herd—would serve as counterpoint, suggest an idea, and supply the finishing touch. Not inconceivably, the natural conclusion of the pilgrimage would be a planned picnic. That would serve for ellipsis points . . .

All was clear, right up to the title. *Awaiting Monkeys.* Good! Who's waiting for whom. Ambiguous. The tooth, the Rafik, the skirmish between the Greek and the anti-Semite, the frostbitten tails, the well-grown manes . . . What else? All was clear, just as it was. No sense in going, just to write something I would write in either case. I decided to write my "journey" without ever embarking on it.

I was in great shape—fit and ready. Sit down and write.

Nowhere to sit.

Whether Tamysh had died, or I had, or someone else there had died . . . I didn't have the strength to return to my baby chicks. I moved on to Tiflis.

But something really had happened. That is, it was happening around me, in actual fact, beyond the rim of my writing desk. My desk was a chair. On it stood a typewriter. I sat on the bed and typed a composition on the very subject of whether a poet did or could have a *home*, apropos of my visit to yet another house-museum. "The Homeland, or Tomb" the composition was called, and the key to it was the comma in the title. I was writing in downtown Tiflis, on the ninth floor of a hotel, once again the Abkhazia, in Room 14, and I was reflecting on the fact that always and everywhere I ended up precisely in Room 14. In Erevan, too, it had been Room 14 . . . What kind of residence permit was this? They couldn't possibly overhear anything in my room except the chirping of the typewriter. But all the same, something was happening around me. While I typed, the ceiling seemed to be collapsing, or rather, getting lower, and when I stood up I almost bumped my head on it. A strange darkening all around, as before a thunderstorm, but the thunderstorm had not taken shape, or as at sunset, but sunset, too, was still a long way off. A shiver inside. Before my eyes a sort of shallow silvery wave, like a fish scale. As though I were turning into air; only a sort of final insolubility prevented it. When I looked at a man, I was very surprised that he also saw me. He approached and introduced himself: Valery Givivovivich, Givivich, Givich, Givovvich . . . Unpronounceable! You can just call me Leroy, that's what everyone calls me. I peered into his muscular pink face with pleasure. There was something attractive about him. I felt like telling him something I had so far told no one. But I didn't know what, and he himself suggested it to me: Was it long since I had seen my brother? I replied readily, going into details I had forgotten forever. The trouble was, I said, that when I first fell in love and began to need money, I sold our joint collection, and at that time my brother was far away, and now where is he? now, too, he's far away, in another country even, but he'll be back soon, only this was a long time ago, we even had ancient Roman coins, and did you have dollars? or pounds? what, haven't you heard about the Korean airliner?

He did, as it turned out, inform me of what had happened beyond the rim of my desk when I felt something happening. It had the aura of a Caribbean crisis and some other sort of anxiety, as in an attack of hay fever. All the flowers had long since gone by. When's the last time you went anywhere? At that point I blurted out everything to him, how I never had a chance to travel abroad. "What do you want with America!" he exclaimed. "You must walk all around your homeland. All around it, on foot, in sneakers!" That's what he said: in sneakers. He was wearing excellent sneakers, Adidas. We were standing at the summit of Jvari, quite apart from the tourist crowd, like initiates, confessing to each other our mutual love for our homeland, at the very spot "Where the rivers, roaring, flow together, / Embracing like two sisters." The roar itself was not audible, but for a long time we watched how the Aragva and the Kura, after they flowed together, continued to flow as two different-colored streams in one bed. "Gray goose, white goose, two sneaky geese." In sneakers, in sneakers! the first goose exclaimed, and the second goose kept glancing at the first one's red feet, unsure where he would get sneakers like that. He would go to his grave in white ones. Adidasov kept proposing that I walk all around my homeland, like Gorky, and I kept consenting to drive all around it, like Gogol. That was how we left it.

What made me especially proud was that I did an end run around Valery Givivovich, Colonel Adidasov—tricked him like a baby. I so sincerely yearned to participate in the roundtable on the Georgian novel, so keenly felt the injustice of their refusing me even this, my human right, that I had planned to go to Sukhum —but there were no tickets. Now, the Colonel could easily help with this. But here, too, he dodged: "What do you want with that stinking Sukhumi? Better Batumi." "I'm interested in the monkeys," I insisted sourly. "Plenty of monkeys there. Go to Batumi, I have a house there. You can stay with me." Again he proposed that I go there "in sneakers." I played stubborn and did not consent to Batum. "This has been very difficult," he hinted to me the next day, "but you may now take part in the roundtable. Just refuse television, it's not worth it . . . You may move into the Hotel Abkhazia today. They've booked a room for you along with the participants." Marvelous, that "along with"! As if he didn't know I was already staying there! They transferred me from one floor to another. And it was the same room number, fourteen. They were already waiting for us on that floor. Two unshaven men of junior rank. Adidasov consigned me to them with a too noticeable eye movement, and they nodded. "I'm leaving you alone," he said, after escorting me to Room 14. I was delighted, and I swelled with self-respect: were they doing this so overtly on purpose, or out of ineptitude? In either case. Here it was, the secret formula of the psychocannon! Inside the computer sits a sergeant . . .

If they were pointedly noticing me, I was pointedly not noticing them. In my hotel room I was writing "The Homeland, or Tomb," as if preparing to report on the difference between the Latin American novel and the Georgian, as exemplified by *The Tin Fleece of Victory*, and giggling at my perfidy, which no one expected of me. It was the eve of the November Seventh holidays; the roundtable participants were to assemble on the ninth; I had time, and I used it. I did have one loyal friend, my Georgian brother, who had volunteered to help me. I hadn't explained everything to him, however—he was glancing over his shoulder as it was—just the difficulty with the tickets. My friend didn't particularly like these anniversaries, either. He, too, had once been baptized by Father Tornike.

On the night between the sixth and the seventh, after making sure I was not under outside surveillance, I slipped out of the hotel. It's good to travel light! For a long time now, I have carried nothing with me except manuscripts and socks.

We puttered about in the semi-darkness like thieves—packing for the trip, trying not to wake the household, driving out of the courtyard in a whisper. Tiflis was growing light as we drove out of the city. It was the most deserted, pre-holiday morning, without even a single policeman—everything was asleep until the parade. The highway was equally empty. The houses slept, the trailer trucks slept by the roadsides, the Traffic Patrol posts slept. Nature alone opened her eyes ever wider. Good heavens, what a morning this was! Hard to believe that all this had been just around the corner. Why hadn't we hurried, all our lives, to wake a little earlier and go a little farther? I was seeing the mountains. No one else—not Pushkin, not Tolstoy—could say more. This was "it." When you no longer ask yourself the question, What is it? You simply inhale and don't exhale. Blessed was the earth on the morning of November 7, 1984, on the road from Tiflis to Kutais!

Autumn had made a special effort, giving forth all its colors, and every leaf shone with a separate hue. Persimmons flamed in the thinning treetops. Autumn was gathering its last, its final harvest—the harvest of colors. "Do you notice how *different* this red is?"

We were terribly pleased with ourselves and each other. We had *escaped.* My friend, fortunately, did not guess how right he was. He supposed we had escaped the parade. While everyone back there would be gathering in columns and carrying signs . . . Freedom. It's eternity. That was what we were leaving for. In sixty-six years, for all their efforts, they had succeeded with nothing. Look, a cliff! look, a stream! look, the sky! look, the leaves . . . Nature is not a Bolshevik. You'll never teach her to do shoddy work.

Thus we lavished praises on each other. Content, my friend began to doze off and surrendered the wheel. I drove and was happy all over again, this time alone. The sign said "Gori," but we didn't need to go to Gori. The sign pointed not to the right or left, however, but to the sky. I was forced to wake my friend in order to choose a direction. He sleepily waved to the right.

A town came into view. Something was wrong here, but I didn't want to disturb my friend again. It bothered me that the road led ever more steeply down into a hollow, to a city built up in an ever more extravagant and ugly style. At the bottom was a square. I didn't know where to go next. There was no one to ask—the city was still asleep. Could I have gone astray and somehow returned to Tiflis? That would be like me. I stopped the car in the middle of the deserted square and got out.

All I could see from the car was a flower bed. When I got out, I saw a pedestal. It was a huge pedestal. Sliding my gaze upward, I saw the boots. They were gigantic boots! And then, all this: the skirts of a greatcoat, the hand beyond the cuff, the gaze into the distance, the service cap, the mustache. He seemed to be licking his chops, an iron cat . . . Then came the sky. The monument had been so designed that when you were at the foot of it the Leader's head was projected against the sky, higher than the surrounding hills. The smile of the Gori cat floated like a cloud.

"Look!" I yelled.

"How did you land here?" my friend said, waking up.

The whole thing struck us as momentous and symbolic. The discussion lasted all the way to Kutais. "Look at that, what force! He reached us even from there. We shouldn't have boasted so." I agreed: no place to frigging hide. And we thought we'd escaped! . . . And so, *we* were the first in all the land, the only two men on our entire sixth of the earth, who had managed to greet both the dawn and the only monument not yet taken down. Stalin had been born here. We had visited his Mecca. *"I'll get you!"*

We needed to purify ourselves. We had no plan, and we didn't discuss it. The road itself led us. Wordlessly, we found ourselves at Motsameta. Autumn, as best it could, had warmed the day. I caught the fragrance of the cloister—cedar, juniper, laurel. There was a silence as still as a pillar. The blood rang in my ears like a cicada. I had not been here since that day . . . If I counted that day as the day I was truly born, I could appear here a second time only to die. I was quite willing. I lay down on a flat, warm stone overgrown with lichen. A cloud passed above me, like my whole life. What do people mean when they say that their whole life passed before their eyes in the last second? Probably just that: not life's sequence of insignificant events, but its equality to a single instant. I wanted to die, as a way to live, not as anything else. As though, of all the modes of living, death alone remained. This was unfrightening, secretly treasured and welcome, as though I had been waiting and it had come: Now death will enter, forgiving you your life, she will put her arm around your shoulders, and you will go willingly, you will trust her completely. The state of expectation—this I didn't want to change, not for anything. I lay there, supine on the warm stone, almost without breathing, merely steeping myself in the rosined dry air, everything I could see consisted of sky—my eyes were neither open nor closed. It was strange to blink all this away. But yes, I had blinked at last, and my Georgian brother instantly got up from his stone: to confess his sins and take communion. I agreed with him immediately. Just right. The one did not contradict the other. And yet, the desire to take communion was not what had roused us! That was why I was unconsciously surprised at myself while we hunted for Tornike all over the cloister and he wasn't there. That was it: Who had ordered me to stand up? Who had said that it wasn't time yet? Who had said, "It would be nice to die here"? "Don't wish for too much, Rezo . . ." It was I who had said this, to him. I had merely thought I was ready. I proved unready, and stood up. What force! What tribulation . . .

No Tornike anywhere. No people. A few hens. How much they looked like kerchiefed parishioners waiting for the church to open—pecking sedately, as if gossiping. A brindled Great Dane pup, Tornike's pet, ran past without looking or barking. So Tornike must be here, too . . . We knocked at the house. A young monk opened the door with an air of displeasure and resignation. Tornike was away: he was vacationing at the Central Committee's cardiology sanatorium in Borzhomi. I greatly desired to write him a letter—despite all, I was his godson. And suddenly the brother admitted me to Tornike's study without hindrance. True, he hung over my shoulder. I twiddled my pen in torment, and he walked away after all, though he kept me in sight. On the walls hung icons, canvases painted by Tornike himself: Queen Tamara, the severed head of John the Baptist . . . "Hung" is the wrong word: they had been stuck up at the corners with thin bits of church candle, as with Scotch tape. On Tornike's desk, a pretense of unfinished work had been neatly tidied: an open, much-thumbed Georgian book— the Gospel, none other—and a faint Russian typescript, samizdat, the nth copy. I couldn't help peeking . . .

The brother relaxed when he saw that I was writing, and even left me alone. I scribbled faster and faster, overwhelmed with . . . *"Come ye therefore, brethren, hear the voice of Christ, and let us ever be watchful in obedience. This parable the Saviour saith for our salvation: he came not for the sake of the righteous, but for the sake of the sinful, that they might be saved. Two men, he saith, went up into the temple to pray: the one a Pharisee, and the other a publican . . ."*

Thus I wrote and wrote, with a strange assiduousness and emotion, as though the words were my own, and from outdoors my friend impatiently hailed me to drive on, while the brother more and more patiently refrained from disturbing me. At last, folding the sheets of paper, I rose and told the brother I had changed my mind about confessing in writing; I would stop by in person on my way back, when Tornike would have returned from the sanatorium. The last thing I remember was a cheval glass cluttered with French perfume. What a shame I couldn't kiss Tornike on his fragrant beard! My friend put me on a bus going to Sukhum, and we parted secretly displeased with something in each other.

No *Monkeys*! *Soldiers of Empire*—that was what I had to write, immediately! The whole past day—or was it a month, or a year —was compacted into a neat little slab, like a chocolate bar, and marked off in rectangles as taut and domed as the belly of a physical-fitness buff. After that, everything happened of itself. I definitely wasn't going back to Tamysh, but as ill luck would have it, I had left my Sukhum addresses back home. I went out to the embankment, certain that I would be surrounded by old friends within a minute. Nobody. Even at the Amra there was nobody. The only one to come along was Dragamashchenka—he arranged everything, then and there. An hour later I was sitting in my own room in the snow-white Abkhazia, which is impossible to get into, and writing this sudden novel. My plywood Room 14, which, by a tenacious irony, I had inherited from the Englishman, resonated with my typewriter like a percussion machine. Conspicuous on the ceiling, in the middle of the fake Finnish gloss, was an authentic white Soviet square. The cat and the rat lived above it as before, supplementing my orchestration with live sounds. Out on the embankment a tour guide was touting a sea excursion, in the nasal voice of a muezzin.

We were writing. Not I alone. "We were many in the bark. Some raised the sail . . ." I gave forth a steady drumming, HE sustained the pauses, the mouse and cat put in the punctuation marks. Everything fitted.

Soldiers of Empire! I, too, had reached the Pontus. Not metaphorically—I could see it from my window, and it certainly wasn't streaked with blood. I had no time to look out at the sea with any kind of thoughtful expression, either. I wasn't having thoughts, I was leading my detachment. This was it:

Dryunya, in a chafing loincloth sewn from two Pioneer neckerchiefs, like swimming trunks, as in that childhood when there were no swimming trunks for sale, when all of us got baptized as we emerged from the little river at camp, and the cross gleamed like a sword in the blinding sun;

Saltyk, stumbling over his guitar and taking offense at the nickname Anacreon, just as he had when I once called him a "Russian Fet"—taking offense not at what was said, but who said it;

The Eye, who had retrained himself to hold his sword in his left hand so that he could see it;

The Afghan, munching the last of his brainy flat bread;

My Georgian brother, who had grown a beard, which was why he was being transformed into a woman;

The Murmansk drifter, dragging behind him a baby carriage full of manuscripts, the chronicle of our expeditions;

Tornike, who baptized us all from one glass, as was proper for a company, but we were a platoon—we got some extra drops;

Victoria, our Victoria! with her blind guide embracing a harp;

Zyablikov, our navigator, who lapped up our reserve supplies but stuffed us with dinosaur egg and other marvelous legends;

The Inventor Brothers, incessantly drawing the Trojan horse in any sand they came to;

Colonel Adidasov, constantly resoling his sneakers;

A barbarian who had attached himself to us, constantly lamenting his homeland, a Voronezh of foggy second-category Albion;

Million Tomatoes, who easily carried each of us under his arm across the wild torrent . . .

We were many in the bark! And Victory awaited us, victory over the Georgian usurper who had appropriated the tin fleece! And then, of course, the liberation of the monkeys, our little brothers incarcerated in so-called freedom and democracy.

Good heavens, they were all alive! They moved. This came hard for them, and they didn't overexert themselves. Each had his heroic feat, but they weren't seeking room for it. How gloriously they rested before battle!

My harmonious crew were enough for me. I needed no one else. Once a day, like Jason, I went down to the shore of the Pontus Euxinus to indulge in a cup of coffee—and even there they dogged me.

I saw no one. Fleetingly I glimpsed Dragamashchenka. Again, I thought I glimpsed the man from Murmansk, as if he had jumped down off the page. I imagined I noticed Valery Givivovich, too. But I only imagined it. Then I did, for sure, encounter the two of them together on the embankment, holding each other by one finger like children—the Murmansk drifter in the embrace of Colonel Adidasov. Ah, you don't say! was my only thought. I indulged my subordinates' weaknesses. The main thing was, not even one more warrior must be lost! I must bring them all through to the end, alive. Alive . . .

They were alive as it was. But how much I had arrogated to myself in becoming commander! In reducing them to the rank of characters, what responsibility I had shouldered for the fate of my novel's personnel! Power! That was what the literary critics failed to consider in the scheme of literary devices. That was what had oppressed me for a whole year as something lost, that was what finally inspired me as something found: all this was mine. Mine! And you wanted to take it away from me? Not a chance! I won't hand it over. *Now* I understand what you were all demanding of me, what you were trying to get, why you were after me. What will interest the powers that be, apart from power? Nothing—and this is their secret and strength.

I, too, was interested in nothing. I shared all the hardships of my subordinates: I didn't eat, didn't drink, didn't sleep, didn't wash, didn't undress. Sometimes I brewed coffee on the windowsill, and then I would be amazed that there was a sea outside the window. Sometimes HE furtively munched something in the corner, strewing dry crumbs on himself; HE, too, slept without undressing, as he so loved to do—slept twelve, fourteen, sixteen! hours a day. I would jump up without dressing or even urinating, go to the typewriter, and begin to type out the next chapter, which was all prepared in those twelve to sixteen hours—where had I gotten what? The fewer the impressions left to me, the better suited they were to enter the text directly: I glanced out the window, and there was Million Tomatoes, already chatting about something with Valery Givivovich. About what? And my coffee boiled over . . .

I didn't even have a Bible at hand. I had the three short pages copied from Father Tornike. *"The two men are the heart and the soul. And within the soul are truth and sin. For truth is brought low by arrogancy, and sin devoured by humility . . . For the heart is a Pharisee . . . And the soul itself taketh the name of publican . . ."*

Two men went up into the temple . . . *"Two horsemen, he saith, a publican and a Pharisee. And the Pharisee hath harnessed two horses that he may come unto eternal life: the one horse, a virtuous one, is fasting and prayer, but the other horse is pride and vainglory and condemnation. And pride hath cast a stumbling block before virtue, and the horse chariot is broken, and the conceited rider hath perished . . ."*

Then and there, the novel acquired a new turn. In the broken car, with the stocking streaming like a flag, as we were trying to save Tishka and escape from pursuit, my brakes failed me, and the author plunged into the abyss, dove into a wall—just at the very moment when I had finally given Tishka a lifesaving injection and contrived to get away from my pursuers. The live Tishka was meowing over me at the end . . .

". . . for no man, he saith, taketh this honour unto himself but he that is called of God. For the apostle saith: Sitting on the branch, thou bearest not the root, but the root thee."

And I rejected this finale, for I was not the root. The trunk was the plot, the branches the heroes, and the Author had seated himself on the main hero's branch. I decided to name the main

hero Author: Author-Khan, of mixed barbarian, Scythian, and Kip-
chak origin, became leader of the detachment. It was he, however,
who managed to lead his detachment through the blazing conflagration of Empire N. He led them out of the barbaric Baltic swamps,
skirted seething Muscovy, bypassed the vicious Kipchaks over the
smoking steppes, and for some reason found a Pontus other than
he had calculated, the Hyrcanian. He needed another long while
to reach the narrow spaces of Iberia, and a long while to master
these spaces, too, before once again reaching the swamps, this time
of Colchis.

But that was all superficial, nothing but envy and mastery of
the Georgian novelist's experiment. The essential point was that a
conspiracy was ripening within the detachment. No one in the
detachment even suspected it yet, not even the leader, or even his
author, because the conspiracy was ripening within the author. The
authorial "I" came up against my own "I"—and they were off!
Who was more important? who had done what to whom? who was
HE, who was I? And already it was a struggle for power. *"But let
none be led into temptation, forasmuch as man's reason is divided
in two. The thought is cut off from the word, for, he saith, the flesh
warreth against the soul. Two adversaries there be in us, ceaselessly
contending: for greed riseth up against fasting, vainglory against
virtue, drunkenness against chastity, fornication against spiritual
purity; hatred and wrath against love; pride against humility;
against truth—falsehood and calumny and other wickednesses."*

A conspiracy! No wonder they were on my trail. It wasn't me
they were after, it was my novel. That is, my detachment. Nothing
could stop me anymore. I must lead all my men out and save them.

And before I could put the final period—Givivovich was
knocking on my hotel-room door, at the crack of dawn, dressed
for the march. In sneakers! Our sneakers would be a Rafik furnished
by Dragamashchenka, who had volunteered to escort us to the
monkeys himself. Valery Givivovich, as I myself must understand,
had not had an easy time of it, getting all this organized especially
for me.

This was fame already! All the earth's vainglory resounded triumphantly in the author's triumphant soul. "Two men . . ." A certain friend once said in answer to my lament, having understood me in his own way: Why strive for world fame? It's enough to achieve it on the scale of a region or district, he said, for the wise man to see what it's worth. And then? For this very friend, even world fame was not enough.

We were going. To me, there was no novelty in this, or in my future fame. This had all been lived out, burned out. Simply, they had stopped me, yet again, from getting them written, my *Monkeys*. I was ready again—and they prevented me again. Before, they had prevented me from reaching the monkeys lest I know what to write about. Now, when I finally knew what about and was actually already writing them, they were forcing them on me, so that I would be unable to write them for a new and different reason: they wanted to stop me by making my imaginings real. One way or another, but I mustn't write them. That was their devilish mission! And yet . . . wasn't this too sophisticated?

With this thought on the sophistication of evil, I submissively boarded the van. Right again: a place of honor had been set aside for me next to the driver, and he, too, alone among them all, was a Russian man. A Russian man driving their van for them. Nothing new! My thought on the sophistication of evil was succeeded by a thought on its primitiveness. What is evil, after all?

The transparent thought was revolving, propellerlike, on its sharp point. I was ready to catch it like a dragonfly . . . "Look to the right." To the right was a long, dismal cement wall, but my thought was already gone. Wasted terrain, barbed wire topping the wall, a tower. "The largest juvenile colony in the Union," Valery Givivovich said, commenting like a tour guide. Oh, this I knew a lot about, thanks to the Eye's manuscript. Which I promptly reported in full, under the polite scrutiny of the group, under the reproachful eye of Valery Givivovich: Why say any more than necessary in his presence? force him to remember? " 'Do not fire on a juvenile!' " I recounted. "Do they have such a regulation? I never heard it before." The reluctance to receive information was a professional habit in Valery Givivovich. "Brake here!" And he disappeared through the entrance gate to the colony. Perhaps they also had an adult division here? A prison gate—this was a fine place to wait! . . . Two shy, overgrown youngsters brought out a pail and a box. Valery Givivovich showed them where to put the things.

We drove on.

And this became a journey in its own right. Outside the window a landscape appeared, picked up strength. Come to find out, Valery Givivovich was a simple man: his grandfather was an Armenian, his mother a Jew, his uncle a Russian, he himself a Georgian. Generally speaking, he was an alien—a Titan in a previous birth, later a Babylonian priest . . . but more on this later. It turned out I had been wrong about him. Givivovich was doing everything from the best of motives. Arranging my participation in the roundtable, my trip to the monkeys. I had been wrong that time, wrong to flee—had exposed him to, done myself a great deal of. One could do business with him: not flee, not say too much in front of outsiders. One could reach an understanding with him. Oh, and of course, one had no problems with tickets, with hotels. Do you think they'd have let you into the Abkhazia? Ah, so that's how . . . What did you think?

We were stopping. There was someone already waiting for us. Yet another associate. An interesting man. A Greek by nationality. With a heavy box, from a Sony TV.

We were stopping. There was no one waiting for us. A fuss and bustle. Several times someone ran into the transport depot and back to the Rafik, promised to return in a minute and disappeared for twenty. At last he brought a tall stack of hot lavash. But did not come with us.

We were accumulating new companions. They were all monkey-colony associates, people of various interests. A historian, a biologist, a physicist, a speleologist, a salesman—we would have sufficed for a series of jokes. An Armenian meets a Ukrainian and a Jew; a Jew, a Russian and an Armenian; a Ukrainian, a Jew and a Tatar. Except that we had no Chukchi. In place of the Chukchi we had a man of still rarer vintage, part German, part Ossetian—a musician, a drummer by nationality.

Even Dragamashchenka proved to be an interesting person. He had come with us not only because he headed the scientific group and accordingly supervised the resettlement experiment—he also proved to be the only human boss over the monkeys. He was the alpha male! And that meant: wild beasts, you know! little lions! fangs this big! bite through to the bone! arms more powerful than your legs! gregarious animals—they obey their leader implicitly! together they can tear apart anyone they want! armed and very dangerous! the leader recognizes just one man, but forever! and that man is the alpha male! Dragamashchenka, that is! only with him could we approach the herd!

Dragamashchenka, it turned out, was our pass to the territory.

After discussing the customs of animals and people, after rejoicing in their similarity, in the triviality of their differences, we entered the nicely situated little town of Kamany. Someone was supposed to meet us here but did not. Givivovich declared a half-hour rest stop and set off with Dragamashchenka on reconnaissance.

We stretched our numb legs. Before us was beauty, somewhat marred by a small concrete-products plant and a quarry. But there were other places to look. The ravine, which we were supposed to penetrate further, was inviting; it promised absolutely untouched nature. Off to the left, soaring and reigning over the whole village, on a separate hill, a ruined church gaped with holes—but even in that form it was stunning in its proportions and appropriateness. I conceived a desire, and the group started slowly up the hill, overcoming their reluctance so as not to leave their guest unsupervised.

The ruin was best observed from a distance; up close, one could see its structure too plainly. Especially if coming uphill. As we grew near and out of breath, the proportions were obscured and the holes acquired shapes. And—what had we wrought!—the dome, along with its cross, was missing. It lay collapsed on the floor, and its stones were overgrown with tall weeds and coltsfoot, forming an independent landscape, a sort of dwarf Japanese rock garden. We entered not through the gates but from the side, where the path led us, through a hole that made a more convenient entrance. But it was cozy inside! And no papers, bottles, or trash heaps—that was the surprising thing. In a corner under the surviving portion of an arch, where the rain penetrated less, stood a lectern fashioned from discarded stools and night tables that someone had carried up here. A homemade icon of very inept workmanship, but which someone had painted himself, reminded me of Tornike's paintings. And—there were candles burning! Brought here by someone not long before we came, and lighted by someone! It was a functioning church!

And it possessed its advantages. From inside we could continue to admire the landscape, each time revealed anew, framed anew —through each of the holes. Like the past, present, and future. I saw the road we had come by, our Rafik at the foot of the hill, the path we had climbed . . . When I looked at the ravine we aimed to visit, an undisturbed landscape opened up in the future . . . And through the third wall, my glance fell on the present: the concrete-products plant, the quarry, and a certain grayish compound enclosed by a wall exactly like that of the juvenile colony, only without towers.

I obtained the necessary explanations. It may indeed have been a prison compound at one time, but now it's an old-age home, an asylum. In summer, they do all right—lots of pilgrims come and give alms—but in winter they're cold and hungry. Yes, yes, pilgrims flock here from all over the Union. This is where the apostle John Chrysostom was murdered.

In the upshot, I didn't believe a single word, especially since my escort of historians had obviously confused Chrysostom with St. John the Divine, calling him an apostle. "But how could that

be!" I said indignantly. "The apostles—that was the first century!"
"Well, and what if it was," said our Armenian.

To them, the first century was nothing. In proof, a little old
lady in black was scrambling up the mountain toward us with a
little black goat, now pushing it, now clinging to it. A pilgrim, no
less. Look, dragging herself up, they explained to me—down below
they can see if anyone comes up here. Not a pilgrim, then. The old
lady proved to be from the poorhouse. She had come for alms, and
she was insistent. My ruble was not enough. Even three she looked
at without pleasure. "I've come so high," she said. The old lady
was Russian. The goat grazed inside the temple.

I wanted to die. What did I care about monkeys? I was completely out of money. I flatly refused to borrow from Valery Givivovich. I would have to flee again. Good God, why couldn't I give
her everything? The little old lady tottered. Her gaze was firm—
she was clinging by it. Whatever gave me the idea she was a "nice
little old lady"? All churchly old women are vicious. And rightly
so.

But why can't you? HE said to me, snatching my wallet. Our
escorts observed the scene with interest. Immediately on receiving
my last twenty-five kopecks, the old lady quickly ran downhill,
managing the slope with some agility. The goat barely kept up with
her. Off to the store, they explained to me.

And we descended to the sacred spot. Nestled close to a yellowish gray cliff, the spring formed a creek and became a head-
water. The stones around it were red. Which served as the main
proof that this was where the "apostle" had been murdered. A
ferrous spring, they explained to me. The pilgrims never fail to
immerse themselves here. Very good for gout. I dipped a finger and
pulled it out red—such was the temperature—the water was icy.
But I went further—splashed my face, wiped my brow. Somehow
it felt like a Muslim ritual.

My escort of historians was already disputing how he had been
murdered. Had they cut off his head, or had they stabbed him?

Cut off his head was somehow more convincing. Over there on that red rock. They were confusing him with yet another John, this time the Baptist. Now they were disputing which rock. A huge one towered above the bank, with just its base submerged in water. The sole convincing point in its favor was its greater convenience for butchery. Another rock was fully underwater and therefore historically more justifiable, for the spring itself had formed as a result of the murder, from the blood of the "apostle," which was why it was red. The small lake forming from the spring had covered the sacrificial rock with water. According to tradition, he who could lift this rock would be forthwith cleansed of all his sins.

Such a possibility could not but inspire HIM. Like any normal person, he instantly believed in the red rock. I could do nothing about it: HE was gripped by a violent ecstasy, I by a sacred terror of life. In the twinkling of an eye he had stripped off all his clothes and was standing in the creek, straining to lift the rock. I had never seen him like this: a mad gaiety illumined his face. The whole business was undeniably foolish. The rock was unliftable. There was no way he could grasp it, he broke all my fingernails . . . and suddenly his seeking fingers *found* two hollows, as if specially made, convenient as handles almost . . . the vein swelled on his forehead. "Died of the vicissitudes of travel," I thought. But the rock shuddered and moved, more and more easily. Oh, yes, Archimedes' law, I thought. But the rock had barely lifted its red brow above the surface when it became decidedly heavy. My escorts deemed this sufficient, however, and unanimously remitted all the athlete's sins.

If anyone was happy, they were. How they loved HIM! How they congratulated him! Somewhere they found a towel. And promptly found a glass of *chacha*, too. HE sopped up the *chacha* like a sponge. "Verily I say unto you: you have your reward." HE had earned it.

The rest happened of itself. Adidasov and Dragamashchenka arrived leading the man who had been "waiting for us here." He was solid gold: his chain, his tooth, his watch, his watchband. Not a man—a ring. He was solid white: his shirt, his suit, his shoes, his face. He was pompous and annoyed, though it was hard to tell the one from the other. We boarded the Rafik together, however, and the Rafik filled with deodorant, and we immediately braked by an entrance gate. It was the entrance to the old-age home, and he was its director. A little old man, staggering under the weight, brought us yet another box. The box kept clinking. Adidasov exchanged a handshake with the annoyed director. Our old lady and her drunken goat happened along.

She called me aside. I had no more money, but that, it turned out, wasn't what she had called me aside for. "Be patient another year or so. You should've seen 'em jump off the mausoleum!" The old lady turned away, shyly wrapping her giggle in her kerchief. "It was awfully funny. God forgive me!" She had seen a vision: St. George on a white horse in Red Square. The way he rode at the mausoleum! The way he brandished his lance! They all went jumping off the grandstand helter-skelter, losing their hats. "You should've seen 'em!" the old lady said merrily, pointing at the director, who was trying to herd her and her goat back into the poorhouse.

And we drove on. The Rafik surmounted increasingly steep hairpin turns. Last year there had been an unheard-of snowfall here. It had been impossible to get through. That was when their tails got frostbitten—it had been impossible to help. Whose tails? Why, where we're going. Ah, so we're going to the monkeys after all . . . I didn't want to go to the monkeys. HE wanted to. Why hadn't I had a heart attack when HE was trying his strength with the rock? "Died of the rigors of travel"—a wonderful epitaph! "Two men . . ."

The shady, overgrown road led us up a ravine. On the left, deep below us, seethed a river: the smell of water reached us. So did the smell of moldering leaves. These smells mingled, giving rise to a smell of earth—newly dug. Small stones sprayed from under the wheels and plunged gaily down into the abyss. We, too, had a chance of plunging down after them, into that fresh grave. But the river was not for that purpose. Its purpose was to divide free monkeys from unfree people. Previous experiments had shown that monkeys must not be settled anywhere near man. Underfed monkeys destroyed crops, and peasants naturally killed them off. Here the river divided them from people and formed a reservation for them, between itself and the mountains. Hydrophobia, the fear of water, fenced the monkeys off from man. No, not all monkeys are hydrophobic, but the ones who live here are.

Conversation in the rear:

"Excuse me, of course, but how many *r*'s do you have in your language, please?"

"What do you mean?"

"Just the letter *r*."

"Hard *r* . . . soft *r* . . . trilled *r*, r-r-r . . . Three, I guess."

"Then our language is more ancient than yours: we have four."

The theory proved somewhat doubtful, but not devoid of . . . That the first letter was *r*—a development from the growl—and that forms of the letter *r* were the first language. And Dragamashchenka supported this by the example of his monkeys.

"Then your language isn't more ancient, it's more primitive," Givivovich said in a conciliatory tone but with finality, for he was rather stung that he had one *r* less. Either way, though, he considered himself more ancient, inasmuch as he had been a Titan priest in a previous birth. He remembered this for sure—the next incarnation was the one he was hazy on—but all the same he was an internationalist as a result. He had come to a remarkable conclusion: we would keep being reborn in each other, until every people had been every nationality! In what sequence? . . . And Givivovich took revenge: "Other nations are reborn any old way —some even as Estonians. The Armenians alone are just Armenians."

"And the Jews?"

"Oh, the Jews . . ."

"And the Abkhazians?"

And again the conversation turned on 1978 . . . Oh, where is the beginning of that end! . . . "You got your television?" (Valery

Givivovich's voice.) "We gave you the university?" "You? gave? us? twenty minutes you gave us! one department you gave us! you didn't give, we took!" "You didn't take, we gave!" A discordant chorus.

Whose was the land?

It was Armenian first. No, Georgian. No, Abkhazian. No, Greek. Whose was the land—his who came earliest, or his who came latest? The Russian driver and I exchanged glances: the land, of course, was Russian.

Hydrophobia or geography? The natural boundaries of mountains, seas, and rivers had not sufficed to keep men from killing one another—nor would church boundaries suffice. Whose was the church?

His who had built it? His on whose land it was built? His whose faith had been accepted here? And again, not what is within us . . .

And yet again: Whose kingdom was earliest? Of what nationality was the king, or of what nationality his subjects?

Tamara wasn't an Armenian? Why did you remove the Armenian stone from Jvari!

Melancholy . . . "*For in thy sight shall no man living be justified. And again he saith: I humbled myself and he did save me . . . For the heart is a Pharisee, who hath not preserved virtue but magnifieth himself concerning corrections and exalteth himself over the most idle, for he knoweth not what is written of him: Boast not yourselves, he saith, speak not of heavenly things in your pride, nor let empty verbosity issue from your lips.*"

We stopped at a very pretty spot on the bank of a small river and started to unload the boxes. I had already guessed, of course, that the monkeys would be absent. But I certainly hadn't supposed that it would be to this extent. That they would be this absent, the monkeys.

No, we didn't immediately set about demolishing the contents of our cartons. The show Givivovich had staged for me wasn't over yet. Four of us, Givivovich, the alpha male, the drummer, and I, crossed the Hydrophobia River by a ropeway. The bucket was rated for one occupant, so we did this four times. First the alpha male, then I went. It was fun putting on the work gloves, going hand over hand along the rope, looking down from on high at the white waters and whirlpools of the alpine monkey river Hydrophobia. It was scary, of course—I understood the monkeys. They wouldn't even go near the river. In any case they weren't there when I dismounted. Even so, I was very excited—if we had not attained our end, we had reached an end point. I dismounted on the bank, and the alpha male greeted me by sounding a gong. The gong was a rusty rail, which hung on a convenient branch of a convenient tree.

"We're a bit too late," Dragamashchenka explained. "They waited for us until one o'clock."

My skepticism was justifiable. The monkeys may have been here at some time—board huts the size of beach cabanas stood in a row like exaggerated beehives—but on each little door hung a rusty padlock. A long counter stretched in front of the huts, perhaps a high bench, or a low table—completely empty. Yes, not without reason had everyone else stayed on the bank. They knew. Givivovich couldn't leave me alone; Dragamashchenka was in on this, though possibly the drummer was not.

"Hurry, hurry!" Dragamashchenka shouted, as though to the monkeys who had departed into the forest, but actually he was also hurrying the two men who were following us across, as well as those who had stayed on the other bank to engage in what subsequently proved to be our main business.

"Hurry, hurry!" he shouted in a repugnant alpha-male voice, and beat on the rail. The sound waves raced up the knolls and foothills, penetrating the forest and alarming the phantom monkeys. Then Dragamashchenka grew tired and lit a cigarette. "They've gone far," he lamented.

He was pretending that they usually came by one o'clock, on the chance that someone would bring feed. But if no one was here, they would go back and graze: acorns, nuts, roots . . . I grinned. Sure: mushrooms, berries . . . That's summer, now it's fall, he explained. I asked Dragamashchenka what was man's first gar- ment, and he couldn't answer me. Givivovich became very inter- ested, and I got him to say that it was a holster. The drummer took up the topic and stated as a certainty that the first music, and the first art in general, had been the drum. Why, even the drummer turned out to be an interesting person. He and I talked a while about the great Tarasov. Givivovich pricked up his ears: "Vladimir Petrovich?" Ah, I had forgotten that I mustn't name names!

"Hurry! Hurry!" Dragamashchenka muezzined again. The drummer and I had stepped aside, away from Givivovich, and were chatting about ecumenism. For convincing effect, Dragama- shchenka strolled along the huts and shook the padlocks. It's still warm now, we'll open them toward winter, he said apologetically, catching my glance. So that I would believe him, he opened one of the padlocks, took a handful of something like—as he explained —"granules" from an empty sack, and scattered them on the mon- keys' empty bar with a generous gesture. Then he thought a mo- ment and scattered another small handful. "Is that enough?" I asked. "Enough for now," he said. "For the time being, pasturage has to suffice them."

The drummer had found places on the rail that he could hit for three notes and was picking out a monkey variation on the "Dog Waltz."

By now people were calling from the other bank.

"They must have gone too far," Dragamashchenka said apologetically.

"It's probably not worth waiting for them any longer," Gi- vivovich agreed.

"No, let's wait," I declared firmly, and started off to meet the monkeys.

"Stop! You can't go there!" Dragamashchenka shouted. "Without me, they'll tear you to pieces!"

"Who will?" I could restrain myself no longer.

"Why, the monkeys! You've no idea how strong they are. You mustn't go one step closer to them than the alpha male does."

"Where do you see any monkeys?" I continued.

"Why, they could appear at any moment!"

"You don't say? . . ."

I took another step and froze. Something stopped me. I began to listen. Nothing. Or so it seemed. But something hung in the air, like yet another silence. It tensed, tautened like an invisible barrier, and sagged in my direction. I peered into the thinning foliage of the small oaks that ran uphill, and in the configurations of the branches I spied a monkey, as in the Nabokovian picture riddle of my childhood: Find the sailor and the little boy. I saw them outlined, first there, then there, suspended in uncomfortable poses, waiting, perhaps, for us to leave. We were waiting for them, they for us. By now there was a monkey hiding behind every tree trunk. But how they could wait! Not a twig stirred, not a leaf crackled. The whole slope was strewn with these shrilling leaves—you couldn't set foot here without a deafening rustle. How had they sneaked up? . . .

I wasn't going anywhere. Period. Not until they came. And since they would never come now, since Givivovich and the fake alpha male were displaying the crudeness of their scheme with increasing urgency, openly inviting me to play their game, since there was no sign of any monkeys—all the more would I see them come! All the more! I wasn't going anywhere, ever! Again I wanted to die, as a way to live. Right here!

And this was the third temple in which . . . The closed church without Tornike, the hole-riddled church with the old lady, and this one. In the end, on this very day, for the second time in my life, I was without sin! And how was this any less than a temple, when . . .

When around me—here was the all. *The all!* Whether you understand or not, it's *all!* . . . Just everyone go away. Everyone go away, for Christ's sake! In Christ's name I beg you, for the last time: *go away!* leave me alone! eat and drink on the other bank, if you're impatient . . . Vanish, scatter . . . Get thee hence!

O Lord, with what gold Thou hast showered my last step! What Dutchmen painted this landscape for me, in colors instantly three hundred years old, in paint not yet dry! how this brown dusk shines! Hallowed be Thy Name! What silence Thou hast draped upon these branches! Yes, Thy Kingdom come! Oh, shut up, you bastard, forget words! pray, you bastard! Hurry, hurry! Pray, you son of a bitch! Weep, laugh, sob, exult, you senseless pig . . . Thy will be done!

The silence was swollen and saturated with expectation, like a sponge. What downpour would be disgorged from this invisible storm cloud of silence? . . .

And I heard the silence break, with a distinct minus-sound, giving birth to the next, still riper silence.

I waited. Soon now. Just a little longer. Hurry, hurry!

I waited and didn't want them to come. I wanted to wait like this eternally, impatiently, for monkeys who weren't even there. The main thing was, I didn't want . . . and even now I don't want . . . this to end as it must end, in the way that it will inevitably end, according to the design, the plot, predestination, my weakness, and HIS inclination. I don't want to go to blue blazes! I want to stand solidly, right here, on these same dry leaves, and I won't shift my weight even once, won't turn my head, except for turning my eyes now and then to see this same *all* all over again: the hidden monkeys stock-still behind Thy tree trunks, in Thy leaves. I myself will stand like a tree. May a little monkey hide behind me, too . . . O Lord, take me at this very moment! Seize—I beg Thee, in God's name—the moment! I don't even ask of Thee what Goethe asked, I don't ask Thee to stop everything around me because, if you please, it's beautiful, I ask Thee only and merely to stop *me* at this moment, so that I will pass when it does, if indeed it is fated to pass . . . Not eternal life—eternal death I ask, curse my tongue for saying so! *"The soul itself taketh the name of publican, because it was created pure by God but hath become defiled in the body*

and doth not wish to behold heaven, but, being tormented in the
bosom with conscience of wicked deeds, it crieth out with heavy
sighs and unceasing voice: O God, freely have mercy upon me . . ."

I peered and peered into the motionlessness of the leaves, which
hung on the autumn oaks as still as in a funeral wreath. All around
stood an indescribable silence: the river roared, the leaves rustled
underfoot. "Hurry! Hurry!" squealed the alpha male, hammering
at the rail with all his might. "Hurry, hurry!" they shouted from
the other bank, and the drummer beat an appropriate rhythm on
the monkeys' bar, as on a tom-tom. But suddenly, not even suddenly but within the word "suddenly," something, or even not
something but something located within the word "something"—
happened, moved, occurred. The picture slid sideways as if coming
unstuck, it hung by one corner, it rolled up, the heavens curled at
the edges in the manner of a Chinese pagoda, the alpha male froze
with the rusty bolt poised over the rail, the drummer failed to finish
his rhythm, and even the river hushed. And within this very silence,
and not the preceding one, was born another silence, it tensed and
swelled like an immense bubble, like a vein on the Divine brow,
and when it burst with a minus-sound, like a dehermeticized vacuum, it gave birth to a sound until then unprecedented in my life,
alive, multiple and total, implacably nearing and growing, like a
tree, like an avalanche, like a torrent, rushing at us—and nothing,
well, exactly nothing changed before my eyes—nothing moved, not
a leaf, but I couldn't take my eyes off this indescribable sound
. . . No words . . .

3. The Cock

. . . Have we already discussed this with someone, the nature
of the indescribable? It wasn't Pavel Petrovich, was it? None other.
I seem to remember talking with him . . .

Now an indescribable terror grips you, now an indescribable

ecstasy. You've taken up your pen, so write, if you're all that much of a writer . . . But what to write about, if not the indescribable? The undescribed—anyone who happens on it will write about it. But the writer bumps against both these walls, of ecstasy and terror, as he forces his way down the narrow corridor of narration (narration is narrowtion, an Englishman once told me). We want to expand to full breadth: who has painted the sea? or the mountains? the forest? the sky? Turgenev and Bunin tested their skill a bit, back when we had time. And again, Turner (as Pavel Petrovich suggested). Again, indescribable silence: the cicadas shrilled and the surf roared unceasingly, a violin string snapped in the fog, and someone blew plaintively into a bottle . . . If it's indescribable, we say, write it beautifully. The more indescribable, we say, the more beautifully. What, is the ugly describable? With the ugly, it simply seems permissible to write a little worse . . . All the same, the beautiful is like . . . and the ugly is like . . . We can't do without the "like." But language isn't comparisons, it's words. Words are encased in the dictionary. And we are encased in words. A fly, so to speak, in amber. So which is beautiful, the amber or the fly? Words vanish from the dictionary, precipitating out as if from a supersaturated solution. The indescribable animal, the horse, has at last been described: for his every joint we have chosen, with love, a primordially Russian word. And now what? The horse is leaving the dictionary, part by part. First the cannon bone, then the gaskin, then the fetlock, then the pastern, then the coronet— all that remains is the mane and hooves, his corneous integument. Also vanishing part by part, after the horse, are the cow, the house, the songbirds, and the grasses. What kind of collectivization is this? The commissars, we say, came and removed everything from the farmyard. But no, it wasn't the commissars alone who did it. We did. And the words that have appeared in exchange—these are anonyms, not words. What do I get from "automation" and "disaggregation"? Not a kopeck. Well, "airplane" is a good word . . . What will I see if I look out the window, not of a house, but of an airplane? Not a fence, not a hen—I'll see an indescribable beauty, which no one ever saw before the airplane. Rosy white, unbroken, whipped up, boundless, swirling, and above it a sort of, how best to express it? a deep, deep blue, azure, sky-blue, well, just like, oh, just like . . . just like the sky. But where are you? I'm flying in the sky. So what's indescribable about it, if it's the sky? What are the clouds like? Like cotton . . . And they're nothing but cotton. The Arctic, the cosmos. Well, all right: An indescribable silence. All around stood an indescribable silence, I'll write. A good Russian construction. No, better: All around stood silence. More pregnant, somehow. Stood like a pillar—another good idiom. Better yet, let the pillar stand like a silence. More fitting for the pillar. Silence. Maybe that's enough. Silence—and it's all there.

Silence.

Indescribable, however.

"But silence stands in our room like a spinning wheel . . ."

Then it is, after all, describable?

But a spinning wheel? Before long, in what dictionary will you be able to look up this word?

And besides, you won't find silence.

Until it comes over you irrevocably. Until "an elephant treads on your ear" and leaves you tone deaf.

Silence came on like an elephant . . . Is that good?

It's not good . . .

A year passed, and I literally stood on the slope of that oak mountain, waiting. The country awoke and looked around unrecognizingly: Who were these people? It had not survived 1984 after all . . . First thing in the morning it began a new life. It forbade itself to take a hair-of-the-dog, and it cut down the vineyards. There was no sense in returning to Tamysh. Hacked-up coils of pipe lay scattered on the famous lawns. The fiery heart of the farmyard had been torn out. The populace was digging its weapons and, in the same garden rows, burying its stills. At the Seventh or Fifth Zantarias', the Fifth or Seventh Zantaria took his sawed-off shotgun, sweetly redolent of kerosene, and shot the local policeman point-blank as he dismantled the still.

It no longer made any sense to go to Tamysh, because now we could go to America. There we rested up from it all by telling all about it. What did *they* understand about this?

"Five more years have passed, / And a hundred rocket blasts"—Daur's five-year-old son was already writing excellent verses, but I was still standing in the monkey grove, not moving from the spot. People found ways to drink, of course, but the vines had been felled and the weapons dug. History ripped the pages from my unwritten book, one after another. As soon as it became permissible to joke, people lost the desire, and little by little they began to kill each other. Only in the beginning did it seem that they had ceased to joke because hope had dawned. All my premonitions turned into reality, and I was too late with my prophecy. To tell the story of the Rafik with the Armenian and the Georgian, the Jew and the Russian, had become irrelevant. But what else did I know? My knowledge of monkeys was poor. When I remembered, I tried to close my ears. To have been acquainted briefly with the monkeys' leader and more closely with the alpha male was obviously not enough. As the years went by, I was no longer even sure that they were specifically called hamadryas baboons, and not something else. Well, how can you write about a tribe if you don't even know their name? They weren't Americans . . .

And why were things so bad, when they were finally going so well for me? People entered, as always, uninvited, but sober and shaven. They had used the nailbrush first thing in the morning, they smelled of made-in-Hong Kong, and they said, Everything is permissible. What was permissible they didn't say. "Now you may write your *Monkeys* . . ." But who the four-letter needed my *Monkeys*!

Better they hadn't smiled. They entered with caressing tiger-smiles, they unlocked the cage . . . The zoo, it turned out, was not on the outside.

Where are my *Soldiers of Empire?*

Where is Dryunya? Selling atrocious *matryoshki* at the Brandenburg Gate. Where is the Eye? Published his best-seller in Paris. Where is the Drifter? On a yacht in the Mediterranean, with an intellectual friend. Where is Zyablikov? Fled to Mongolia. Where are the Inventor Brothers? Opened a patent office, jointly with one of the emirates. Million Tomatoes? Auditing shops. Einstein? Washing dishes in Princeton. Saltyk alone sings his old songs. And Colonel Adidasov is at his old job.

Did I lead them out to the shore of the Pontus? Or did they burn up in the conflagration?

Where are my *Live Souls?*

What are you laughing at? Not the television . . . Yourselves? I have walked in sneakers all over the Empire, and I am weeping, like Gogol. Comrades, we have entered a new historical period! The freedom to laugh at our own selves.

They had gotten their way. HE had burned up in this conflagration, and I had taken to drinking alone. HE or I? I was left like Robinson without Friday. It was no joke to stand idle for seven years without moving, always in the same ringing uninhabited grove—snow did not fall, summer did not come. Within, the autumnal splendor of emptiness. And all around, only changes! A home at last, a wife, a child. I've returned from America to a dacha. I'll just dig my potatoes and take off for Paris. *Glasnost.* An enveloping muteness . . .

Fullness. Emptiness. Not a line. What am I without HIM? What is Friday without Robinson . . . I have surrendered. Joined the herd. Hurrying on before, the leader continues to roll ahead of him a kind of monkey Tao. If anyone thinks I know what that is, the TAO, it's the Tuva Autonomous Oblast . . .

But how the primordial birds have pecked my head!

A restlessness took hold of me. No urge toward a change of place. No part of me left alive on the map. Only Albania. Luckily I couldn't go there. An aching sensation of mediocrity. Recollections of youth.

There are women of whom you're unworthy,
There are women whom you have not saved.

I was gripped by the premonition that I had missed my time.
That is, that I had missed a premonition.

I have no God, I have no Mom—
I hold a pistol in my palm.
I have no God, I have no Mom . . .

And so, I was passing time at the dacha, just outside Moscow.
All evening we played cards and watched television. What did
Ruslan Imranovich say again to Rafik Nisanovich? "Rafik Nisanovich," said Ruslan Imranovich to Rafik Nisanovich. And this
time what did Rafik Nisanovich reply to Ruslan Imranovich? "Ruslan Imranovich," replied Rafik Nisanovich to Ruslan Imranovich.
And there was method in this: my wife doubled the stakes. I had
two sequences of three and she had one, but hers was higher, and
I lost.

And went upstairs to my room. Downstairs the children were
asleep, my wife was getting ready for bed. I took the typewriter
out of its case and inserted a sheet of paper. The keyboard was
overgrown with gray fur. Mechanically I looked at my hands. I
remembered: dust on his hand . . . What was that from?

Not like this, all at once. Seven years—and all at once. As
though *perestroika* had taught nothing . . . Standing in the grove,
I stretched my stiffened legs.

I lay down. Someone's unread manuscript crackled underneath
me like leaves. Everybody was writing now—and I was supposed
to read it . . . Pencil to write notes. Pad to write them on. Angrily
I knocked the manuscript together in a ragged pile . . .

AWAITING MONKEYS

I wrote, on the back of the young author. And underlined it.

Never had I taken such a risk! Never had I written the title before writing at least a page. Lest I stumble, right at the start. A blank page looks dreadful with just the title, all by itself at the top! Worse yet if there's an epigraph. For example, "Linger a while, moment!" At this point a Russian Faust comes along. Stops dead in his tracks.

"Ah, but who," I wrote fearfully,

is awaiting whom? Ape-man, alpha male . . . The first and the last . . . In what beginning is my end? . . . Obligation. Obsession. For oh! yes, O! is the mega-letter. The ovum. Oval. Zero. Onus Opus Onan Odium   It's so elegant   So intelligent   What shall I . . .

Oh, I already hate them!

Not those innocent, or rather blameless, mammals—I hate the very necessity of writing about them.

Why, strictly speaking, am I Obligated to write about them? And where does this Obsession fit into the plot?

The page ended. I wrote the number two and lapsed into a reverie. "Description of Waiting," I wrote, and again lapsed into a reverie. I put three periods as ellipsis points, like this . . . And promptly put the number three, as if omitting the description temporarily. As if to say, that's a technical question.

They were right, those critics! In my own example, I was becoming convinced that any kind of formalism was evidence of paucity of thought and poverty of content. If writing a few words beginning with *O* indicated a thought, what was my "description of waiting"? I definitely had nothing to describe—that was the problem!

Well, I'm waiting. There was meaning in that. I remember there was some meaning. But then it would have been better if they hadn't come running . . . Immediately they were nothing special. People. Ordinary people, just like us. Except slightly handsomer than we are, perhaps, from their point of view. Wonderful manes. The chest and arms. When they come pouring down the mountain at you with this uniquely alive, powerful rustle, face on, so to speak, growing rapidly larger as they come closer, and it's not they who are running but you running at them . . . this is amazing. Like a movie. Because a movie is something you haven't seen in real life . . . but here it's real life! And that, let me tell you, is something! That's life, not the zoo . . .

But now he's right beside you. The baboon. He's the chief baboon, because the first. He suddenly becomes smaller than his own size. Probably he just seemed bigger when he was running so fast. But also because everything he has behind somehow doesn't compare with what he has in front. Behind, the baboon is somehow unfinished. As if he'd been run over. There are unfortunate dogs like this, with paralyzed hind limbs . . . smooth-haired breeds, the Great Dane, bulldog, boxer . . . with disproportionately narrow rear ends . . . that was how Linda died, God rest her soul! What is it like, there in dog paradise? Probably like here . . .

So he's half lion, half dog. Inhospitable, glowering. You shouldn't meet his glance, they warn you about that. That is, it's all right to meet it, but avert your eyes immediately. Don't stare straight at him, because he'll perceive it as aggression. Might even grab. His fangs fill you with . . . Wouldn't grab the alpha male, of course. He bragged endlessly, that Dragamashchenka . . . You're not advised to stare at the females, either—this, too, the leader might take personally. I kept having to remind HIM of this . . . Aha! At last I remember! I was still with HIM then. We were together then, at the monkey colony. HE . . . Well, how could HE help staring, when she had God knows what going on behind! The whole thing was turned inside out, unconcealed, and shone with all the colors of the rainbow. It might even change hue depending on maturity, ripeness, and readiness . . . Never in my life had I seen anything uglier! Although, on second thought, the question is purely aesthetic, which is to say, debatable. These frightful genitalia are presented as the main argument, for good reason. And painted,

possibly, with love. Yes, exactly. With love! Without love, it would
never make sense. Evolution didn't toil over this makeup without
purpose. In the end, you can't deny that it's . . . You and I have
hidden it all—the only thing left is the photo on our passport.
That's where the marriage stamp goes. But they . . . Even on their
faces they have something similar, like the ischial callosities, but
a trifle more modest . . . what's the term? anyway, those things on
the cheek, near the nose . . . also striped red and blue. Clowns,
masks, the carnival, the revealed secret—the secret *is* the mask.
So when they look at a portrait, that is, at a face, they're already
forming an idea of the charms that await them *there* . . . I must
give HIM his due: he had always perceived nature more keenly and
vividly than I. I would have to distract him somehow, because the
leader was already watching disapprovingly.

But so far the baboon was busy demolishing the "granules."
They did, in fact, prove to be a treat, despite their unprepossessing
appearance. There were actually enough of them for one. He raked
them all into a pile and seated himself on the bar. Hovering around
him were females and flunkies. A certain female was the most
flirtatious, another male the most pesky. They, too, got something:
she a granule, he a beating. HE was observing the female, I the
flunky. In particular, the flunky informed on a young whipper-
snapper who dared, behind the leader's back, to eat a granule that
the leader had accidentally dropped. Reprisal was instantaneous.
First the flunky got beaten, then the next male within reach. The
next-within-reach began squealing something about justice and got
it again, but this time the guilty party was presented as proof, and
he, too, got it, rather indulgently, as a matter of form. With an
exaggeratedly plaintive howl, testifying to the heaviness of the sov-
ereign's hand, he ran off to apprise everyone of the existence of
justice. At last the fink was given one of the granules. The leader
was wise and just, he was weary of his subordinates' petty squab-
bles. Having attended to justice as casually as to a call of nature,
the leader turned away—and caught HIM staring immodestly at the

royal favorite. For some time they eyed each other, but at last even HE understood . . . averted his eyes and didn't get a beating. For the leader, this was enough. He apparently considered it an acknowledgment of defeat, if not a victory.

And that was all, I think. I don't think there was anything else. After that, we sat on the bank and did what we had come here to do. Reclining by the campfire not far from the Rafik, under the arching branches, we gobbled kebabs made of meat taken from the juvenile delinquents, sipped young wine taken from the old folks, glanced across the river at the other bank teeming with monkeys—and, in embarrassment, averted our surfeited glance from their hungry one. From the look the leader threw the alpha male, I understood that the leader was wise. He was the first to realize that there would be no more, there were roots and acorns for now, and he shouldn't count on more than a one-time incentive for the leadership in plain view of his subordinates. He understood all this about Dragamashchenka, and, preserving a sense of his own dignity . . .

. . . Omitting the description of waiting, I covered the back of the young author's next page, under the number three:

Output without input. O – I. 0 – 0.

O. It's a hole, a void, a vacuum, it vacuums out all my thoughts. And I resist (make faces, stream like a flag) this wind and whistling, wave my arms, slowly twist, untwist, and twist again, the only part of me alive is my suit with its flapping double entendre, trousered double-breastedness—and the necktie on my shoulder. A movie hero . . .

Two zeros, two holes. In one, out the other.

O is flat, O is a mirror . . . I shatter my face against my own reflection.

Reflection . . . rejection, dejection. L'Étranger misérable. Camus and Hugo all in one. The novel Whom?

The old monkey in Krylov's fable holds a child-sized oval mirror and makes faces at me in it. He has grown "weak in the eyes"...

In infancy I understood the fable thus: "The monkey is old and grows to be eyes..." I didn't know then that he would grow to be my eyes.

I could have no suspicion that I would grow old.

The page ended, and I wrote the number four.

"Fire," I wrote below it. "Description of the Conflagration."

That's *it*! That's the thing I not only couldn't but also didn't want to describe! And besides, what can I write if I don't remember anything! I remember only the black hole of the sea, and charred seagulls on the shore, like moths around a great lamp. The lamp was shaped like a rooster. I remember I was alone. Without HIM. I turned away to keep from watching. Several flaming brands shot quite far out and fell into the water like spent rockets, barely lighting up a greasy black sea with seagull corpses floating in it. For some reason I kept thinking that by some miracle HE would suddenly surface out of what was happening behind me. Grubby, insolent, kindred, he would say something cheeky to me, something especially rude and insulting—and I would agree with him and be happy as never before. "It's your own fault," HE would say, for example. "Don't forget to turn off electrical appliances when you go out. And besides, your novel was . . . well, it'll burn like blue blazes!" "Blue?" I would ask, and force myself to turn and look. But the flame bursting from the windows is not blue, or even red, but black, like the sea . . . But the white walls are pink and the black sky is white, and in the sky, high above the conflagration, at the pinnacle of the coiling spire of smoke, there is something fluttering like a flag—now red, now gold, a red golden cockerel. He flaps and screeches, fanning the fire with his wings . . . "To hell with it!" I would say lightly, of the manuscript. *"We're alive . . ."*

But HE never did come, and I never did turn to look, merely

repeated without cease the sole prayer I remembered—the publican's prayer:

God be merciful to me a sinner.

God be merciful to me a sinner.

God be merciful to me a sinner.

No strength to lift my head, no strength to lift my hand and cross myself, standing in that same monkey grove.

One, two, three, four . . . Mousie's tugging at the door. One, two, three, four, five . . . Bunny's glad to be alive. Five. I crossed out the number and omitted—after the monkeys—the fire as well . . .

> *O . . . Omissions, omens, orisons . . . Nymph in thy . . . Opprobrium, opium, oblivion. A nobody. A zero without a stick. Without balls. Orchidectomized. Orphaned.*
>
> *O is the Tao! Ta-da, the Tao! I didn't know what the Tao was, had no idea—and that, again, was the Tao. "Word," incidentally, is the most nonexistent word. How can it name itself? Word equals Tao. Word minus Tao equals O. O equals Tao minus word. The word "word" is already a koan.*
>
> *No complaints against the author, however! What is the title of this piece?* AWAITING MONKEYS. *So wait!*

Ominously I dated the first page, above the title. By now it was the morning of the next day—August 19, 1991.

Papa was believed to be working upstairs. Ordinarily my wife's voice woke me from below, as she shouted at the children not to make noise and disturb Papa.

But I was wakened by a suspicious silence. My first impression, when I saw them downstairs, was that they were kneeling and praying to the television. Later this impression was corrected and explained, but only in part. They simply weren't dressed yet, and their long nightshirts and . . . Oh, children know full well when to keep quiet! The announcer's voice alone sufficed. The kind of announcer ousted by democratic changes, he had been brought back to read the text of an urgent emergency message from the government. It was not yet a declaration of war, but it was already a sentence. I suddenly felt that my whole life, overnight, had been made into a not very esoteric film, with cliché layered on cliché: nightshirts, frightened children, wife clinging to the stirrup . . . I couldn't bear it even a second longer.

I drove out to the highway—but the movie continued. A wind that was not wind, silence that was not silence. Desert. All it lacked was a camel. It did have sand. Somehow the sand began by crunching in my teeth. I put up the window—but then the serpentine swish against the glass became especially audible. As if there were a dune up ahead where I was going, and all these curling strands were blowing from its crest . . . I was driving alone. The absence of traffic in either direction was inexplicable. The air was opaque, despite clear and cloudless weather. And actually there wasn't even a wind. The sand simply hung in the air, and I drove through it. Moreover, the sand grains were coarse: you could almost say they were pebbles drumming on the windshield. I wanted to wipe it clean. But what needed to be wiped was the sky. The dusty sky crackled around me like an old movie, in which I, apparently, had been filmed, going somewhere *over there* . . . Strictly speaking, my car was standing still, and the threadbare landscape was rushing past on either side, as is proper in a film studio. *As though* I were driving. I pretended to turn the steering wheel. I was going nowhere. I was waiting. Waiting *as I once had* . . .

Wait—it doesn't matter what for. For a bus, for the woman you love. It's a formula, not a reason. You wait because you are predestined, because you have been described, because you are inside the description. I wasn't waiting for the monkeys themselves. I had landed in a text that described waiting for them. This was it—the state when it's not you but something happening to you. The state from which all literature comes. Its essence. You don't write literature, or read it, when you become an element in it. This was the elegantly termed déjà vu, when you feel that this exact instant has already happened, and this space, and this time, and you in it, that you were left hanging in this familiar and unrecognizable instant forever. It has happened, already happened . . . Of course it has! The ordinary recognition of the unwritten text.

I seem to remember having had a vehement squabble with HIM. I was stuck over there in that glade, trampling leaves redolent of cognac—although I had long since crossed to this bank and was unburdening myself on the subject of silence, in conversation with the drummer. "I understand you," he said, agreeing. "Otherwise, why would I drum?" They all understood me now, agreed with me. I was exceptionally right. This irritated HIM.

By now I was drinking alone, without HIM. Today I could indulge, and I was quickly getting drunk. This, too, could only irritate HIM—that he wasn't being served. They came and sat beside me by turns, first Pavel Petrovich, then Million Tomatoes, then Doctor D., and then Valery Givivovich, making sure everything was in order. It was. Victoria hummed her arias to me. I found a kind word for everyone, I who today, toward morning, had successfully led them all out to the Pontine shore!

"But Simyon . . ."

"Yes, we lost Simyon," I said, ignoring HIS rejoinder, "and nevertheless we endured all the hardships of narration and came to the sea, because we were together."

"Together? . . ."

Again I ignored HIS empty, pleading glass. "Yes, yes, precisely. *Together.*"

"Well, and what next?"

"The free element! . . . What's the matter, freedom's not enough for you?"

"Freedom your mother . . . What next, I ask you?"

And HE went off to gather brush for the dying campfire.

Something made me turn abruptly toward the river. A large

baboon on the other bank had come right down to the water and was looking in our direction. I thought this was the leader, and it struck me that he was staring at us. Of course, his eyes were impossible to make out at such a distance, but I could feel that stare. It was the same stare with which he had first met me, wary and fearless, submissive and burning. As though he had averted it so quickly not because he feared us, but in order to keep us from guessing that he did not. Now he wasn't afraid that I would understand this . . . Finally, as if having made sure that I was looking in his direction, he picked up a fallen tree from the bank and carried it to one side, where he threw it on a pile. And another baboon promptly aped him, adding his mite.

They're building a fire! I guessed.

They were copying HIS movements!

Doctor D. undertook to disabuse me of this.

"Understand, it's not a fire they're building, but a pile! You're not about to claim he'll strike a spark now by rubbing two sticks—"

"Beat a jackrabbit and he'll learn to light matches," Pavel Petrovich said, seconding me in his own way.

"These Russians!" Million Tomatoes said. "They always have to beat a jackrabbit, break a birch tree. Where else? What other nation? A leafy tree, so you go out and break it—"

"Shall I tell you what you are?!" HE broke out indignantly. "You . . . you are a person of the Abkhaz persuasion!"

HE could not have said anything more offensive. But Million Tomatoes possessed one unfortunate characteristic: he was so strong that he couldn't hit a man without killing him. Therefore people were always hitting him. Therefore he did not take offense but started laughing, as if at a joke.

"An unlucky nationality we are . . ."

"You, an unlucky nationality?" Givivovich flared. "*We* are the unluckiest nationality—because of you!"

"Who will dispute that the Armenians are the unluckiest nation?"

The opinion sounded so indisputable that everyone fell silent. Who else had a territory so small that it consisted of history alone?

"And who will pity Greece?" said our own Greek, the monkey-colony electrician. "Greece, which created the whole of culture, the whole of Europe, the whole of the present-day world?"

"The whole of it?" we asked in surprise.

The Greek presented his proof, and the Armenian's ironic glance was as nothing to him.

"What about it, were the ancient Greeks really the same as present-day ones?"

"They were blond and blue-eyed."

"The Armenians were blond and blue-eyed, too!"

"Then surely it's not the Russians," Pavel Petrovich said.

"What do you mean, it's not the Russians?"

"I mean, it's not the Russians who are to blame for everything. The Russians were blond and blue-eyed, too."

"As were the Jews, however."

"Even now there are more blond and blue-eyed people in Israel than in the homeland of the blond knaves."

"That's what I'm saying, the Russians are the unhappiest nation."

"*We're* an unhappy nation?!"

"Unhappiest of all are the Germans," the drummer said in a sorrowful whisper.

He understood the nature of sound, and everything became quiet.

One of us said, however, "Why don't we quarrel about which of us is happiest?"

Can it be that language began directly with the vowels? But then how was the first vowel born? A-a-a-argh! This is *pain.* O-o-o-ow.

"But do you know," Million Tomatoes said, "what became of the horse? Do you remember the horse?"

"The one who ate the apples?"

"Why, yes. They shot him."

"Shot such a horse!" Again, HE took the whole thing personally. "Out of envy, was it? Or before the races? . . . Right at the
races!?" His imagination was running riot.

Million Tomatoes laughed. "Certainly not. They simply shot
him. He broke his leg, and they shot him."

"And ate him, I suppose?" HE said angrily. "The only thing
you pity is the Russian birch tree?"

"But the doctor has eaten a crow!" Pavel Petrovich said, settling the ethnic conflict then and there in Doctor D.'s favor.

We talked a while about horsemeat and pork, about the great
land where the cow is not eaten—and about religions, naturally.
Our religious disagreements again developed into ethnic ones, and
Pavel Petrovich led the conversation into the homestretch: cannibalism . . . Now, that was a topic! I had never thought people gave
it so much thought . . .

It became clear that what distinguished civilized men, among
whom, I will note in parentheses, were all who had gathered here,
both the Armenian and the Georgian, both the Georgian and the
Abkhaz, both the Abkhaz and the Russian, both the Russian and
the Jew, and also the sole Greek among us, because, I will note in
a second parenthesis, there were two of each of us, and sometimes
even three . . . the difference between civilized men and the savage,
of whom, I will note in still another parenthesis, there was for some
reason just one, and imaginary at that, but for some reason iden-
tically imagined by all: a black man, in a little skirt and a nose
ring, which to all appearances uniquely prevented him from eating
a man . . . well, it became clear that the savage kills his enemy
and eats him, but neither kills nor eats a person like himself, while
the civilized man kills his enemy but does not eat him, yet devours
a person like himself willingly, and moreover alive, by very diverse
methods, such as the family, society, and other so-called human
relationships . . . Moreover, to my great displeasure, HE was the
one who took the initiative in this discussion. How had I let HIM
slip past me?

"Now, would you eat an Armenian?" HE asked.

"Me? eat an Armenian? never!" Valery Givivovich said indignantly.

"And would you eat Valery Givivovich?" HE asked Million Tomatoes.

Et cetera. And Pavel Petrovich again stopped the gastronomic disagreements from becoming ethnic, the squabble from becoming slaughter. He reined in the headstrong argument at full gallop, over the abyss of the Jewish question.

"I," he stated categorically, "would never classify meat according to an ethnic criterion. I'd eat everyone indiscriminately . . . This would be useful in every respect, the ecological above all. I'd eat man if he were tasty. But he tastes revolting, I'm sure, for a more rotten creature does not exist in nature. Yes, I will venture to say that he is also by nature the most imperfect creature. Perfection follows a descending curve in relation to evolution: the fly is more perfect than the elephant, and the infusorian more perfect than the fly. And everything that tears itself from its habitat and runs is more imperfect than that which is rooted—more imperfect than a plant. Only a plant abides in the earth and in the sky, in darkness and in light, in death and in life . . . And everything is more perfect than man! Man's imperfection is indeed his sentence. He's a failure! A failure. Creation was abandoned at this stage. Evolution was discontinued. The only thing left to us is degeneration, mutation—"

"Pavel Petrovich," HE put in suddenly, with ingratiating courtesy. "Remove the hair from your lip—"

Pavel Petrovich automatically pinched his lip, in search of—

"—lest it hinder you from bullshitting," HE said distinctly.

"What, what?" I hadn't quite heard.

"Turn off the kettle and simmer down."

In the ensuing silence Doctor D. could be heard sobbing. "I don't want to talk about evolution! I don't want to talk about mutation! I want to talk about diplodoci! They were jolly and kind, they rejoiced in life . . . loved to dance . . ."

"Sure. Blond, blue-eyed."

Something flashed on the other bank, then flashed again. Impossible to make it out in the gathering dusk. They couldn't have struck a spark?

"What did YOU just say??" I didn't recognize my own voice.

"I simply said, didn't you forget to turn off the kettle."

"But didn't YOU turn it off?"

"I did not."

"Really?"

"Really."

Those were *eyes* glinting! The eyes of the leader on the other bank . . . But how brightly!

"I can't believe you wouldn't eat me," I heard from the bushes.

"I wouldn't eat YOU even on a desert island!" My voice rang with pride.

"Too squeamish?!"

The bushes were snapping, the leader's eye was glinting, and the boiled-dry *jezve* on the windowsill was growing red-hot . . . I, HE, Pavel Petrovich, and Doctor D. . . .

"A ban on a particular meat, the imposition of a taboo on particular animals, is essentially that same membrane—the pre-prohibition against eating the meat of man . . ."

"The membrane from a beefsteak? Ha, ha . . . There's no commandment 'Thou shalt not eat.' The commandment is 'Thou shalt not kill . . .' Why doesn't the number of commandments match the number of deadly sins?"

"If it's gluttony, if you go ape over meat—only then is it a deadly sin. You have to want terribly to eat a man!"

"A glutton is not a gourmet."

"Man is like a tower. There's a reason why he's vertical, walks upright . . . An animal keeps its eyes on the ground . . . But our tower has holes. Mouth, nose, eyes, ears, and so on. Seven holes for the seven sins . . . The holes are armed with membranes . . . Commandments, prohibitions, taboos, chastity . . . If a membrane is ruptured, man is dehermeticized—temptation, sin, and evil enter freely through the hole. The devil leads the assault . . . Battering rams, ladders. Arson. The man flames up from within . . . A conflagration . . . The tower blazes . . . Sparks fly from the windows and embrasures, flame shoots out . . . Bruegel has these towers, Bosch has them. As many as you wish . . ."

"Does the number of holes match the number of sins?"

"If you count a pair as one, there are six. But there are seven sins."

"The eyes don't have holes."

"As a child I was sure that the pupil was a tiny hole. I even tried to insert a needle in it, in front of the mirror."

"Well? What happened?"

"I got scared. Everything's backward in the mirror."

"Man is imperfect because he's supposed to perfect himself. On his own. With God's help, of course. It's not a sentence, to be a man. It's a purpose."

"You don't mean to say that man is a profession?"

"That's exactly what I mean."

"A profession, a purpose, a tower—next you'll say a vessel of sin. Holes . . . The doctor is right. The worm invented our body."

"I am slave, I am king, I am worm, I am God!"

"Two holes. In one, out the other."

"Two men . . . The one was a publican, and the other a Pharisee . . ."

"You're a Pharisee, Pavel Petrovich!"

"Who, me?! I have tasted of tribulation in public houses all over this land!"

"It makes no difference what hole pride enters by. You've got no reason to boast. Nowadays the Pharisee is much more of a publican than you. The Pharisee has become a publican, and the publican a Pharisee."

"Two men went up into the temple . . ."

"And neither came out."

"No, both came out. Two publicans went into the temple, and two Pharisees came out."

"And what we got was Prometheus!"

"Not Prometheus, but Danko. Prometheus was before the Birth of Christ."

"Oh, go sit on your progress! Fire, the wheel, the lever . . . Slavery—that's man's only invention."

"Prometheus didn't invent fire, he invented the home still. That's why he had liver trouble. Cirrhosis is 'eagle,' in translation."

"Translation from . . . ?"

"The medical."

"Is drunkenness gluttony?"

"A controversial question. 'Eat, drink. This is my Body and my Blood . . .' Who said that?"

"On first thought—"

"There's never just one. Two holes—"

"There's *only* one. How does that go? 'Until the alive becomes the dead, and the dead the alive . . .' "

"The outer the inner, and the inner the outer . . ."

"The man a woman, and the woman a man . . ."

"And has this already happened?"

"Why, of course. All of it has. You just *think* you're turning yourself inside out with effort. You'll no more see the Kingdom of Heaven than your own ears!"

"Is the ear, at least, a hole?"

"You're talking damned nonsense, but you yourself took meat from children, wine from old men, and fruit from monkeys! . . . And you ate your God."

"Beg your pardon? Ate?"

"Literally. As a body. He descended, and you ate Him."

"Will you finally shut up!"

"Ate Him! Ate Him!"

"Don't blaspheme, you fool!"

"Pharisee! I hate—"

I lunged for HIM. He went crashing through the bushes like an animal fleeing pursuit. A large one, though . . . Suddenly, in silence and darkness, I was groping around on all fours as if I had lost my glasses. Suddenly, I heard . . .

Sobbing, on all fours, rear end sticking up in unseemly fashion, face buried in the moldering leaves . . .

"O Lord, if I am a formula, I curse Thee, that I may continue to believe in Thee.

"O Lord, if Thou art not, I curse Thee, that Thou mayest exist at least in my curse.

"O Lord, if Thou art, and I am not a formula, is this not too much for happiness?"

"That was when it all happened," I recalled, my tires crunching along the highway. The desert stretched on. The sand flew coarser and coarser, struck the windshield more and more ringingly. And then, as I compared that silence and this one, that rustle of fallen leaves and this whisper of sand, that sense of expectation and this, and found them identical, I realized that I was waiting, and for what. In my unmilitary mind, the insight was blinding: I had never seen them free, the tanks, any more than I had seen the monkeys . . . I realized that the tanks had traveled down the highway ahead of me. They had ground up the asphalt and sent dust and sand rising to the sky.

Yes, that was when it all happened. HE was struggling to get to the other bank with a box of groceries, to feed the monkeys. Pavel Petrovich was teaching Doctor D. to puke, Valery Givivovich had his arm around Million Tomatoes . . . But I was seeing a flaming tower, with fire shooting from all its holes, and that tower was— the Hotel Abkhazia. Manuscripts burn splendidly, and the conflagration was starting from a manuscript! Especially with such a lot of plywood around it . . .

On the way back, Pavel Petrovich babbled some more nonsense about a descended God: Since we had not fulfilled our purpose, and He had already given us freedom of choice, He was no longer able to interfere or correct, but neither did He divest Himself of responsibility. He sent us His Son and we didn't understand, we assigned the heavens and the churches to Him and carried on as before. He had no choice but to share our lot, to descend to us and dissolve in us. In this sense, He is among us. And is even, perhaps, one of us. And we never know with whom we are dealing—every time we meet a man, not inconceivably we are meeting Him . . .

But I understood that all was over. Not just the hotel had burned, and not just my manuscript, but *live souls*. The empire had ended, history had ended, life had ended—I didn't care what happened next. Didn't care in what sequence the debris and burning brands went flying, or at what velocity.

Somehow everything had become too clear about the future.

It didn't matter. It didn't matter what happened now. Because what had been would never be again. When what has been vanishes, what would have been vanishes also, along with it, because not even an atom of what has been will be contained in what will be. You will not be. What's the difference.

Both when I finally saw the first tank and when I saw the burning Abkhazia, both when I came up against that armored dune and when the heat of the fire stopped me, perhaps the sand got in my eyes, or the smoke, but I cared so little, pitied myself so little, that I started to cry.

"And you privately think you're free of vainglory?" It was HIS sickening voice.

"Vainglory!" My blood boiled. "What's that got to do with it!"

"You don't regret your labor. When did you ever labor? You regret the lottery ticket—which might have been a winner, at last. Anything could suddenly happen . . . and suddenly didn't. By the way, you abuse that little word 'suddenly.' "

Oh, HE knew how to get me! I blew up. "Who are you to say this to me! Purulent pederast!"

"Fie! Intelligent, the man thinks he is. An intellectual."

So much poison HE put into the one root . . .

"Who, me—an intellectual?" I said indignantly, just like HIM.

"But *I'm* not," HE parried regally.

I couldn't argue with that.

"And then," he said, resentfully and smugly. "Judge for yourself, how could I be gay?"

"Did I say it, or did you? In your opinion, if someone's intellectual he's homosexual?"

"What, aren't they synonyms?"

"You know the word 'synonym'?"

He burst out laughing. "Who can say what burned in the library at Alexandria? Were there many masterpieces? Maybe Bulgakov destroyed it so that he could speak his famous phrase? Was Heraclitus all that good, apart from the quotations? Gogol . . . It's definitely the masterpieces that burn. Easier for us that way. How inconvenient without a conflagration—we have to lose our manuscripts by the suitcaseful, like Hemingway . . . So let me tell you: that's definitely your masterpiece burning now. *Live Souls!* Why *Soldiers of Empire*? I'd advise you to rename the book. Stick to this version. Even better, burn with it. A most happy finale! Right away you'll be a genius. Myth is a splendid advertisement. People will start reading you, finding out what burned, your unrealized potential . . . Who can say that it wasn't vast? You have to leave a trail of potentialities, not texts. It's not enough to be better than others. Takes too long. Much easier to get what doesn't belong to you, all at one go. Death—and right away your whole future, entire. And you don't have to stick your neck in a noose, shoot yourself, burn your masterpieces, or lose your suitcases . . . That's not your work or worry anymore—*they* will take care of the mourning and the money. They, too, have to exist somehow. They'll *work*! For you, by the way. Just leave it to them. Give in. Walk away. Why keep on existing and existing? Make widows of them, go ahead, do it! Let them screw on your grave with the gravedigger—now, that's recognition! Real recognition. Glory. And it has nothing to do with the tsar, or society—it was fate, the elements! A better co-author

. . . No. Drunken nobodies get hit by a tractor, the great man never!
I dare you!"

I lunged toward the fire so that HE would stop me, and he did:

" 'Co-author,' 'tractor'—do they rhyme?"

"As you wish," I said, slain. "Better, 'provocateur.' Is it true
that none of them ever perished in an accident?"

"Unclaimed by fate. That's why they dramatized it."

"Just now my text is in flames—this is no dramatization."

"What do you think, did the rats and cats manage to escape?"

"What the . . ."

"Because you'll be the culprit in their death. Maybe one of
them was a Copernicus."

"Not Copernicus. Giordano Bruno."

"What difference does it make? Even *people* bother you less
than your manuscript. But don't worry—nobody burned."

"How do you know?"

"It's no special trick. I observe life. There's just one man who
can still burn in this historic conflagration—"

"It just won't be you."

"Again, notice: I'm the boor, but you're the one who always
makes rude remarks. Always to me, moreover. You'd be scared of
a boor."

"I'm not scared of you!"

"Very clever. Even you can sometimes reply without fishing
in your pocket."

"Only my breast pocket."

"Why are you always so afraid you'll be suspected? Take pride.
You've whipped up a pretty fierce fire—even if not worldwide.
When Gogol cremated his dead souls, he froze for good. Never did
get warm."

"He *himself* burned, as a live soul."

"You think so?"

"I don't think anything! It's *my* novel that burned."

"Your baby?"

"Exactly!"

"Your favorite?"

"You don't understand these things."

"These things, those things . . . What do *you* understand! Have you ever once given thought to anyone? understood anyone? You call me 'HE' and yourself 'I'—is that fair? When we drink vodka, it's us together, but when we puke, it's me? What's the big surprise if I don't care . . . Your novel can go to blue blazes! *That's* fair. Have it your way: I didn't write it, you did. No skin off my nose. I should have your problems, Teacher."

"That's . . . how a master of old jokes would write it!"

"I can't write." His voice was unexpectedly gentle.

"You don't say! Well, at last. You admit it."

"I don't mean in your sense. Not in the writer's sense. I can't sign my own name."

"You're kidding!"

But I knew HE wasn't kidding this time. "Well, so you've helped me in other ways. You might have observed things. Remembered them. Since you're so observant. Or you might have read a book about monkeys and told me about it—"

"I can't read."

"That either? You're logical, though, in your own way."

"Yes," he said smugly, "character is my prerogative."

"Prerogative . . . Where have you picked up these words. Like old jokes."

"There you go again. I'm your wastebasket. But actually, that's all you have left now, the crumpled things from the wastebasket that I've smoothed out."

"You saved those!"

"Why, of course! Rough drafts—they're a high for me. I can make them out without reading them. Like claim checks. Like streetcar tickets."

"Do you really love me so?"

"So . . ." HE said scornfully. "Why must I love you *so*? Like loving a Jew. Can't I just *love*? Is that too little, not enough? I hate you! But always more than you hate me. After all, I'm not as unfeeling—"

"As I am . . . Listen! Remember in that marvelous Georgian town, the time you got so drunk . . . the time you and I got so drunk . . . the time I and you . . . oh, anyway, the time we got drunk and I was dying, I'd been beaten up by the local Armenians for my pro-Georgian speeches, which they perceived as anti-Armenian . . . Remember?"

"Nah," he said. "I don't remember."

"You don't? You're kidding . . . I lay there in my hotel room, dead drunk, beaten to death, dying. My heart kept stopping. I counted. It beat again after all. And now it failed to beat. I had died. No light, no corridor, no tunnel . . . A warm, nauseating darkness, like terror. Like being stuffed back into the womb. And then I was lying naked and washed, on my belly, but I saw the whole room, as if I were on my back. And I saw myself, me, hovering at the ceiling . . . Was that YOU?"

Now HE turned his other side to the conflagration, partly to cool the current side, partly to warm the previous one . . .

"I remember a yellow lightbulb, with YOU circling around it. The light was peculiarly yellow, like a body . . . like YOUR body. And like mine. You were watching with such curiosity! As if seeing for the first time . . . Whom did you see?"

"Why are you trying to shake me, like a detective in a movie . . ." HE retorted lazily.

"Was that you or me? Did you return me to life, or did I return you?"

"I don't remember."

"You were flying above me, and you were very excited. And I was dead."

"Sure. 'Then in the desert you lay dead . . .' "

"That fits—that's how it looked. Only worse. In the bed. Or more accurately, on the bed. Because this was a corpse. The live man lay *in* the bed, the dead man *on* the bed. Don't you agree?"

"We didn't finish high school."

"It's not the grammar. I mean, there were two of them, identical, like twins, like two peas. A dead man and a live one. And they merged. It grew dark. I opened my eyes. It was dark. The dead don't open their eyes. I groped in the darkness. And the first thing I felt was this object . . . Round, warm, and elongated. Hard. Standing upright. Don't you remember?"

"I don't do that, myself."

"Fool. The object wasn't part of my body."

"Well, all the more, then!"

"Fool! It was the neck! The neck of a clay jug, filled with red wine!"

"Well?" He was interested. "And what happened?"

"What do you think happened? I touched it caressingly."

"Well?"

"And applied myself!"

"And threw up."

"No, I didn't, I drank my fill and was resurrected. I turned on the light. Note that it wasn't on. Note that it wasn't nearly so yellow. But I was stark naked, and I'd been bathed, and the jug hadn't been there before! Did you bring it?"

"The Georgians sent it to you, for your anti-Armenian speeches."

"No, it was you!"

"Typical delirium."

"Delirium . . . Illiterate, but how you pick up the words."

"From you. But tell me, what happened next?"

"Next . . . Next I summoned you, and you drank the rest."

"Better you'd croaked," he said, resentful again. "This whole act, who's it for? What's this role you've assigned to me? You create, you write and read, you're as spiritual as Beethoven . . . Me, I just drink and sleep and . . . Why, you're like Venichka, you don't even go to the bathroom. And I haven't even got a proper name! Slavery. That's the only thing your kind have managed to invent! Slavery!"

"My kind?"

"People!"

"And what are YOU?"

"You know."

"Not an angel?"

"I never said that . . ."

"Did you think that up yourself, about slavery?"

"I suppose *you* did? Where would you get MY experience? You always talk down to me, but in fact you *hold* me down. To the role of pig, drudge, scum. I swear, it's like you're taking revenge."

"Why?"

"You know."

"I don't know!"

"Because I've got spirit, and you don't! Because I've got talent, and you don't! Because I'm the one the women love!"

"So that's why we're quarreling. A woman!"

"I'm not about to quarrel with you. You're no rival of mine!"

"That's a fact. Strange . . . It just occurred to me! Listen! Why is it we've never fallen in love with the same woman?"

"Your women never appealed to me. And you were shy with mine."

"Do you think so?"

"What's to think."

"Well, but was there never one who would have suited us both?"

"That's called love."

"Well, but have we never loved?"

"*I* have, but you haven't."

"Because you didn't share with me. Kept it all for yourself!"

"Who, me? But all my efforts were on your behalf!"

"Oh, come off it! But don't we have the same soul for both of us? She's not yours or mine, is she?"

"Mine!"

"Exactly. Animal!"

"Computer!"

"Listen, aren't you sorry for our gentle soul? We batter her, we've worn her out completely—"

"We tear her to pieces, crumple her, wipe our feet on her!"

"We've dragged her down, humiliated her—"

"Screwed her!"

"We should be sorry for her, not ourselves—"

"It's too late to be sorry. We must save her!"

"A live soul—"

"Barely alive!"

"Not rejoicing, not exulting—"

"No wonder. Hardly breathing!"

"Is this good?"

"This is not good."

"But who's to blame?"

"You!"

"There you go again! When was the uprising of the slaves in Egypt?"

"Twenty-seven fifty B.C."

"You remember!"

"How could I forget! Old Mr. Ivanov! When he wanted to pull a *D* up to a *C*, he always asked that question. And you were a *D* student, a lively little boy. It was only later that you became this slaveholding, self-righteous pain in the neck. This mediocrity."

"Fool. I'm not the only one in trouble, you know—you are, too. What are we to do, if there's one of her for two of us? Can't have a duel! If I shoot you, I'll hit myself."

"You'll miss. It'll be suicide."

"What are you doing, egging me on? Look out, I'll shoot myself, so as not to miss—and hit you for sure!"

"Don't you threaten me. My situation couldn't be more solid! Yes, I'm scum. But I'm alive. I say my prayers. But you, what have you accomplished? What have you achieved, I ask you. Only indifference. Do you imagine you've improved yourself, matured, shed vices? All you've done is shed unnecessary vice, because it fell off by itself. You haven't become better—you've only become worse. You've covered up your ugliness, you don't display the sore. You're a mask. My mask."

"Why do this *today*, when my novel has burned up, when at last I feel some sort of emotion, as you understand it—why be angry with me *today*, when at last you ought to pity me?"

"But when else could I say anything to you!? You don't hear anyone! . . . Why have you told me this, why? As though you . . . you . . ."

"Come now, come now . . . Don't cry. It's the other way around. More likely, YOU . . . ."

"I'm just your coat hanger. You'll drape yourself on me, no ironing needed. You'll drip dry, assume a shape, which, take note, you don't have, by definition. You'll start acting vain again, as if nothing had happened. Sanctimonious prig!"

"Without my sanctimoniousness, you'd be a drunken old sot!"

"Thanks a lot. That's just what I'm having no luck with! No way can I be a drunken old sot!"

"Now don't go off half cocked."

"Say, would you have any left?"

"I've been wanting to ask you—"

"You? Ask me? I don't have any."

"Look, I'm asking you who don't have any . . . asking you as my conscience, my soul, not as my slave . . . *did* I, this time, write it well?"

"You! again you! always you! and once more you!"

"We. Did WE pull it off?"

"How to tell you . . . On the whole, it wasn't bad."

"On the whole . . . ! What do YOU know."

"You forget, I simply can't read. But I have to feel for both of us."

"Have you reversed roles? Why, you *are* a slave! Give you freedom, and you're already on my back!"

"See, you're putting me down again."

"You're quick. Caught me. Well, I'm sorry. I agree. I know it myself. They're not *Dead Souls.* Let them burn. Live ones give more heat."

"Oh, don't be intimidated by Gogol," he said dreamily. "You had some glorious pages!"

"Truly? Do you think so?"

"I do. Dead souls are burned as firewood. Live souls burn with their own fire! This was the best thing we . . . you . . . You'll see —this will be a historic conflagration! The Hotel Abkhazia is only the match. Someday you'll say: I saw *how it all began.*"

"You set the fire?!"

"Suppose I did . . ."

"And you say this to me! Son-of-a-bitch Herostratus! A lot of honor this will . . . It was sheer laziness! You just didn't take the kettle off!"

I made a dash to save the manuscript, but HE grabbed my arm. HE had always been stronger than I.

I cowered and howled in pain.

"Really, was the thing so very precious to you?" he asked, as if in surprise. "Wait a minute."

But I did not succeed in restraining him. I simply wasn't strong enough.

He vanished in the smoke and the fire.

He was agile as a monkey. An instant later I spotted him on a third-floor balcony. Impossible to see clearly . . .

But who else could it have been?

The muzzle was aimed straight at my forehead, and somehow this reassured me. Because the muzzle was too large, or because we're used to seeing it more often in the movies than in real life. Strange that a piece like that could also shoot, and not merely in order to intimidate. A submachine gun is somehow more dangerous, a pistol still worse, but nastiest of all is a knife . . .

Yet they had knives and submachine guns, too, these soldiers who had abandoned their APCs to stretch their legs, smoke a cigarette under the clear sky, and lounge against the warm August armor, and their faces were also unfrightening with regard to the submachine gun and combat knife, which they didn't even plan to use, which they were merely supposed to wear like badges and chevrons, but looking at them you could have no faith that they wouldn't fire the cannon when the order came. The businesslike courtesy of their gestures and tone in contacts with civilians was such as to suggest that they had been briefed not to yield to provocation. They were executing this first order well, which meant they were also capable of firing the cannon. The public conversed freely with them, and from the car it appeared they were making some arrangement for this evening, after . . . I liked the soldiers. Unexcitable. They had nothing against the people whom they would be ordered to shoot.

That was what I was thinking, I who knew nothing about this, as I turned into the embankment detour in order to get across to the other bank, and became stuck in a traffic jam. I studied each oncoming face at length, because there were some people who for some reason had the same urgent need to get across to this bank. And it was always the same face, not only because the traffic jam was moving so unthinkably slowly, dragging along like a low storm cloud, its color blending with the asphalt, and not only because the other bank, which I could see across the river, was just as clogged as this one, but because each successive oncoming driver maintained so much the same expression that it was truly amazing—what had shaken them so, united them so? . . . Their same, shared face said, I don't know who you are, staring at me right now, but you didn't see me and I didn't see you, and how I feel about what's happening, am I for that bunch or this bunch, you'll never find out and never tell . . . Only their knuckles were white on the steering wheel, as if gripping it harder than usual. Their sullen impassivity, their universal upper-echelon secretiveness . . . that was what frightened me. Not one expression of annoyance, indignation, fear, despair—they had all known all of this by heart for so long! It was they who were soldiers . . . all to a man. Halt! Breathe exhaust fumes! But not a single expression of exultation, either, I thought with glad melancholy. Not one!

When I had squeezed across the bridge at last and parked fairly near the cordon, I gently crept out to reconnoiter. Deserted and sunny. Neither cars nor people. Had they been chased away, or had they fled? The benevolence of the police put me on guard. I could see why there were no cars, but if there were no people, it turned out, it wasn't because they weren't being admitted. A few curious people, as wary as I, were pretending they had wandered over here with a non-political purpose. I felt neither terror nor gaiety. Nothing. A Bruegelesque idiot, in a winter cap with one earflap missing, was traversing this dismal canvas in a direction of his own choice, or at any rate crossing through it. He was carrying the heavy iron headboard of a bed, and I imagined I saw in his manner something surprisingly familiar, even kindred, even painfully so . . . Pavel Petrovich!

"How are you?" he said.

Meaning "how do you do," nothing more.

We took hold of the headboard together and started to carry it. He in front, I behind. He seemed to know where he was going with it . . . For some reason it was very nice to see the back of his head, his thinning hair. A little old man in worn-out Adidas . . .

"Say, where'd you disappear to?" he said to me.

"Who, me?!"

"You haven't gotten any younger," he said with satisfaction.

"Whereas you look splendid," I parried.

"All the same, I'm frightfully glad to see you, Doctor Doctorovich . . . Well, what about it, finish the novel?"

Well, wasn't he the scoundrel? As if it hadn't been seven years. I almost dropped the bed.

"Say, did you bring any with you?"

He hadn't even cared about my answer, it turned out . . .

"Come on, don't feel so bad . . . I brought it."

This was said with such kindness, suddenly, that I realized he knew all. And he did, in fact, know all . . .

"The fire at the Abkhazia started in the stovepipe in the kebab restaurant. They never cleaned it—they kept the fire inspector supplied with kebabs. Lamb fat and soot are a very good fuel mixture."

"How would you know?"

"I was there."

Again I almost dropped the bed on my foot.

"You recently saw *City Lights*?" I guessed.

"What's that, a Charlie Chaplin?"

"Where are we going?" My voice sounded ungracious.

"We're eagerly awaited."

"Are you sure?"

"You'll see."

We threw our burden on a pile of scrap metal. It was the barricade.

"It's that easy?" I asked in delight.

"What did you think?"

And he glanced disdainfully at the tanks. We settled down cozily with a view of the tanks, as well as of the Moscow River and the Hotel Ukraine.

"Are you a democrat?" I asked.

"Who, me?" he said indignantly. "Of course. Who do you think I am?"

He built a fire out of boxes, then and there, and produced from the pocket of his oversized smock . . . What all didn't he have there! Before I could think, he was extracting "it."

He was extracting "it," but I was looking at his hands. It was hard not to look at them. His characteristic fingernails, half type-writer keys, half claws, had curled down even farther, and his hands were covered with ghastly pink spots. Psoriasis, none other . . . "Vodka knows its job," as he himself had once said.

"A burn," he said, noticing my glance.

To tell the truth, I was dumbfounded.

"I was repairing an iron . . ."

And really, that burn couldn't have been this fresh.

"Now . . ." he said vaguely. "Now," he said, concentrating, and poured us each our first.

We had time for seconds, too, while the *chifir* was coming to a boil.

"Found it!" Affectionately he scratched under his shirt, where his heart was, with his terrible hand. "Found it . . ." And he glanced affectionately at the reality around us, as though it had changed into a small kitten. "You keep interrupting, I've never succeeded in fully expressing myself to you . . . The poor, poor thing! How it turns itself inside out with effort! For whose sake? And what can we offer it but never-ending, gasping work. . . . Four chambers. Always leading from one to another. Not a second's sleep. And death in every pulse. Keeping count of death . . . keeping count of every second, a little more quickly than the moment passes. The heart—it's faster than time! How short a distance left to run . . . It breaks the finish tape! A record! An ovation! And you're gone. You didn't run—you only thought you were running. Your heart ran! And your heart finished, not you. Why do you feel so sorry for yourself? Take pity on your heart, your heart!"

And he poured again, for himself alone.

"Wasn't it you, Doctor, who used to quote to me from Thomas . . . 'Until the outer becomes . . .' On your lips it all sounded strange. Like some sort of paradox: the outer becomes the inner, the man a woman, life death, and vice versa . . . Nothing strange about it! It's merely a description of the heart . . . Merely! What a thing to say . . . How it struggles, your poor heart . . . Hear it struggling? It beats—and you hear. That's the whole story. The music comes after. The rest is silence. A pause. The abyss. The cosmos. The heart doesn't beat, it stops. Each second flies into the abyss, dies, faints there. And you also used to discourse on clocks! . . . The heart alone measures time in nature. Ever see the connecting rod on a locomotive? Think it turns the wheel? The usual technical sleight of hand! Because they have it hooked up to a feeble, shy little rod, in such a way that no one can notice that the connecting rod doesn't move by itself. The little rod pulls it up, to make it move from the dead point—and the locomotive goes, fat and important, he puffs, pretends it's him, thinks he's the one. The heart—*this* is the main lock! It closes the whole chain: the universe with its holes, parsecs, and dwarfs, and the Earth of that Universe, and on it life, with its amoeba and man . . . and on man, this padlock! What is less artificial than the heart, with its ventricles, auricles, valves, and aortas? The whole of it was invented. By whom?! This is my blood, and this is my flesh . . . An eternal infarct! An eternally ruptured and healing membrane . . . The heart—*this* is virginity! Chastity! Because He blew Himself to bits for each one of us! Spare your heart, they say . . . but you can't use God sparingly . . . simply pity it. It's incorrigible, the heart!"

I was suddenly ashamed of my travels abroad, my dacha, my car, my potatoes, and I expressed too hastily my agreement and delight, noting, however, that the blood is enriched in the lungs . . . How indignant he was!

"Through the lungs, you say? . . . Through everything! What do you breathe? You assume you breathe air . . . But I say to you: Not in the lungs is the blood enriched, but in the heart. And with that enrichment it arrives here." He rapped his forehead scornfully. "Our most public place, most polluted outhouse. Everyone's noggin is like a thing. The head and the balls—these we have on the outside. But the heart is inside! It's incarcerated in us as in a prison. That's why we all have the same thoughts, and yet our hearts are lonely. Space vehicles, flying through the darkness of flesh . . . Our hearts are separated, but not our thoughts. A thought is a very superficial thing, and it never touches the essence. The brain doesn't sing or dance, it doesn't weep or rejoice, it's a cold jellied mess. Why are we fixated on this bowl of mush? The *brain* is the very one who has never spared the heart, for he smugly imagines that the heart serves him. Everything, if you please, is subordinate to him—which means that everything also waits on him. And then, since everything waits on him, well, everything's under his control. And then, since everything's under his control, well, he can do everything. And since the brain can do everything, Come on, he says, let's make an artificial heart! They built a ministry the size of the White House. Right Ventricle Department, Left Auricle Department. They hooked it up to a dying man: Go ahead, live! But I said: I don't want to! The brain got angry at the man: Why not? we've provided you with everything, first-class supplies, what don't you have enough of? missing your heart, you say? . . . They busied themselves with improvements, along the line of redistributing departmental functions and reducing staff. They made significant progress. The heart was quartered in a city block instead of a precinct. At this point a thoroughly wise man came and accused the doctors, not without justification, of stupidity. You're archaics, he said. Why try to copy nature? You'll never pull it off. Let's proceed from purely technical parameters. To start with, they caught a calf. Installed a small electric motor in him . . . Do you know? He lived! The blood circulated normally. Supplied everything it was supposed to. And do you know what was missing? The stops! The blood brought supplies, but no notification of life and death. The calf had no pulse! His count of time was lost. He expired but didn't die. For the heart's every beat is . . . a battle! My God! What are you battling for? . . . Oh, Lord!" he exclaimed. "But how good it all is!"

"What's good?" I said in astonishment, catching sight of the tanks again.

"The weather. The holiday. Despite all, it's Transfiguration."

" 'The sixth of August, Old Style . . .' And I had forgotten!"

"What, not patronizing the churches anymore?"

"I didn't patronize the churches!" I said, hurt.

"I ran to church first thing today."

"You?"

"I can get a hair-of-the-dog from the watchman. And what should I see but this bed."

"You're eternal! You're a phoenix! Thank God . . . And of course you know what's going to happen?"

"What's going to happen? Not a frigging thing! There'll be a thank God. A great holiday."

"I don't mean that. I mean them . . ."

"Which, those?" He didn't even glance at the tanks. "Scrap metal. But don't mind them. See there!'"

With the spoon he was using to stir the *chifir*, he pointed skyward, not looking.

At first I imagined . . . But then I thought, No . . . I glanced down at the tanks once more, and then up at the sky. No, it couldn't be! But . . .

"And I saw in the air an army . . ."

Leaning on white-hot spears as if on shovels, wearing quilted jackets over their white wings, the angels dozed in the sky. Their Russianized, Düreresque faces were spacious as fields, creased by lightning, and smoothed by the unquestioned inevitability of martial labor. Their swollen, blacksmiths' fists, forged along with their weapons, inspired trust, like their faces. My heart was eased, not troubled: it was they whose fingernails had grown through their hands, they who were shackled to the clouds with ascetics' chains, they who had the heavenly trash of Russian villages stuck to their wings, like chicken droppings masquerading as a patina—log cabins, fences, cart tracks, wells, the ruins of churches and tractors . . . The sleep of the angels was leaden, and light as their wings. They startled and snorted like horses; their breath made our campfire flicker a little, a puff of smoke would reach up to them, and then it would seem that the angels smelled of the fire of their tireless battle. O God, how forbearing Thou art toward us, and harsh toward them!

"O Lord, help *them*!"

. . . ~~He thought or I said?~~

(February 28, 1993, Forgiveness Sunday)

FROM THE TRANSLATOR
The Boundaries Within

On April 8, 1944, Hero of the Soviet Union Lieutenant Lapshin and his rifle platoon, in a sudden attack from two sides, took the bridge in the zoo, killing 30 Nazis and capturing 195. This decided the outcome of the battle for the zoo.

> —Inscription on a monument at the Kaliningrad Zoo

Andrei Bitov wrote the three tales in this novel between 1971 and 1993, while the Soviet Union moved from peace to war to collapse. The first tale was published in 1976, but the second did not appear—and the third could never have been written—until after *glasnost*. As time flows through the novel, the changing fortunes of the author, the hero, the censor, and their country generate a very complex set of ironies.

On the simplest level, *The Monkey Link* is a novel in three acts, a comedy of ideas. Bitov originally intended to pose three questions: What is man's role in relation to other biological species? To God? To humankind? The story was to end in the early eighties—that is, before Mikhail Gorbachev, before *glasnost* and *perestroika*, in the so-called era of stagnation, when, as Bitov wrote in a synopsis in 1990, "time and the Empire itself were frozen like eternity, and the boldest mind could not have guessed the course of history." But history overtook the novel. The events of 1991—the failed coup against Gorbachev, Boris Yeltsin's sudden ascent to power, and the dissolution of the Soviet empire—forced another question: What is a man's role in relation to *himself*?

An empire inevitably shapes the mental landscape of its citizens. The pride of empire distorts their moral boundaries to include dominion over others, while tyranny and terror divide people against each other and against themselves, forcing them to betray friends, country, and conscience. For people of Bitov's generation the problem is compounded by the trauma of a wartime childhood. His fictional heroes tend to suffer from a painful, multifaceted alienation: a sense that they do not know who they are, that they do not belong in their own time and place, that they are distant from "the people" and from life itself, that they live only in books or movies. Like some of Dostoevsky's heroes, or Thomas Mann's, they cannot be sure which of their self-contradictory identities is real, where their deepest loyalties lie, or whether they serve God or the devil.

Hidden at the center of the hero's problems in *The Monkey Link* is the image of the Bronze Horseman, Peter the Great (1672–1725). Bitov was born in Peter's capital, and his writings are steeped in the Petersburg literary heritage. Nevertheless, his heroes have expressed a profound ambivalence toward the brilliant tyrant who designed the city and shaped the destiny of the empire. In *A Captive of the Caucasus* (1983), Bitov's book about his spiritual quests in Armenia and Georgia, he formulates the problem of imperial pride and envy very simply: "This journey begins from afar . . . From Peter the Great—half benefactor, half Antichrist." The Antichrist of contemporary Russian history, of course, was Stalin, and an identification of the two men was the artistic premise underlying Bitov's use of imagery from Pushkin's "Bronze Horseman" in his first novel, *Pushkin House* (1971).

In *The Monkey Link*, another figure lurks behind these two. Not mentioned, but implicit in the structure of the book, is the three-faced Lucifer of the *Divine Comedy*, who stands waist-deep in the frozen lake of hell and gnaws on the three worst traitors of all time (Judas Iscariot, Cassius, and Brutus). Bitov's personal map of the twentieth century might be described as a three-dimensional design with its horizontal surface covered by a thick layer of Soviet ice. Wherever the hero finds himself in space and time, a vertical axis runs up to heaven and down to hell; his life journey traces spirals around it. He exists at that spiritual center, waist-deep in the ice like Dante's Lucifer, and his ego relentlessly punishes him for his various betrayals (of God, of Caesar, of self). He must acknowledge the part of him hidden in the ice, recognize and forgive his own capacity for betrayal, understand that Stalin is within him—he must, like Dante the Pilgrim, climb down past Lucifer's hairy loins before his soul can complete another spiral upward through time.

The Monkey Link begins, psychologically, at the end point of *Pushkin House*. Lyova, the hero of that novel, feels that his life has traveled in a circle; he is trapped within coils of deceit and betrayal. Although powerless to free himself, he gives "the author" a copy of his grandfather's journal, containing a message of salvation. In an essay titled "God Is," written in the early twenties on the eve of his arrest by the new Soviet regime, Grandfather asserts that *under other conditions he might never have looked up and learned that he was free*. This insight establishes the framework of *The Monkey Link*.

The setting of *Birds*, the first of the novel's three tales, is a peninsula in "East Prussia." Königsberg, the historic seat of the princes of East Prussia, fell to Soviet forces in 1945 after a long siege. Founded in 1255 by the Teutonic Knights, the city had retained its German identity through centuries of struggle among neighboring empires for control of the lands along the Baltic coast. Between the World Wars, East Prussia was an island of German territory within Poland; on today's map, Königsberg is the Kaliningrad District, an isolated scrap of the Russian Republic, with just the northern tip of the Kurish Spit extending beyond the international boundary into Lithuanian territory.

When Bitov went there in the late sixties to work on *Pushkin House*, the Kurish Spit was the westernmost reach of a monolithic empire. The Soviet system had rigidified again after the relative thaw of the Khrushchev years (Bitov has commented that Leningrad never even thawed as much as Moscow). Leonid Brezhnev's regime seemed unshakable. In August of 1968 the flowering of the "Prague Spring" had been crushed by Soviet tanks. Writers like Sinyavsky, Brodsky, and Solzhenitsyn were being cruelly harassed and would soon be exiled. Pacing the beaches of the long, narrow sandspit and writing about the sequelae of a Stalinist childhood, Bitov was balancing on a geographical and political knife blade between East and West.

Revisiting that shore in *Birds*, the author-hero finds his thoughts returning to human aggression, to empires, boundaries, anti-tank barriers, to images of pursuit and flight, concealment and confinement, exile and homeland. He is trapped, like the feathered prisoners who blunder into the nets erected on the Spit by ornithologists, and the only way out is up. Hence his impulse toward God—toward the ideal, the "supreme thought." (This, too, is appropriate to the setting: many an eighteenth-century philosopher made the pilgrimage to Königsberg to study under Immanuel Kant, who lived and taught there all his life.) In dialogue with a Soviet "priest of science," the hero's sense of exile is transmuted into a discussion of man's abandonment of his primitive niche in nature. But in his private reflections on the ambiguous paradise of the Spit, he stops barely short of equating ordinary Soviet life with spiritual death.

That equation is stated more explicitly in the novel's second tale, *Man in a Landscape*. The germ of this tale is an incident in the final chapter of *A Captive of the Caucasus*, in which the author-hero, on his way home to Leningrad from Georgia, visits a historic site. Depressed by the shoddy restoration effort, he suddenly perceives God's original design in the Russian landscape and feels that the reality around him is like the back of a painting: he has momentarily fallen through a hole in the canvas and landed in the paint layer. He is inspired to write a new "journey," to be called *Man in a Landscape: New Information on Birds*.

Man in a Landscape was thus conceived as a mischievous reversal of "reality," a view of the Soviet paradise from below. The allegorical setting is a somewhat fantastic preserve outside Moscow, dating from the time of the early tsars. With an artist as his quasi-supernatural guide, the hero journeys into the medieval heart of Russia. From there he descends further into the darkness of modern treachery (the lowest, ninth circle of Dante's hell), and finally, in an autumn sunset in 1979, arrives at what may or may not prove to be the threshold of paradise.

At that pivotal moment in history, Soviet forces were preparing to invade Afghanistan. For Bitov, as he has since told an interviewer, the invasion marked the end of the twentieth century—and the beginning of the end of the empire that the Soviets had so stubbornly dragged behind them. When he wrote this story in 1983, however, public protest of the Afghan debacle was still impossible. Cold War rhetoric was intensifying under the new regime of Yuri Andropov. Bitov himself was in trouble with the authorities for allowing *Pushkin House* to appear abroad (1978) and for co-editing the samizdat anthology *Metropol* (1979). He was virtually unable to publish.

The author-hero of *Man in a Landscape* hints at similar circumstances, and they emerge undisguised in *Awaiting Monkeys*, the novel's third tale. By the time Bitov undertook to write it, his previously suppressed works (including *Pushkin House* and *Man in a Landscape*) had at last been published in Russia, he had made several trips to the West, and he could openly parody the Soviet utopia. He chose to parody his pre-*glasnost* self as well.

In another era, he might have described this phase of his hero's pilgrimage in terms of a journey to the holy sites of the Mediterranean region. But his hero, in 1983, cannot hope to travel abroad, and for Russians the Caucasus has been a traditional substitute. Abkhazia is a particularly fitting locale, on a number of counts. Its native name, *Apsny*, means "Land of the Soul." It still boasts a remnant of an ancient forest to which Christians were exiled from Rome and Constantinople. It is also the shore to which Jason voyaged with his Argonauts, in quest of the golden fleece that would regain his throne from a usurper. For the last thousand years the nation's political fortunes have been bound up with those of neighboring Georgia—and in the twentieth century, therefore, with Stalin. Its capital, Sukhum, has been the site of Greek, Roman, and Byzantine fortresses, Ottoman and Genoese slave markets, Russian and Soviet health resorts, and now also a research institute's monkey colony. A visit to the "free" monkeys becomes the goal of the author-hero's travels: he will exploit the colony for satirical purposes.

The first two parts of *Awaiting Monkeys*, "The Horse" and "The Cow," stand in the same relation to each other as *Birds* does to *Man in a Landscape*: a journey to an equivocal paradise, followed by a journey to a netherworld where the hero gains partial insight. In "The Horse" (perhaps because the date is given as August 23, anniversary of the Nazi-Soviet non-aggression pact of 1939), the hero travels back in memory through the Stalin years to the collectivization of agriculture, which emptied the Russian village and turned the populace into a nation of policemen. His earlier sense of society's spiritual death thus acquires a symbolic focus—the peasant, repository of the Russian soul—and in "The Cow" he begins to see his own complicity in the Mephistophelean bargains of Soviet history.

The pattern is repeated again in the third part, "Fire." From Moscow, where the evil of the socialist paradise is so banal as to be its own parody, the hero plunges into an unreal world of filmmaking and literary criticism in Azerbaijan and Georgia; there, fleeing demons in 1984, he finds himself at the source of evil and comes close to genuine insight. The plot then spirals back and forth between Moscow and Abkhazia, from the illusory freedom of the Gorbachev years to a moment of self-confrontation to a moment of revelation.

All the points visited in this novel are stages in the hero's quest for a spiritual homeland. But if those points are plotted on a map of the Soviet Union, the line obtained gives his journey an added subliminal significance. In the Great Patriotic War of 1941–45, German forces failed to reach either Moscow or the oil fields of Baku; Leningrad withstood a 900-day siege (Bitov has written of being evacuated, as a child, over frozen Lake Ladoga). The boundary of the German Occupation was thus an irregular diagonal line starting below Leningrad on the Baltic shore, passing just west of Moscow, extending almost to the Caspian Sea in the south, and from there turning west across the Caucasus to the Black Sea. In its own way, this book is a tour of the front and an exorcism of childhood trauma.

It is also an epic poem: the hero is Odysseus returning from war, Jason dethroning the usurper, Aeneas hoping to found a new empire—the empire of the soul, as Dante's Virgil called it. The poetic structure of the book grows organically with the narrative. On the first page the hero sets sail in Lermontov's "air-ocean," where demons roam and angels watch unseen; along the way the demons and even the angels become increasingly visible and real. The components of the opening metaphor (modern man as an armored creature who lives on a boundary line and never looks up unless compelled) become actual elements of the final scene at the barricade. The gyrations of the bird in the trap become the loops of the hero's journey, the shadow cast by the painter's Gogolian nose becomes the author's alter ego—image after image seizes life and plays its role in the narrative.

Bitov's allusions to other literary works complement this structure. Whether quoting openly or writing in "invisible ink," like Akhmatova, he is taking the azimuth, as it were—measuring off arcs that connect the fictional moment with an outside reality and thus define his location, or his hero's, or ours. As more of these sight lines are added, they intersect to form an airy design of their own, enveloping the narrative in a sphere of relevant human experience. Fundamentally, Bitov draws on our shared literary heritage: the Bible, the *Divine Comedy*, *Don Quixote*, the Faust legend. He also uses elements from Russian classics, but they undergo a late-twentieth-century metamorphosis, and his hero exists in a world that knows Mann and Grass, Solzhenitsyn and Nabokov.

There is special beauty, impossible to translate, in the ties between this book and the twentieth-century Russian poets—Blok, Akhmatova, Mandelstam, Zabolotsky, Kuzmin, Pasternak, Brodsky. The Western reader will hear in their names a litany of persecution and exile, but what must also be remembered is that these people salvage the human spirit from the flames of their century. Many of them knew each other, knew the Caucasus, translated from the Georgian; their work spans the Soviet era. Like the invisible beings poised silently in Bitov's mountain forest, they are a living presence in the novel.

In its deepest structure, this "pilgrimage novel" is a drama of salvation—a battle between good and evil for possession of the hero's soul, and for the soul of his nation. The hero's journey is not done: it is the eternal struggle upward, toward

God. But it takes place in time, our time, and its end point in this novel is an unforgettable moment of hope in our history.

The notes that follow should be consulted only if the reader feels need of further information in order to gauge Bitov's irony. I have tried to provide relevant details that might be part of a Russian's general background of awareness. Since Bitov delights in what he calls "rhymes"—seemingly accidental correspondences that give added meaning to life—I have also included a few "rhymes" from my own recollections of the century and its literature. The reader will undoubtedly find many more.

For advice and encouragement in the preparation of this translation I sincerely thank Rosemarie Tietze, the author's German translator; Professor Michael Connolly of Boston College; Irina Ryumshina, Vladimir Gurin, Boris Hoffman, Rima Zolina, and all the very kind friends who commented on my manuscript.

NOTES

3 *That is, I wouldn't want* ....
  When Bitov revised *Birds* in 1993, he "censored" his own opening and
closing remarks by substituting symbolic rows of dots, as poets from Pushkin
to Akhmatova have sometimes done when lines were cut by official censors.
  Bitov also eliminated some of the ecological argument, reshaped the text
typographically in a way that suggests his hero's tendency to intellectualize,
and inserted mention of East Prussia and 1968 (see translator's comments,
page 356).

3 *the air-ocean*
  In Mikhail Lermontov's "The Demon" (1841), the stars sail in the air-
ocean, indifferent to earthly passion. The demon of the poem is a fallen angel
trying to seduce a Georgian maiden. He pursues her to a convent, but she
dies in his embrace, and when he tries to claim her soul the angels bear her
away.

5 *"But this shore had already been won . . ."*
  From Alexander Pushkin's *Journey to Arzrum* (1835). Never allowed to
travel abroad, Pushkin unofficially accompanied the Russian army to Armenia, crossed the river into Turkey, and was chagrined to find himself "still
in Russia."

17 *"One thought after another! Pity the artist of the word . . ."*
  From an untitled poem by Evgeny Baratynsky (1840). He goes on to
say that for the "priest of the word," thought is a naked sword dividing him
from the life of the senses.

24 *Grandpa Krylov*
  Ivan Krylov, much-loved fabulist (1769–1844).

35 *"Animals have no name. Who ordered them named?"*
  From Nikolai Zabolotsky's poem "A Stroll" (1929), which continues:
"An equal suffering is their invisible lot . . . All of nature smiled, like a tall
prison . . . And all of nature laughs, dying every second."

36–37 *"White the lonely sail . . ."; "as though the storm brought rest."*
  From Lermontov's famous lyric "The Sail" (1832).

37 *"Give me nothing more! . . ."*
  The author notes that this is from the poetry of Galaktion Tabidze, a
well-known Georgian writer (1892–1959).

46 *"now touching her wing to the wave"*
  From Maxim Gorky's "Song of the Stormy Petrel" (1901), a romantic allegory urging revolution.

60 *the sun . . . "will send us its light," "its fiery greeting."*
  Phrases from Soviet songs.

61 *the meaningless word "Amsterdam"*
  In *A Captive of the Caucasus*, Bitov writes of Amsterdam as "a city whose name, to us, means Peter the Great."

63 *a catechumen*
  That is, an unbaptized convert, still receiving training in Christian doctrine. In the Russian Orthodox Church, catechumens are "strangers" who may listen to the sermon but must leave before the sacraments.

69 *Behold the stone . . .*
  The epigraph is taken from the Gospel of Thomas, Saying 66. In Marvin Meyer's translation (HarperSanFrancisco, 1992), it reads: "Jesus said, 'Show me the stone that the builders rejected: That is the cornerstone.' "
  The Gospel of Thomas, although cited by some of the early church fathers, was lost until 1945, when a Coptic version came to light in Egypt. It is a collection of sayings attributed to Jesus, with many parallels to the canonical four gospels. It includes no promise of a second coming, however; in this gospel, Jesus teaches that the kingdom is to be found here, around us and within us, and counsels us to "Be passersby." The author of the gospel identifies himself as the Apostle Thomas, called Didymus ("The Twin"). Some Christians have believed him to be literally the twin brother of Jesus, but modern scholars generally interpret the name as a metaphor meaning that each person should strive to be as a twin to Jesus.

72 *the log cabin in which Peter the Great stayed in Archangel*
  Peter's cabin has been moved from Archangel to Kolomenskoe, a former estate of the Grand Princes of Moscow, overlooking the Moscow River. The dominant feature of the estate is a tall church built in 1532 to celebrate the birth of Ivan IV (the Terrible). There is also a Church of the Beheading of John the Baptist.

77–79 *Shishkin . . . Ayvazovsky . . . Levitan, Vasiliev . . . "Doesn't Repin have a Cossack laughing?"*
  All of these Russian artists had ties to the late-nineteenth-century group called the "Wanderers." Shishkin is best known for his paintings of the forest, Ayvazovsky for his seascapes, Levitan and Vasiliev for their emotional landscapes. Repin painted a variety of subjects; one of his historical canvases, *The Zaporozhye Cossacks Write a Letter to the Turkish Sultan*, shows the men gleefully defiant.

84 *"Genius and villainy are two things . . ."*
    From Pushkin's play *Mozart and Salieri* (1830). Apropos of rumors that
the playwright Beaumarchais had poisoned two wives, Mozart remarks: "But
he's a genius, like you and me. Genius and villainy are two things incompatible. Isn't that true?" At this point, Salieri drops poison into Mozart's
glass.

89 *"But that's the candy!"*
    One of Shishkin's best-loved paintings (*Morning in the Pine Forest*,
1889) includes some bear cubs. The painting is reproduced on the wrapper
of a popular Russian candy.

90 *". . . 'Farewell, free element' . . ."*
    Ayvazovsky and Repin collaborated on a painting in which Pushkin is
shown gesturing with his top hat as he stands on some jagged rocks, dan-
gerously close to the pounding surf. The painting's title is taken from Pushkin's poem "To the Sea" (1824).

94 *that "Man with a capital letter" . . . Danko . . .*
    From works by Maxim Gorky, founder of Socialist Realism. The "Man
with a capital letter" was Lenin. Danko, the hero of "Old Woman Izergil,"
rips his flaming heart from his breast and uses it as a torch to lead his people
through a dark forest. (See also note to page 46.)

101 *" 'Everything, even the dilapidated birdhouses . . .' "*
    From Anna Akhmatova's "Seaside Sonnet" (1958).

103 *"Is he Semyon or Simyon?"*
    "Simyon" is not a standard Russian name. The spelling suggests the
pronunciation of the name Simeon, a biblical form of Simon (Semyon).

104 *St. Cyril and St. Methodius*
    The ninth-century Byzantine missionaries who created the first Slavonic
alphabet ("Cyrillic") and translated the Bible.

108 *" 'So stone by brick we tore that factory down . . .' "*
    From an "urban ballad" sung by the author's friend S. G. Saltykov.

111 *Emperor Paul's anti-profile*
    The Emperor Paul (Pavel Petrovich, great-grandson of Peter the Great)
had a quarrelsome disposition and a snub nose. He was assassinated with
the complicity of his son in 1801.
    Mentioned by Dante (*Inferno*, Canto II), and perhaps also relevant here
in this anti-world, is St. Paul's experience of visiting paradise (II Corinthians
12:2–4): ". . . Whether in the body, or out of the body, I cannot tell: God
knoweth."

114 '*. . . He himself looks very like an ape . . . O vanity! . . .*'
     Adapted from Lermontov's long moral poem *Sashka* (1839).

124 *I had traipsed along after him like Gogol's Mizhuev*
     In *Dead Souls* (1842), Mizhuev always protests against, but then submits
     to his brother-in-law, the braggart Nozdrev. (The name Nozdrev derives
     from the Russian for "nostril"—the hero is following his own nose, so to
     speak.)

140 *August 23*
     Anniversary of the Nazi-Soviet non-aggression pact of 1939, which pre-
     cipitated the Soviet takeover of the Baltic countries and led directly to World
     War II. The fiftieth anniversary, in 1989, was the occasion for a protest
     demonstration in which two million people formed a human chain across
     Estonia, Latvia, and Lithuania, seeking independence from the USSR.

144 *try the* chacha *he had just distilled*
     Popular in the Caucasus, *chacha* is a strong homemade liquor distilled
     from grape pressings.

147 *the poet who said, "Ever more often I see death, and smile . . ."*
     Alexander Blok, in "Free Thoughts" (1907). Blok died in 1921, a victim
     of hunger and disease in the aftermath of the Civil War. His ambiguous
     poem "The Twelve" shows marauding Red Guardsmen as apostles of the
     Revolution.

149 *Senyok, our drifter*
     Senyok is a familiar diminutive of the name Semyon. The slang word
     translated here as "drifter" originally referred to a seaman who had lost his
     berth on a ship. The word is now broadly applied to any vagrant alcoholic.

149 *"loved the smoke of burnt stubble."*
     From Lermontov's poem "Homeland" (1841), in which he professes to
     love Russia *not* for its "glory bought with blood," but for its landscape and
     the homely details of the countryside.

151 *Prince Myshkin*
     The hero of Dostoevsky's novel *The Idiot* (1868).

152 *Rio de Janeiro*
     The unfulfilled dream of Ostap Bender, the great schemer of Ilf and
     Petrov's satire *The Golden Calf* (1931), was to abscond to Rio de Janeiro
     with his suitcase full of money and walk down the street wearing white pants
     like the mulattos.

153 *the unforgettable Venichka*
     The alcoholic narrator of Venedict Erofeev's painfully comic novel *Mos-
     cow to the End of the Line* (1977) maintains that "Privy Councillor Goethe"

secretly wanted to drink but instead forced Faust and Mephistopheles to
drink on his behalf.

153 *Academician Shchusev*
Among the many other structures designed by A. V. Shchusev (1873–
1949) was Lenin's mausoleum.

155 *"Damn Lavrenty! How many we might have been . . ."*
Lavrenty Beria (1899–1953) played a leading role in Stalin's purges as
head of the Soviet secret police.

156 *Voronezh . . . was a third-category city*
That is, designated to receive a much smaller supply of food and con-
sumer goods than the first-category cities, Moscow and Leningrad. (Voronezh
is the provincial capital to which the poet Osip Mandelstam was exiled in
the mid-1930s.)

157 *"The Lady with the Lapdog"*
Anton Chekhov's familiar story (1899) of ill-starred, middle-aged love.

164 *" 'Rather skinny, but her calves were round . . .' "*
From Joseph Brodsky's "Letters to a Roman Friend" (1972).

166 *Armenian Radio . . . the Chukchi jokes*
Soviet "Armenian jokes" were often cast in the form of reports from
Radio Erevan. The Chukchi, a frequent target of ethnic humor, are a remote
Arctic people.

172 *"This is an ancient quarrel of Slavs among themselves"*
From "To the Detractors of Russia" (1831), Pushkin's patriotic reply to
Frenchmen who were siding with Polish agitators against the tsar. You hate
us, he says, because we toppled your idol Napoleon, but the Russian land
—from Finland to Colchis (Abkhazia)—will rise up united against anyone
who interferes in our family quarrel.

176 *Ermak, "nach Osten"*
Ermak Timofeev (d. 1585) was the Cossack ataman who began Russia's
conquest of Siberia. The *Drang nach Osten* was the "drive to the east" of
the medieval Teutonic Knights.

178 *"in his fine red shirt, such a bonny lad . . ."*
From a Russian folk song. But the motif also brings to mind the beautiful
red-shirted youth who is the hero's rival in Mikhail Kuzmin's novella *Wings*
(1906; see also note to page 261).

178 Toilers of the Sea
A novel by Victor Hugo (1866), in which a fisherman trying to raise a
sunken ship battles a giant octopus.

184 *"With rosy dawn the east was mantled . . ."*
    From "The Cherry," a bawdy poem classified among the *dubia* of the youthful Pushkin.

185 *as Voroshilov did in Iskander*
    The reference is to a banquet in Stalin's honor, as recounted by Abkhazian writer Fazil Iskander in his novel *Sandro of Chegem* (1973).

189 *the suicidal exodus of the Abkhaz*
    The prince of Abkhazia sought and received Russian protection in 1810, but the Muslim tribesmen of the highlands resisted infidel rule for the rest of the century. Deluded by promises of religious toleration, thousands emigrated to Turkey.

192 *Anapa*
    This town in the Russian Republic, just over the northern border of Abkhazia, was a center of Partisan resistance against the German Occupation during World War II.

195 *Triton and a naiad*
    During the calamitous flood in Pushkin's "The Bronze Horseman," Peter the Great (*"He"*) is metaphorically linked with an angry Triton destroying the people.
    For his naiad, the woman named Margarita, Bitov draws on the Faust legend. In Goethe's version (1832), Faust's seduction of Margaret leads to her death, which causes him to repent his bargain with Mephistopheles. In Mikhail Bulgakov's *The Master and Margarita* (1940), Margarita gladly enters into a compact with the devil in order to free the Master from a Soviet mental hospital.

196 *August 25*
    On this date in 1940, as Germany appeared to be on the verge of gaining the whole world, the hero of Mann's *Dr. Faustus* died; in 1968, a small, brave, futile demonstration against the Soviet invasion of Czechoslovakia took place in Red Square; in 1991, Gorbachev resigned as head of the Communist Party.

210 *the mousling and the froglet . . . and the unknown beastie*
    An echo of Pushkin's fairy tale "King Saltan" (1831), in which the queen reportedly bears a child of indeterminate sex and species.

226 *"De . . . de . . ."*
    The Russian words for "death" and "laughter" begin with the same syllable, *sme*. Bitov's wordplay recalls Velemir Khlebnikov's "Incantation by Laughter" (1910).

229 *Grigory Skovoroda*
    A wandering Ukrainian philosopher and poet (1722–94), who wrote

dialogues treating biblical problems from the point of view of Platonism and Stoicism.

232 *Grandpa Chukovsky*
Kornei Chukovsky (1882–1969), distinguished author, translator, and critic.

234 *"Give the stick back to Engels."*
Engels said that the monkey became man when he took a stick in his hands.

241 *the unforgettable year 1984*
Vsevolod Vishnevsky's *The Unforgettable Year 1919*, about Stalin's role in the Civil War, received the Stalin Prize in 1950 and was made into a film, with music by Dmitry Shostakovich.

243 The Knight in the Tiger Skin
The great epic poem by twelfth-century Georgian poet Shota Rustaveli.

243 *In 1978 . . . the Abkhazian events*
In 978, after two hundred years of independence from Byzantium, the kingdom of Abkhazia was absorbed by its powerful neighbor Georgia. At mass demonstrations in Sukhum and Lykhny in the spring of 1978, Abkhazians threatened to secede from Georgia and join the Russian Republic.

243 *a fresh wound on the skull*
In 1991, the body of a man who had been frozen in a Tirolian glacier for some 5,000 years was damaged by Austrian rescue workers. A jurisdictional dispute with Italy ensued.

244 *both that he was Shota and that he was Avtandil*
Both author and hero of Rustaveli's epic. (Avtandil is not, in fact, the knight in the tiger skin, but rather his spiritual brother; with a third knight, they rescue a maiden from demon country.)

250 *another November anniversary*
The anniversary of the Bolshevik Revolution of 1917 was regularly celebrated by a two-day holiday featuring massive parades.

252 *The Korean airliner had just been downed*
On September 1, 1983, en route from Anchorage to Seoul, a Korean Air Lines jet was shot down by the Soviets near Sakhalin with 269 people aboard, most of them civilians.

254–55 The Tin Fleece of Victory. *A translation from the Georgian . . . Colchis . . . Jason . . . "The Pontus."*
The title of this fictitious book parodies a contemporary genre of patriotic Georgian novels. Colchis is the classical name for Abkhazia, to which Jason, in order to regain his throne from a usurper, voyaged in quest of a golden

fleece hanging in an oak grove. The Black Sea was known in ancient times as the Pontus Euxinus.

The plot of the book is a pastiche of details from familiar works on the themes of betrayal and usurpation. The cloak with a red lining is emblematic of Pontius Pilate, in Bulgakov's *Master and Margarita;* the broad-chested Ossetian is Stalin, in the poem (1933) for which Mandelstam was arrested and exiled.

255 *like a Grand Prince . . . the Kura*
For political reasons, the princes of medieval Russia often postponed baptism until they thought their time had come. The river Kura is in Georgia.

256 *"the heroic feat for which we always have room in our lives."*
This often repeated phrase is from Gorky's tale "Old Woman Izergil" (see note to page 94).

260 *a Nadenka*
That is, a beer hall—so called after Lenin's wife, Nadezhda Krupskaya.

261 *Kuzmin*
Mikhail Kuzmin (1872–1936), an esoteric writer, openly homosexual, with an interest in classical and religious themes. His poetry reflects his spiritual quests in southern lands such as Italy and Egypt. (See also note to page 178.)

261 *a drifter . . . homeless*
See note to page 149. Homelessness, or the lack of a residence permit, was a crime in the Soviet Union.

262 *Saltychikha . . . Shchedrins*
Saltychikha was an eighteenth-century landowner famous for torturing her serfs. M. E. Saltykov, who took the pen name Shchedrin, was a nineteenth-century novelist.

268 *"The Soviets have their own pride."*
From a Soviet song, often quoted ironically by people wistful for bourgeois material comfort.

269 *Ilf and Petrov*
Immensely popular satirists of Soviet bureaucracy; joint authors of *The Golden Calf.* (See note to page 152.)

270 *Engineer Garin*
A mad scientist bent on cornering the world gold market with his death ray, in a novel (1925) by Alexei Tolstoy, who was a distant relative of the great Lev Tolstoy.

273 *Well done, Pusskin, well done, you son of a bitch!*
Adapted from Pushkin's self-congratulatory exclamation on finishing his drama *Boris Godunov* (as recounted in a letter to a friend in 1825).

276 *Neuhaus*
H. G. Neuhaus (1888–1964), eminent and influential Soviet pianist. (His daughter became Boris Pasternak's second wife.)

281 " *'How sad our Russia is' . . .*"
Pushkin is reported to have made this remark on reading an early draft of Gogol's *Dead Souls*, the theme of which—the purchase of lists of dead serfs, to be mortgaged for a profit—Pushkin himself had suggested to Gogol.

282 *the Fontanka River*
In St. Petersburg (Leningrad).

284 *"Why did you dream all this up?"*
On October 26, 1983, *The New York Times* reported that journalist Oleg Bitov (the author's brother) had defected from the USSR in September and had been granted asylum in Britain. He reappeared in Moscow a year later, claiming that he had been abducted from a film festival in Venice and held involuntarily by British agents (*New York Times*, September 19, 1984).

284 *The lap robe, the piano, the couch . . .*
These details suggest a central scene in Thomas Mann's *Dr. Faustus:* an I/he dialogue between the hero and his changeable devil, who emanates a bone-chilling cold despite the summer warmth of Italy. (Zyablikov's name derives from the Russian for "chilly.")

288 *I put my arms around her, and what did I see over her shoulder?*
Adapted from an untitled lyric by Joseph Brodsky (1962)—printed in 1990 as the opening poem of the first extensive collection of his émigré works published in Russia.

290 *did Dostoevsky create his* Demons, *or the demons us?*
The demons of Dostoevsky's novel (also known as *The Possessed;* 1871) are radical revolutionaries, precursors of the Bolsheviks.

290 *Did Dahl indeed create a* Dictionary of the Living Language . . . ?
Vladimir Dahl's dictionary was published in 1880–82.

290 *Rafik*
The Rafik is a light van; its nickname derives from the initials of the Latvian factory where it is produced. By linguistic coincidence, Rafik can also be a personal name or nickname in several of the Caucasian lands.

292 *Valery Givivovivich . . . Unpronounceable!*
Although he has an ordinary Russian first name, Valery Givivovich's

patronymic is strange to Russian ears because it derives from the name of
his Georgian father.

292 *Jvari . . . "Where the rivers, roaring, flow together . . ."*
    Jvari is the site of a sixth-century cathedral overlooking the confluence
of the Aragva and Kura rivers in Georgia. The quotation is from the opening
stanzas of Lermontov's poem "The Novice" (1833), where he mentions that
the Georgian king had entrusted his nation to Russia, and describes it as
blessed by God behind Russian bayonets. The poem is the story of a rebellious
young monk who tries to flee to his native mountains rather than take
monastic vows. He travels in a circle, back to the monastery, and dies an
exile.

293 *"Gray goose, white goose . . ."*
    From a children's counting rhyme.

293 *Sukhum . . . Sukhumi . . . Batumi . . . Batum*
    The short forms of these names are older, often used by local people;
the Georgian forms ending in *-i* were accepted as standard by Soviet
authorities.

296 *"I'll get you!"*
    From Pushkin's "Bronze Horseman." The poem's angry hero addresses
the threat to the statue of Peter the Great, whom he blames for the death
of his beloved in a Petersburg flood. The "idol" then pursues the hero through
the streets until he dies.

297 *Who had said, "It would be nice to die here"? "Don't wish for too much,
Rezo . . ."*
    Here the name Rezo is substituted for Vano, in an exchange of remarks
taken from one of Erlom Akhvlediani's "Niko and Vano" stories (1969). Of
these modern fairy tales Bitov wrote in 1973: "Niko and Vano are one man
simultaneously, they are pronouns of a kind: I and he, he and I, I and they,
I as he, he as I . . ."

297 *Queen Tamara*
    Ruler of Georgia in the twelfth century, when the country was at the
height of its power.

297 *"Come ye therefore, brethren . . ."*
    This passage appears to be from a seventeenth-century Church Slavonic
translation of the writings of St. John Chrysostom (d. 407). He began his
religious life as an ascetic in the desert outside Antioch, but eventually became
Archbishop of Constantinople and gained fame for his eloquence in con-
demning the sins of the mighty. Banished by the empress in 403, he was
recalled at the insistence of the common people but was soon banished again,
first to Armenia and then to what is now Pitsunda, in Abkhazia. An old man,

forced to travel on foot, he died on the journey, in a Pontic town called Comana, whose exact location is now unknown.

298 *"We were many in the bark. Some raised the sail . . ."*
From Pushkin's poem "Arion" (1827), about a legendary Greek poet of the sixth century B.C. Like Orpheus on Jason's *Argo*, Arion had only one task on the ship—to make music for the crew. (He survived the wreck of the ship when a dolphin enchanted by his song guided him to shore.)

299 *a "Russian Fet"*
Poet Afanasy Fet (1820–92) was of German extraction.

302 *the Hyrcanian . . . Iberia*
Classical names for the Caspian Sea and Georgia. ("Author-Khan" and his men follow roughly the same route as the narrator of this book, from the Baltic to Abkhazia, via Moscow, Baku, and Tbilisi.)

315 *what Goethe asked*
If Goethe's Faust prays for the moment to linger, it is time for Mephistopheles to claim his soul. (That moment comes when Faust—who has devoted his life to good works after repenting his fatal seduction of Margaret—admires a landscape that he has reclaimed from under the sea. Despite his old bargain, he is redeemed.)

317 *someone blew plaintively into a bottle*
The phrase recalls the opening of Chekhov's story "The Student" (1894). Beside a bonfire on a wintry Good Friday, a divinity student talks about the long, chill night during which Peter denied Christ three times before cockcrow. The student is comforted by the realization that Peter's betrayal and grief are linked to the present day by an unbroken chain of events.

318 *"But silence stands in our room like a spinning wheel . . ."*
A variant of a poem by Osip Mandelstam (1917), on the themes of distance, time, and exile, with allusions to the voyages of Jason and Odysseus.

320 *A restlessness took hold of me. No urge toward a change of place.*
Adapted from lines near the end of Pushkin's *Eugene Onegin* (1831). In Nabokov's translation (Bollingen, 1975): "A restlessness took hold of him, / the urge toward a change of places."

321 *There are women of whom you're unworthy . . . I have no God, I have no Mom . . .*
Lines by the author's friend Gleb Gorbovsky.

321 *Ruslan Imranovich . . . Rafik Nisanovich*
That is, Khasbulatov and Nishanov. Both are politicians from the Caucasus; they figured in the televised parliamentary struggles over the status of the Soviet republics—struggles which led to the failed coup against Gor-

bachev on August 19, 1991, and ultimately to Boris Yeltsin's accession to power.

326 *a red golden cockerel*

The phrase recalls Pushkin's sardonic fairy tale "The Golden Cockerel" (1834). Perched on a tower, the cock crows thrice to warn of approaching danger. The danger proves to be a woman; the king's two sons kill each other in battle over her; the king wins her. Insufficiently grateful, he is pecked to death by the cockerel.

On quite another level, the image recalls Mandelstam's poem "Tristia" (1918). In literal translation: ". . . Who can know . . . what the cock's crowing promises us when fire burns on the acropolis, or why, at the dawn of a new life . . . , a cock, the herald of the new life, beats his wings on the city wall?"

330 *beat a jackrabbit, break a birch tree*

The first phrase is from a modern proverb; the second, from an ancient Russian folk song.

332 *Our religious disagreements . . . ethnic ones . . . cannibalism*

Stalin said, in 1931, "Anti-Semitism, as an extreme form of racial chauvinism, is the most dangerous survival of cannibalism."

336 *" 'The outer the inner, and the inner the outer . . .'" "The man a woman, and the woman a man . . ."*

Based on the Gospel of Thomas, Saying 22. In Marvin Meyer's translation: "Jesus said to them, 'When you make the two into one, and when you make the inner like the outer and the outer like the inner, and the upper like the lower, and when you make male and female into a single one, so that the male will not be male nor the female be female . . . then you will enter [the kingdom].' "

339 *Bulgakov . . . his famous phrase*

"Manuscripts don't burn," says the devil in *The Master and Margarita,* and from a pile of manuscripts he retrieves the Master's novel about Pontius Pilate and Jesus. (The Master himself had burned it, in fear and anger, because he could not publish it in the Soviet Union of the 1920s.)

340 *When Gogol cremated his dead souls, he froze for good.*

Nikolai Gogol, after completing his novel *Dead Souls,* turned to religion and tried to write a sequel depicting a moral, reformed world. He burned his drafts shortly before his death in 1852.

342 *" 'Then in the desert you lay dead . . .' "*

Adapted from Pushkin's famous poem "The Prophet" (1826), a grand statement of the poet's sacred mission to "fire the hearts of men" with God's word. Untranslatable echoes of the poem are worked into Bitov's dialogue, for an irreverent comic effect.

347 *Herostratus*

   In 356 B.C., in order to immortalize his name, Herostratus set fire to the
temple of Diana at Ephesus (on the night Alexander the Great was born, as
it happened).

351 chifir

   Tea brewed so strong as to have a narcotic effect—a concoction favored
by prison-camp inmates.

353 " '*The sixth of August, Old Style . . .*' "

   From Boris Pasternak's "August," one of the poems in *Dr. Zhivago*
(1955). The Transfiguration of Our Lord, which under the pre-Revolutionary
calendar was observed by the Russian Orthodox Church on August 6, now
falls on August 19. The holiday is traditionally associated with the apple
harvest.

354 "*And I saw in the air an army . . .*"

   The quotation is adapted from a medieval account of Prince Alexander
Nevsky's successful battle to drive the Teutonic Knights from Pskov in 1242.
Above the carnage on the bloodied ice of Lake Peipus, the Russian warriors
see "God's army" coming to their aid.